D1053277

LAST CANTO
OF THE
DEAD

LAST CANTO
OF THE
DEAD

AN OUTLAW SAINTS NOVEL

BOOK 2

BY DANIEL JOSÉ OLDER

HYPERION

LOS ANGELES   NEW YORK

First Edition, May 2023
1 3 5 7 9 10 8 6 4 2
FAC-004510-23090
Printed in the United States of America

This book is set in Baskerville MT Pro/Monotype
Designed by Phil T. Buchanan

Library of Congress Cataloging-in-Publication Data
Names: Older, Daniel José, author.
Title: Last canto of the dead / Daniel José Older.
Description: First editon. • Los Angeles ; New York : Hyperion, 2023. • Series: An
outlaw saints novel ; book 2 • "Rick Riordan presents." • Audience: Ages 12–18. •
Audience: Grades 7–9. • Summary: Simultaneous battles rage in the Caribbean
and Brooklyn as sixteen-year-olds Mateo and Chela, two gods-turned-teenagers,
try to get to the bottom of what is keeping them apart.
Identifiers: LCCN 2022021455 • ISBN 9781368070904 (hardcover) •
ISBN 9781368070928 (ebk)
Subjects: CYAC: Magic—Fiction • Ability—Fiction. • Cuban Americans—Fiction. •
Jews—United States—Fiction. • Brooklyn (New York, N.Y.)—Fiction. • Caribbean
Area—Fiction. • Fantasy. • LCGFT: Fantasy fiction.
Classification: LCC PZ7.1.O45 Las 2023 • DDC [Fic]—dc23
LC record available at https://lccn.loc.gov/2022021455

Reinforced binding
Follow @ReadRiordan
Visit www.HyperionTeens.com

SUSTAINABLE FORESTRY INITIATIVE

Certified Sourcing
www.sfiprogram.org
SFI-01681

Logo Applies to Text Stock Only

For Poppy—teacher, friend,
and the greatest diviner in the galaxy!

DAY
ONE

A needle.

Feather.

A tiny splash of ink. Milk. Coffee. Blood.

Crumbs, long forgotten.

Ash. That silky, fleeting thing between your fingers:

Impossible to hold, still leaves a stain.

—*The San Madrigal Book of the Dead,* Canto IV

CHAPTER ONE

MATEO

CHELA HIDALGO.

She sits beside me in this little motorboat; the wind makes a huge and glorious halo out of her beautiful hair. All around us, the crashing waves of the sea. Up ahead, the three peaks of our homeland rumble upward into the sky. Our lost island has returned, and so have we.

A few weeks ago, Chela was just a girl in my neighborhood whose bat mitzvah I'd played piano at. I barely knew her. Now I will fold my life in half and break open the world to keep her safe and right here by my side.

I know. . . . Both dramatic and *fast*, Mateo. But listen: our . . . whatever this is—love, for sure, although that barely seems to encompass it—goes back centuries. Not being poetic here. Chela and I were spirits once, just spirits. And we surged across the water searching for safety and found it by creating this island—San Madrigal, the first freedom seekers called it when they landed here, refugees like us. And as the strange city at the foot of those three peaks grew and sang and came to life, so did our love, our partnership, our bond.

We were just spirits, ethereal things of the salty air, and we knew one day we'd enter human forms, find true homes in those bodies, in each other, and we did, we did.

But somewhere in there, other forces came into play: sabotage, empire, disaster. Our memories were shattered, those three peaks sank, and the people of that lost island found a new home in Brooklyn, New York: Little Madrigal.

Well, that's about as smoothly as I can put it all together, anyway. Like I said, at some point the spirit I am, Galanika the Healer, became one with the boy I am, Mateo Matisse, brilliant pianist and chaotic teenager, thank you very much. Everything that happened before then comes to me only in scattered shreds, and usually only when I'm close to Chela.

Chela. The short, fierce girl beside me holds so many truths at once:

Okanla the Destroyer.

San Madrigal the Creator.

Burakadóra, she who punctures holes, to her gangster cousin, Tolo.

To my higher spirit self, that buff old island santo Galanika, she is a million mystical memories—warrior, lover, confidante, muse.

But to me, Mateo, she is just Chela, the blazing, unstoppable force of nature at my side. The one who gets me, who sees through me, believes me, checks me. She is just Chela, and that's all I ever want her to be. She's a terrific dancer and a terrible singer. She saves her smiles for when she really means them. She doesn't get shook by demons or bullies, and she'll tell you the truth even if it means cutting your throat. She's also *very* good with blades, of which she has two.

And that's another thing I'm grateful for right now, since we're about to land on the shores of a long-lost island that's probably inhabited by demons in the thrall of a two-hundred-year-old maniac named Archibaldo, who happens to be my ancestor. Uh, long story.

"It's time," Chela says as the beaches of San Madrigal rise to the surface of the frothing water up ahead. The sandy embankment leads to a grove of trees, and beyond that, the stucco rooftops rise and fall around the two bell towers of the old synagogue that Chela's father, Rabbi Hidalgo, used to run.

It's real, San Madrigal. This isn't a corny poster or simulation. This is the place where I, Mateo, was born, but I barely saw it. (I was only one year old when it sank.) The place, lifetimes ago, that I, Galanika, helped found and became one of the leading saints of. The beaches glisten; water pours from the windows and doors of the buildings. There's not a single sign of life from what I can see, but what does that mean in a world of ancient spirits and creepy old guys named Archibaldo? Nada.

Standing hand in hand, Chela and I turn to each other, and in her eyes I see that special look she saves just for me, that easy glint of affection. A sly smile, eyebrows raised. *It's so much*, that glance says. No one but us has done this, understands this, will live this moment.

I nod.

The bottom of the boat wedges against the sand with a bump.

Now all we have to do is survive.

I drop anchor and leap over the gunwale, feel the warm Caribbean waves slosh against my knees. Step onto the shore. Madrigal.

Immediately, a song rises within me.

I recognize it. It's the same lonesome, joyful hymn that I felt come to life within Chela when I went to heal her, the night I realized I had feelings for her.

This, though, the song of the island—it's like a variation on the theme. Whereas with Chela it came in sonorous, reverberating harmonies, the San Madrigal version arches upward in a single melody line that seems to stretch over the thunder of a hundred pounding drums. A phrase, a pause, another phrase. Lonesome, full of love, full of life.

The world is made of music—mine is, anyway. It's what holds it all together. So I take note of the song, store it away in my memory banks to play with later when I'm back at the keyboard.

Right now I'm home, in a weird, off-center sort of way. But what is home? I spent most of my childhood in hotels all over the world, waiting for my parents to finish their shifts saving lives in local clinics. It's only recently that our little enclave in Brooklyn truly became a place where I felt like I belonged, and even that is all tied up with me being a big-deal spirit and kinda-sorta saving the day. My tía Lucía's apartment felt like home, but ever since everything went to hell and she was killed there, it hasn't felt like anything but a morgue.

Truth is, the only time I really feel home, besides on the inside of a song, is when I'm with Chela.

It's weird: we've been inseparable these past few weeks. We've grieved together, loved each other. We know things no one else does, see the world like no one else can.

But there's still so much we haven't said out loud, like what exactly we even are, what our status is. It seems absurd to think about that in this moment of moments, but that's how you know it matters. And when has anyone ever accused love of making sense?

I turn back to tell her all this and freeze.

She's still standing in the boat, her eyes wide, mouth hanging open. But now it looks like she's about to scream.

"Chela! What's wrong?"

CHELA

Mateo Matisse Medina wants to know what's wrong.

As if I could explain. Even he, the one person I know who also happens to be some kind of weird embodied spirit of our lost island, would have trouble wrapping his big head around this one.

For a moment, he wears that wide-open face of his—same one he made when he saw me take out that first bambarúto a couple of months back on the night of the Grande Fete. The night everything changed. That face . . . He's just a kid, really. We're both just kids. I saw him grow. . . . Right in front of me, the boy became something else—came into his own, really—and what a thing it was to see. Still is.

You wouldn't know it to look at him, but Mateo loves order, needs it to survive. Have you seen his bedroom? Mateo Matisse is the only teenager I know who folds up his pants and puts them away after taking them off. That's why music has such a hold on him: he can write it down, fit it into a staff and time signature. It helps him make sense of this broken world, he'll tell you poetically. As if. There's no sense to be had, only chaos.

That's good for me, though, because chaos is the only thing that makes sense to me, dissonance the only harmony I know.

And chaos is what's erupting all around, right now, except no one can know the full extent of it but me. Not even Mateo.

Why? Because even while whatever it is—I'm not exactly sure yet—is very much happening in the world out there and will soon be all around us, it's also happening inside me, through me, from me.

When I don't answer, Mateo's face goes from surprised to concerned. Eyebrows scrunch like they're trying to meet in the middle, and he cranes his neck, squinting at me.

I don't answer because I can't. There is no answer. It's all so much more than words, even music (don't tell Mateo) could encompass.

It's bigger than everything, what I feel.

When I open my mouth, nothing comes out.

It started as the three peaks crested the waterline.

I thought it was just the thunder of all my power working—power I barely understand. Felt like a faraway train passing, a distant whisper that shook the foundations of the world, but the faraway was deep within me.

As the island rose, so did the feeling. It rose and expanded, a flower opening in my gut. Then another. The impossible sense of falling while standing still.

Surely, it's my powers, I kept telling myself. Reassuring myself.

There are two spirits within me, who are me: Okanla the Destroyer and Madrigal the Creator. They're opposites, and they're the same—*we're* the same. These are the riddles, divine and confounding, I've been living with recently. The Destroyer, I get. I've known, in some distant way, I've always known that Okanla lives within me, that I am her, even. I sense her flickering to consciousness in very particular moments, sometimes utterly mundane ones—at a club, when the beat really hits, in the midst of an extra-competitive soccer match. She simply rears to life; a howling, unstoppable ferocity surges, a wild and tactical ruthlessness takes over.

Then, more recently, there've been actual battles for her to relish, and that's a whole other kind of holy terror I won't even get into.

But Madrigal—that gently glowing, floating patron saint of the island, that serene and benevolent creator—who is she? How is that me? What's that got to do with me?

I know what. I possess the power to make life. To bring flesh to shadowy spirit forms. I've seen it happen. *Felt* it flow through me.

But it doesn't make sense. She doesn't feel like me, not the way Okanla does.

Of course, life doesn't make sense. This broken world. We are one, we three, and the island is part of us, too. Madrigal created it, after all. It's what creator spirits do. She, I, we, imbued it with that sweet, sweet creator-spirit essence, and so it's an extension of this tangled mess of spirits and girl that is me.

And now, right now, I can feel the island come to life like a trembling earthquake in every cell of my body.

That's what this is. Not my powers, not my fears. Not my death. It is the living island rebirthing itself, rising from the depths of the sea after fifteen long years of sunken hibernation.

I feel every shimmer of water slide off each leaf, the crumbly creak of stones and concrete resettling, cracking. Eyes open—many, many eyes—and blades of grass reach toward the sudden sky. Geysers of ocean course through the streets of me, gush forth from my houses and temples. I am once again whole, returned to a fullness I never knew I possessed.

And now I know why I've come, why San Madrigal had to rise. Why the spirit Madrigal had to return to the place Madrigal.

It wasn't just because I can.

This land is me, unstoppably, undeniably me.

And I won't have it overrun with beasts and some maniac who's lived past his expiration date.

We vanquished a god several times over.

We witnessed visions of the past, saw my aunt Mimi betray the empire pirates she'd secretly aligned with, saw the storm I'd gathered to block Vizvargal's return, the beginning of the end of this island, of our own amnesia as we entered these human bodies.

And now we've returned ourselves to ourselves, and San Madrigal to the surface.

Whoever I am, whatever the fullness of my powers entails, there's no version of this where I cede a single inch of this island without destroying anything that tries to take it from me.

"Are you . . . ? Can you come?" asks Mateo, ankle-deep in the waves, hand outstretched.

His voice, his eyes holding mine, the wholeness of him and what we are—an ancient and brand-new thing that has no name—it all pulls me to the surface.

The shouts and rumbles awakening within me simmer to a whisper. I stare at Mateo, trying to memorize him in this moment: his tan skin and long arms, his broad shoulders and the glint in his eye that says he's trying to find the humor in all this, a way to shake me out of whatever I'm going through. He's coming up short, though. I want to tell him he doesn't need to comfort me or do anything funny or heroic; he just needs to be him, be near, and that's enough.

As our world in Brooklyn fell apart these past two months, I watched Mateo step bravely into himself. Saw him rise to meet the madness of our time and stand by my side against the impossible. Immediately, he saw me. Knew me. Knew how to care for me, be silent when I needed a refuge, be brave when I needed a warrior at my back. He lost his aunt, and instead of crumbling or throwing it all away for revenge, he came and found me, fought even harder. And won.

Yeah, yeah, we've had centuries of being spirits together, a celestial love beyond mortal understanding. And yes, Mateo saved my life, took a blade to the chest for me. Literally died. For me.

All that is myth crap, though. It's epic. It looks good on paper. It's breathtaking in the moment. It'll sweep a girl off her feet, yeah. Even an ancient destroyer-creator archangel girl.

But that's not what makes a partnership, not necessarily. He could've done all that and still been a total drip, or one of those dweebs who doesn't know how to listen, or whatever, and none of this would've worked.

No. Mateo Matisse is my person, and I will reshape the world into a better place for him if I have to. But not because he's a hero or a god or any of that mess. It's because he's Mateo. It's the silence between us, the particular knowing we have. The tiny ways we move with each other, the way he holds me. The way I know he'll tell me the truth no matter what.

"Mateo . . ." is all I manage to get out before the catastrophic symphony of rebirth screams to a fever pitch inside me. Eyes spring open in the dark as bursts of soil and water and debris reinvent themselves into new shapes, and each one is a tremble, a burst, a pulse inside me.

I try to reach out my own hand, clasp his.

Instead, I feel thunder crash within me, sense a sliver of shadow along the crest of my shoulder, see a young girl with haunted eyes, her black hair blown into a swirl around her face. And then there's just nothing, nothing at all.

CHAPTER TWO

CHELA

ALL ACROSS THE TUMBLING DUNES AND HIDDEN CAVERNS, THE awakening hisses and growls and writhes. I rumble and rise and flesh stretches across bone and sudden gulps of air gasps of life lungs filled hearts tremble then shake then thud to a grumbly start and all around all around teeth and claws guttural cries and the opening of pathways sliding mud unstoppable water gushing and shushing through it all, falling away, away, always away.

Chela, wake up, please. . . .

Unstoppable the water unstoppable the sea unstoppable me.

Nowhere to turn because I'm everywhere, everything, life itself.

Sneakers thump the sand, underbrush rustles; a chest rises and falls against my face.

Crumbling destruction and brand-new caverns, ancient caverns, lost secrets, hideaways now dust as new crevices form new histories written across the island that is my body.

Life, unimpeded and uncaring, rages forth.

Chela, please.

Through the slithering darkness, the steady rumba of drips and drops, and the never-ending shush of the sea.

Through the impossible tunnels, past makeshift nesting grounds, splatters of blood and ichor, the scribbled ravings of a broken mind.

Chela, I need you!

A heinous green glow as the black water sloshes away.

A creaking and sputtering.

A crease in the darkness. The two chitinous curtains unclasp from each other, the towering beasts step away, and within, an ancient, half-decayed face crinkles into a smile beneath bright green glowing eyes.

MATEO

Chela holds my gaze as she slides downward, like if we stare hard enough at each other, somehow she won't collapse. I lunge toward the boat, making it tilt precariously, and manage to snatch Chela before her head cracks against the hull.

"What . . . ?" I try to ask, but I don't even have the question.

She's still kind of awake. . . . Her eyes blink up at the sun, then return to me. "So . . . many . . ." she mumbles, lost. "So, so many."

"So many what?" I grab the satchel with her blades in it and drag her to the shore.

"Eyes . . . Eyes, Mateo."

Lay her down on the beach.

"So many opening eyes."

I'm a healer. A whole entire spirit of healing, in fact. I've faced off with death itself and won.

But this . . . This is different. Bigger, somehow. I don't even know where to start. Chela lies limp in my arms, shivering, soaked, eyes half-closed.

When I was lost, first learning how to heal, it was Chela who told me to find the music, that the music would help me know how to move. And it did. I'd close my eyes and let the song rise and guide my hands, my focus. I can reveal a hidden aneurysm out of the shadows; I know the way a melody crinkles around a broken bone, the jangly, off-rhythm cadence of oxygen-starved tissue.

It's different with Chela because Chela is different. She's something else, and she's someone else to me—the beating heart of my world. How am I supposed to . . . ? None of this makes sense, and I hate it.

Death must be stalking me from the depths of vasculature, it's everywhere and nowhere at once. Over the past couple of months, I've seen more of it than I had in my entire life. The violence sweeping through Little Madrigal claimed my tía Lucía, and she left a dead man on her apartment floor for me to find—one of her attackers. Before that, I took a life, even though I didn't mean to, and I saved someone else immediately after. The sightless, empty gaze of Arco Kordal still glares back at me on nights when I can't sleep.

And sure, Chela and I are immortal, supposedly, but so was the demon Vizvargal, and I killed him, too. It just seems like I have been running and running since October, and I thought we'd made it out, that our happily-ever-after was at hand. But I was a fool. You can't outrun death, even if you're immortal. And now it's catching up to us.

"Ba . . . bam . . ." Chela mutters, then trails off. Pretty sure I know what the rest of that word was supposed to be, and it's not good. What I don't know is whether it's a warning, a clue, or just confused rambling.

Music, Mateo, find the music.

The waves crash and hiss behind me; the wind whips all around. My knees press into the soft sand of San Madrigal. Up ahead, rooftops rise over a dense forest that gives way to more buildings. The city snakes partway up the sides of all three peaks. I've seen this image on hundreds of posters, lock screens, album covers . . . and there it is, real.

Something moves in the trees up ahead. Not just fronds swishing in the wind—this is branches and trunks being shoved out of the way.

We don't have much time. As far anyone knows, Chela's aunt Mimi was the only person to drown when the island sank. But it turned out my creepy old ancestor Archibaldo was still alive and probably survived, and who knows what other monstrosities he's been keeping around all the while.

And if the rest of that word she started to say is *barúto*, we have a serious problem. Back in Brooklyn, we didn't know what to call these towering creatures with labyrinths sprawling across their ichorous skin and mouths as big as a human torso. They had no name when they showed up uninvited in our neighborhood, so we called them bambarúto, or *bogeymen* in Ladino. The honor guard of the demon Vizvargal, they were mostly just spectral at first, their horrific visages hidden behind body armor. But then a few of the creatures managed to take corporeal form using Chela's powers of creation, and they became even more terrifying.

One shredded my face, in fact, nearly ripping out my eye and leaving me with a scar I'll carry for the rest of my life.

"Chela, we gotta go. Chela!" I'm trying not to yell in her face, but she doesn't seem to hear me, hear anything. Her eyes slits, her mouth opening and closing with a whispered mumble.

I can't heal like this. I've done it in the midst of battle, but I knew what was happening then, wasn't caught off guard. And Chela was watching over me.

Chela.

I can't lose her. We've only just found each other—again? For the first time? Doesn't matter. What matters is we get out of this alive, both of us, so we can be together.

The first bambarúto bursts out of the trees ahead with a horrific shriek. It skids to a halt in the sand about twenty feet away, its long snout raised to the salty breeze. Then it turns to see me huddled in the sand over Chela, and it snarls, all those hundreds of teeth glistening in the Caribbean sun.

Chela is just a slight thing, easy to toss over my shoulder and run with. Still, the sand is uneven beneath my pounding feet. I'm terrified and have no idea where I'm going and get winded in about ten seconds.

Behind me, the snarls and shrieks grow louder as more bambarúto come charging out of the woods.

CHELA

The sickly green light glints off cold cavern walls; the darkness seethes.

Deeper. We are so much more gigantic than anyone could've imagined. A whole city of tunnels beneath the city by the sea. They stretch, wind, connect, and pull apart. Tributaries lead to vast sunken storehouses, crumbled stalagmite kingdoms, an impossible labyrinth of whispering shadows.

Measures were put in place to conceal all this.

A desperate, ancient magic.

All of this was hidden from us.

It is part of us.

Frantic etchings cover some of the walls. Music notes and a jagged, angry alphabet. Code. Or ravings. Both.

Deeper. A tunnel veers off to the side, away from it all.

Away from it all and deeper still, a place apart from these hideaways, cache within the cache.

The stone corridor narrows, then juts steeply upward, and we climb, we climb, past the forever dripping and flowing and swirling of these underground tide pools, and here, near the surface, speckled sunlight enters through a grove of trees above. Out in the world, a tremendous rush seems to pass overhead; a freight train of memories, lost loves, battle scars, hopes and fears—all thundering closer and closer through the sky.

Will it smash into the mountain? Will it devour us all?

Instead, it gets more and more intense, until I can almost make out voices, muffled chitterings of excitement, wonder, expectation.

And then, very suddenly—it all goes silent.

I'm surrounded again by the drips and hushed sighs of this cavern.

Down here, something stirs.

Another peel of green light opens as the shadows give way around it, unfolding themselves in dim silhouettes, then stepping aside.

Another face emerges from another chitinous coffin.

A face familiar from both photos and the murky depths of memory . . .

CHAPTER THREE

MATEO

BEST I CAN FIGURE, HERE'S HOW MY POWERS WORK:

—It starts when somebody gets hurt; let's call him Fulano for this example.

—On a regular day, when Fulano is okay, his body emits a very quiet song that only I can tune in to. Some people can feel energy or see people's auras or whatever. I can hear their song. Cool.

—But boom! Fulano gets hit by a car!

—Fulano has a broken femur! The bone clipped an artery, and now Fulano is bleeding out!

—The bone shards and sudden change of blood flow warp the melody; it's not as simple as harmony or dissonance. It's just something that *feels* off, out of place. It feels different depending on what it is, whose song, how long it's been going on, etc.

—Here I come, lean, mean, and ready to . . . uh, medicinally clean? Prevent gangrene? Whatever—I'm a composer, not a lyricist, okay? I show up, and the first thing I do is listen. I usually have to wave my hands over the person, but that may just be what helps me focus. Soon, the song emerges. Even if I haven't heard it before, I can tell when something's wrong. The off-ness jumps out at me, like a drummer with no rhythm.

—I go inward, both within myself and within Fulano. It's like my spirit is moving within his, and when I tune in right, I can reach that song, and I can fix it, slide the melody back into itself, ease the beat toward cohesion—whatever's needed.

—Resolving the problem with the song ricochets back to the problem with the body, solves that, too. They're interconnected, and healing one causes a chain reaction in the other. Hey, hey!

———◆———

That's the healing part. Here's where it gets really interesting:

—Having healed Fulano's broken bone and severed artery, I now carry them. They're mine. It's not like the injuries happened to me, but these things do build up, and the collected ailments can weigh me down if I let them. It's like racing to catch a plane while carrying other people's luggage.

—This is where cleansing comes in. Tía Lucía taught me how to clean, about the power of intentionality. You have to release the things that have a hold on you, the work of this world, other people's crap. This is a spiritual act Santeros are particularly good at, the clean-off. It's called a despojo.

—The day the empire pirates killed Tía Lucía, I added my own innovation to the despojo: I weaponized it. (Don't come for me! I can do that kind of thing since I'm also a spirit, though I didn't know it at the time.)

—This means that in battle all I have to do is work on the casualties, healing them and collecting their various wounds, and then I can whip the injuries back at whoever caused them. Boom! Two birds murked with one proverbial stone—me. I'm the stone.

It's pretty awesome when you stop and think about it, except I don't have time to do either of those things at the moment, because my skill set only works when people on my team are getting hurt. Right now it's just me and Chela, and she's out of commission in some weird spirit coma that I don't know how to cure. I've still got her slung over my shoulder, and I'm busting ass through winding jungle paths; there are about a half dozen bambarúto on our trail.

To use my cool smack-back-with-someone's-injuries move on these monsters, I'd have to hurt one of them first and then I guess heal it, so what's the point?

I'm tall and I have some muscle to me, but I'm not nearly as tall and muscly as those creatures.

Problem is, I'm just about out of both breath and options.

And this jungle path has led me to a sandy embankment between two unscalable cliffs, so now, on top of everything else, I'm at a dead end.

I ease Chela to the ground—she's still limp and mumbling—and pull the beaded ceremonial blade from her satchel. This is the steel that recently killed me. The demon Vizvargal shoved it straight into my chest. Yes, I let him do it so I could use my own death to murder him right back (and it worked—ha!), but I can still taste the sudden emptiness in my mouth as my insides were shredded and my heart simply ceased to beat. I don't carry my own death around, but the memory of it doesn't fade—the breathlessness, and most of all the pain, that tearing as arteries and organs ruptured against vicious steel.

Doesn't matter. The blade is in my hands now, and it's specially sanctified to deal death to exactly the type of creatures running up on me right now.

"Rest, Chela," I say, even though I'm pretty sure she can't hear me. "I will keep you safe." It's a promise as much to myself as to her.

I have to keep her safe, because I'm the only one here and I won't lose her. I refuse.

The rumble of those approaching feet grows louder, so I rise and turn, already swinging the blade. The first bambarúto catches it right between the eyes, halted in mid-snarl. The beast doesn't die, though; it just collapses with a shriek, spewing black blood everywhere, and rolls to the side as the others charge over it.

I can't let them get to Chela, but that also means I don't have much room to maneuver. I slash and hack wildly, trying to clear myself a little space. The blade slices through claws and bones, sending one or two more monsters howling in retreat. I'm still hemmed in, though, and the remaining three are pissed.

Two come at once; all those teeth and flailing limbs are just a blur of darkness. I swing, stab, miss, then feel the air leave my lungs as one of the bambarúto smashes directly into me and we both clatter into the sand. My fingers are still curved around the beaded handle of Chela's blade, though, and I have just enough room to drive it directly through the monster's open mouth and then carve upward through its skull.

Ichor, blood, brain probably—all of it explodes onto me in a single wet splatter. I roll the dead thing to the side just in time to see the other leaping at me and then . . .

With a growl, something huge rams into it from the side, and both go tumbling away.

I stand. Glance at Chela—she's unhurt, still out—and then blink at the mess around me. More bambarúto are surging out of the forest, but these are attacking the ones that were pursuing me.

I see two of them chase down the creature whose face I slashed earlier. They pounce on it, thrashing the monster to pieces. Guttural howls and shrieks ring out all around, and . . . maybe, across the island? I can't be sure. Either way, something huge is happening, and I have no idea what.

When the last of my attackers has been gruesomely dealt with, the bambarúto who came to the rescue approach. There are nine of them, and they are no less terrifying than the ones who almost killed me just now. Not to be that guy, but I can't tell bambarúto apart. Not yet, anyway. Judging by what just happened, that might be a skill I'll need to develop.

Before I can do anything about it, one hoists Chela on its shoulder, and when I start to flail at it, the others stand in front of me.

Then they all head off as a group, pausing only to look back at me with a single tilted-head glance that can only mean one thing: *You coming?*

CHELA

I step back, back, until I'm enmeshed in shadows again, wandering between the folds of time, the world an impossible blur.

And then a small hand wraps around mine.

I look up, ready to pull away, to fight whatever demon has me.

Instead, I'm face-to-face with a girl—the girl with the black hair and haunted eyes. She's several years younger than me, pale, with sallow cheeks, and she wears an old-fashioned dress and buckle shoes.

She blinks at me with wonder, awe even. I must be looking at her the same way.

Then she tugs once on my hand, turns, and hurries off into the mist.

So I follow, a waft of air driven forward by pure intention in the midst of this world reborn, which is me, reborn within me.

Down, down, into the darkness, the depths; down we go.

For a while, I lose sight of her in the infinity of time.

But I keep going, following the slight trail of dissonant air her presence leaves in its wake.

Deeper now, and there: another scurry of movement in the emptiness. Across space and now time we travel, an endless pursuit, and as the world blurs and then unblurs, I glimpse a solemn meeting—the Cabildo, I think—although there are more council members than the three we have now. Then it's a mess of crowds, mourners, victory celebrations . . .

The world slows around me, and it's nighttime in another era. Angry scars crisscross the surface of this small island, this body nearly broken by battle.

Smoke rises from Galerano rooftops. So do desperate shouts and screams . . . and laughter from the depths.

I sweep across the bloodied beachfront.

Take it in.

Breathe.

The plain truth of what's to come fills me.

These fallen, broken, writhing bodies . . . They spiral toward me, or maybe it's me who moves, but it doesn't matter.

Charred skin, splintered bone, gushing wounds. Memories, the caress of the breeze on closing eyes, a million moments gone in a flash of artillery fire and the sudden empty space where a heart once was.

Up ahead, the spirit girl runs through the carnage.

I must follow; I know she holds secrets. She's trying to show me something, trying—

A wall of sheer, impossible darkness rises ahead of her, breaks the world itself in half.

She whirls to face me, her eyes even bigger now, mouth wide open to scream, and then the barrier seems to swallow her whole. The girl is simply gone, and there's nothing at all where she once stood.

I speed over more death: charred bodies, torn flesh. Reach the wall and slam into it with everything I have. All that does is send little shocks through my spirit form.

The girl is unreachable, along with whatever she was desperately trying to show me. And I'm left here, a hundred or more years in the past, surrounded by corpses.

CHAPTER FOUR

MATEO

SAN MADRIGAL HAS A SMELL.

It's earthen and moist, like when you stick your head in a bag of fresh soil and inhale. (Not that I've ever done that! Who would do that? Okay, once. Anyway!) But there's a tangy citrus scent threaded through it, too, and then something flowery—jasmine, I think. And, of course, that salty seawater and fresh-ish fish vapor underlies everything.

Anyway, it's a whole lot, is what I'm saying, total sensory over-load, because the forest is full of bright green leaves, red fruits and flowers, weird bugs, glistening streams . . . plus, I'm panting and heaving, can barely keep up with these huge, sprinting monstrosities.

One thing I am absolutely *not* gonna do, though: leave Chela alone with them. Sure, they may have saved our asses, but for all I know it was so they could cook her up and eat her themselves! I have no idea what kind of internal bambarúto dispute we've stumbled into; all I know is wherever they take her, I'm going, too.

They wanted me to come, though, so I guess that's good. Or they just don't see me as a threat.

Either way, I stay at a steady jog to at least keep them in sight. We bound along a dirt path through the tropical forest and then up some stone stairs. And, just like that, stucco buildings rise around us and we're in the middle of San Madrigal City, where my parents grew up, where I was born, where all these weird, piled-on-top-of-one-another histories and myths took root.

No time to ponder all that, though. The bambarúto don't stop to sightsee or get nostalgic. They leap through the muddy streets, toppling carriages and lampposts and not showing any signs of stopping.

The one with Chela slung over its shoulder is up toward the front. I'm watching it like a hawk when howls erupt all around us and I almost throw myself onto the soggy street with shock.

I don't know why I didn't think we'd get attacked—guess I was just too busy trying to keep up to worry about much else. But now two more bambarúto are lurching out of alleys and rounding corners and launching themselves with snarling grasps at the ones with Chela.

And, of course, at me.

I don't know if they know who I am—what I am—but it hardly matters. They've already tried to kill me once, and I don't see why they wouldn't again.

The group I'm with picks up the pace, anxious not to be goaded into a fight, I think.

We race down a winding side street, around a tower, then up another steep stairwell. (San Madrigal and these stairs, man! Why?! Invest in ramps, people!) The pursuing bambarúto close on us, their gnashing teeth and guttural laughter ever nearer. Worst part: I'm falling behind. I was already out of breath when the group saved us, and we've been going nonstop since.

And then two creatures in my frantic procession slow their strides so they're even with me. One of them waves a huge clawed arm at something ahead—a tall, impressive structure that looms over everything around it. San Madrigal's synagogue. Now I just want to live long enough to see Rabbi Hidalgo's face when I tell him the local monsters showed me right to the door of his old house of worship, (hopefully) saving his daughter's life.

I can see why we're heading there: a fifteen-foot cement wall surrounds the place, a remnant from the years of war that once ripped San Madrigal almost to shreds. A perfect fortress. I sprint toward the open gate as the creature carrying Chela disappears inside.

I'm only a few feet shy of safety when a terrible screech rends the air. I skid to a halt. Something orange and gigantic—four times the size of a human—has apparently dropped straight from the sky and pinned one of the two creatures that made up our rear guard.

This thing, it . . . It's shaped something like an oversize bambarúto itself—that hairy hunched-over back and almost-human face. The arms are disproportionately long, but also there are way too many appendages. They hammer down on its pinned prey so fast and ferociously it's impossible to count how many there are.

All that would be bad enough, but something about this monster strikes a chord deep inside, igniting a kind of terror I didn't feel even when I was facing down death back in Brooklyn. This fear is something different; it's like a wrongness that chimes through me—two notes played too close together on an out-of-tune piano.

I want to run. Hide. But I can't seem to move.

The other bambarúto in the monster's hunting party stay back, cheering it on as it thrashes their fellow creature into a bleeding disaster of shredded flesh. Then the enormous beast looks up as the second rear guard charges it.

I realize I've just been standing here staring with my mouth hanging open like some monster-movie extra who's about to get squashed.

But I'm not some extra; I'm a powerful spirit holding a powerful dagger, and I know what's about to happen, what I have to do.

And I hate it.

I hate it with every fiber of my being, but that doesn't stop what happens next: in a split second, the orangutan-spider-monster launches itself at the other rear guard, smashing both of them through a nearby stucco wall.

The other bambarúto hurry over to watch the fun; they don't see me crouching beside the shattered, blood-soaked misery of the first rear guard lying in the mud of San Madrigal.

I reach out, still hating this. Yes, this bambarúto helped Chela and me get away, but that doesn't make it an ally, doesn't mean it won't kill me the second it gets a chance.

Doesn't matter. Right now, I need the havoc that was wreaked on its flesh.

The other times I healed bambarúto, it was in the heat of battle back in Brooklyn. I was conscious of what was happening around me, sure, but I'd also entered a kind of flow state that allowed me to heal and wound in close succession with barely a thought, like breathing.

It all happened so fast, so naturally, I barely caught a trail of the monsters' songs.

That simplicity seems a million miles away now; it's like I have to learn it all over again from scratch.

But I know it's within me to do. I just wish Chela were available to keep those other ones at bay.

There isn't much time.

I reach out my hands, do my best to quiet my frantic mind.

Then, instead of a song, I hear a tiny, high-pitched wheeze.

When I look down with a start, a single eye opens from that battered mass. It looks right into mine.

I hadn't realized this creature was still alive after that thrashing.

My first instinct is to put it out of its misery, but that's what people who don't have what I have do.

I let the world fall away as my hands hover just above its slightly twitching face. The song rises, and I'm so startled by what it is, I almost lose focus once again.

What pulses through this creature is the melody of Madrigal, that gentle hymn of our island.

Da-da-deee daa-da . . .

It's faint, and tattered like the bambarúto's flesh, but I'd know it anywhere.

And that makes it easier to do what I have to do.

———◆———

Five bambarúto stand with their backs to me. Beyond them, a desperate fight rages amid the rubble of a small house.

The first sliver of devastation leaves my fingertips and slams like a battering ram into the one nearest to me. The other four turn at the sound of cracking bones and suddenly pulverized flesh.

They're too slow to dodge the splatter of trauma rippling out in waves from my swinging arms. Two collapse where they stood, senseless and howling. The others manage to stumble off in terror.

By now, the oranguspider has noticed something's up. It turns, midway through grappling with the other rear guard bambarúto, and then howls, charging me. I had been feeling pretty good, had almost gotten back into my battle trance, but no amount of confidence or badassery can prepare you for the feeling of being attacked by all those hideous legs and that gaping mouth.

The thing comes barreling toward me, launches through the air with a hiss, and even when I leap out of the way at the last second, its hairy carapace still manages to crunch against my shoulder.

We both stumble. Towering legs surround me like a vile, skittering forest. I dodge one swipe, get clipped by another. Finally get a grip on one of those flailing appendages and manage to release a blast of damage into it. Shock waves reverberate through the thing; it screeches and bucks, knocking me over before I can get in another hit.

Then a bambarúto smashes into it from the side. This one is wounded, so it must be the second rear guard. I take advantage of the confusion to unleash another symphony of pain into the multi-legged monster. The bambarúto I healed comes thrashing in from above—it must've climbed to a rooftop for an optimal revenge angle—and clobbers the hell out of ol' oranguspider.

That does it.

The massive orange creature has the good sense to know when it's outnumbered. After a flailing, messy extraction, it clambers off and disappears into the back alleys of Madrigal.

I turn to my new allies, the creatures I once had to fight against for my very life. We regard one another solemnly with, I think, a new, strange respect.

When we turn together to head to the synagogue, I realize a figure stands in the entranceway, watching. She is tall, slightly hunched over, and her skin and eyes glow with an eerie green pallor.

"Galanika, you fool," Mimi Baracasa says, her face a mix of shock and vague disdain. "You never should've come here."

CHELA

The girl is gone, and me—I'm just a spirit alone, tossed along this impossible tide of history I have no idea how to navigate. This has to be, what? The eighteensomethings. It's hard to tell. The world seems so very dark. I stumble into the shell-shocked heart of the city. Here, voices of dissent and confusion rise, and with them cheers of victory that mix with the wailing of those who've lost loved ones.

Down narrow streets and across plazas, I manage to find myself in a cavernous chamber in the heart of Madrigal City, where several cloaked figures confer in hushed tones as a crowd waits anxiously out in the streets.

The Cabildo meeting . . . I passed it along the way; believe that made it easier to find, somehow.

I can just make out snippets of their words as I approach.

"Are you sure? It can't be. . . ."

"They were explicit, Baba. There is no . . . But anyway . . ."

". . . known that the Divine Council has been with us since the dawn of . . ."

"They can't simply . . ."

". . . in two, just like that? Seems brash. Still, we must . . ."

And then I'm among them, two women and a man, all tense and middle-aged and unsure of what the future holds.

"It's settled, then?"

"It is. We have no authority to challenge them, even if that was what we wanted. It's simply . . . out of our jurisdiction."

"Very well. Are we agreed?"

"I don't know what to think, Imelda. I truly don't. But if this is the way, so be it. Okanla will henceforth be split off, a separate entity from Madrigal."

This is it—the moment that my splitting in half was officially decreed. What is this Divine Council, though? I've never heard anything about it. From the sound of things, they dissolved immediately after passing this decree, but . . . it still seems odd.

"All documents or traces of anything saying otherwise will be destroyed at tonight's celebration."

I watch, an invisible witness, and a coolness enters me, a calmness. There's nothing I can do, after all. This is history—it's already been written. Yet there's an eeriness to these proceedings, like bearing witness to your own vivisection.

"And Vizvargal?"

"The same, of course. Destroyed without a trace. It was the one condition we levied on them, for all the good it'll do. His name will be banned, his visage erased from all records, official and not. It's the only way."

"Last matter?"

"The splitting of Okanla and Madrigal—it will facilitate the final decree: that if Galanika and Madrigal-Okanla ever become embodied . . . they must not join forces in any way. Absolute chaos will reign; the world will be thrown off-balance. Only calamity can result from it."

What?!

"Disaster."

This I did not know. This is not . . . possible. This cannot be.

"Indeed."

What chaos? What imbalance? Mateo and I have been teaming up for months, and it's only made my life infinitely better—his, too. We saved Little Madrigal. This doesn't make sense. It's abhorrent.

But the conversation wraps up quickly after that, and then the figures step out into the open air to the cheering crowds and announce a great bonfire will be held tonight, and on and on, and all I can do is fade away, phantom that I am, dislodged in time and place, and now, simply, utterly lost.

CHAPTER FIVE

MATEO

"WHERE IS SHE?" I DEMAND, STILL PANTING FROM EVERYTHING that's just happened.

"I'll be asking the questions," Mimi Baracasa croaks.

The air in the synagogue is musty, even with the double doors wide open behind me, the salty sea breeze flowing in.

Mostly, this vast hall is shadows, splintered pews, shattered stained-glass windows. Things lurk in the darkness around me, though. More bambarúto, I'm sure. They stir, ever ready. Whatever happens next, it will not be easy to get through.

But I will. For Chela, I will.

The two bambarúto that fought off that oranguspider with me quickly disappear into the shadows. Mimi and I face off in the long square of sunlight pouring in through the doors.

She wears a crimson shawl over skin that looks like it was once a rich brown but has turned sallow, pale. She's been underwater for the past fifteen years, so I guess that makes sense. As much as any of this makes sense . . .

"You get no answers from me till I know Chela's safe."

"Mmm . . . worse than I thought," Mimi mutters to herself. Then she turns those alarming glowy-green eyes on me. "She is in the inner sanctum, mmm. If I'd wanted her harmed, I would've left her to Archibaldo's fiends, eh? But I didn't, did I? Now—"

"Archibaldo . . . My . . . Archibaldo Medina . . . He survived?"

Mimi nods irritably. "I'm sure he did, yes. That heinous old bat just won't die. He's powerful enough to live for centuries, eh? A decade and a half underwater won't do much, unfortunately. I'm sure his creatures protected him just as mine protected me. He's already messing with the spirit world—I can feel it in the air all around us, that static—and he's surely sending more attacks our way, since he knows I betrayed him. So we don't have much time. Now tell me . . . My husband and son? Where are they? Why didn't you bring proper resources with you? What the hell happened?"

All the wild improbability of this moment slides into sudden focus as I try to figure out how to explain. . . . "Si was killed a few years ago," I blurt out. "Some territory dispute with a rival gang in Brooklyn, from what I heard."

Mimi's tight face doesn't flinch, doesn't move at all. She just slides onto the nearest bench, her breath suddenly heavy. "Was it all for nothing, then . . . ? And Tolo? He must be around your age, eh?"

I nod. "Took over things after his dad died. Been running the club and has a whole side hustle smuggling weird folklore and rare books. He's . . ." How to describe the thunderstorm of a personality that is Tolo Baracasa? "Everyone loves him" is the best I can come up with.

A wry smile crinkles across Mimi's face. "Ah, well . . . He's probably ashamed of me. And so he should be." She looks away, expression shrouded in shadows.

"These bambarúto . . ." I say. "They do your bidding?"

She doesn't look up. "Hmm? Oh, is that what you call them? Heh. Appropriate name, actually. The real word is unpronounceable by a human tongue anyway, so I suppose it'll do. And yes . . . Well, you could say we work together."

"All I've known these things to do is try to kill me and the people I love." I take a breath. "They almost succeeded, too."

Mimi appraises my scarred face, creases the edges of her mouth to indicate she's vaguely impressed. "Mmm. That would make sense. Come." She stands suddenly and heads with a creaky, off-kilter stride toward the darkness. "There is much to discuss. I will bring you to Chela while we speak."

Finally. I knew, deep down, I knew Chela was okay. But everywhere except deep down, I'd been fighting off a thousand different images of her horrible death. And when it wasn't that, it was me trying desperately to get to her, failing every time as we both disappeared beneath a sea of monsters.

The simplicity of Mimi's statement, *I will bring you to Chela*, almost knocks the wind out of me. I have to hold back tears. Fortunately, the old woman is not paying me any attention.

I hurry to catch up, and together we slip deeper into the darkness of this abandoned synagogue in the heart of our once-drowned city.

CHELA

The city is so quiet.

Streets empty.

The only sounds the endless crashing of waves, the occasional caw of night birds.

Darkness. The last glimpse of daylight a vanishing tease at the edge of the sky. Stars are already out; a crescent moon rises over the three peaks, gigantic.

Then, from the center of the city, a mighty yell rises, and the sudden roar and crackle of flames. An attack? A celebration? A little of both, perhaps. Through these winding streets, around corners and up narrow stairwells, a rustling of leaves on a banyan tree; wind chimes let slide their gentle song from a balcony.

There.

The plaza beneath the central peak writhes with crowds. All Madrigal is out, bustling, chatting. The dire threat of invasion has finally lifted; the heaviness of all that might have happened releases from furrowed brows, tense muscles. The war is over. The island is still shaken from the brutality of it, but there will be time to confront those ghosts later. Tonight is for celebrating. For surviving. For all that lies ahead.

And for bringing in a new era in San Madrigal.

The Grande Fete, they call it. *And,* someone adds importantly, *it will forever commemorate peace, the triumph of Madrigal, and freedom.*

CHAPTER SIX

MATEO

"Do you know what *BAMBARÚTO* means?" Mimi asks me as we work our way along a slippery corridor amid dripping water and moss-covered walls. She sounds almost kindly now that she's warmed to me. Can't say it's mutual. Not yet.

"I figured it was just one of those nonsense words. Just means *bogeyman*, right?"

"Nope. *Cheap bread.*"

"Huh?"

We reach a staircase, begin climbing in a nauseating spiral. "The baker would march up and down the street calling out, *¡Pan barato! ¡Pan barato!*"

"Pan barato—bambarúto."

"Cheap bread. And he was a sight to behold, I'm sure, his skin blackened from the oven smoke while he hollered at the top of his lungs. The children were terrified."

"So he became the bogeyman."

"Eso mismo."

"But that's not what these creatures are, not really. What are they?"

"Well, in a way, they are. The bambarúto, as you call them, are creatures made of fear. Madrigal is the creator principle, right? That's how the many gods and demons that people brought here became flesh and blood. But our fears are perhaps more vivid than our prayers. . . . They, too, took form, became incarnate beings. They hid in the shadows, mostly, away from the world."

"I had no idea."

We reach a landing. Mimi nods to the shattered window. Beyond, the city stretches out in tiled roofs and bursts of greenery. We're facing east; the sun, just beginning its path back to the horizon, throws the long shadow of this tower across the rubble of a nearby building. Farther off, the edge of the far peak is just visible, sloping upward with a sprinkling of houses amid more tropical forest.

"Disparate as folks here are, most of San Madrigal shared certain terrors: the terrors of empire, of oppression. The hell of persecution was a very real memory for almost all of us, or just a generation removed. It lives on in our bodies, and in a very real way, it has always lurked in the underbelly of our city."

"But not everyone felt it," I say as we head up some more stairs.

Mimi nods, grave. "The cult of Vizvargal lived on in the shadows, too. They had very real fears, but they were different. They feared everything that Madrigal stood for. They were terrified of what it meant for the world—an uncolonized island, a haven of resistance, an outlaw state. I know because I was one of Vizvargal's followers for years."

I can only grunt at that. From what I'd seen, it may have been Mimi who helped stop the empire pirates' final plot to take over the island, but she'd been along for a lot of the ride.

"The bambarúto born from the fears of the empire pirates . . ." Mimi goes on, "they recognized the truth in my heart. They saw that I brought you and Madrigal in spirit form to the secret ceremony to raise Vizvargal on that fateful day. They knew what that meant."

"And when the island sank," I finish for her, "they formed a monster cocoon around you, saved you from drowning, kept you alive with their weird monster nutrients all this time, just like the other ones did for Archibaldo."

"And now . . ." Mimi's voice trails off, and a wicked glint flashes in her pale green eyes. She shakes her head. "And now we wage war against one another."

The door opens with a shrill creak, and inside, Chela lies on the floor, still unconscious.

My knees land beside her, my hands lift her to me.

"What's wrong with her?" I whisper.

"The island," Mimi says in a sad and gentle rasp. "It's . . . It's too much for her to take in. The two of you coming here has triggered an unimaginable series of catastrophes, I'm afraid. But we'll discuss all that soon. First, you must revive her."

"I . . ." There's no point in talking. Finally, there are no monsters attacking, no impossible decisions to make. Chela's a gravity well; all I want is to cascade forward and collapse in her arms. But she needs me to be at my best.

"Be careful," Mimi is saying, but her voice is already a hundred miles away. "I know that look in your eye. . . . Should never have come . . ."

I have one thing to focus on, one thing to do. I must heal the woman I love, and I must do it now.

It's just a whisper at first, but slowly, slowly, her song rises.

And then it's the only thing I know.

"¡Nunca conquistado!" a drunken troubadour yells.

"¡Nunca vencido!" the whole city roars back, deep in their cups.

But while they've gathered to mark a memory, to commemorate, this is also a celebration of forgetting. A rending. A forcible expulsion.

Me. I'm the one being torn. Cut in two. This is the tearing. A party.

I suppose that's one way to go.

Closer.

The flames of that bonfire are not fed only on logs from the cypress forest. No . . . there are tomes in there. Paintings. Sculptures.

Closer.

Most of them show the demon Vizvargal. Here he is devouring a cluster of screaming virgins; here he vomits out an island that becomes the world. Time-worn pages of secret incantations and praisesongs sparkle at their edges, then turn gray-black and disintegrate, become ash.

But it's not just him. Here I am, with my two opposite faces: Madrigal, bringer of life, and Okanla the Destroyer. The one divided into two, forever torn asunder. A whole mythology altered in the space of a night.

At least, that's what they believe.

Nothing really works that way, though.

"¡Adelante, mi gente! ¡Con la trompeta, Chancho!" someone yells, and a wild, outrageous melody devours the night. Dancers spin, fall in love, find new partners, love harder. Sweat-soaked bodies move through, eyes alight with the rising flames, the thrill of victory, the wonder at all that is yet to come.

Only I know what lies ahead, and even that is only in scraps and shards.

And what any of it *means* is beyond me.

I am, in my wholeness, nothing, after all. A memory. A curse. A walking sin. *Too powerful.* Something to be feared, destroyed. Torn in two.

Doesn't matter.

The words that won't stop echoing, that keep slicing through my gut, that refuse to go away: *If Galanika and Madrigal-Okanla ever become embodied . . . they must not join forces in any way. Absolute chaos will reign; the world will be thrown off-balance. Only calamity can result from it.*

Ramblings of a madman? Bad divination? Cold, calculated political positioning?

I'll probably never know. I just know that boy is the only one who's gotten me through the devastation of these last two months, and he's the only one who really gets me.

I move through the crowd, a ghost, bearing witness, only witness.

The me of this time is surely somewhere, sulking or celebrating—I don't know which. I have no memories of this night. Of so many things.

But everywhere around me, the first Grande Fete rollicks in full swing, and who am I not to let a small smile of despair slide across my haunted face? What's not to celebrate? Who else gets to witness the world they helped create as it collectively decides they should be torn in two?

I let myself slide into the swirl of revelry; a song picks up, swinging from a mournful bolero into an insatiable waltz. I know it's not because of me, invisible me, joining the fray—all this has already happened; it's all a memory, written and printed. But in my head, they feel me, they feel the full wretched fire of me, my entirety, perceived as a single complex entity for this one final night. They feel it, and it moves them. The ragged street orchestra pushes this dizzy rager harder than it's ever gone; the dancers respond in kind, a ferocious rumble builds. We amp it up, we don't stop, and as the bonfire roars, the night takes on a dangerous, impossible urgency, that heady, pounding feeling that marks the end of one world and the beginning of another.

The bodies twirl through me; they draw closer to one another, then push away. Laughter, screams, panting . . . They're singing along in three languages, now nonsense, now howling as the trumpet cries out a staccato solo over the driving tom-toms.

You, a voice says as warmth envelops me. A ghostly hand wraps around my ghostly waist.

And everything stops.

No—the dancers keep spinning; that murderous waltz simmers on. The fire keeps turning my face to ash.

But somehow, it's so far from me. Because he's wrapped around me; he's holding me close, and he knows who I am, the whole of me, and what I can do, what I can destroy.

He knows me, and he's not afraid of me.

And I know him.

I smile into the faraway flames and dancing revelers, then let him spin me so our translucent faces almost touch.

The tiny sliver of night between the tip of my nose and his, both glowing with the bright ethereal power of whatever we are in this Never Land of memories, ghosts, and fire.

———◆———

You have so many names, I say, smiling into his smile. *I never know which one to use.*

He smiles, too, and it's like a miracle, that smile. After all we've been through, more than even we can fathom. *You're one to talk.*

Ah . . . My grin doesn't falter, but in some tiny, inexplicable way, my face must fall.

He knows me too well. *What is it?*

How did you . . . ? I let it trail off because the answer doesn't matter. Not now. I don't even know how I got here.

Long story, he says. *And I'm not totally sure myself—I think you sort of pulled me in when I tried to heal you. And your aunt helped.*

Mimi? Real-world things—aunts and islands—they all feel so distant, a fairy tale. My eyes flit away.

He pulls me closer. *What's happening here?*

The Cabildo's pronouncement comes thundering back to me. These vapid impossibilities, politics. Human shit. I despise all of it—all of them, for their follies, their rules, their unwinnable games. They can burn. *It's the first Fete.*

I lead him back to the wildness at the heart of the city. We must've spun away in our embrace; I barely noticed.

That's . . . They're burning pictures of you. . . .

It's the night of the dividing. When Okanla ceased being a praise name and became a spirit unto herself.

He blinks through the flickering bonfire. *But . . . why?*

Not sure. The lie comes out of me before I can think too hard about it. Barely feels like a decision. The silence that follows, though, that's all me. I did that. Every opportunity to correct the record presents itself in those next five unbearable seconds, and I firmly, consciously reject the entire notion.

Why? Because I'm not even sure that what the Cabildo decreed is true. I'm not sure whether it's all some ruse created by Archibaldo to divide us, or whether I'm losing my mind. But I'm sure Mateo will take it to heart, fall away from me, do the "right" thing. That's who he is. And I love him for it—and maybe, just a tiny bit, hate him for it, too.

But already, the revels, the fire, the ashes of who I was—they're all fading, sliding into an indistinguishable blur, and soon the only thing that's clear is the only thing I wanted to hold on to anyway: Mateo.

And then he is gone, too, and I'm floating in the mire of nowhere at all.

CHELA! A sharp voice finds me. Not Mateo's . . .

CHELA!

Whoever this is, she's not taking no for an answer. *You have to slam the door on all that. You have to leave the island. Slam the door. Slam it forever! You can't have it both ways!*

I don't know what she's talking about . . . or why she's yelling. But there, in the distance, an old wooden door opens to the bonfire, the night of the first Fete, the old world. And then, suddenly, it's all very, very close again: the sounds of wild laughter, that spiraling music reaching out like a siren's song, the crackling fire, the delicious smells of seafood grilling. . . .

From somewhere farther away, I hear a terrifying, never-ending scream. Thousands of voices joining in panic and horror . . .

Chela! Slam the door!

I do, barely realizing what's happening.

"Wha . . . ?" An unrelenting ache racks me as I find myself back in my physical body, a cold floor pressing against my shoulders. Afternoon sunlight pours through a shattered window; the blue, blue sky. "How . . . ?"

Mateo shakes his head, trying to clear it. He looks lost. "We're in the temple," he manages, then nods at someone standing a few feet away.

"Sobrina," says a voice like crinkled paper. "At last you have returned to us."

My elbows find the floor, and Mateo helps me prop myself up on them. "Tía Mimi."

"You were lost within the island," she says solemnly. "You cannot go in there. You could be gone forever. There is no in-between there—you must decide to block it out or it will consume you, eh."

I can barely follow her words.

It was so dark in my own strange vision of her. I recognize the shape of her face from family photos—those sharp cheekbones and pouting mouth—but . . . she doesn't look quite human. It's not just that pale green glow emanating from her eyes, her skin. Her angles and proportions are all just the slightest bit off, like someone broke her and then put her back together from memory. I try to ignore it, but the off-ness keeps jumping out.

I pull a hand across my face, trying to ground myself, and Mateo lets out a little gasp.

"What is it?" I ask as he gently takes my arm and turns the underside toward me. A shiny, whitish streak stretches from my shoulder to my elbow. It looks like my skin has been pulled apart slightly to reveal a marble statue beneath. "What the hell?" I recoil in horror, glancing at my other arm, my legs. Doesn't seem like it's anywhere else. It won't come off when I brush it.

"Let me try," Mateo says, doing his best to sound calm. He closes his eyes, preparing to heal.

"Your Galanika magic won't work on that, boy," Mimi rasps.

"Why not?" I demand.

"It's not an injury. You've been marked by the island. The island is dying, and you burrowed into its depths. What did you think would happen?"

It doesn't hurt, and I don't really believe that Mateo's powers can't heal it; I don't believe anything this old bat has to say, so I just grumble, "Okay," and start looking around for my stuff.

"You don't sound very happy to see me, mi niña."

I have to get up. Can't have a conversation like this from the floor. I grab Mateo's arm, grateful for both his presence and his silence, the attentiveness and respect he gives this ghoulish reunion. "From what I understand"—I manage not to groan too loudly as I heave myself upward, anchored to Mateo—"you didn't give me much to be happy about, Tía."

She considers this. "Mmm, well, regardless of that, we are at war now, and I'm all you've got." She glares at Mateo. "Time to go."

He glares right back. "Sure, no problem. You're welcome for raising the island, see ya later."

"Just you," she says. "This one stays."

Mateo's mouth falls open. "What?"

She looks back at me like I'm the answer to her problems. "Chela, why don't you talk to Mateo about everything you know and then come back so I can tell you the rest."

My ears must be on fire. My fists tighten. I'm sure I look ready to explore the full thrust of my destroyer powers. Mateo puts a calming hand on the small of my back, and it's the only thing that keeps me from leaping across the room, finding Mimi's neck between my fingers, and squeezing.

What right has she? After all she's done, after whatever it is she knows—how dare this barely human traitor lord half-truths over me?

"Leave." I whisper to keep from shouting. If I shout, it'll bring down this whole tower, crumble my father's synagogue. And I'd like the chance to see it for real now that we're here.

My aunt flashes an exaggerated frown. "You won't let this island fall into Archibaldo's hands, my girl. This I know."

"Maybe I'll drop it back below the surface where it was," I snarl.

"You can't. Not now. You've set everything into motion."

"I think you underestimate my ability to not give a damn."

Tía Mimi does not look impressed, or even vicious. She just keeps glancing around the room and blinking too many times. I don't even know why I'm bothering with this lady. She wipes some drool from the corner of her mouth and stares at me. "Then why don't I tell Mateo—?"

"Stop." I hate it when people call my bluff. There are a few things I give a damn about, and whatever it was that happened in history, I need to find out more before I talk to Mateo about it. "Mateo . . . give us a sec. Please."

He blinks at me, opens his mouth to say something, then shakes his head and walks out the door, closing it firmly behind him.

"You have three minutes," I say, standing uneasily and gathering my stuff.

"Now that you raised it," Mimi says, "what happens on this island is inextricably linked to what happens in Little Madrigal."

"Basura," I grunt.

"You think a place is just a place? Don't be naive, child. A place is also its people, of course. And a place as rooted in spirit and magic as this one, well . . . just imagine. Sink the island again—go on. Then see what remnants of everyone you loved are left when you get back to Brooklyn."

"You're a damn liar!" I snap.

"Am I?" She turns away. "Under this tower there's a tunnel that will lead you to the beach. Hopefully the boat is still there for Galanika to leave on. You're welcome." And she's gone.

"What was she talking about?" Mateo asks, eyes wide when I walk out into the shadowy corridor. "Are we leaving?"

"No," I say. "Not the island, anyway. But we're definitely leaving this dungeon. Come on." I lead him down the stairs, trying to ignore the feeling of the world falling out from under me.

CHAPTER SEVEN

MATEO

"It's the whole island at once, and parts I never imagined existed, not in any version of who I am," Chela says as the tunnel starts to climb steeply toward the surface.

I've never known Chela to unleash such a torrent of disconnected thoughts like this. She's been rattling through various topics the whole time we've been in the tunnel, barely letting me get a word in. I'm not complaining, it's just . . . whatever it is she's *not* telling me clearly looms larger for her than anything she's actually saying.

We both know there's something giant on her back, between us, all around. We both know it matters, that it won't be denied. Whatever Mimi was going on about, it touched a nerve. I want to pull Chela close, whisper that it'll be all right, whatever it is, but I'm not a good liar, and I really have no idea if anything will ever be all right.

"Truth is," she goes on, "I've never *felt* like Madrigal. Not the way I feel like Okanla. I mean, that was a no-brainer. I've always loved destroying things. It all comes natural, a language I learned before I remember learning. And yeah, this creation magic can be pretty straightforward, sure, but it doesn't fully feel like me. And maybe it never will, who knows?"

Back in Brooklyn, the phantom bambarúto used Chela's powers to incarnate themselves before she even knew she had them. Once she figured it out, she brought to life a whole army of golems in Tolo's basement—secret weapons Mimi'd had shipped off the island right before the fall. But Chela hasn't tried to do much with her creation magic since, and it's not the kind of thing you can just casually practice.

Destroying, on the other hand . . . that's practical to learn *and* handy in a fight.

"I've never had it like it is for you," she goes on. The sound of the ocean grows louder from up ahead. We're close to the top. "I don't *see* the other parts of me—they don't show up from the future."

That was how I realized who I was—Galanika kept appearing to me as he's depicted on prayer candles and paintings all over Little Madrigal: a ripped old dude with a scarred eye and white beard. He's me in some distant future, I guess. (Who knows how time works for spirits, right? Not even me, and I apparently *am* one!) I finally put the pieces together when that bambarúto almost ripped my eye out.

"It's probably like the way you understand music, I'm thinking." I don't want to say Chela is *rambling*, because that seems rude and dismissive. But if I'm being honest, Chela is definitely rambling. "Like . . . you learned it, sure. You know the ins and outs, the technical stuff. But you also *feel* it. There's an instinctive aspect at play. I can see that. That's why it helped you figure out how to heal, too. You had to see healing through the lens of something that made sense to you intrinsically."

We step out into a tropical nighttime world. The waves slosh onto the beach up ahead. Based on where the three mountains are, I'm guessing we're not too far from where we came ashore, what feels like a lifetime ago.

"But I don't have anything like that—something to help me understand how Madrigal works inside me. This . . ." She swings a reckless arm over the rise and fall of jungle peaks, the gulls circling over rooftops, the certainty of monsters lurking within. "This place. It all came rearing up at me when we landed, all happened at once, like every cell, every plant, every secret and crevice and landing and alley of this island was yelling inside me at the same time."

"Damn," I say, trying to empathize but only managing to worry about why she won't look at me, what she's not saying. Whatever it is, you could fill a vast ballroom with it. This moment isn't about me and her, though. This is bigger than the two of us. "Do you want me to, ah, try to heal your . . . whatever, now?"

She squints at me like I've just asked her what my own name is.

"The thing on your arm."

"Oh!" She glances at it, seems confused, distracted. "It's fine. Later, maybe. It doesn't hurt. It's just weird. But *what was I expecting*, right?"

"What did your aunt mean by *the island is dying*?"

Chela shakes her head, annoyed. "Mateo, I don't think we can give too much importance to anything that woman says, unfortunately. Seems pretty alive to me."

Soft glints of light begin sphering through the air like the first gentle snowfall of winter. We glance all around, squinting to make out these strange bubbly figures against the dark sky. They're everywhere.

Then it hits me. "*Iwin*," I whisper, awed.

Chela cocks an eyebrow. "Huh?"

"They're little creatures from the spirit world that like to hang out with people and get all up in their affairs. There's songs about them in almost every culture. Iwin is just one of their names, from the Santeros, I think. But I've never . . . you know . . ."

"Imagined they're real?" Chela says.

"Exactly." We both blink at the hundreds and hundreds of little floating spirits filling the night. Sure, we've battled monsters together and done things most people would call miracles. Sure, we're living incarnations of spirits ourselves. But that doesn't stop the wonder of getting to stand next to someone you care about and watch a marvelous bit of magic unfold before your very eyes. I didn't even notice she'd slid her hand around mine until she squeezed it.

After a little while, I ask, "But now—the thing with the sensory overload—is it better?"

She shakes her head, eyes on the dancing translucent creatures. "Still there, just less." Shrugs. "Guess my body and mind adjusted to being on the island that is a part of me. Or something . . ." Scowls. "I don't know how to do this."

This. Does she mean *us*?

I don't know how to do *this*, either, but my *this* is: figure out how to be a divine being who is also a teenage boy while fighting for my life on a mystical once-sunken island.

In fact, the one thing I *do* know—maybe the only thing I know— is how I feel about Chela. Love only barely gets to it. Love seems like too fragile a word for what I feel, thinned from overuse. I don't remember most of the hundreds of years we've been at each other's side, learning each other, fighting for each other, growing together, but they still live inside me; they are with me when I look at her, when she smiles.

Maybe that's not true for Chela, though. She was just talking about how the spirit parts of ourselves work differently. Maybe she looks at me and sees some kid who happens to be along for the ride, who she's stuck with, puts up with.

"What is it?" Chela asks, because now I'm the one blinking out at the darkening horizon.

My attention snaps back to the girl in front of me; I gaze down at her, find her eyes, and know instantly I was making up ridiculous stories a second ago. Her expression leaves no question about how she feels about me.

"We never . . ." I'm not sure what words I need, so I take her face in one hand, and she closes the distance between us. I exhale, try again. "We never said what we are."

She rolls her eyes, but not cruelly. "Aw, man—who knows? We're spirits, we're teenagers, we're gods, angels, demons, whatever. I'm over trying to—"

"No," I say, laughing through the sudden bout of nerves that rises within me. "Not that." I almost didn't cut her off because I love when she gets going on a little rant like that. But who knows when something's going to come try to kill us or recruit us to its freakish cause? Time is weird and unstable here. "Not what we, each of us, are. What you and I *together* are. What *we* are, Chela. What are we?"

Chela's puzzled face breaks into the widest smile I've ever seen on her. "Mateo Matisse Medina!" She gawks, pulling closer to me now. "After all these hundreds of years, are you . . . Are you asking me out?"

"I . . ." I hadn't thought of it like that. I'm not sure how I'd been thinking of it. We've never talked about it! We just . . . We just both knew. Before we knew what we were, we knew we shared a oneness, an ease beyond the fluttering and crushing. We knew we loved each other, and in a way it was simple. And in some other way, absolutely the opposite of simple. But hey, every story contains its opposite, as Madrigal lore reminds us again and again. "I guess I am!"

She scrunches her face wryly. "Um, no, sir, you certainly better not be guessing about something as important as this. You asking me out or not? Say it with your chest, son."

My turn to roll eyes. She knows that's not what I meant—it's not like there's a precedent for this. And anyway, I may not know exactly what I meant, either, but whatever it is, it's much more than just asking her out. Pretty sure I'm not going to figure it out without saying it, though (which is actually really unfair, but what else is new?).

One word at a time is the only way this'll happen. "I'm not . . . asking . . . you . . . out. . . ." I almost give the whole thing up when she blinks away a sudden pained look. Why is this so hard? The rest comes out in a torrent, desperate for clarity. "I'm asking you if you'll be my . . . my person, Chela. I'm saying I want you, that you're more important to me than what everyone else thinks or what happens next, that to me you're bigger than this damn island and all the terrible history we've seen but lost."

Her eyes go wide; she finally understands.

"I'm saying," I manage through what turn out, unhelpfully, to be tears, "that you're like music to me. That's what you are."

We both startle out of the moment as the deep clanging of a bell rings across the evening sky. "What the . . . ?" Chela gasps.

"It's coming from the synagogue," I say. Then it hits me. "'The Midnight Toll for Lonely Lovers'!"

Chela shoots me a *Huh?* look.

"It's an old Madrigal pirate ballad that everyone used to sing in barrooms. The legend is those bells ring at midnight every night to commemorate some tragic love affair. But the story itself isn't in the song—the song's about some side buccaneer using the bells to woo his beloved, et cetera, et cetera."

"Men will forever be the corniest pickup artists, huh," Chela quips.

"Yes, but also . . . the legend is real? Unless it's Mimi ringing that bell." I squint toward the two towers that rise over the treetops, trying to make out a swinging bell. "She doesn't seem like the sentimental type, somehow."

Chela puts a finger on my chin and brings my face back to hers. "Repeat what you just said," she says over the chimes.

"She doesn't seem like the—"

She swats me, and I deserve it, so I get serious. "You're like music to me."

She raises one hand, palm out, then the other. I meet them with my own, and we put our foreheads together.

I try to imagine what it would be like to live in a world that loved us back, that wanted us to win instead of throwing every problem in our path, whichever way we turn. I try to imagine a world built from a love as strong as the one I feel between us. What would things have been like if Vizvargal and his worshipers weren't constantly trying to undermine and destroy this place we built?

I open my eyes as the last chime begins to fade, and Chela opens hers. That faraway look crosses her face, and I wonder if she'll float away to that distant place again . . . except instead she reaches up around my neck and pulls me into a kiss.

It's a deeper kiss than we've ever had before. It's the moon and the stars, the slowly turning globe, the spirits dancing in the night.

Everything else is nothing at all.

When it's done, I hold her for a few moments, my lips near her ear, hers near mine.

"Let's go," I say. "Get away from this place, this past, this mess. Not Brooklyn—somewhere where we can just be, just you and me, Chela and Mateo, and that's it."

I'm not sure if she's laughing or crying when she whispers, "That's quite an ambitious first date, Mateo Matisse."

"Yeah, well—" I start, but my words are cut off by a sudden rumble that rips through the night, getting louder and louder until the whole island shakes with it.

And then one of the three peaks of San Madrigal shatters to boulders and dust, and it cascades into the dark sea.

DAY TWO

Death is a doorway,

the dead our only escort through.

The end never comes, is always there.

Only those who have left can see you through,

return you to all you once knew.

All you will never know.

The dead are a doorway,

Death our only escort through.

—*The San Madrigal Book of the Dead*, Canto VII

CHAPTER EIGHT

CHELA

EVERY ONCE IN A WHILE, WHEN I WAS LITTLE, MY DAD WOULD relent to all my begging and let me spend the day at my cousin Tolo's house. Tolo wasn't the problem, of course. His dad, Si, my father's brother-in-law, was a notorious gangster. But even that wasn't the problem, not really. Si was the one who performed the initiation ceremony on me, the one that clinched my connection to Okanla (and thus Madrigal, though I'm sure no one knew it at the time). He did it behind my parents' backs, and I can see how that would piss them off. And then the island sank, that very day, and everyone moved to Brooklyn, where Si had already set up his criminal empire *and* made sure there was plenty of room for the diaspora Galerana.

And my dad, even though he's the head rabbi of Madrigal and always insists the whole community—Jewish or not—is his congregation, he swore never to speak to his brother-in-law again after that day. But he didn't want to deprive me of spending time with my favorite cousin. The whole family shouldn't be torn apart just because he had a vendetta—that was his philosophy.

And every time, as the playdate was coming to an end and my dad was on the way to pick me up, I'd pretend to fall asleep, wishing and praying that it would force him to come inside and finally, finally spend some quality time with Si.

Usually, Tolo and Si would tickle me till I couldn't pretend anymore and then send me out to where Dad waited, tall and stubborn and stern in his overcoat, and off we would go.

But one night Si heaved my tiny body onto his giant shoulder and marched toward the front door.

The thick, tangy smell of some designer cologne filled my nose. My heart felt like it was pounding right through me and against Si, like he was a door it was desperately trying to get into.

"Mira, nena," he said in a gravelly whisper. He had to know I was awake; I wasn't fooling anyone. "Todas las cosas que eres, sélas. Sélas enteramente. Esa es la única manera de ser."

All the things you are, be them.

I wonder if he knew how important those words would be to me all these years later. He couldn't have had any idea that Madrigal and Okanla are one. I don't think anyone knew that—not any humans, anyway. But he could already see how many different things I was at once. He saw me, and I didn't even really get it, what it meant, not yet, but I *felt* how true it was, how important it was. I remember smiling into his shoulder, my eyes still squeezed shut; I remember feeling seen.

Then the door swung open with that squeak and groan, and he stepped out into the winter night.

For a long time, the two men just stood there staring at each other, their breath rising into the sky as the snow cascaded in wild spirals all around us.

Be them entirely.

This is the only way to be.

Now, as I stumble in a half daze through the beachside jungles of the island that is a part of me, all I can think about are Si's words. Dawn simmers at the far edge of the sky. I've been walking all night, moving through underbrush, over sand dunes, past ruins and stone figures. None of it makes sense; none of it matters.

Have I ever fully been all the things I am? Is that even possible when I didn't know the half of them until very recently?

It hardly seems like a fair demand on someone so full and so empty at the same time. I barely know how to be Chela, let alone Okanla, Madrigal, a spirit divided, an entire island. I love Si, but what a typically useless adult thing to say to a child. Pretty words, big sentiments; in practical terms: shite.

A few hours ago, I put Mateo back on the boat, gave him his mandate, the info that would lead him to answers, and sent him on his way with a vague demand he think of me at midnight.

I should've explained everything; I explained nothing.

There wasn't time, I keep telling myself. Another lie. I just needed him gone, as fast as possible. If he lingered any longer, I never would've let him go. And he had to go; that much was clear. I don't know how true any of these things are—nothing Mimi says can be trusted—but obviously there's *something* going on; something about the Galanika-Okanla connection is now throwing the natural world into disarray and imbalance, and I need to know why. If there are answers out in Little Madrigal, Mateo will get them. Or, more precisely, Tolo will get them and give them to Mateo. My cousin took over his dad's operations when Si was killed, and that included the most extensive library of Madrigal books and lore anywhere.

And if there are answers here, I'll find them. I'll shatter that crooked old man at the heart of this mess and get the information we need, and Mateo and I will break this curse, or whatever it is, and we'll live out the rest of our endless immortal lives in love, and that will be that.

Yeah, right.

I stumble down a tall dune—hadn't been looking where I was going, of course. Lost in thought. Halfway to the bottom of the slope, my foot snags on a root and I topple forward, catch a mouthful of sand, and roll the rest of the way.

"I should probably be more careful," I say from the ground, my voice breathy and half-choked. This whole island is covered with monsters. Some of them want me dead; others think I'm a god. One is even my aunt.

How did the world get this weird?

I'm on my feet, lurching toward the waves, grabbing tree limbs and bushes to steady myself, failing and flailing.

Right before he left, Mateo had leaned down to kiss me.

I'd stepped back, then just offered up my cheek instead. Those wide eyes. He'd looked so startled. Not even hurt, wasn't trying to guilt-trip me. It was clear it had completely caught him off guard.

And then he'd nodded like he understood even though he didn't—he couldn't—and gotten in the boat and zoomed off across the waves.

If we'd had time for me to tell him what's going on, we would've joked about it, found another way, figured it out together. We would've tried, at least. But inevitably, the night would've led us back into each other's arms; that inevitable, irresistible pull would've taken hold, the gravity of us. It would've yanked us closer and closer, and then more mountains would've collapsed, and who knows what other hell would've been unleashed both here and in Brooklyn.

I know myself. I know Mateo. He would've tried to resist, but I would've won him over. That's why he had to go, immediately.

Don't come back till you have an answer, I told him, hating the words, myself for saying them, the look he gave me. Suddenly I was the cruel one, the Destroyer incarnate. The problem.

Is the world so fragile? Or is our love that strong? Doesn't matter. All that matters is we find a solution.

I wind along a sodden path back into the jungle, down another incline, and then up to a heavily forested plateau, the crashing waves in the distance.

Something shines on the ground up ahead. A bare patch, I realize as I approach. It's off-white and glistens slightly . . . not unlike the strange marking on my arm. I take another step toward it, then feel a snap against my ankle as the ground spins wild loops around me and I'm yanked up into a tree.

Dammit.

And there I dangle, upside down.

I was carrying my satchel in one hand when it happened, and that's *definitely* still on the ground; must've dropped it in surprise, like an absolute newbie.

I am 100 percent off my game, and this is what I get for it. Swinging twenty feet over the forest floor upside down in the middle of a jungle full of monsters.

Way to go, Chela.

Still . . . this contraption the rope is attached to—it's beaded with a yellow-and-blue design that spans a large cowrie shell. Santero work, clearly. Are they here? The mighty orishas? That'd be something to see.

Whatever it is, it's not a bambarúto that's trapped me.

That's all I need to know.

It's been a long day, and hanging upside down is surprisingly more comfortable than I ever would've imagined. Besides, I'm a god of destruction, chaos queen, and this island is my island, is me.

And anyway, everything is terrible.

Perhaps it'll be better when I wake up.

CHAPTER NINE

MATEO

THE DIVINE COUNCIL.

And my own great-whatever-father, Maestro Archibaldo.

The Cabildo during the peace accords.

Find out everything you can, she said. *Everything.*

I've never seen her like that, not even in the thick of battle. Chela is the definition of cool breeze. Even when she's upset about something, she merely morphs into a grumpy variation on the theme of cool breeze. This Chela . . . This was something else entirely.

When the mountain collapsed, we ran. It didn't make sense. We weren't close enough to get crushed by it, but somehow standing there felt wrong. Huge bursts of dust and rock exploded into the night, and the air around us filled with tiny shards of debris. None of it was moving fast enough to cause much damage, though; it just raked against our skin and made everything cloudy.

And then we stopped, because the rumbling had ended, and the whole peak was just gone. Gone. There was only sky where it had been.

I turned to Chela, and she had the strangest look on her face. . . .

Understanding is the only way I can put it, like she knew; somehow she knew. But there was a haggard kind of terror etched into her, too. She grabbed my arm, ushered me to the boat we'd come in.

"You need to leave," she said before telling me what to research. "You can't . . . We can't . . ." She'd looked away, shaking her head, tears welling up. "I'm sorry, Mateo. There's no time to explain. Find out what you can. You'll know when you find it. But"—she squinted up at me like she'd been slapped—"don't come back until you have an answer."

I nodded. I hated all of it, but I knew, and still know twelve hours and a thousand miles later, that I'm capable of doing quite literally anything for Chela Hidalgo, even dying and coming back to life. So whatever it is, I'll do it, cool. But I hated it then and I hate it now, and I hated it even more when I went in for a goodbye kiss and she gave me her cheek instead.

"Think of me at midnight" is the last thing she told me. "I'll find you there."

Cryptic. Delicious. Maddening. Chela to a tee.

But long-lost folklore aside, if the bells really do strike at midnight every night, that'll be Chela's only way to check the time, our only way of linking at the same moment. It's not like she'll have anywhere to charge her phone.

I don't know what the cheek-instead-of-lips thing meant, whether we're done or not, what I'm supposed to do with that. We barely— no, we *didn't* even get to have our talk about what we are. So how can something that doesn't even have a name be over? Did it ever begin? Maybe I was a fool to think that just because we've been lovers for centuries, just because our spirits created a whole island and made new forms of music to better express how deeply we felt for each other, because of all that, we were automatically going to click and be a thing now that we're in our human forms.

All this is spinning through my head for the fifteen thousandth time—uselessly, I might add—when I step back onto the streets of Little Madrigal, Brooklyn, for the first time since we'd raised the island.

It's winter—blistering, blasted winter—and the dirty brown snowscapes ripple through the street edges, forming gnarly tide pools of filth between parked cars.

I haven't slept since I don't know when, and I'm still achy from my run-in with that spider monster. My brain has been so racked, I couldn't even be bothered to fully heal myself. The whiplash of it all.

But Chela gave me a mission, however vague, and if getting answers is what will get me back to her, then that's what I have to do.

Times like this, it's helpful to have a checklist.

1. I'm gonna go to the library, where I'll
2. find the info we need, then
3. do with it whatever must be done and
4. get back to San Madrigal, where I'll
5. find Chela and help her defeat Archi if she hasn't yet, leading to
6. me and Chela living happily ever after, boom!

See? I already feel better just mapping it out like that. Especially because step one is so easy. And once it's done, step two will seem much more manageable. Bam! It's like music! All those dissonant chords collapse back to the sweet harmony of the one, and everything slides into its place.

I point myself down Fulton Street toward Tolo's club and start walking.

First thing that's different: a cop car idles up ahead. We never had to bother much with the police in Little Madrigal. A deal Si and then-councilwoman Anisette struck with city leadership kept them out of our business. But now Anisette is gone, crushed by one of the golems Chela brought to life, so I guess the deal is off.

My breath catches a little when I see it, and I duck into a doorway without even thinking about it. Instinct, I guess. I'm not doing anything illegal. But a lifetime of being brown in America and coming from a hidden pirate nation has enshrined distrust of the law into my DNA.

When I peek out, another cruiser is pulled up alongside the first. I hear laughter; then they both peel off in a hurry.

I step back onto the sidewalk, mad at myself for hiding and acting guilty when I have nothing to conceal. But also just a little shaken up.

It's a small thing, cops in Little Madrigal, but it adds to the creeping sensation that the world is spinning too fast under my feet.

I have to stay focused.

Tolo will know where to look. He might even know exactly what I'm talking about. The guy is a library of lore unto himself, and he has the physical books to back it up, all stashed in his weird mystical library beneath the club. Even farther down, an entire army of golems stands stock-still, waiting to be brought back to life. Chela ignited them to action when we were fighting the bambarúto and Vizvargal, and they immediately shut back down once the battle was over.

The streets of Little Madrigal feel cavernous, vacant; the silence of them howls.

That week the empire pirates staged their coup and took over the Cabildo, it had felt like this, too—an emptiness that was all the more pronounced because we normally live half our lives cavorting through the streets, yelling, singing, laughing, carrying on into infinity.

I stop. Let the quiet surround me like darkness closing in on a sudden winter night.

Did something happen? I realize I haven't even checked in with anyone from home since I left. My best friend, Tams, would've told me if there'd been an attack, I'm sure of it. My parents, now back from their endless save-the-world globetrotting, certainly would've let me know. Right?

I spent the trip back too caught up in my head to let anyone know I was coming, but I had my phone on.

I'm starting to break into a run when something shimmers into existence just in front of me. Some*one*.

He's very old and very frail. It takes me a few moments of gaping to realize who this is: it's me—Galanika, many, many years from now.

But something's different this time.

In the past, whenever Old Galanika appeared, he'd look the way he's depicted all over Little Madrigal: an old dude who hits the gym a little too hard.

Now this visage shimmering in the middle of Fulton Street—it's definitely me as an old man, with the scar down the side of the face that can't be missed—but . . . he's . . . *I'm* . . . dying.

I'm not totally sure how I know. It's more than just a physical thing, although he looks alarmingly weak—on the verge of total collapse. No, it's something else. Death lurks in the small moments, the nuances and details that can't quite be described or tallied but are unmistakably there nonetheless.

Maybe it's those eyes. They seem to glare at me with a certain hungry desperation that I've never seen in this phantom of myself before. He's always looked calm, badass, stern. Never scared, never weak, never this.

Galanika reaches out one hand to me, his younger human form. It's like he's pleading with me, asking me to save him.

I don't know what he wants, what I'm supposed to make of this. *Use your words!* I almost yell, but what good would that do? If he could talk, I'm sure he would've by now. Instead, I just stare until he slowly vanishes back into the ether and all that's left is the ghostly mist of my breath, the parked cars, the dirty snow.

I must've done something wrong. It's all I can think. Future me was once proud and healthy, ripped even; now he's at death's door and silently begging me to save him.

I have to get to Tolo's. I need answers. My feet have already broken into a run as I realize how desperate I am. They carry me all the way down Fulton, past so many quiet shops and darkened windows.

And then I stop because I can't make sense of what I'm seeing.

There's sky where Tolo's club is supposed to be.

Sky and, on the ground, a pile of cement, Sheetrock, wood, and rubble.

———

A single tall figure stands at the edge of the rubble: Safiya Alaqba—Tolo's right-hand woman. Safiya barely flinched when the first bambarúto revealed itself in Tolo's office, not far from where we stand now. She's a warrior through and through.

But now her shivering hands grip a paper cup of steaming bodega coffee, and her face scrunches in on itself like she's still trying to make sense of what she's looking at.

And I get it. Tolo's club was more than just a music venue or hangout spot. It was the beating heart of the community. It's where we gathered to celebrate one another, for vote nights—that sacred and often corrupt pirate ritual—and for the Grande Fete. We all have so many memories from this place; the walls must've known all our secrets, our jealousies, our whispered love affairs.

And, I found out recently, the walls had their own secrets, too. Si had built tunnels all throughout this block. An underground hall held the magnificent golem army. Tolo's office alone was home to a vast library of archival tomes from Madrigal, including, I'd hoped, the very information I need to bring back to Chela.

And now all of it—the books, the secrets, the memories—has been reduced to shattered rock and twisted steel.

"What . . . What happened?" I ask, stepping up beside her.

She barely seems to register my presence, just shakes her head. "No one knows. It collapsed. Sometime last night."

Tolo's club is usually rocking late into the night, which means . . . "Was anyone—?"

"There was a bembé for Sango at Baba Mo's. He said everyone in the community had to come by—part of this whole unity thing they've been pushing. I guess the santos are in on it, too. But look"—she nods at the rubble, eyes still wide with disbelief—"it saved some lives. Another weird Madrigal miracle for the books."

"Weird miracles seem like all we've got," I say.

Something shifts in Safiya. She looks over at me for the first time, blinks. "Galanika!"

I roll my eyes. "Just Mateo, please, Safiya."

She nods, pats me on the back, and returns her gaze to the rubble. "A triumphant reentry from your heroic adventures to our lost homeland."

I scoff. "Hardly."

"Is it true . . . ? That it's back?"

I nod, shrug in that Galerano way, scrunch my face. All that means *Yes, but it's complicated*, and I'm so grateful when Safiya returns the gesture. She doesn't need me to explain any more than that.

There's so much to do, especially now that my step one has been demolished before I could even begin. But I have no idea what I'm looking for yet, and in a strange way, all I want to do is stand here with Safiya and take it all in. Feels like I haven't stopped moving in months.

"Speaking of weird miracles . . ." Safiya says after a few moments. "Must feel strange, no?"

"What's that?"

"The god thing, or whatever. Santo. Being that. Or finding out."

I guffaw, because yes, it is, but somehow it feels like one of the least weird things going on. And I like that she asked me direct instead of wondering quietly. After we've both had a good chuckle at the absurdity of it all, I say, "It is pretty strange, yeah. But even though I don't know the words for it—not even sure there are any— what I can tell you is that it's simply true. I know who I am like I know I have a hand. It's just there, that reality."

Safiya nods, then frowns. "Guess you can't really go to therapy to deal with stuff that comes up, being an immortal or whatever."

It's the kind of thing someone else would say as a corny joke to break the tension of impossibility, but I can tell she really means it. Hadn't even occurred to me, to be honest. "Do you go to therapy?"

"Of course," she scoffs, then sips some coffee. "Do you have any idea how many people I've killed?"

Nothing to say back to that, so I wait.

"Sure, they all had it coming, but still. Therapy is awesome."

"And you can . . . You talk about that stuff?"

"I find creative ways to get what I need out of it, let's put it that way."

I consider for a moment. "I guess maybe I could, too, sometime."

"Well, let me know if you ever need a reference. Or just want to talk. I'm a pretty good listener, quiet as it's kept."

Weird miracles indeed. "Thank you, Safiya." And then it hits me that we are literally the only people out right now. I haven't seen a single other Galerano since I've been back. "Where is everyone, anyway?"

"The unity event," she says like it's the most obvious thing in the world. Then she catches herself. "Oh, right—you've been gone, sorry. There's an, ah, event going on at the synagogue. I want no part of it, to be honest, and I don't think Tolo does, either, but he's more committed to politics than I am."

That sounds bad. "Unity event?"

"Yeah . . . reconciliation . . . something, something . . . hearing out the empire pirates . . ."

My eyes must boggle, because Safiya rolls hers. "Tell me about it. Worst part is— Mateo? Where you going?"

CHAPTER TEN

CHELA

A RUSTLING OF LEAVES BELOW YANKS ME OUT OF TROUBLED SLUMBER.

My head is throbbing. For a moment, I panic. Why am I upside down? How . . . ? Then the strange night slams back into me: the kiss that toppled a mountain, the dread and coldness of that goodbye, the wandering, and, at dawn, this damn trap.

Somehow, I had lulled myself into a feeling that whatever happens, happens, that I can handle everything. But down below, I see the long, loping strides of several bambarúto, their labyrinthine skin glistening in the early afternoon sunlight that cuts through the canopy of banyan leaves above. And the look of hurt on Mateo's face—it keeps pounding through my head like a hangover, the impossibility of our situation, the steep sense of gravity between us.

I can't handle any of this, let alone *everything*.

Sure, I'm immortal and probably very hard to kill, but there are much worse things than dying, as anyone with any imagination whatsoever will happily remind you.

And anyway, my bag.

It's nestled in a bush directly below, the beaded handle of my blade sticking out, shiny and easy to catch a glint of.

There are four bambarúto. They stride with confidence, with the certainty that the divine light of their vile, dead demon god still moves through them.

And they're about six feet away from my stuff.

They'll find it . . . and know I'm near. Scanning the forest, they'll finally look up, and here I'll be. All bound up and nursing a confusion-and-heartbreak headache, just dangling here for the taking.

Here's something else I haven't talked to Mateo about but probably should've: I don't really know how my powers work.

Mateo's a good listener, and the only other being like me in the world, as far as I know. But more than that, I helped him learn how to heal. Still remember that lost look on his face as he crouched over a wounded body in the streets of Little Madrigal. It seemed really straightforward from where I stood—music is the window he sees the world through, so of course his healing power would be related to that. I told him to listen to the music inside him. But I knew he was lost in the panic of the moment, and nothing made sense, let alone some new secret magic. I understood being lost and having more power than you knew what to do with, literally.

Point is, we've talked it through since, as he's worked on it and honed his skills, but I've never gone in depth about mine.

I just kind of focus on whatever I'm touching and try to send my energy into it and keep a clear sense of what I want to happen and . . . boom! Sometimes it does!

Sometimes being the key word.

But I don't know why it works when it does. I don't know how I'm supposed to be any use in a jam when I can't consistently do the very thing I'm an actual divinity of! Hello!

And who has time to practice when disasters keep happening?

I'm about to try to swing my body up and reach the rope around my ankle—maybe destroy it even, who knows?—when a colorful shaft whizzes out of the trees nearby and does the job for me.

The rope snaps, and I plummet and probably scream as I go, because once I manage to angle my face down it's only to see all four bambarúto looking up at me, huge mouths open wide.

I don't have time to do any cool surprise attacks or spiffy landings. I just clatter directly on top of one of them in a flailing mess. The impact knocks the wind out of me . . . and doesn't even topple the damn bambarúto! But that's all right; got something else for its maze-faced ass. I clamber up the huge creature's slimy, sharp body toward that horned head. I may not have had the full element of surprise, but still, I'm sure it wasn't expecting a girl to drop out of the sky.

Both my hands land on its pulsating temples, and as its mouth opens in a scream, I send all the destruction and pain I can muster into my palms and . . . the thing just flinches, grunts, then swings one arm. A nasty crack across my face sends me spinning sideways through the air into a freaking tree trunk.

Stars. I literally see little dancing flashes of light as I collapse to the damp soil and then scramble out of the way as the thing comes charging, claws-first.

And then it stops a foot or two away.

If you pause too near your enemy in a battle to the death, you die. That seems like it'd be rule number one, no? Not my problem either way. I close the distance between us before it can reconsider. Both hands out, I can already feel the power surge through me as my palms land on the thing's torso. That thick chitinous flesh shatters first, and then some gooey internal organs explode outward, splattering me. Suddenly unsupported, the top half of the bambarúto drops straight down between its own legs, which fall to either side. It doesn't even have time to squeal before it's dead.

I'm still panting when a thick net covers the sky and then me.

I can deal with this. This is a thing I can destroy.

I better do it fast, though, because the other three bambarúto are making their way toward me at a brisk, snarling run.

Just gotta get a good piece of it in my hand and . . . Nothing happens when I call on my destruction powers. Nothing at all.

I try again, and of course, still nothing. They're all around me, muttering and grunting. I'll have to kill them from inside this net when they come for me.

I'm gathering my strength, taking deep breaths and getting ready. I'm a divine being, and I cannot be stopped. Just a little wonky at the moment is all.

But I'm ready. I'm absolutely ready for anything.

I look up when a sharp swishing sound cuts the air, ending with a juicy *thwunk*. Another colorful shaft—an arrow, just like the one that freed me from the rope trap—is suddenly sticking out of the nearest bambarúto's face. It drops to its knees, howling as two more arrows find their marks in the others.

The creatures aren't dead, but they're definitely tapped out. All three stumble away with shrieks and growls.

A few moments of heavy breathing pass, and then soft footsteps approach.

I turn myself around, blinking through the heavy netting.

A girl about my age emerges from the forest. Her skin is golden, her face wide with sharp cheekbones and bright yellow eyes. Two antlers rise in elegant, thorny arches from her head.

"Well, well, well," my savior says, very pleased with herself. "Look who decided to show back up!"

"Well, whoever you are—are you going to help me out of this, or are you going to walk in circles looking smug?"

From the look of that too-pleased smile and those arched eyebrows, this wild elk chick is going with option two.

"Depends," she drawls with a wink and a thick Galerano accent. "I'm not sure I trust you yet, eh."

"Well, that's mutual, at least, so why don't you go ahead and level the playing field. We can sort this out like women."

She laughs—a cruel, beautiful sound made of cobwebs and icicles. "How very mortal of you."

"I'm *not* mortal," I growl, and it comes out with more wrath than I meant it to. I may be unsure of many things about myself, but that's not one of them. Not anymore.

"Ooh, ooh! It's a nerve I have struck!" She twirls just out of reach, not that I can get very far with this net tangled around me. I've only managed to disintegrate one small section at a time. Not enough to pull free. Partly because I'm trying to do it without Elk Chick noticing, but also because my powers are still only working when they feel like it.

"Look," I say, the frustration bleeding through without my permission. "You're . . . You're a spirit, aren't you?"

She doesn't answer, keeps circling in slow, deliberate strides. She's full flesh and blood, this girl, not some wispy apparition. But this is Madrigal, the island built from my essence, where spirits incarnate and monsters roam.

From those horns and that bow and arrow, she must be one of the hunter santos, probably associated with the orisha Ochossi.

"What do you want? What's your name?"

She bows elaborately and smugly. "Odé Kan, I am called. The hunter of hearts. Or the first hunter. Depends on who you ask, or how I'm feeling, really."

"I'd say nice to meet you, but . . . it hasn't been so far."

She giggles. "Honesty. I enjoy that. It pleases me." Then a somber look crosses her wide face. "And what I want, in fact, is less important than what *you* want. . . ."

I stand to my full height, which isn't much, but it's better than being all hunched over trying to quietly untangle myself. "I'm listening."

"You are, I think, Okanla the Destroyer, incarnated into the body of a human girl, hmm?"

"I am," I say easily. Because that part is easy. This second bit, less so: "I am also Madrigal the Creator, incarnated into the body of a human girl."

Her stare is impossible to read.

I add a little "Hmm?" at the end in the same pitch she uses.

Odé Kan snorts through a vibrant smile, then gets serious again. She points a long golden finger directly at me, and it would be comical if her frown wasn't pure business. "Are you here to unite our forces and lead us against the armies of Vizvargal—yes or no?"

"I . . ." Words slip away. I know I'm supposed to sound certain right now; thing is, I'm anything but. Gotta go with the truth—this one looks like she could hit a lie with one of those arrows from ten miles away. "I'm not sure."

She lifts her chin and squints, but she's still listening.

"I raised the island again . . . just like I brought it down fifteen years ago. But . . . I don't remember that other time. I don't remember anything that happened before the moment we—*I* became one with this form."

Odé Kan lets out a thoughtful murmur. Don't know what it means, but I keep going.

"We took out Vizvargal in Brooklyn. Galanika did, really. And yes, I will bring down anyone who tries to carry his banner, starting with that deranged old maestro who's clearly lived two centuries too long."

Odé Kan spits a guffaw.

"But I don't know what's happening on the ground. I barely understand the history that's happened in my lifetime, let alone all the back-in-the-day crap that I played some huge unknown role in.

And I don't know how I'm supposed to unite forces I just found out about. Plus . . ."

Odé Kan looks up suddenly; her great yellow eyes widen, then sharpen to slits.

"Wha—?" I start, but I'm cut off when she leaps forward, snatching my blade from the ground as she goes, then cleaves the net with a few quick swipes.

"You liked my speech?" I ask, pulling the remaining strands off me and emerging at last.

"I did like it okay, yes, but also our friends are coming back now and have brought more friends for us to murder."

"So, you trust me?" I offer my open hand.

"Eh." She makes a noncommittal shrug, the Galerano one. "I saw you in action, and I could probably use a hand." She flips my blade so the beaded grip faces me, passes it over. "Trust takes more than a few earnest words, however true they may be. But I respect someone who can admit they don't know, I'll say that."

She lowers herself into a squat, about to leap, I think, but something pale catches my eye from the ground, and I shout, "Wait!"

Odé Kan looks back at me.

"What is that? On the ground?"

"I don't know yet." She scowls. "That's why I set up that trap you fell into. To find out more. It is connected to this fool Archibaldo and his monsters, I know that. It has their stench. I already found a few scattered throughout the island. It seems like a kind of death."

The island is dying, Mimi had said. I trace a finger down the back of my arm, shudder when I feel nothing along that sliver of pale emptiness. Behind me, the grunting and trundling gets louder. It sounds like there are a *lot* more friends now.

"Okay, it's time!" Then she's gone, leaping through the trees like some impossible shadow, letting off arrow after arrow as she goes.

I turn, blade ready, and gasp. There are more than a lot more.

A wave of bambarúto comes cresting over the top of the tree-lined hill. Maybe two dozen total. I ain't doing this.

"Odé Kan!" I yell, breaking into a run. "That's a lot of friends!"

"Yes! Too many!" She's blitzing along through the trees above, leaping across branches and slipping in and out of foliage. "Follow me, and we'll regroup to make a plan, eh?"

Don't have much of a choice, really.

I charge along below, take a hard left when she does, and then follow her into a rocky streambed and through a series of small tide-pool-speckled tunnels.

"You said *unite the forces*," I pant once we've put some distance between us and the monster army. "So, they're divided?"

"It's just me, actually. Having a great warrior like myself on your side could really do some damage, you know?" We emerge into a sunlit field of sand and towering weeds. "And then there are some people you would really do well to avoid making alliances with, eh." The rooftops of the city rise toward the two remaining peaks up ahead.

The call of a shofar, mournful and defiant, howls through the afternoon air.

"Heh, speak of the devil, yes? That'd be her right there."

"Isn't that coming from the synagogue?" I ask. "You mean—"

"Mimi Baracasa, that insolent traitor hag? Yes, her."

CHAPTER ELEVEN

MATEO

"AND SO WE MUST HEAL," RABBI HIDALGO DECLARES IN HEAVY, somber tones as I walk into the temple. "And healing is hard work. It is not pretty, not a straight line. Requires courage, hmm? Tenacity."

The whole neighborhood must be crowded into this place.

This is where all our bar and bat mitzvahs happen; these walls have witnessed countless wedding vows and funeral speeches, and I was there matching the mood on my keyboard for plenty of them. I've lost track of how many times Rabbi Hidalgo has brought the whole congregation to tears or had them falling over with laughter with his speeches. It must feel to him like his whole life has led up to this one.

"I wish it were otherwise, but I don't have the answers, don't know the path forward. I'm sorry. I wish I did. These are treacherous, urgent times. We still don't know how my nephew's club was destroyed last night, and it is only by the grace of God that no one was there when it happened. We've never lived through a time like this, and I have yet to find the Torah portion or wisdom from our elders that provides light for what's ahead."

The ornate wooden pews are full, and Galeranos squeeze into the aisles, lean against walls, perch along the short staircases by the stage. Pirates, Sefaradim, and Santeros have all shown up in force. Everyone wants answers, a sense of direction.

I manage to stay unnoticed in the shadows of the back wall.

"The new Cabildo members insist we must hear one another out to heal."

I wonder what new Cabildo members he's talking about. As long as I've been alive, the Cabildo has been a triumvirate made up of one representative from each of the three communities. Rabbi Hidalgo and my tía Lucía repped the Sefaradim and Santeros, respectively, and Anisette Bisconte took over for Mimi as the pirate leader once we arrived here. Instead of passing her seat to Tolo like everyone expected, she tried to install Maestro Gerval, a renowned musician and my hero right up until he turned out to be a horrible demon incarnate. That's how the fighting broke out—fighting that killed both Anisette and Tía Lucía, along with about a dozen others from both sides.

Tolo has probably taken his rightful place on the Cabildo at last—he won the vote before Mimi's coup, after all, and if there's one thing pirates swear by, it's voting. (Except those who swear by empire demons, of course.) Sure enough, I catch sight of him up on the bimah, his face clenched, brow stern. There are a few more folks up there, but they're farther back and I can't make out who they are from this distance.

"I'm not sure that's such a good idea." Rabbi Hidalgo looks around, his eyes glassy. He's probably worried about Chela, and he doesn't even know the half of what we're up against. "But the Cabildo was split down the middle, so we agreed to give them a chance."

Split down the middle? That's not possible with a three-person council. What's happening?

The rabbi sighs. "I yield the floor to Aberdeen Cangrejo."

That's when everyone else sighs, too. At fifty-two, Aberdeen swears he's seen it all, and he's one of those talkers who will wander in fifty different tangents around the actual point without ever getting there.

I work my way toward the bimah, catch sight of my parents looking very uncomfortable beside each other in the front row. They confer quietly, then both light up when I nudge my way between them.

"Mateo," my mom gasps. "We didn't . . . You're back!"

Everyone around us is whispering and muttering, too—Aberdeen's blathering about equality and mutual respect does not command much attention.

My dad squeezes my shoulder and then pulls me into a hug. "M'ijo . . . what happened out there? Is Chela okay? Is . . . Is the island really . . . ?" He shakes his head, like the idea is somehow too much for him to bear.

I spare him the trouble of finishing. "I'm not sure how Chela's doing, to be honest, but I know she'll be okay." Do I? I have to believe that, even though it doesn't feel real. "And yes—San Madrigal is back. We . . . We did it. We raised it."

My parents shake their heads in shock. "I can't . . . I can't believe it," Dad says. "After all this time."

Mom has both hands on her face like she's about to burst into tears. God, I hope she doesn't. "Seems impossible."

"I've given up letting what is or isn't possible stop me from doing things," I say, not as a gotcha but just a straight-up fact. I used to think I knew, and the world kept proving me wrong. Hell, *I* kept proving myself wrong. So why bother? "Anyway, what is this mess about?"

"We have to put this community back together, Mateo," Dad informs me in the daddest dad voice of them all.

I scowl, for so many reasons. "Yeah, but, like—"

"And the *only* way we're going to do that," he goes on, steam-rolling over whatever I was going to say, "is by listening to one another."

Escucha—Listen—Tía Lucía's most important lesson. But I'm not sure how she'd feel about listening to the very people responsible for her murder. Actually, I'm pretty sure she'd feel like it sucks. That's how I feel, anyway.

"We barely made it out of November alive, Dad," I say. *And some people didn't* sits there unspoken but implied. I'm not gonna rub that in his face, but there are other things I can. "You weren't here. You don't know."

His face stays perfectly still, but I can see how much effort it's taking him to keep it that way. And I'm enjoying the strain, just a little. "I will not be lectured by my own son about where I was or wasn't. I may not have been here during the fighting, but at least I wasn't taking part in it."

He must've felt like he was landing a low blow with that one. Besides wrapping their whole personalities around being doctors, my parents are militant pacifists; they hate fighting more than almost anything else in the world. Me? I did what I had to do and made my peace with it. I start to say, "I was—"

But Dad cuts me off. "You showed up out of nowhere after being gone most of your life and proceeded to join in the violence."

Now that actually *was* a low blow, and a hypocritical one at that. "Because *you* had me living out of hotel rooms across the world my whole childhood, Dad!" Our whispers have risen to growly hisses by now, and people are starting to notice. Fortunately, Aberdeen wouldn't know how to read a room if it were a picture book, so he just prattles through his closing non sequitur, still oblivious.

"Excuse us for giving you a firsthand global education," Dad says. Mom puts a firm *Shut the hell up* hand on his leg, and he takes a breath. Then he cuts off my retort. "My point is, the only way to heal is to hear one another out, even—"

He's interrupted by Rabbi Hidalgo's voice from the bimah, sounding like molten lava. "And now, Vedo Bisconte, you may proceed."

Vedo *gets to talk? Into a mic?* This kid—Anisette's son—he'd always just seemed like a harmless nuisance; he had an obvious crush on Chela, wrote bad poetry, that was about it . . . until he aligned with his mom and Gerval and the other empire pirates in their coup attempt. Over the course of a week, Vedo hardened, some hellish fire lit inside him, and all the worst parts of him were turbocharged.

I'll never forget how he watched, his expression ice, as one of their men tried to run over me and Rabbi Hidalgo. He saw me inadvertently take that man's life while trying to protect the rabbi, saw me try and fail to revive him. Then he silently walked away to keep organizing the violence that would take so many more lives, including Tía Lucía's.

And now he's up there on the bimah, unfolding a much-abused piece of printer paper with trembling hands and sending watery, pleading stares out at the neighborhood he tried to destroy. He looks mostly the same—short, pale, uncomfortable in his skin and that button-down shirt. But now, inexplicably, he wears a green cowboy hat. It makes me even madder. "I . . . I just wanted to say, you know . . ." he squeaks, barely audible, and someone yells, "Louder, coño!"

The auditorium erupts with laughter, but I just want to scream. Vedo shouldn't get to speak at all; he's had his say. I don't even understand how he still gets to walk among us, given what he did. We don't call the cops on folks—it's built into us not to, and I wouldn't wish prison even on this clown. But he shouldn't get to be here. Not here with us. Certainly not in this sacred space.

"S-sorry, I . . . Here." He gets closer to the mic, which promptly feeds back a nasty screech. "Ah, okay, sorry, sorry. Okay." Finally he's found a safe position to speak from, and he immediately starts reading. "We—we are Madrigal, one people, one island, and even though we are three peoples, we are one people."

I could swear this was the terrible poem he shared at the fete last year when everything first started falling apart.

"And even one people makes mistakes; even sometimes we get greedy, selfish, mess up."

What does that even mean? I know Tams is somewhere in this crowd rolling her eyes, too. At least I hope she is.

"We have made actions with unintended consequences," Vedo rambles on nonsensically, "and the things that were done should never have been done. If anyone felt hurt or harm from the unintended consequences of the actions that were done, we . . . we wish they didn't."

"¿Qué carajo dice?" a viejita grumbles, speaking, I hope for all of us—*What the hell is Vedo saying?*—but someone else quickly shushes her.

"Finally, if we are truly one people, a people who accept all, who open our doors and hearts to those of us who are hiding, scared, lost, to all beliefs . . ." Vedo's voice seems to crystallize as he speaks, like he's found his rhythm, however ungainly and wack. "My mom told me one man's demon is another man's saint. And you may not believe in what we believe, but that doesn't make it wrong, you know?"

Is this kid really using Madrigal's creed to be a safe house for the persecuted? To justify his worship of an actual demon?

"For many generations, my people lived in hiding among you all just like you once lived in hiding in your homelands." He's comparing us to the Inquisition, to slavers! Never mind that those are the very people his secret cult aligned themselves with against Madrigal. Against *us.*

People are getting irritated; I can feel the crowd bristle at the implication.

"All I ask is that you welcome us and not oppress and persecute us anymore!"

"¡Basta ya con esa mierda!" someone yells, and others join in. But many are listening quietly, too, and I wonder what they're thinking.

"Ah," Rabbi Hidalgo says somberly, "perhaps we should hear from one of our new Cabildo members, eh?"

I'm looking around the room when my dad stands up and just walks right up onto the stage like that's a completely normal thing to do. He can't be . . . Can he?

"Thank you, Vedo Bisconte," my dad says loftily. "I know we are all sorry for the loss of your mother, even though the circumstances were fraught and complicated."

There's no way this is happening. I want the earth to open up and devour me whole.

"And as a new member of the Cabildo and someone who also lost a beloved relative in the fighting," Dad continues, "I want to say this: I forgi—"

"STOP!" a voice yells. "STOP THIS RIGHT NOW!" It's my voice, I realize as I approach the bimah. That's me yelling.

CHAPTER TWELVE

CHELA

"SEE, YOU KNOW WHAT YOUR PROBLEM IS?" ODÉ KAN FLASHES A wry smile as we maneuver side by side through the muddy cobblestone streets toward my father's temple.

It's the kind of non-question I normally roll my eyes at, and I do now, but I'm smiling, too, because this girl barely knows me but still feels the need to give me a full read-down of who I am and what I've done wrong. Can't help but admire the audacity. Can't pretend it's not the type of thing I would do, either. "Bet you're about to tell me."

"As a matter of fact, I am!" She slides to a halt, stretching out one hand to block me from going any farther. "Mind the babachúcho."

"Bambarúto," I laugh as a posse of them rumbles past and then cuts a hard right down another alley. "They're heading for the temple, too." From stolen glimpses and the direction of their clamor, I can tell the main group of empire bambarúto is sweeping through the city behind us. Others have been trundling by in small clusters.

"Answering Mimi's alert," Odé Kan says with a dead-eyed glare at the bell tower. "Come on."

We hurry down the street, trying to ignore the ever-growing stomps and war cries behind us. "Why do you hate her so much? Besides the obvious, I mean."

"Never mind that. We were talking about your problems, eh?"

I smirk. At least having someone to banter with takes the sting out of probably being about to die on some faraway island without any of my loved ones. "Please, go on."

"Everything is all-or-nothing with you, isn't it? That's very mortal of you."

"Says the girl who won't even talk about why she won't form an alliance with the only other viable force around to fight a demon-empire army."

"This island—" Odé Kan waves a long slender arm at the rising and falling rooftops, the two peaks beyond them. "It is you?"

I answer as honestly as possible. "I dunno. Kinda, I guess?"

"You see?" she says archly. "Uncertain."

"Uncertain because it's not clear! Because it's both, not all-or-nothing. Isn't that what you . . . ?"

We slide down a steep incline where all that's left of a stone stairwell pokes out from the slippery mud. Up ahead, the temple looms. We're close. And so are our enemies. I imagine them rolling over us like an ocean tide—vast, unending, impossible to stop.

"¡Exactamundo!" Odé Kan declares. "The fact that it's not one thing or another makes it an uncertainty to you! So you are unsure!" She's stopped now, inexplicably, and has pulled me to a halt, too, so she can poke my chest with her finger to emphasize her point. "You do not know!"

I swat her away, anger and fear flushing through me, competing for the pilot seat in my brain. "Stop! Can we talk about this when we're not about to be overrun by an army of monsters?"

"This is the most important thing," Odé Kan insists, but she follows when I pull away and head for the temple. "It is more important than all those bampalúpos combined."

I'm annoyed she's managed to make me laugh while I'm trying to be vexed with her, but what can I do?

"This island is either inside you . . . or it's not," Odé Kan prattles on. Both of us are panting now from running for so long. "You can either feel . . . its every movement . . . and memory . . . or you feel nothing! Eh?"

Up ahead, a squadron of Mimi's bambarúto stand around the entrance to the temple. It occurs to me once again how strange it is that this was once a place of joy, where my dad would welcome his congregation, counsel those unsure of their faith, hold celebrations and ceremonies. Now it's the site of his unhinged sister's last stand.

The towering beasts peel to either side as we approach, and the hunched-over, glowing figure of Mimi Baracasa limps toward us between them like some ridiculous Moses parting a sea of monsters.

"So, you've finally come to your senses?" She chuckles. I'm not even sure which of us she's talking to. The woman has lost it. "Well, it's too late. We're all going to be destroyed. And *you* . . ." Her gaze turns sharp as it lands directly on Odé Kan. Their eyes meet, and Mimi's whole face suddenly softens. Whatever she was about to say evaporates on her lips. "Just get inside, both of you. Hole up in the bell tower. At least from there you'll have a front-row seat for the end of the world, eh?"

I don't have any response to that. What do you say to ravings? But a tower seems like a pretty good place to be with an ace archer at my side. I nod and start to head down the corridor of bambarúto.

"How do we know you won't give us up?" Odé Kan demands, squaring off with Mimi.

My aunt—my strange, mystical, glowing aunt—just shakes her head sadly. "I couldn't even if I wanted to."

Something inside the hunter's spirit seems to break; she looks like she's about to cry. Instead, she crinkles her face, sniffles once, and shuffles in after me.

CHAPTER THIRTEEN

MATEO

THE WHOLE ROOM, MY WHOLE COMMUNITY, STARES AT ME.

It wasn't that long ago that this very thing would've shaken me to my core. I carried a ghost on my shoulder—not a real one, like my tía Miriam, who faded for good when Tía Lucía was killed. This was the kind of ghost you can't get rid of with just a despojo. It was much worse—a nasty phantom of my own making that only whispered to me that I didn't belong because I'd spent my childhood overseas. I didn't belong because I'd learned our music mostly from books and recordings, not the streets like everyone else. I didn't belong, I didn't belong.

Then, in a last-ditch effort to discredit me, Gerval gave voice to that phantom in front of everyone. But by then any remaining shred of admiration for him had fallen away, and I finally managed to do what Tía Lucía had been telling me to do for so long: listen. And what I heard was a community of people who saw me for exactly who I was, am: their son. Just as messy and imperfect as they are, as much a part of this weird, fractured diaspora world as the next guy.

Something broke in me that night. It was the best kind of breaking—the kind that sets you free. Maybe that's the only thing I have to thank Gerval for, but really, he wasn't the one who did it. He was just the catalyst. It was everyone else who reminded me that I've always been home, and I always will be, no matter where I am.

So now . . . now it's barely a glint on my radar that all eyes are once again on me and I've shattered the fragile facade of unity, or whatever it is my dad's playing at. My names, both of them, ricochet through the crowd along with whispered wonders about where I've been, where Chela is, what we have done.

My *STOP THIS RIGHT NOW!* still echoes when my dad looks right into my eyes and growls, "What gives you the . . . ?" A curse hangs on the edge of his sudden silence—not sure which one, but he can't seem to finish the thought without it, and my dad *hates* it when people swear in public. His already red-tinged light brown skin has gone full scarlet now; coupled with those carefree blond curls, it makes him look like a surfer bro who took too long a nap without sunscreen. Possible I've never seen him this mad. His whole face is clenched—like when he exhales, streams of fire will hurl forth and incinerate me. Or . . . try to, anyway. I don't think there's a fire in the world that could match my own right now.

"That's exactly what I was wondering about you," I say. "What are you even doing up there? Since when are you a Cabildo member?"

"I figured it was about time, given everything going on, for them to make a seat for those of us Galeranos who worship the secular gods: science, reason, logic."

"What—both of you?" I scoff.

I realize, as the room erupts in laughter, that I might've cut a little too deep with that one. My dad looks a couple fast heart-beats away from a total meltdown. Instead, he does that annoying deep-breathing thing he always tries to get me to do and steadies himself. He's probably "decentering his ego" or practicing some other useful lingo maneuver, because then he goes, "This actually has nothing to do with your mother and me."

(Never mind that he basically just acknowledged they're the only two atheists San Madrigal has ever known—he didn't need to drag Mom into this. Between the enraptured onlookers, I catch her worried glare in the front row.)

"But it has everything to do with *us*," Dad continues, thinking without basis that he has the upper hand. "This community, this neighborhood, and everything that happened, everything that you were a part of last month . . . *son*." That last word was meant, I'm sure, as a sharp reminder of my place, but it just makes him look petty.

"I only wanted a chance to explain what we were doing." Vedo says it softly, but into the mic. "There are a lot of different understandings about what happened."

I finally turn to him, this boy who once seemed like just a nuisance, a hanger-on, and became much more as our streets swirled into crisis.

"You sided with a demon against the people of Madrigal," I hiss.

"The way many people see it," Vedo informs me calmly, "*you* sided with a demon—the Destroyer—against the people of Madrigal. And anyway, I know what you did, what you've become."

He's talking about what happened to Arco "El Gorro" Kordal. The man I killed. Arco had been about to finish off Rabbi Hidalgo when I tackled him from behind. He fell and cracked his head on the curb, dying instantly. I tried to bring him back to life with my healing abilities, but I'd never done anything like that before. I'd only fixed broken bones and struggling hearts, never resurrected anyone. When the vast abyss of death's gaping maw seemed poised to swallow me up, I pulled back, terrified. By the time I realized it was within my power after all, it was too late for Arco. He was *gone* gone.

Sure, I sometimes see that gray face and those empty eyes when I'm trying to go to sleep; yes, I often wonder how his loved ones felt when they found out, and what he might've done with himself if he'd lived. But I also know that my actions kept the rabbi alive, and I did everything I could to help once I realized Arco was dead. I don't know how to explain any of that to a crowded room; it all feels like some impossible secret. Chela's the only person I've ever told. I knew she would understand, hold the space without judging me or trying to pretend it was all right when it wasn't. And she did.

Suddenly I feel utterly exposed, backed into the worst corner.

"And Chela Hidalgo . . ." Vedo continues once he's seen in my eyes that I have no quick rebuttal. "Okanla. Madrigal. Whatever—a liar. Who brought down the island, Mateo? Who did that?"

Chela did—or the spirit who later unified with baby Chela, anyway. She brought down a storm so powerful it sank the island, stopping the full resurrection of Vizvargal. Then his high priest, my ancestor Archibaldo, used young Gerval's body to incarnate the demon instead.

But again, how to explain all that? How to make it seem rational to a room full of people who've spent the past decade and a half pining for their sunken homeland? Gerval had tried this same tactic on the night of the vote, the coup, and I'd managed to flip the narrative on him. There was so much we didn't know then; Chela and I were still figuring out who we were, what it meant. Now that we have unlocked our memories of how the island fell, it has somehow become even more complicated, even harder to explain.

As the eyes of the community flick to me once more, waiting for an answer I have no idea how to give, my thoughts turn to Chela. It's such a simple thing, so small and meaningless, but in this moment, I miss her. Maybe it's because I never have to explain the complicated stuff—she just gets it. Maybe it's because no one looks at me and *sees* me the way she does. Maybe it's because it's her name that's on everyone's mind now, for all the wrong reasons, because of all the wrong people.

I close my eyes, try to do what my tía taught me: *escucha.*

At first, all I hear are the faraway waves and squawking gulls. Then there's the rustle of many, many bodies from somewhere nearby. No idea what it means, whether I've tapped into whatever Chela's doing on Madrigal or I'm just imagining things. Either way, all it does is heighten my longing.

"Chela," I whisper to myself, a near-silent prayer. I feel the faintest trace of her within me, like she's emerging from a thick mire and reaching out. All I want to do is linger, grab on to her essence or whatever it is I feel and hold tight, never let go.

I know I can't.

When I open my eyes, the world feels clearer. The impossible remains impossible, but I know I'll find my way through somehow. Also, I finally catch sight of Tams, her face wide open and worried, brow furrowed.

"These stories are bigger than a tit for tat," I say. "And I know Vedo will make that sound like a dodge, but if we Galeranos know anything, it's that stories have more layers than they first appear to. And I also know this: Chela raised the island. For the first time in fifteen years, San Madrigal has fully risen."

Gasps and cheers break out all around me. Rabbi Hidalgo and Tolo both stand, their eyes haunted with a million questions.

"And she needs our help," I add when the noise settles down.

"What happened?" someone yells. "What can we do?"

"I'll tell you everything, but not here. I know my dad is earnestly trying to make things better with this forgiveness thing"—our eyes meet, then he looks away—"but I won't be part of it. This isn't the path to healing. Not like this. I'm out. Join me if you like. We'll find a way forward together."

As I leave, the sound of many stomping feet follows in my wake.

CHAPTER FOURTEEN

CHELA

"You knew me . . . before . . ." I say as we head up the winding stairwell inside the bell tower.

Odé Kan shrugs. "Of course. We all did."

"And was I . . . ?" Maybe she's right about me. I can't even find the words to describe what I am or am not. Was or wasn't. It barely registers as something real in my brain, true though I know it to be.

Instead of rubbing it in, Odé Kan decides to be magnanimous. She chuckles to let me know she sees what I'm struggling with, then waves it away, telling me not to bother trying to language it. "You were always both. You've always been both. And this place . . ." For the first time, her tone loses all that mirth and mischief and becomes something very different: reverent. "Our world. You've always been our world—Madrigal, Okanla, the island, the spirit, the girl. It's always been you."

"So . . ."

"The division is people's problems, Okanla. Basura de los mortales. That's for them. We, the spirits, know you for all the things you are."

I can't help but think about Mateo, the only one who truly seems to know all the sides of me. Who lives my complexity, too. Or something very like it. But then my parents' faces surface, and Tolo, Tams. . . . They understand in their hearts even though they can't totally wrap their heads around it.

"The problem is . . . as spirits, we are inextricably linked to what people believe about us," the hunter says. "We don't get to just brush it off. There's an infinite continuum connecting the fiber that makes us who we are and the worshipers who sing our praises. It is beyond even my unassailable understanding, but that doesn't make it any less true, eh."

A creaky door swings to the side, releasing us from the dank stairwell and into the fresh afternoon air, the smell of the sea, the wide-open sky.

Down below, a mass of empire bambarúto cluster around the outer wall of the synagogue. At the front of it, some kind of huge orange spider creature carries an ancient, cloaked rider toward the gate.

"Mimi Baracasaaa!" Maestro Archibaldo Medina's crinkled-up-paper voice rings out across the sky like a Klaxon.

"Can he even kill us?" I whisper to Odé Kan.

"Ah, it's not easy, but yes. And there are worse things than death he can do, I'm afraid."

"So, we . . . We can die for real." I already know this. I was there when Vizvargal died for real. But it seems like a faraway truth. Even though I've only just come to understand it, my immortality has become a part of me, unambiguous.

"We can be killed," Odé Kan corrects. "Especially in our incarnated forms. It's much easier to kill something with flesh and blood—even if it's a spirit deep down—than to kill something that's barely there. But even with all that, if no one kills us, we don't die."

Archibaldo's army takes an uneasy step back, and his mount

rears as the front gate swings open. Mimi and her cohorts pour out, forming a single file in front of the temple with her at the center. Despite the fact that her force is smaller, they face the opposition with steely determination.

What is she doing?

"Very simple, very simple." Archibaldo snickers. "Nobody likes conflict, hmm? Nobody wants war to tear apart this island yet again. Especially given what happened last time, heh. We can all live in peace, yes? We both know disaster here means disaster for all your loved ones in the diaspora, eh. You do still have loved ones, don't you?"

I'm not sure exactly what Archibaldo means by all that, but it lines up with what Mimi told me earlier and . . . she does indeed have at least one loved one out in the world: my cousin Tolo. The prospect of these two vicious armies clashing, splattering blood all over the temple grounds—it suddenly feels imminent, like at any moment an errant breeze could tip this whole standoff into all-out war. And what would that mean for Brooklyn? For my family? I have no idea.

Mimi hasn't said a word, though; she hasn't moved a muscle. Her bambarúto fan out to either side, poised to leap across the ten or so feet between the two armies and commence the killing.

"There's only one thing you have to do to avoid more blood being spilled, more death, the end of our people forever," Archibaldo says, and then he chortles an aside. "Because let's be honest, there aren't many of us left, eh? A massacre or two, an unforeseen disaster could wipe us out completely, and you well know it."

"The thing you have to understand about Archibaldo," Odé Kan says distastefully, "is that he was the last initiate of Vizvargal before the purge. So, just like his demon god, the maestro is obsessed with commerce, exchange, expansion, domination. He leeches the bambarúto, using the power of the island itself—*your* power, Madrigal—to turn their life essence into his, granting himself near immortality."

I let out a low growl that seems to rise from the island itself.

"Everything near him is a resource, something to be exploited."

"The island is dying," I whisper.

Odé Kan cocks an eyebrow at me. "Eh?"

"Something my aunt said. I wanted to blow it off, ignore it, but . . . those strange empty spots you've been finding." *It's reached me, too,* I almost say, but I let the words simmer and vanish in my mouth. It feels like a secret I must keep for some reason. Or maybe now's not the time.

"Exactly that. I haven't worked out what it is he's pulling from this place yet, but I can promise it's destructive and profitable. And I know he—"

"Must be stopped," I say, my jaw clenching. "We have to stop him."

"Yes, that, too," Odé Kan agrees. "But to do that we have to survive."

"My dear Mimi," Archibaldo says, then pauses dramatically, eyeing the pirate queen from his mount. His speech didn't seem to get the rise out of her he was hoping for. "Just give us the Destroyer and your little hunter spirit, hmm? Those are the terms, the only terms. And we can avoid all this . . . ugliness."

"Your?" I whisper into the whipping wind that fills the sudden quiet.

Odé Kan scowls, and some pieces fall into place. All the other spirits left Madrigal after the cataclysm. They followed their people, the Santeros initiated to them, the adherents to their sects. But not Odé Kan. She stayed. She stayed and so did Mimi. But that would mean . . . "Tía Mimi is an initiated Santera?" I ask.

The hunter hasn't taken her eyes off the battlefield. "I promise I'll explain everything if we survive this, but for that to happen, you need to listen carefully to what I say right now."

The two armies stir, readying. Mimi still hasn't responded, but she's consulting with one of the bambarúto nearby.

"Mimi's going to try to die a martyr," Odé Kan says in an urgent whisper. "That flair for the melodramatic has always been her downfall."

"You sure are the expert in everyone else's problems."

I expect Odé Kan to roll her eyes, or clap back at me, something. Instead, she turns so we're face-to-face, her expression dead serious. "You can't afford to be unclear or vague right now. Do you understand me?"

"No."

She doesn't even look exasperated, doesn't miss a beat.

"Are you Okanla?"

"Yes."

"Madrigal?"

"Yes."

"The girl?"

"Yes."

"The island?"

"I . . . Yes."

Down below, I hear my aunt's bellowed response: "Never!" A massacre is about to commence, and its ripples will tumble all the way to Little Madrigal. I don't know how, but I know it's true. I have to stay focused.

"You can feel its memories, its aches, its growth?" Odé Kan whispers.

"Yes."

"You know what it needs, where it's been."

"Yes."

"Why?" prods the hunter.

"Because it is me, and I am it. We are one. The island is a part of me; the island is me."

We stand there, this hunter spirit and I, and then she takes my shoulders and points me to the battlefield below. "Then act like it."

With a whoosh, the doors within me swing open, and for a second, everything is chaos as reams of information, growth, sunlight, shadow, stream through.

Odé Kan's voice cuts through. "The only thing you still don't understand is your own power."

I can control it. It doesn't have to be all-or-nothing. It is me, and we are one.

I flicker back to the here and now, glimpse the two armies launch toward each other. It all seems to happen in slow motion, but an inescapable gravity yanks me toward the moment, sends the whole world reeling.

The island is me, and I will do as I please.

I raise my arms, my glare fixed on the ground below, the world flickering in and out of existence. The front lines of each army are inches apart. A wrenching pain opens in my chest as cobblestones, dirt, and wood burst upward into the sky, send bambarúto hurling in either direction as both sides collapse backward in shock.

My rib cage feels like it's being split in half as flames race through my chest and out of my mouth.

Someone is screaming; the scream tears the sky, burns the air— it's me, my scream, my body being torn asunder, my flesh and soil shoving out of the way, coalescing, breaking.

"Madrigal." Odé Kan's voice again. "Okanla."

And then another voice, from very far away: "Chela," Mateo says in a calm whisper. I don't know if it's a memory or if he's reaching out somehow, but that clinches it. I spin back to the world; the world spins back to me.

Down below, an earthen barrier has sprung up between the two armies, twenty feet tall. Its sudden appearance sends them all scattering.

The raging pain in my chest simmers to a dull roar. My ribs never split, no fire came from my mouth. But I still feel the singe of it; the memory of that tearing throbs through me.

I blink against the ebbing pain, breathe as it passes.

Odé Kan is staring at me with wonder in her eyes. "That's what I'm talking about!"

CHAPTER FIFTEEN

MATEO

I NEED TO TALK TO TOLO.

As I storm out of the synagogue, the fresh January air hits me like a slap in the face. Behind me, countless Galeranos march and cheer and chant and argue. A movement takes shape in the span of seconds, but it has been building, growing, seething under the surface.

People don't believe in that reconciliation-and-forgiveness talk. It's not that any of those ideas are bad, it's just . . . they haven't been earned. Not really. That much is clear from what I saw on the stage.

I need to talk to Tolo, find out if there's any way some of his archives didn't get destroyed. Or, if they did, find out where else I can look. I need answers.

But first I gotta keep moving, not let this momentum fizzle.

Out in the street, a nasty pileup has gridlocked traffic in either direction. Must've been black ice; no one goes fast enough to do much damage on Fulton, but several cars have flipped and icy water geysers out of a raised rift in the blacktop.

Must've just happened, but no one seems badly hurt. Anyway,

this doesn't concern me; now that the keep-the-cops-out pact has apparently fallen apart, they're all around and ready. Ambulances are already screeching up as grim-faced patrol officers divert traffic.

Keep going. The crowd behind me swarms through the streets, alive and awake, my spirit name on their lips as a chant rises, becomes a song; it carries us.

I'm not sure what's happening, this spontaneous eruption, but all I can do is move with it, flow. A glance behind me reveals Rabbi Hidalgo living his very best life, dancing a wild rumba amid a crowd of drumming Santeros as beside him Tams clacks two wooden sticks together—the claves. Tolo must be in the crowd somewhere; I'll find him when things simmer down.

But it doesn't look like that'll happen anytime soon. More revelers join in as we go, shouting, yelling, still arguing but without a break in the celebration—very Galerano of them, to be honest.

Somewhere back at the synagogue, my dad is *heated*; I know it. And Vedo is probably huddling with his buddies about how to ruin something. Many miles away, Chela wanders our lost island. When I reach for her at midnight, will she be there? Or will it just be a lonely meditation on how much I miss her?

"Mateo!" Tams has passed the claves to Rabbi Hidalgo's wife, Aviva (she's killing it), and caught up to me. She wraps her long, loving arms around me and squeezes as hard as she can, neither of us losing stride. "I missed you, short stuff."

Short stuff. I'm the only person around as tall as she is, and she knows it. My best friend's got jokes.

I pull her even closer. "I missed you, too."

"And," she says, falling into step alongside me, "I was worried about you."

I try to explain best I can, but I keep bumping up against the hard truth of the situation: there's so much I don't know. Our spontaneous parade winds through the side streets of Little Madrigal unabated. Music pounds into the chilly night as Tams gives me her most dramatic reactions to each bit ("Oh no! But did y'all . . . ? Oh! OH! Oh no! Wait—the whole mountain? *Gone?! How?*").

When I get to the part about Galanika looking like he's dying and reaching out for help, Tams stops me. "Hold up! Thought you were a spirit, immortal and whatnot. What's this dying crap?"

"I . . . I have no idea. I thought so, too."

"Come to think of it, why would you even be growing old? What part of the game is that? In fact, why aren't you still a baby?"

I have to laugh. It's both exactly that absurd and a real question I need the answer to.

"Mateo," Tolo says with that gruff friendliness of his as he rolls up out of the crowd. Tolo Baracasa is big in every way. He's tall as hell, wide as hell, thick, fat, muscled; at times gregarious, always a presence—even his silence is alarming. For an eighteen-year-old, he seems like he's already lived several lifetimes. He slides up next to Tams and kisses her on the cheek. I guess a lot has happened since I've been gone. But I'll have to get the bochinche later. Right now, it's business.

"Tolo! I'm so glad to see you, man. I—"

The young gangster startles me with a hug. He's warm and surprisingly gentle, and I feel suddenly very safe. The ongoing parade slides to either side of us, an unstoppable river.

I wait a beat so as not to kill the moment, then ask, "The club—I heard about what happened. Any idea how?"

Tolo shakes his head, crestfallen. "Nada. The guys I know in Fire said no signs of sabotage so far, but . . . you know. There's no other reason for it to just collapse like that."

"Chela asked me to . . . There's some old Madrigal info I need to try to dig up for her. Any chance the books survived somehow?"

"Doubt it," Tolo says gravely. "But who knows? Haven't had a chance to sift through the wreckage myself. What's she got you looking into? You know I'd turn the world inside out for my li'l cuz."

"The peace accords after the 1810 war," I say. "Something happened at the Cabildo meeting around then. . . . We need to find out more. Maybe there's firsthand accounts from witnesses or something?"

"You know," Tams cuts in, throwing an arm over both our shoulders, "there is a way to get info about the dead besides just reading dusty old books. . . ."

"Oh boy," Tolo grunts, but he's smiling now, smitten.

"Go on," I say, although I'm pretty sure I know where this is going.

"Ask 'em yourself," Tams says, excessively pleased with herself. Tams is a Santera, and besides having all their powerful santos, a big part of the Santería practice involves communing with the dead. My tía Lucía had a whole altar for our ancestors set up with old photos and trinkets, and she'd put food and coffee down for them at every meal.

"You think it would work?" I ask. "You can just call up the ones you want to talk to? Is there an online directory or something?"

"You can try, wiseass," Tams shoots back. "And no, but names are powerful things, you know."

I nod. Don't have much else to go on if Tolo's library is dust. "Let's do it."

"Great!" Tams beams. "I'll set it up for tomorrow afternoon."

"I'll come, too," Tolo says gamely. And that's when it hits me—there's a relative he may be expecting to show up as a spirit at that misa, but she definitely won't.

We fall back into stride with the revelers around us. Galeranos will make an epic celebration out of anything anywhere they go, from funerals to protests to someone finally learning how to dance after a lifetime of trying (long story, that one).

"Tolo," I say, trying to work out which words make sense in a situation like this. None of them. There's no right way to do this. "Your mom . . . She's . . . alive. She's on the island still. No idea wha—"

I stop because Tolo is staring murder at me. "My mom died when the island sank," he says simply, like I must've just made a slight calculation error, forgotten to carry the two or something. "So, no."

"Tolo," I say, more firmly now. "I talked to her. It's her. She's alive. She . . . She's not aligned with the empire pirates anymore, but she . . . She was once. It's complicated, and—"

"How . . . ?" His voice is soft, and that's bad. If he was yelling, it'd be fine. Soft is bad.

I'm about to answer, when he holds up a hand to stop me. Shakes his big shiny head. "Stop. Not now. I can't right now. I'll tell you when."

Tams squeezes him close.

"Of course," I say, relieved that it's out of me and on him to decide when to talk about it next. "Just say the word."

"Now that *that's* settled," Tams says, "let's get to . . ." She lets her words trail off, and behind me, the music rumbles to a stop, too.

"*This is the New York City Police,*" a gruff voice growls over a megaphone. "*And you are participating in an illegal gathering. Disperse immediately.*" Up ahead, a row of cops in body armor glares at us through their face shields. These aren't bambarúto—we can see their human features—but their presence in our streets is almost as out of place and threatening. The last time they were here, the night of the Grande Fete last October, things got ugly fast, and they look like they're ready for a rematch.

"These are our streets!" I yell into the stunned silence. I'd barely realized the words were mine as they came out. I'm more fed up than I realized. "You don't get to tell us where we can and can't be!"

Everyone around me erupts into applause and jeers. We're not doing anything illegal. And Little Madrigal has been cop-free since we first came here. None of this is right.

"Who said that?" one of the in-charge-looking cops hollers, spittle flying in all directions.

"I did!" I call back, and I'm tall as hell, so it's easy for him to gaze over the other heads and lock eyes with me. The guy's one of those older, burnt-out-looking sergeants, like a burly Mr. Magoo type who probably should've retired years ago but is waiting around for his pension to get fat or whatever. He squints sheer death at me, and all I can do is smile. There's at least fifty people crowded together between me and that row of riot police. They'll never catch me.

Sergeant Magoo consults with one of his officers, who starts looking at his phone and yammering into a radio.

"Disperse immediately," the megaphone voice yells again.

But now someone has yelled, "Whose streets?" and the whole crowd responds as one: *"Our* streets!" The second time is even louder, a yell that seems to shake the train tracks above us, reach right past all these tired buildings with their rusty fire escapes and clanking radiators, straight up into the sky and out across the world.

"Whose streets?"

"Our streets!"

Tams yells it, Tolo yells it, I yell it; we all yell it together, as one.

"In three minutes, we will begin making arrests!" the megaphone insists. But we are so many, and there are only about a dozen cops. We didn't plan this, so they had no way to be ready for it, and these really are our streets, cops or not. And best of all, we know it. The bass drum kicks up a rugged march in time with our chanting, and soon the whole band jumps in, horns leaping up and down the scale

in harmony with one another and all our shouts. Tolo, Tams, and I start boogying along with everyone else around us as a gentle snow begins falling like confetti over the celebration.

We really are pirates, all of us, because there's no way this doesn't go south somehow, but we'll be damned if we don't make a jolly ol' dance party out of it anyway.

Tolo pulls his phone out of his pocket while twirling Tams and answers it with a gruff "Dímelo." Then he glances at me, nods, hangs up. "We gotta get you outta here, kid."

I boggle at him. "Me?"

He cuts his eyes to the side, where, sure enough, the small crew of riot cops is shoving a cruel path through the crowd; they're heading directly for us.

"What the hell?" I yelp, following Tolo in the opposite direction. Tams runs along beside me.

"That was Safiya," he says in a low mutter. "She's been monitoring PD radio, and they're looking for you, Mateo. Got your name and description, a mandate to pick you up on sight."

"How?" I demand. "I haven't done anything!" The protest sounds naive as it fumbles out of me. What does it matter what I've done or not done? The cops'll think of something. I let my indignation die as we push deeper into the crowd, try to focus on getting away. We can deal with the rest later.

By now, though, everyone's figured out what's happening: a fellow Galerano is trying to get away from the law. Without a word of coordination, people part to either side ahead of us, clearing the way, then close in tight in our wake.

Soon the cops are far behind us, and we dart down an alley and lose ourselves in the crisp winter night.

The question remains, though: What the hell?!

CHAPTER SIXTEEN

CHELA

"THE HELL WAS THAT?" I SAY ONCE THINGS HAVE CALMED DOWN and it's clear Odé Kan and I are safe.

The two armies stayed scattered for a while; confusion reigned. When they did manage to coalesce again, each beat a full retreat in opposite directions. Now the sounds of birds and the rustling whisper of palm fronds mingle with the *shush* of waves sloshing against our shore.

We stayed in the bell tower. It's surprisingly comfy up here— they got a little cushioned bench set up, and you can see in every direction.

I know the answer to my own question; the time to stop pretending I don't is over, but still . . . knowing it is different than accepting it.

Odé Kan raises her eyebrows to indicate exactly that, then Galerano-shrugs. Night begins to settle in across the sky behind her. "I know it's a lot, what you live, what you see. And you start from scratch, eh? No reference points, no memories."

I pull my knees to my chest and rest my chin on them: peak cozy-pout position. "I have some memories."

"Oh yes? Listen." She gets all serious for a moment, that mischievous glint gone like it was never there. "There's a lot I don't know, yeah? But what I know, you will know, okay? I don't play games. Don't speak in riddles. Nobody has the time, you know?"

"Do. I. Ever."

So I give her the rundown. It's clear I can trust her—more than anyone else on this island, anyway—so why not? The one thing I need right now is clarity. "It's true, then?" I ask when I'm done. I hate the quiver in my voice, the way I sound like a lost little girl.

She cocks her head to the side, deep in thought. "Which part?"

"The, uh, Cabildo meeting . . . Most specifically, the thing about me and Galanika not being supposed to, you know . . . team up."

"Ah yes." Odé Kan slides her back down the wall until she's in a comfortable squat. She pulls some kind of crunchy nut-and-seed wafer from one of her pouches, snaps it in two, and hands me half.

"Because, I mean . . . we have . . . you know, *teamed up* . . . numerous times. . . . Or maybe my interpretation is off?"

Odé Kan lets out that silvery spiderweb laugh between chomps. "I don't think it's totally off, no. But you have to understand, Okanla: everything changes now that the island is raised. It became a nonentity when you sank it, yes? It was—we were all—in stasis. And the island—your island, *our* island—it is part of the equation now. Even more so because you are here, on it, with us."

The wafer is chewy with an unexpected sweetness. She must've used honey to hold it together. I cover my mouth so Odé Kan doesn't have to see a bunch of half-chewed seeds. "But . . . why?"

Eye roll. Galerano shrug. Giggle. "Why what? Why this island? Why this sea? Some of these things are beyond us. All I know is, when you were . . . Well, before you entered into your lovely human state, back when we all had to pretend that you were two different entities entirely, it was known . . . We all knew you and Galanika could be whatever you wanted to each other as long as you remained in spirit form."

I tip my chin at her to keep going.

"If you were to become a couple, a pairing, while incarnated, well . . . what you heard is what is said: the balance of our world will be thrown off, your connection to the island severed."

"How can I be severed from something I *am*?" I demand, more confused than angry, but definitely both. "You told me it's not just a part of me, it *is* me. I know that to be true. So . . ."

She passes me more wafer with a sad chuckle. "I said I don't talk in riddles. The world itself . . . well, that's another thing. All riddles, all the time, eh?"

I sag, all my energy suddenly sapped. "Eh."

A gentle night rain sweeps the jungle around us; you can hear each drop speckle the leaves, the tower, the soil. Maybe my sinking mood made it happen—seems I can summon storms and rend the very earth here, so why not also cause a little sprinkle?

Odé Kan insists she's fine on the floor; I take the cushioned seat. My fingers idly caress the strange smooth trail along my arm: A scar? Some kind of slow death? I don't know, but when I get to the spot where I had thought it ended, I almost yelp with surprise. Because it doesn't end there—it's a little bit longer now, stretching toward my shoulder.

I'd reached deep into the heart of the island. *What did you think would happen?* Mimi's voice whispers shrilly in my ear. But it's not just the heart of the island—it's *my* heart, too. And Archibaldo has cursed both somehow, infected them with some slow-spreading blight.

That's fine, I tell myself, trying to settle down for the evening. But it's not fine, not even close. And I can't comfort myself with thoughts of destroying Archibaldo in a million different ways, because I can't fully count on my own powers.

"What is it?" Odé Kan asks, because suddenly I'm sitting up, my quick gasps filling the room.

"I have to . . . We have to . . . How can I stop Archibaldo from destroying this island when I can't even . . . do the things I'm supposed to be so good at . . . ?"

Her eyes glint in the darkness. Her smile isn't cruel; it's mischievous, knows sacred secrets. "Oh, my sweet sister."

"What?" I ask, calming down some, smiling just a little, too, even though I don't know why. No one's let me in on all those sacred secrets, not yet.

"Get some rest, Destroyer. Tomorrow, we train."

CHAPTER SEVENTEEN

MATEO

I'M ROUNDING A CORNER ONTO CHELA'S BLOCK WHEN THE SOUND OF laughter stops me short.

Tolo, Tams, and I split up after ducking through the shadows for a few hours. The police presence thinned out once the crowd headed off, and it seemed easier to stay low solo than in a group. I hadn't even realized I was heading to the Hidalgos' until just now; I only knew I couldn't go home. Some internal compass must've been pulling me this way all along. Even though there's no Chela there, it's about as close as I can get. Plus, I love her family like they're my own.

But a group of figures stands out by the cemetery gate, conferring quietly. Most of them are in the shadows, hard to make out, but that guy in the middle of things is definitely Vedo. And it looks like he's giving orders. I duck back around the corner as they head off in different directions, Vedo coming directly my way.

All right. I've been wanting a word with this kid; here's my chance. But I won't confront him empty-handed.

The small side street I'm on doesn't offer much in terms of ammunition, just some brick walls and trash cans. But I don't need much to make a weapon. I brace myself, hating what I'm about to do, and then lean back and smash my head into the wall with all the strength I can muster.

You know how when cartoon characters smash into something, their eyes get all blurry and little stars dance around their head? Yeah—turns out that's pretty accurate. For a few desperate seconds, the world is all bright flashes and smudged shadows. I wonder if I overdid it and the whole thing's about to backfire, Vedo rolling up on me half-conscious and at his mercy.

But my hands find my split scalp, and my own song rises, familiar like an old friend. By the time he does round the corner, I've already sealed the wound and pocketed that throb and shatter. Vedo stops in his tracks. I'm leaning against the wall like we're not bitter rivals, just cool.

"You gonna secretly record me and play it for the neighborhood like you did Gerval?" Vedo sneers. "Because, somehow, I don't think it'll go your way this time, buddy."

I shrug. "Why bother? You're plenty untrustworthy without my help. At least Gerval had charisma."

"Did you have something to say to me, or are we gonna trade barbs all night? Because I have places to be, actually."

"I just want to know . . . what the hell you think you're doing."

I had imagined a lot of things happening at this point—more sneers, some wisecracks, maybe even an actual hint about his plans. Did not expect an outburst of emotion. "My mom is *dead*," Vedo says, a sob threatening to well up from his trembling throat. "Dead, Mateo. And it's one hundred percent your fault. You might not've brought that golem to life, but you put everything in motion that got us to that moment. *You* did that."

There are so many things I want to point out, so many disagree-ments I have with just that one little thought process, but I'd rather get information than argue, so I hold my tongue.

"All my mom ever wanted was to get us to live up to the creed we've always declared about ourselves," Vedo goes on, his face bright red, eyes watery. "That's it. We're supposed to be open, accepting. But *you* and *your* people want to tell us who to worship, which gov-ernment to support, how to live our lives. You're liars. All of you. And I'm sick of it."

He wipes away some snot, huffing and puffing. And I think maybe he's done, until he locks eyes with me. "And since you had to tell everyone else what to do, Mateo Matisse, my mom is *dead*. Gerval, Vizvargal's chosen incarnate, is dead. Vizvargal is dead. But I am alive, Mateo. And as long as that's true, I'm going to do every single thing I can to make your life as miserable as you made mine."

"Vedo, the police aren't going to—"

"Oh, you think the cops showing up is the biggest problem you got, Mateo?" He manages a blubbery scoff through his tears. "Just wait. Just wait, buddy. All your shit friends, all your shit family, everyone you know and love . . . They're on my list, Mateo. All of them will pay for what you've done."

"Are you sure this whole thing isn't just because Chela wasn't into you?"

Something snaps in Vedo, and he lunges. He's gotten solid in the past couple of months, probably been training for exactly this moment, but I'm ready for him. The first punch whips past my face as I dodge, and when he comes swinging with the next one, I grab his wrist and let loose my own injury, fracturing it.

"Gah!" Vedo howls, already stumbling off, gingerly cradling one hand in the other like it's an ugly baby. "Stay away from me!"

I let him go. What am I going to do? He said his piece; I'm not going to kill him. Now all that's left is to face whatever comes.

CHAPTER EIGHTEEN

MIDNIGHT

We rise.
Together, but a thousand miles apart,
we rise.

Over stucco roofs and steeples,
treetops and mountains,
and suddenly the sea.

Through pipes and concrete, insulation and shingles,
up beyond the rise and fall of towering buildings,
cross streets full of tiny dancing lights.

The cloud-crowded sky.
The moon catches a glimpse of herself in the waves.
We rise.

It's easy to find each other.
Their pulse calls you, it's a beacon in the night,

flame in the shadows.
All is darkness and the speckled stars,
and then
There.
There you will know peace; there is
refuge, sanctuary. Safety.

We are beings of shadow and light.
Barely there, but powerful beyond belief.
Unbound by bodies.
Free.
When we meet, here in the far-off firmament,
new fires are born, new dangers and joys
invented. A new music, every time.
It has been so long, beloved.
We come from long ago, and we are still so sudden,
our consciousness mingled, harmonized, fresh.

It's all so much, Mateo.

I know, Chela. Love.

*There is war here. And more . . . too much to describe. I'm okay,
though.*

Here it's just lies and politics . . . and cops—

In Little Madrigal? What?

*I know, right? They attacked a spontaneous rally that happened after
I got into it with my dad at a Cabildo meeting . . . uh, long story.*

Wow. Did anyone . . . ?

Everyone's safe. Your parents are good. In fact, I'm crashing in your bedroom tonight.

Oh?

We were all out partying late, so . . .

Don't go trying on my cool goth regalia; you'll break it since you're eight feet tall.

Ooh, now that you mention it, I think I might!

Mateo! You'll probably get distracted because the room's a mess and you'll have to clean it.

Yeah, yeah, yeah . . . Chela, I miss you.

———◆———

Feel like we should be trading notes about everything that's going on, but . . .

That doesn't feel right, does it?

No. But I don't know if that's because it's not, or because really, in this sliver of a moment we get together, I just want to be.

Yes. No strategy.

No worries.

No war. Just be.

Yes.

        The night wind whips through us
as we spin slow circles through the sky over the sea,
      bright like the moon and light as snow.

There's something you're not telling me.

A few somethings . . . I . . . I don't know how. . . . . Not yet.

It's related to this whole homework assignment you've sent me on.

Yes.

How am I supposed to—?

I know . . . I know . . . Just hold me.

Can I? Will you turn away the next time I see you in the flesh?

Mateo, I—

The club collapsed.

What?!

Your cousin's.

Do they know how? When?

They don't know anything yet. It happened sometime last night. . . .

Last night . . .

                                        Chela?

I . . .

                        Chela, we can't do this secrets thing.

I'm sorry, Mateo. I don't know how. How to talk about this.

                                Chela . . . can I . . . ?

Stay safe, Mateo. We'll figure this out . . . somehow.

                        Stay safe? Chela, don't . . .

DAY THREE

What is lost is never lost,

But what we leave behind must remain in the past.

Reviving the dead is no simple task,

Reaching forward and behind us at the same time;

Gather the ingredients,

Study each map,

The beyond lies in wait, untouched, ready.

—*The San Madrigal Book of the Dead*, Canto X

CHAPTER NINETEEN

CHELA

"Very good!" Odé Kan yells from her perch in the ancient oak tree. "Again!"

She means it, too. First of all, the hunter spirit doesn't say things she doesn't mean. But also, I can hear the gentle ripple of laughter in her voice that tells me she's truly proud of how far I've come.

Not sure why she would be, though. If anything, I've gotten worse since yesterday. Only progress I can mark is that I've managed to destroy two out of every three of the whirling projectiles instead of just every other one. A poor excuse for a destroying angel, if we're being honest.

And anyway, I'm distracted—still haunted by that faraway spirit conversation Mateo and I had in the midnight skies, and what it all adds up to. The club collapsing for no clear reason the same night the mountain fell . . . It can't be a coincidence. Does that mean we really can't be together? That we'll destroy everything we care about with our love? I can't bear to think about it.

I launch into a forward roll, spring up from it, and catch the first plate in midair as it whips toward me from the tree. The plate shatters into dust in my hands. I leap to the side, avoiding the next one, and then hurl myself across a stretch of empty dirt and roll under a small table.

Must've come in with a little too much heat, though—the table goes clattering to the ground, and as I jump to try to catch it, Odé Kan's next flying plate comes whizzing out of the sky toward me.

I probably still would've been able to handle it, but Odé Kan yells, "You can only break it into four pieces!"

And when I glance at her in shock, the plate zings across my left temple and shatters across the concrete.

"Ha!" she squeals, sliding down from the tree as I sigh and rub the side of my face.

The first streaks of sunlight radiate across the gray skies over Madrigal. The birds sound like they're having quite a celebration in the forest nearby. Odé Kan got me up before dawn. I'd been having nightmares about Mateo disappearing as I held him, and I'd woken up every few hours thinking he was with me. Odé Kan shoved a goblet full of some weird coffee-like concoction into my hands, led me down here to this walled-in plaza behind the synagogue, and started throwing plates at me.

She'd dragged out a bunch of furniture for me to dip and dodge around, not unlike the absolutely unhinged and vicious obstacle courses my gym teacher, Ms. Bonsignore, made us run through back in Brooklyn.

"Training!" Odé Kan had explained enthusiastically, and I couldn't help but smile. The events of yesterday—the battle averted and, I think most of all, us deciding to trust each other—have put her in an excellent mood.

I don't know what she's getting at with this only-four-pieces thing, though. "How?" I ask as she stands over me, arms akimbo, an extra-pleased-with-herself grin across her mug.

"Precision. You'll see."

I take her outstretched hand. "You sure that's possible?"

She scoffs. "I can't wait for you to stop being so human. Things are much more fun when you don't have all that concrete in your brain."

I'm too intrigued to be offended, and then I'm too busy whacking away a plate that's whipping toward my face. "Hey!" I succeed only in clipping it; the plate crashes to the ground. I didn't destroy the thing.

"Think fast." Odé Kan chuckles.

"You're supposed to say that *before* you—"

"I did." She whips another plate at me. "See?"

This one I manage to stop with one hand, and as I send out a wave of destruction, I imagine it slicing clean, precise lines that bisect the porcelain surface once, then again.

Instead, the plate disintegrates against my palm.

"Start from the top," Odé Kan orders, skipping to the far end of the plaza. "I'll run alongside and mess with you!"

"Easy to be chipper when you're the one throwing the plates!" I call, hurrying after her. "And anyway, you never told me—"

"Start quadrisecting, and then I'll start talking." I've barely made it to the beginning point when she frisbees the first plate at me. "You know what happens when someone initiates as a Santero, right?"

"Yeah, it's like—" I leap out of the way, smacking the plate out of the sky and obliterating it entirely. "Dammit!" I land already running and dive under a bench. "It's like a whole new orisha is born for the initiate, right?"

"Correct!" Odé Kan yells with gusto as she sends a plate arcing into the sky like a missile.

"Mimi was initiated!" I realize out loud.

"Correct!" She launches another.

"And you were her guardian angel!" I vault over a fallen coatrack, landing right under the first plate. Shatter it to dust. "Her orisha!" I catch the second one with the edge of my hand and manage to reduce it to about twenty smaller shards. Progress.

"*Am*," Odé Kan adds. "It's a lifetime position, eh."

I stand still, panting. "Even if . . . the initiate . . . doesn't continue in the tradition."

We're about five feet apart when she whips another plate straight from her hip. It catches me totally off guard—all I'm really aware of is the white blur zipping toward me, my hand rising to meet it, and—

Shhhk!

Two jagged lines crisscross the plate, quartering it perfectly.

Odé Kan's smile is radiant as the four pieces clatter to the ground between us.

"Oh my God." I gasp. "I . . . I did it! Did you see that? I did it!"

The hunter spirit cocks an eyebrow. "More important . . ."

"I haven't missed a single one this run, have I?"

She shakes her head, infinitely pleased.

"How? I didn't even . . ." I plant myself on the bench to catch my breath.

She sits beside me, serene. "Okay, see . . . I'll admit this: I didn't actually know if you could cut it into fourths, so this is very cool, no?"

"*What?!*"

"I figured if you were concentrating on something beyond just getting it right, the *next* step, well, then you'd probably start assuming you'd already mastered this first part without realizing it, eh? And it worked!"

"I . . . You said I was being extra human by wondering if it was possible! And you didn't even know it was!"

She tilts her head victoriously. "Exactly! I was right on all counts, eh!"

I got nothing to say to that, so I just take the goblet full of concoction she passes me and drink up.

"So, you were just stranded?" I finally ask after we've taken in how the shadow and light play off the gathering morning. "Mimi went on to become a pirate queen and you—what?"

She raises one shoulder, tips her head all the way over to meet it, and closes her yellow eyes. "More or less, I suppose. Could say I went rogue, eh? A very Madrigal approach to the situation. An initiate, they are responsible for taking care of their spirits, yes?"

I nod, thinking about Mateo's tía Lucía. The elaborate soup tureens she kept decorated and dusted on a shelf in their apartment— that was where her santos stayed, the central focus of her spiritual work and worship. I know there's some complicated ceremony that happens when a Santero dies, but I have no idea what it entails or where their spirit goes. And I've never thought about spirits who are left stranded by nonpracticing initiates.

"Yes, so if an initiate decides to stop, it's better for them to pass the caretaking on to someone else, eh? But in this case, well, she just . . . She just left. Got bored, maybe. She was a human teenager; they are so fickle, you know. No offense."

I wave her off. She's not wrong. "None taken. That's . . . That must've been horrible."

"Eh, at first, yes. Confusing, heartbreaking. I wandered the island for a while, starving. Thought maybe I would just waste away, but no . . . Over time, I became a spirit of the forest, of the island. It sustained me, and I sustained it." She nods, considering. "And you know, I always remained tethered to her on some level. So when she stayed behind, sank beneath the waves in that shell of bambarúto, I stayed, too. What else was I going to do?"

The rising sun crests the far wall of the plaza. Odé Kan dusts herself off, tilts her head at me with a sad smile. "Now, shall we get back to it?"

The plate is already a sharp disk in the dawn sky, beginning its dive toward my head.

CHAPTER TWENTY

MATEO

I HATE THIS PLACE.

Even out here in the stairwell, every missing tile, each tiny imperfection on the plaster, the flickering fluorescents . . . they all come together to remind me of the world I lived in a couple of months ago, the one in which Tía Lucía was alive and this building was our home and Chela didn't have some weird, faraway riddle that seemed to be driving us apart. There's a certain horrible balance to it all—standing here missing an aunt who's dead and gone and a girl who seems even farther from me than the thousand miles away she actually is.

But Tía Lucía's never coming back. Only hope I have is seeing her ghost one day at the Grande Fete or some ceremony, and the idea of that is chilling, not comforting.

And this place will never feel like home again. I didn't live here in any long-term way until a little over a year ago, when my parents decided it was time for me to finish high school in my own community while they kept traveling the world, saving people's lives. And for most of that year, my aunt and I were just cool. Sometimes we fussed; mostly we went about our business, and that was that. Lucía's wife, Miriam, died a decade or so ago, but her spirit hung around, and Tía had her orishas and clients and Cabildo politics keeping her busy.

It wasn't until Tía Lucía's last couple weeks of life that I finally let her in, finally gave a damn, finally listened to her, listened to the world, listened to myself, like she'd been telling me to do all along.

And then a few of the empire-pirate goons came by to round her up—part of their grand plan was to keep all the Cabildo members out of the way so they could go through with their big coup undeterred. My tía was never one to go quietly, though. She stabbed one of them in the neck and died scrapping with the other two.

I try not to think of all the years before I came around as time lost, wasted, moments I chucked unceremoniously out the window of my life without even realizing the true gift that she was. I try not to wallow in regrets. I know she wouldn't want that.

Again and again, I try. And every single time I fail.

That's why I've barely been here since she died.

Most of the time I just crashed at the Hidalgos' house, adjacent to the temple. Aviva and the rabbi love me like a son after everything that went down, and Chela's arms are the only place I want to be any given night of the week.

When I did come here, it was only to stop by for a quick nap or to pick up a toothbrush or something. A neighbor took Tía's dog, Farts, and my parents were sensitive enough to leave me alone about not staying with them. Guess they felt bad about how everything had gone down.

Now, though . . . I've come carefully to this place that was once my home; stopped at every corner to check for cops, feeling ridiculous but knowing I had to do it anyway. It's a frigid January morning and the landlord doesn't heat the hallways, so I'm watching my frosty breaths rise as I stand in front of Tía Lucía's door, the door to Tía Lucía's apartment, the door to the apartment that Tía Lucía used to share with me when she was alive, but now she is dead.

Grief doesn't make any sense, doesn't care about time, certainly can't be bothered to go from point A to point B in anything resembling a straight line. Grief doesn't even acknowledge that point B exists. Grief is simply everything, everywhere, all the time.

And then it is not. And there's no rhyme or reason to it.

Anyone who tells you otherwise is probably trying to sell you something.

Small steps will get me where I'm going.

I put the key in the latch.

Breathe.

Try not to think of the men who stood exactly where I'm standing, preparing to drag an old lady out of her home. They surely didn't realize how death itself was stalking the streets of Little Madrigal that day, laying claim to souls of all kinds. None of them could've imagined that death was waiting for them on the other side of this very door, rippling through the air as they closed in on destiny.

Did the ones who dealt those fatal blows have to grapple with guilt the way I do? Or was it just another day in the life of a goon?

Turn the key.

Open the door.

Breathe.

My parents have redecorated, but that doesn't stop me from being pounded by the silence where Farts's little yip-yipping should be. All of Tía Lucía's spirits are gone, returned to the earth or given to other Santeros. Her tacky artwork is down, probably got tossed (maybe for the best).

Over there by where the altar used to be—that's where a man lay dead when I got here that terrible day.

Now morning light pours through the windows; little dust specks swirl through it. The burble of a coffee maker comes from the kitchen, and then so does my mom. "Mateo? Are you okay?"

I'm instantly annoyed by her overconcern, but I have no reason or right to be. "Fine," I say, trying not to let irritation seep in.

Breathe. She wasn't the one up on that stage offering a performative gesture of forgiveness to somebody who didn't deserve it.

"Come sit. Let's do coffee time."

Coffee time. I'd always know when something messed-up happened in the field, because the first thing my parents did when they got back to the hotel was make coffee, no matter what time of day or night. Then they'd sit, facing each other, mugs in hand, and talk through each step of what had happened in agonizing detail. Sometimes it'd become an argument; other times, they'd cry. They never tried to hide anything from me or talk in secret code, but most of it went over my head anyway. I learned to just let them have their ritual. And yeah, sometimes I thought it was pretty sappy, but I also knew not many people in the world could understand the experiences they'd lived through, the life-and-death decisions they'd had to make.

Now here I stand in the same room where my aunt died. I have taken lives, saved lives. I have lost loved ones, and I've fallen in love.

And damn, coffee time seems like the best idea in the world. I just wish I didn't feel so cold toward my own family, still. But my mom isn't someone I'm good at saying no to; plus, I really haven't gotten to spend any time alone with her since they got back. And, coffee.

She puts a steaming mug in front of me—one of Tía Lucía's corny ones with a cartoon Chihuahua on it. I try not to let my mind spiral down the impossible road of *When was the last time I saw her drink out of it?* Fail. It was during that week of hell, mid-coup, a few days before she died. Before she was murdered. Before they murdered her.

"Did . . . ? I don't even know how to ask about what happened on your journey." Mom sits across from me at the table, just like she would do with Dad in a hotel room. She tucks a few strands of curly graying hair behind her ear, tries to smile to make this moment less horrifically awkward.

I appreciate the effort, I really do. But it's as hopeless as me trying to fight off a million memories of Tía. "A lot happened. I don't really know how to talk about it."

"Is Chela . . . ?"

"She's okay. She's still there. There's some stuff we need to . . . figure out."

"Is there anything I can do?"

I can't help it—I laugh. It's not meant to be a cruel gesture, a hand slapped away, but it is anyway. It's just, my parents really are the most utterly overly-grounded-in-reality people San Madrigal has ever spat into the world. They're fundamentalist agnostics—obsessively, desperately devoted to science, logic, order. Thankfully, it's not as annoying as it could be, mostly because they don't generally lord it over people, and they usually avoid scoffing at other orthodoxies.

Usually.

But then, I scoffed at hers. "I'm sorry," I say, and I mean it. "That wasn't fair."

She waves me off, doesn't even look hurt, but it was an empty gesture, I'm sure. "I know we're not . . . I know your dad and I are mostly outside of what you're going through, Mateo."

Jeez, she makes it sound like I joined the mafia or a satanic cult or something. The truth is much more complicated, of course. I tried, I really did, to explain it to them when they first got home, but they kept trying to rephrase it back to me in a way that still fit their rigid adherence to science. Finally, I just had to let it go.

"But I don't want you to think we're . . . we're judging you or telling you what to do. We're worried about you, Mateo."

As I'm nodding vaguely, it finally clicks what's irritating me so much. Something happened last night on that stage. It was huge and it mattered. And all she wants to talk about . . . is stuff we've already been over.

"Mom," I say, the word singed with vex. "Stop."

She blinks at me, sips her coffee.

"This unity crap . . ."

She puts down the mug, lets out a deep, mournful sigh. Sags. "I . . . I'll be honest with you, Mateo."

"Please."

"Mateo." She cuts her eyes at me, letting me know I'm approaching a dangerous line. Then she swivels her head, gaze now somewhere far away. "I don't like it, either."

What?! "What?"

Now it's her turn to scoff. "You do realize your father and I are different people, right, Mateo? I mean—I'm all for unity, don't get me wrong. And it's good he's pushing for it. But . . . what happened yesterday was a bad idea. Too soon, too clumsily done."

"Did you tell him that?"

"It's all we've talked . . . argued about for the past week." She looks tired. I only realize it now that I'm finally really looking at her, but those worry lines on her face, the slight smudge of darkness under each eye—it seems like they all showed up overnight.

"I . . . I had no idea."

"Yes, you've been gone, Mateo." She doesn't say it harshly, but she doesn't have to. The words do all the work. She shakes her head, slides her hand over my wrist. "I'm sorry. That came out as an accusation, and it wasn't meant to."

I manage not to storm off. I'm not totally sure how I feel about it. "If you want to accuse me of something, just do it, Mom."

"No," she says, and I can tell she means it. "It came out that way because I missed you."

Oops. That gets me. Didn't see it coming and definitely wasn't expecting the gulp of emotion that rises in me. I drop my head and let a sob well up and escape. Truth is, I missed her, too. Missed them both. Everything seemed so simple when I was traveling with them; all this mess started when I settled back here.

But this mess is the truth of the world, and it's the truth of me, who I am. And I'll take it every day of the week over pretending everything's fine when it's not.

And then my mom is there, wrapping herself around me and crying some, too, rubbing my back. We're both apologizing, I don't even know what for. And then we're laughing through our tears at how ridiculous we both are, and she settles back in, pours us some more coffee, and sighs.

"Well, at least—" she starts, and that's when my dad appears in the doorway, face still tight and deep red like he's been cultivating a low-level bonfire inside himself ever since we butted heads last night. "Jorge, I—"

"Do you have any idea what you ruined last night?" my dad asks me in a quiet voice that means certain death.

"Jorge!" my mom gasps.

I stare at him.

"What makes you think you can just come into this apartment after what you did, hmm?"

This apartment. The one Tía Lucía lived and died in because of the person my dad was trying to shake hands with in front of the whole world.

I'm already standing when my dad says, "You're not welcome here," already out in the hall when my mom yells at him not to talk to me that way, already slamming the door on the escalation of their next useless argument.

CHAPTER TWENTY-ONE

CHELA

"WHY US?" THE QUESTION RISES WITHIN ME UNEXPECTEDLY AS I LIE with the cold concrete of the plaza against my back, the bright midday sky in my eyes and a dozen small trenches crisscrossing the ground all around me.

"Hmm?" Odé Kan asks from the bench she's lounging on while she waits for me to recover.

Turns out it's utterly exhausting—plying the very soil of this island that is me into sudden violent shapes. Exhausting in my body, which registers each change like a small earthquake is racking it, and exhausting in my mind, which doesn't know what to do with the overload of information and cataclysmic change.

And every time I do it, yes—the slim line of nothingness lengthens ever so slightly up my arm. But there's plenty of me left, and I'm not going to let Archibaldo's poison stop me from learning my own powers. That would be playing into his hands.

In short, being an island sucks. But Odé Kan is right when she says putting my abilities to good use is the best chance we have of snatching the upper hand from Archibaldo's army.

I clasp my fingers behind my head and pull myself into a sit. "Archibaldo's one demand when he was facing off with Tía Mimi . . . He didn't ask for her to surrender or turn over the synagogue. He just asked where we were."

"Oh!" Odé Kan cartwheels off the bench and is already dancing a little jig around me when she lands. Show-off. "I mean, think about it—he knows I hate him. He knows that even if I haven't figured out how to kill him yet, I won't stop till I do. Would you want me gunning for you?"

I acknowledge the point with a head tilt.

"And you," Odé Kan continues. "He's probably worried about his porcelain dinnerware. You're a holy terror on those plates, man!"

I shake my head, chuckling. "Can't stand you."

"Seriously, though: I don't know what Archibaldo's plotting, but whatever it is, your existence threatens it. At the height of your power, you defeated Vizvargal twice, and he knows that, like me, you'll never bend to his will or compromise. So you gotta be destroyed."

"Yeah . . ." Something doesn't fit, though, some errant piece of the puzzle I can't put my finger on.

I shake my head. Got enough on my plate trying to unravel this mystery of why Mateo and I are theoretically not supposed to be together. "I'm going to . . ." Never sure how to say it—any of it. Language feels wildly insufficient to describe these things I'm able to do, these journeys and miracles.

Odé Kan sees my hesitation, seems to get it somehow without me explaining. Motions at me to try. I like her.

"I'm going to explore some." That works, almost. "Inwardly."

"Ah." She nods. "Good, good. You need a rest from all this maneuvering the earth anyway, eh? I will cover you." She pulls the bow off her back and nocks an arrow, then takes up a position nearby, much like I did for Mateo when he was first learning to heal.

Mateo.

Don't get lost, Chela. Not now.

Midnight can't come soon enough, but is that the only way I'll be able to reach him from here on out? Just as flimsy spirits? I'm greedy; it's not enough. No, I will find a way to make this work.

I sit cross-legged, hands resting on my knees, and close my eyes. Go inward.

Immediately, the gulls, the ocean wind, the whole world falls away and I slip through the darkness, weightless as a ghost, as I feel the constraints of time and place come loose all around.

It seems so random, but as I meander through the swirling memories of this enchanted island, my island, my people, the first conscious thought I have is of Amsterdam.

We went there on a school trip last year—fancy, right? On the final night, instead of sneaking out to the discotheques or coffee shops with everyone else like I had the other nights, I went wandering by myself. The shimmering lights in the dark water of the canals, the comings and goings in the streets, the delicious bakery smells . . . They seemed to be telling me stories I could only barely understand. I don't think I'd ever felt so free—like time itself evaporated the second I veered off down some cobblestone walkway and I just had my random whimsy to guide me through that midnight city.

Sure, it was reckless. And I was scared the whole time. And invigorated. And uncertain. And totally confident. All that at once. But mostly it was just me and the streets and I could be as much me as I wanted to and go wherever I pleased, and it felt like not a cop or teacher in the world could tell me a thing.

That's the only experience I can compare this to. This . . . This weird wandering through the underbelly and history of our home. I let it slip through me, and I slip through it, and years slide past: ships entering the harbor and taking off, shoot-outs in the streets, love affairs and promenades, and rituals, festivals, feasts, debates . . . What a place this was, our home.

I'm not here for idle wanderings, though, much as I'd love to just cavort. I have to find that girl, get her out from behind that barrier, and find out what she knows. It all seemed to happen so fast, but it's there somewhere, a fixed moment in time. And if it's there, I can find it.

The Cabildo meeting will be my anchor point—1810. The last time the Cabildo had six members instead of three. I was there before, so I should be able to make my way to it again.

Time slows around me; the blur lessens as faces and clothing become crisp, detailed. But this isn't right—I'm on a street in the Port District, the crowd milling around me, through me, some people in suits, others in jeans and T-shirts. Big sunglasses and afros. Wristwatches, soda cans . . . I'm in the sixties or seventies.

Could've sworn I was going back much further than that.

The figures blur into motion again. Lives unravel, schemes work backward from their devilish conclusions to their meticulously plotted origins; lovers marry, court, meet, return to before they even knew each other; tragedies untangle themselves; families become scattered loners.

Inside me, inside this chunk of earth in the ocean, there's like a whole library of memories, history, I can wander through. But there's no Mr. Aviles to show me around like at school, no Dewey damn decimal system.

When I stop again, it's definitely earlier—no jeans!—but who knows what fashion was like on a tiny hidden-away island in the Caribbean Sea? Not I. Could be anywhere between the early 1800s and . . . the turn of the twentieth century, I guess?

And it's night; the stars are out but not many people. The crescent moon hangs low over the waves, and there's a gentle breeze on my face, the smell of jasmine, soil, rum. I want to wander, get lost, lose myself. I want to walk these streets with Mateo, fill them with our idle chatter, our easy laughs, our loving silences.

But Mateo is in Brooklyn, trying to figure out why we can't be together without fully understanding the situation. I'm such a fool for not telling him the whole of what I saw. But then, I'm not wrong that he might've taken it too seriously and cut off any contact, any way to figure it out together.

Doesn't matter. There's no knowing. Would'ves and should'ves can go on forever, but what happened, what I did, is done. We move on.

Without me realizing it, the island has spun into motion again, the gears of history churning around me; the people blur through their lives, the sun and moon chase each other across the sky again and again, the world becomes calm as twilight sets in, then explodes into frenzied motion seconds later. The world does not stop, it does not stop, it . . .

STOP!

(It does, but only in a dizzying, off-kilter way, people walking forward, then a few steps back, then ahead again but only some. . . .)

I can't do this.

I am nowhere. Time, place . . . it's all a wash.

Mimi said this could happen, would happen, I realize belatedly. And I hate for her to be right, but . . . there's no way to navigate this. Or if there is, I don't know it. Not yet.

But now my head's spinning, or is it the island?

I stumble forward, and time accelerates.

I can find myself and Mateo, our moment on the beach. From there I can get out. I know I can. I lived that. I, Chela, lived it. It's the memory of a place, even if that place is me. It's a memory from this body.

The waves crash; the world rushes along. A storm comes; the island sinks; a few moments later, it bursts out of the water once again, and there we are, Mateo and me, watching with tears in our eyes.

Forward, forward, slower now . . . The sun sets, the moon rises, the Iwin come floating out to illuminate the night like sky jellyfish. The midnight bell tolls, and there we are, face-to-face, palm-to-palm, palm-to-palm. . . . The mountain falls, and we run. We run and . . .

"Chela?" Odé Kan's voice reaches me in the darkness. A hand shakes me. My eyes open to the strange sky of today, right now, and my friend's face staring down with worried eyes. "You were . . . You were sobbing," she says gently.

I sit up, then turn over and retch my guts out.

CHAPTER TWENTY-TWO

MATEO

EARLY LAST YEAR, ONE OF TÍA LUCÍA'S CLIENTS ASKED HER TO DO a divination for his daughter, who'd been locked up on drug charges and was having a rough time of it. Tía's cowrie shells foretold some heavy problems on the horizon, and she had to go into the facility to do a despojo for the girl. I tagged along to keep her company— and almost immediately regretted it. That place, it gets within you as soon as you enter . . . the deep cold of it, the way it closes in, the finality of those slamming cages, their echoes. I hated it, every second. Felt like I couldn't breathe. And our whole stay was an hour, tops. People spend their entire lives there.

And the way things are looking, I think, my feet hitting the pavement as my eyes dart from side to side, I might be headed back there, who knows for how long. . . .

My mind wouldn't stop spinning at the Hidalgos'—panic kept sweeping over me in vast, unstoppable waves. So I hit the streets— carefully, carefully—and for the past few hours, I've just been sliding around corners, ready to run, ready to hide, trying not to look as suspicious as I feel.

Gradually, bit by bit, I've let my walls down, and the music of the city has risen around me, mingling with and soothing these fires inside.

Over by Atlantic Avenue, a few blocks from Little Madrigal, Brooklyn feels like a whole different place. Cars rush back and forth, to and from Queens, the airport, the rest of the world. Auto shops, fast-food joints, and cheap motels speckle the edge of the thruway.

I've been walking for hours; I know exactly where I am but still feel lost.

The rushing traffic, empty warehouses, parking lots . . . It all blends to form a blur of gray.

What's Chela doing? What the hell will happen to us?

Even with all the monsters and miracles we've witnessed in the past couple of months, even knowing we are who we are, that midnight meetup still feels barely real, barely possible. It was something in the realm of dreams. The rational part of my brain—my parents, basically—keeps trying to file it under *things that didn't really happen.* Keep the boundaries of space and time nice and tidy.

Right.

I can't keep wandering like this. Eventually I'll wander right into the arms of the people trying to lock me up.

I turn and head toward the only place that feels any degree like home these days.

———◆———

There are two old men sitting on the steps of the synagogue when I arrive.

No. That's not right.

One of them is me: Galanika. That spectral visage has somehow strengthened even as my ancient body has grown weaker. Death seems to haunt his every wrinkle and tremble, like if I look closer, its shrill rictus will glare at me from just over that emaciated shoulder. One arm reaches toward me . . . pleading? The hand opens, closes, then pounds on that frail chest once.

And then the image is gone and I'm left blinking at an empty spot on the synagogue steps.

That's when I realize who the other old man is: the person who died trying to run me over that snowy night two months ago, whose very death I snatched and secreted away within myself when I brought him back to life.

"Mateo," Tantor Batalán says, standing creakily and hoisting an instrument case onto his shoulder with a grunt. "Look like you've seen a ghost, joven! Anyway, I owe you a long-overdue thank-you. And an apology."

I don't trust him, and my body doesn't, either—my fists have already clenched without me telling them to, plus my brain is still woozy from the vision of Galanika.

Sure, Tantor's old, but he already tried to kill me once, and that's not the kind of thing the deeper parts of ourselves forget. Anyway, you'd be surprised what these spry Galerano viejitos can manage after all those years living on a pirate island.

"It's fine," I manage, trying to not sound rude and also not invite any further conversation as I brush past him. A small but firm hand catches my forearm, halting me in my tracks.

"It's not fine," he says gravely. My hand lands on his, ready to rip it off, to block whatever other attack may come. But something— maybe it's the very real sadness dancing in his eyes, maybe it's the fact that he brought an instrument—*something* tells me he's not here to surprise shank me and leave me for dead.

For a few moments, we just stand there in the chilly afternoon sunlight, frozen still, arm clutching arm like someone hit pause on our strange waltz of death and resurrection and regret.

The street in front of the synagogue is still torn up from whatever freak accident happened last night—bright police tape warns people away from the sudden canyon torn through the pavement; it turns even a few passing cars into instant gridlock.

"I tried to kill you, Mateo." Voice like an ashtray, but he means every word he says. "It's not fine."

Finally, I turn to face him, and it's . . . It's hard to. The grayish, newly dead version of Tantor comes swimming to the surface of my mind—unhelpful! It makes it even stranger to be standing here talking to him. I've already tumbled all the way into the uncanny valley, though, and there's no turning back. "I'm listening."

"It's not just that." He lets go of me, thank goodness, and looks away, scrunching the flesh around his nose like there's rotting fish nearby. "I thought . . . I thought this Vizvargal thing was a path to freedom somehow." Tantor Batalán shakes his old head, scratches one of the slim gray muttonchops along his jaw line. "I believed all of it, swallowed it whole. All those lies. Tanta mierda." He spits. "The opposite of everything we stand for, and I let it consume me, become worth throwing away everything for. Worth *killing* for."

The city feels silent around us. Almost no one is out, and the air is crisp, so quiet, like all that newly fallen snow has shushed the world so it can hear our conversation more clearly.

"What . . . What brought you back around?"

Tantor looks up at me. "*You* did, Mateo. Well, dying did. But then you. You saved me twice, really. Because I was already half-dead when El Gorro sent that car careening for you and the rabbi. The empire pirates and their vicious god del carajo had already eaten my heart whole and spat it back out." His hands grasp my shoulders. "But it was still me. I was still part of it. I did it, and then you brought me back to life anyway. You didn't have to do that. I was your sworn enemy. When I realized what had happened,

I . . . I could barely live with myself. But ending everything would've defeated the purpose of what you'd done. So I just disappeared from the world, best I could. Hid out in my apartment. Didn't answer calls, didn't speak to nobody. Just hid."

He settles back down. Rubs his eyes. "Rambling. Apologies. Didn't come here to talk about me and my problems. Came here to say I'm sorry, Mateo. For all of it. The target was really the rabbi— that's why we were there that day, and that's why I'm here now, to make amends to him. But I was going to find you anyway. To say this. I am sorry. And I will live what's left of my life working to undo the damage I have done."

The target was really the rabbi.

They'd been trying to take out the Cabildo. That was the plan all along. That's why . . . in another reality, Tantor Batalán could've been the body I'd found on Tía Lucía's floor. He could've been the one to deal the fatal blow to my aunt.

I tense, feel a shadow come over me. Tantor seems to notice it, too, steps back once.

It wasn't him, though.

He didn't kill Tía Lucía, not if what he's saying now is true: that after our encounter he stayed out of the fray.

And I can't live my life based on things that might've happened.

And I believe him.

These words form at the edge of my lips: *I forgive you.*

But all I hear is the echo of my father trying to say the same thing in front of the community, how false it had felt, how wrong. This morning I stormed out of my own home on the strength of how much I'd hated him saying that.

With Tantor it feels very different, but the resonance and the dissonance of the words remain. And they're not something I ever want to say if they're not true.

So I swallow them and nod my acceptance, meeting his old watery eyes. "Thank you, Mr. Tantor. That means a lot to me. You should go 'head and see if the rabbi's in."

"Actually . . ." Tantor says, looking somewhat impish. "I thought, perhaps . . . we might . . ." He hefts one shoulder, indicating the instrument bag slung over it.

I didn't realize how badly I've missed playing music until he raised the possibility. It's been *weeks*. Feels like I've been holding my breath without even knowing it.

Behind these doors is the big auditorium we were in yesterday. There's a grand piano on the edge of the stage and an organ in the corner; the acoustics are brilliant. I don't even know what Tantor's got in that bag—something stringed, if I had to guess—but I don't care. Music is music, and I'm starving for it.

Without meaning to, I smile. Those are the best ones, right?

CHAPTER TWENTY-THREE

CHELA

ODÉ KAN DROPS TO A KNEE BY MY SIDE AND HELPS KEEP ME UPRIGHT.
"Easy, Okanla, easy."

"Yeah, I just . . . I'm okay." And I am. It's dizzying, sure, like getting off a boat after days at sea—nothing feels quite right. But already my body and mind are adjusting back to the present tense. "For real. It's not . . . It's not as overwhelming now. Not like that first time, when it felt like the earth was swallowing me whole."

"And?"

She helps me stand. I don't think much time has passed. The bright sky and high sun make it early afternoon at the latest.

I rub my eyes, stretch. "You're right."

"My favorite words, but about which part?"

"It's definitely possible to go back in. Mimi was acting like the door could either be open or closed, that's it." Odé Kan starts to say something, but I beat her to it. "Mortal crap. I know."

She laughs, shakes her head. "Yeah, but also Mimi crap. Even among an overly this-or-that species, she's exceptionally wedded to all-or-nothing. How do you think I ended up a rogue spirit on a sunken island?"

"Thing is, Mimi was also right. Trying to move through time, it's . . . dangerous. I almost got lost in there. Like, for good."

"Bah."

"Damn." The walled-in plaza spins a little when I try to stand on my own, so I head to the bench, ease myself onto it.

"Still adjusting?" Odé Kan hovers nearby, ready to catch me. She acts tough, but what a sweet softy, really.

I manage to smile. "Yeah, I'll get there."

"Problem is . . ."

"I know. What good is this skill in a fight if it leaves me winded and woozy?"

"Eso es." Odé Kan nocks an arrow and fires it into a nearby tree. I'm alarmed at first. Sure, her face displays the same easy nonchalance as always, but then, she would be the one to be utterly unfazed in a fight—I've already seen it. "Maybe with practice, though."

And that's when I realize it: *she's* practicing. It's second nature to her; all day she's been randomly running up trees, stretching, bench-pressing actual benches. The girl is just constantly working out. I gotta introduce her to Bonsignore one day; they'd love each other.

But there are more pressing things at hand. Like the awkward secret that I'm not sure why I've been holding close all this time. I stand, an urgent, nervous wind suddenly shoving me into motion even though there's nowhere to go. "Also . . ."

"What is it?" Odé Kan is busy slinging arrows through falling leaves.

"That emptiness you've been finding around the island," I say.

"Mierda desgraciada del carajo," she spits. Then she stops what she's doing and turns to me. "What about it?"

A moment passes, and Odé Kan waits patiently, apparently aware that this isn't easy for me. Finally, I raise my arm and pull down the sleeve of my shirt. The line has reached my shoulder and spread some. "It's not just on the island."

Odé Kan's eyes widen. "Wha— How?"

I shrug, scrunching my face. "Not sure. But every time I connect to the island it gets a little bigger."

"Well, then you ca—"

"No," I say firmly, and then I realize that this is why I've been hesitant to bring it up. Because of course she will try to stop me from going back in, connecting to the place that is me, my home. But I *have* to. This power, this connection, it's already saved us all once. Who knows what else we'll need it for? And it's no good to us if I barely understand it. Plus, we're outnumbered and scattered; we need all the help we can get. "I have to. If nothing else, I have to *because* he did this. We *have* to stop him. I'm not giving up one inch of who I am or what I can do. That's exactly what he wants. Either we destroy him or we're all dead, so this is what it has to be."

She doesn't look happy about it, but I can tell she's not the type to tell someone else what to do with their body.

"Anyway, it's not moving that fast," I point out. "Just a tiny bit at a time."

Odé Kan tries to smile. "There's not *that* much of you, shorty."

I wave her off with a grudging guffaw. "Yeah, yeah. When Mateo gets here, he'll heal it all up, I'm sure. It's what he does. But look, there's something else. . . . I can use the connection for other things besides battle and historical research. . . ."

"Eh? We are at war. What could be more important than—?" I actually see the realization slide over her face like a sunrise. She releases one more arrow and spins to face me. "Reconnaissance!"

I don't smile big. It's just not how my face works. But this time, I'm pretty sure my grin is almost as wide as this wild forest spirit's.

"You sure you're ready to go back in so soon?"

We're in the bell tower (mostly because it has a nice view), and Odé Kan has been clucking and fussing over me since I decided to jump immediately back into the island's-eye view. I can tell she's worried about the slowly growing line of nothingness along my skin, too, but she doesn't want to bring it up. Her eyes keep darting back there, then quickly away.

"I won't be if you keep distracting me," I growl.

She flinches with mock offense. "Yow! Attitude! Eh, eh!"

"Yeah, yeah, less fussing and more nocking arrows in case we get attacked while I'm out of it, as my old gym teacher would say."

Odé Kan nods approvingly, nocks an arrow. "Very well, very well."

Off to the right, a cluster of elegant weather-worn estates nestles into the jungle slope. Farther down, the Port District hugs the edge of the sea. It must have been a bustling, magical place once. I'm sure if we'd stayed here, Mateo would've loved wandering down by the docks to let the secret songs of the sea whisper to him, or some other poetic-type thingy. He makes it all seem so natural, like music rises up around him.

Enough. *Focus, Chela.*

This world is empty of everyone but monsters now, and Mateo is a thousand miles away.

And I have a job to do.

I breathe in, breathe out.

And go inward.

The beginning is always a jolt. That first time—being totally overwhelmed, the full-overload experience—spins back to me, and I always lose my breath in a sudden panic. But I was ready for it last time, and I am again. This go-round, I zip past it even faster, bat the whole mess out of my way, and slide into a ferocious single-minded focus, buzzing along treetops, swishing through the underbrush, launching upward into the clouds as I make sure I've got the hang of this weird, impossible motion.

And I do. I do. Small wonder, as it is me. Huge wonder, as I am within the sea-soaked, trembling, and ever-growing consciousness of an entire island.

No movement through time now. Stay firmly planted in the present.

The cloud-speckled skies whirl around me; the two mountains poke up from below, the wreckage of the third now just tide pools and rock piles.

Dive.

The island spins within.

A steady thud in the distance. It reverberates from somewhere deep in the nearby peak.

I slip through sky, canopy, leaf, underbrush, soil. All along the jungle and toward the sheer rock face of a mountain. As the rubble of the third peak appears beyond the trees, a shrill, ambient wail gets louder and louder. It's screaming, I think. Many, many voices screaming together. I slow.

A form on the ground just in front of the rubble catches my eye. I swing closer, slowing even more, then recoil in horror. It's a long figure, each limb bound to stakes in the dirt, its flesh rotting in the Caribbean sun. A bambarúto. No way to tell which master it belonged to, who did this. A ritual sacrifice of some kind? A warning? A tiny flutter of white pulls my attention. It's not bone poking through desiccated flesh like on other parts of this monster's corpse—it's a flower petal. A few other petals lie scattered around.

I don't know what to do with this sight. It's just there, and horrible, and asks way more questions than it answers. And that screaming . . . I surge forward, breaching the rubble, going through tunnels, more tunnels, diving deeper as that heavy pounding grows louder and louder and the screams recede. And then, with a whoosh, a great cavern opens around me.

It's crowded.

Bambarúto writhe and howl.

No. They're . . . That's *dancing*. Or something akin to it.

Near the far wall, several of them are smashing sticks into dried hides stretched across giant tree trunks. There are so many of these creatures—more than I could've imagined. It's hard to tell in the darkness, but it must be at least a hundred or a hundred and fifty. But that seems impossible. . . . How could there be this many? And why didn't they all come out to get us?

And these ones seem different, from what I can make out. They're even more hunched over; their flesh dangles like curtains from pale exposed bones. They stagger around the cavern, aimless. These *Dawn of the Dead*–looking bambarúto don't have the sharp precision of the others, but they're terrifying in a whole other way.

And then, somehow, it gets worse. A hideous, creaking scream sounds above the thunder of those drums. At first I think they're sacrificing a goat . . . but no. Following the high-pitched whine, I realize that's a melody, or it's supposed to be. And it's coming from . . . there! At the far end of the cavern, a hazy green light emanates from Maestro Archibaldo's stooped figure.

He's clanging away at an ancient organ made from mostly rotted driftwood and bones. Each note blasts out of a long tube pipe, filling the cavern with that desolate scream. I don't really have an ear for music, but I'm pretty sure this is that cursed song Mateo was playing on vote night, the one Archibaldo encoded his secret messages into.

It's awful.

But I'm here for information, not music criticism. So I brace myself and then close in on the maestro.

There's a book beside him on the bench.

Closer.

His near-dead body seems to convulse with each note, that old face all scrunched up with concentration.

The San Madrigal Book of the Dead is written in elaborate letters across the front of the old tome.

The music pounds on, screeches on; I can't take much more of it.

Perhaps I've gotten what I came for, though.

I'm just turning to leave when something pale catches the edge of my vision.

There in a corner . . . a person!

Several people! From what I can tell, they're in their thirties or forties. One has slicked-back hair and a white suit. Another is balding, frumpier. They're all very uncomfortable, clearly, but . . . what are they doing here?

Okanla.

I'm about to swing closer to see what I can find out when a hand lands on my shoulder. . . .

My shoulder?

Madrigal.

I have a shoulder.

I do, and there's a hand on it.

Odé Kan's hand.

"Chela."

I blink as her wide, solemn face eclipses the hell rave.

"Okanla. Madrigal. Chela. Come back. Come back."

I blink again. The sky is around us, the swishing trees, the stomp of approaching feet down below.

"Chela?"

Approaching feet. "What's happening?"

"Someone is coming," she says. "Lots of someones."

CHAPTER TWENTY-FOUR

MATEO

IN CASE YOU'RE WONDERING HOW THINGS ARE GOING WITH THAT checklist I had going, here's the update: garbage. One hundred percent basura. Of the six items, I've done crap-all. In fact, there are more items now, if we're counting the misa later. Item one was discovered to be a pile of rubble, and that about summarizes the whole endeavor.

On the plus side, though, there is music. Music is always the answer when the world refuses to make sense, when all checklists are upended from jump, when nothing is working out. Also on the plus side: turns out Tantor Batalán's instrument is a balalaika and he knows exactly what to do with it.

I glanced over when we were getting set up, when I was taking my own moment to relish the sheer bliss of sitting in front of these keys again. Sure enough, the old man was grinning down at the wooden triangle with the kind of glint in his eye that most keep reserved for long-lost friends.

I let him start, because I'm courteous and I had no idea what he knew how to play, so following along made the most sense. Tantor took a breath and then sent a magnificent tapestry of jangling, tangled melodies cavorting through the empty auditorium. The song seemed to dance a mean tango with itself, layers of harmony rising and falling, mingling and separating.

It wandered like a stranger in a new city, and for a moment, it seemed like all those tight turns and slurred notes would never resolve into anything I'd know what to do with. It was beautiful, don't get me wrong, but still somehow impossible; remote, a thing unto itself with no room, no need for accompaniment. Then the song ambled gradually toward a familiar tune: an old Ladino classic called "Los Bilbilicos," *the nightingales.* See? Music brings order to the chaos of the world. We'd all be lost without it. Okay, I'd be lost without it. Tantor wound through the main melody one time with long, dramatic pauses between each phrase, drawing out the notes and wrapping them around each other as they cascaded with mesmerizing gravity back toward their one.

I joined in as he rolled into the main verse again, leaning heavy on the bass notes since it was only us two. And then, without warning, it wasn't: a steady *thump, thump* rang out from the kit at the corner of the stage. Tams must've wandered in without either of us noticing. Wild smiles were exchanged, and then the song took off; it just went.

And now, fifteen minutes later, it's starting to feel ready to ease itself down to a close. We dipped into a whole rumba, teased "El Manisero," of course, that most quotable of old Cubano riffs, made our way through a wicked drum solo with Tantor and me dropping back to staccato hits so Tams could take the lead. Then we returned gloriously to the head, with even more verve this time, and now Tams's enthusiastic close-out smashes are taking us somewhere toward thrash as we bring it home.

Tantor tips his chin at me, and I nod at Tams, and we crash and bang it all to a sweeping, violent collapse. Tantor lets out a cigar-stained cackle as the cymbals shimmer toward silence. "¡Coño, mi gente! That was incredible." He shakes his head, wipes his eyes, and stands, gently leaning the balalaika against his chair. "And now this old bladder has to empty itself, ahahaha!"

Tams snorts. "Down the hallway, third door to the left." When he's gone, she looks at me.

I shrug. "I dunno, T. He apologized and seemed like he meant it. What am I supposed to do? What are any of us supposed to do?"

She shakes her head. "Wish I knew."

"Speaking of my dad . . . Looks like I'll be crashing here tonight."

Her mouth falls open. "Yours, too?"

"Wait, wait, wait . . . What? *Your* dad kicked you out?"

Tams shakes her head, eyes wide. "No! What the hell? I wish he would try! I stormed out because he was being such a stubborn asshole and I'm fed up with his crap. *Your* dad kicked you out?"

I bop my head side to side. "He tried, yeah. My mom intervened, but I stormed out! Ha!"

We both laugh; I'm pretty sure neither of us knows why. It's all just so ridiculous and terrible. What else can we do?

"You can't evict me—I quit!" Tams yells.

"Basically! What's wrong with our dads?"

She falls into an urgent little march on the snare. "They're old and out of touch, I guess. And probably terrified because their community is falling apart around them."

I join in with a dramatic mambo. "I mean, so are we? But you don't see us cozying up to the people who tried to kill us."

"Er, you don't?" She nods at the doorway Tantor ambled through a few minutes ago.

I make a face and send the mambo into a chaotic free-jazz meltdown. "Okay, whatever. Point is, I'm taking Chela's room."

"Ew! So you can try on her freaky goth fits? Have at it. Tolo and I are staying in the guest room, anyway."

The whole song crashes to a halt. "Wait! It's moving *that* fast?!"

Tams keeps right on playing. "Hmm?"

When I left, she'd been midway through a whirlwind extra-intense . . . something or other with Maza, one of the Alameda twins. They'd both been openly lusting after Tolo, sure, but everyone does that. Then again, Tams famously gets what Tams wants, no matter who else wants it, too. Still . . . I'm so behind on everything.

"What about Maza?"

Tams scrunches one side of her face. "Oh, you know, they . . ."

"Died?" No way she'd be this casual about it if that was the case!

Tams busts out laughing, still not missing a beat on the march. "No! Good grief, Mateo. They kind of edged over to their sister's side of things, politically. Maza's not pro–empire pirate, per se, but they definitely think we should all just get along and pretend none of this ever happened."

"Ugh."

"Tolo and I are hoping they come around, or at least stop giving us the silent treatment, because—"

"Everything was going so well!" Tolo's deep, gravelly voice booms across the auditorium.

"Exactly!" Tams confirms. "Hey, gorgeous!"

Tolo Baracasa moves down the center aisle with the fluid, unstoppable grace of a ballet dancer who might shank you at any moment.

"Don't stop on our account," Rabbi Hidalgo calls, coming in behind his nephew with a bag of groceries in one hand and his cell phone in the other. "Please, keep playing! Although we do have to get ready for the misa soon; Baba Johnny and Iya Lisa are on their way."

Tolo leaps onto the stage easily and looks like he's warming up to give Tams a big ol' kiss on the lips when a stoniness comes over his face. I follow his glare of imminent death to the back of the stage, where Tantor Batalán has just walked in the door.

I'm standing, reaching out, opening my mouth to tell Tolo no, but it's all too late. He crosses the floor like a freight train moving at light speed. The flash of his blade is a blur as he draws it. Tantor yelps, but there's nothing he can do—Tolo already has him pinned to the wall, the business end of a bowie knife tickling the old man's throat.

"What . . . the hell . . . is he doing here?" Tolo growls.

Tantor can only gasp. "I . . . I . . . Please . . ."

"He's with me," I say, trying to approach from an angle that won't startle anyone and get me shanked. "He apologized. And I believe him."

"He tried to kill my uncle and *you*, Mateo. And now he's walking out of a hallway that leads to the rabbi's office. Does that seem like a good thing to you?"

"He went to the bathroom," Tams says. "Which is also down that hallway."

"Is true," Tantor whispers.

Tolo is unmoved. "Keep quiet, you. Tío, see if your office is locked?"

The rabbi passes without a word; his face reveals nothing as he clomps down the hallway.

Tolo glances at me without taking his blade off Tantor. "Didn't you *just* get through cursing out your dad over this same thing, Mateo?"

"I . . . Yes, but this . . . is different?"

"Enlighten me."

"It's not a big public display, for one thing," Tams points out. "He came privately."

"And he actually apologized," I say. "Which Vedo didn't do."

Tolo considers this with a grunt.

"Also," Tantor squeaks, "I didn't come empty-handed. I know things. . . ."

I think all of us go *Huh?* at the same time. That part is news to me.

"Office is locked and nothing's been disturbed," Rabbi Hidalgo says, stepping back in from the hallway.

Tolo eases up with the dagger some but still has his enormous forearm shoved up against Tantor's sternum, which he could probably shatter without breaking a sweat. "We're listening."

"First of all, thank you, and yes, I came to apologize to the rabbi, yes," Tantor says in a hoarse and desperate deluge. "I saw Mateo first, and we decided to play music while we waited, but—"

"Info, now," Tolo prods. "Apologies and explanations later."

"Yes, yes," Tantor squeaks. "Of course. I started hanging around with Vedo's crew again the past few weeks, because I knew I'd be coming here. Wanted to have something to offer you. A gift!" he adds hastily. "Not a trade! A gift."

"Go on." Tolo releases Tantor's arm but remains looming over the much smaller man. I'm the same height as Tolo, and I personally would do anything he told me to if he were standing near me like that. Pretty sure Tantor feels the same.

"Vedo, the empire pirates, they're in league with some . . . I don't know exactly who they are. Shady, very wealthy, and well-connected people is the best I could gather."

"For what purpose?" Rabbi Hidalgo asks.

"They did a presentation of some kind last week. It was a video call with a bunch of these guys. Vedo—I'd say he was going off a script his mom left behind before she died. Think it had all been in the works already and he was just picking up the reins. He showed footage from October, when the . . . the bambarúto attacked that rally in their riot-cop gear, you remember?"

Of course I remember. It was the night Tía Lucía taught me how to cleanse myself spiritually. The night I realized how deep my feelings for Chela were.

"Did they say why?" Tams asks.

Tantor raises one shoulder, then the other. "Was a business arrangement of some kind. That's all I could gather. No one was up-front about anything; you know how these cats roll."

Do I ever. And the more I know, the more it sounds like these plans must've been in the works since well before we raised the island.

CHAPTER TWENTY-FIVE

CHELA

I STAND PERFECTLY STILL IN FRONT OF THE SYNAGOGUE GATE AS THE trees up ahead shiver and rattle and the ground shakes with approaching stomps. The first few towering creatures appear on either side of a half-dilapidated shack; more stomp toward me behind them, then more.

The thing about bambarúto is that even when they're not coming to murder you, they're still a terrifying sight to behold. There's something about their inexplicable enormity and staggering ferocity that makes the brain short-circuit a little. It's not that they give off apex-predator vibes; more that it seems like any given apex predator would be no big deal to them. But they're not cold and robotic, either—they're so very hideously alive, full of wrath and hunger and a drive to kill, kill, kill. And enjoy it.

So when Tía Mimi's strange little form limps achingly out of their ranks, I find myself exhaling a little bit. I'd known they were hers already—Odé Kan's sure-shot eyes had spotted her from the bell tower (where the hunter spirit still stands ready, arrow nocked), and I'd confirmed it through the island. But still . . . Everyone is tense, so anything can happen.

A bambarúto struts along either side of Mimi as she approaches me; they glance around warily, fall a few steps back at a signal from her.

"Still alive," Mimi says without much warmth. "Menos mal."

It's a weird time to be so standoffish, but I don't have time for unpleasantries. "Tía, listen, I—"

She railroads right over me. "Still, you did save us from possible destruction, and for this, I am grateful, eh."

"Tía—"

"We have come back to the synagogue, and we can gather tonight and decide what must be—"

With a shrill whistle and a thunk, an arrow shoves itself into the dirt a few inches from Mimi's sandaled foot; she stumbles back in shock. The bambarúto on either side roar and close in around her, facing outward.

"Shut up for two freakin' seconds and let the girl talk, coño!" Odé Kan yells from the bell tower.

"¡Desgraciado espíritu de mierda!" Mimi hollers back.

"Tía, *listen to me!*" I shout. She's about to yell back—her whole face is primed for a curse-out delivery—so I keep going. "Archibaldo has more bambarúto than we thought! Like, hundreds more!"

That stops her. She steps forward from her bambarúto protectors, their beady eyes glued to mine. "Pero . . . ¿cómo? It's not possible."

"I saw them, Tía. I went looking through the island, and—"

"He would've . . . He would've brought them yesterday. There were only fifty or so. Why wouldn't he bring his whole force and finish us off with one go? He's arrogant but not foolish." Her gaze wanders as she tries to work out the impossible calculations behind all this madness.

"We think—"

She snaps her gaze back to me, one finger raised. "No. No se puede. You know what happened? I know what happened. You went back in with the island and the past and present mixed together. It's easy to happen, no? You saw the past when you first got here; you don't have control over it, fully. I told you to keep that door closed, that he would manipulate you through it, and here we are, pues."

This whole conversation is basura. She's barely present in this reality, and here I am trying to convince her of something I know to be true. "Tía, I know what I saw. It was real. It *is* real."

"The bambarúto are made from fear, mi vida. Fear. The fear of people. Humans. You're looking at the only other human on this island besides that old fool and you, if you even count."

"That's the thing," I cut in firmly. "There were people there, too. In the cavern."

She looks disgusted. "Huh? No es posible."

"You better start listening to your niece," Odé Kan warns, walking up from the synagogue entrance. Guess she figured no threat we faced was any more dangerous than my tía's wack gaslighting. Pretty sure she's right, too.

"Or what, eh?" Mimi spits. "What are you going to do?"

Odé Kan gets all up in her face. "Trust me on this: I have had plenty of time to think of creative ways to cause you pa—"

"Both of you, stop!" I shout, shoving them apart. "I don't know who those guys are or how they got here, but I know they are here now, on this island. And I know there are more bambarúto than we had any idea about."

To my utter shock, Mimi actually listens to me and immediately seems to launch into strategy mode. "Pues, they had to get here somehow, no?"

"So, unless they were dropped off and have some way to call for a ride," Odé Kan says, taking Mimi's cue, "which seems unlikely, their way off the island is probably still here somewhere, eh?"

"Eh," Mimi confirms. Both of them are already strutting toward the beach.

The bambarúto turn as one, and suddenly I'm immersed in a walking, breathing forest of creatures. Ugh. "I'll see if I can figure out where it is as we go," I call, hurrying to catch up.

CHAPTER TWENTY-SIX

MATEO

"VEN ACÁ," TÍA LUCÍA SAID TO ME ONE SUNDAY MORNING WHEN I was, of course, literally sitting right next to her. *Come here* when you can't get any closer—it's one of those habits Galeranos kept from our Cuban roots. I didn't go *I'm already here!* that time, just looked up to show her I was listening.

This was during that horrible week when the bambarúto had the run of our snow-covered streets, and everyone stayed home as much as possible. We—Tía Lucía, Aunt Miriam, and I—were all pretty fed up with being stuck inside, but we were grateful to have one another, and Tía was using the time to teach me what she could about the tradition.

Of course, looking back, it's clear she knew she didn't have much time left.

"Ju know why we have the espirits over there?" She pushed her lips toward the corner where a bunch of old family photos sat on the floor behind a chalk semicircle along with a stick and various old-timey knickknacks. "Y ¿los orishas por allí?" She nodded to the altar with all her santos in their tureens and their elegant implements.

"Same reason we had to keep Farts in his crate when we were dog-sitting Chancho Cabrón from down the block?"

That got a good chuckle out of her, which was all I was hoping for. Lord knows the mood needed some lightening.

"Más o menos, sí," she allowed. "There aren't many straight lines in this world, even fewer in the espirit world, eh? Pero one separation that must be made is between los santos y los muertos. The santos are evolved spirits, some from heaven, others from earth. But they are very different from the basic ancestral spirit. ¿Entiendes?"

"Más o menos, sí," I said. "There's dead-people spirits and there's nature spirits, and they're different, and the difference matters."

She nodded, pleased. "Eso es." Sipped some of her cafecito. "Bueno, pues, some santos were people once, pero esa es otra historia. Point is, there is a place for the dead, and a place for the santos. That's why when you have a misa, hmm, it's for the dead y ya. Más nadie. And when you have a bembé, eso es para orisha, santo. Los muertos no se invitan."

"No orishas at misas, no dead folks at bembés. Got it."

She chewed on her cigar and tipped her head, eyebrows raised, to allow for an addendum. "Bueno, pues . . . some santos show up at misas—the ones who deal with the dead, pero esa es otra historia, ya."

"So, in summary," I said, laughing because she was, too, knowing I was about to make it more complicated than it had to be, "the santos and the muertos have to stay separate even though some santos were muertos once, and no muertos are allowed at santo parties, and no santos are allowed at muerto parties except the santos who are."

"¡Eso es!" Tía Lucía yelped with a little mambo. "Más o menos." By this point, Aunt Miriam had floated in from the bedroom, and we all shared a good laugh together. One of our last.

It's still echoing through me as I take a seat in the Hidalgos' library dressed in my whitest whites and prepare myself for the misa to start. Okanla is surely a spirit of the dead—in some stories she collects the souls of those killed in battle. Does that mean Chela might show up, the way she did at midnight? Will Tía Lucía appear? Aunt Miriam? Truth is, I'm wholly unprepared for any of those things happening. I'll probably break down in tears if they do. Sometimes spirits mount people at these things, possess them and speak through them. What if Chela possesses me? Can I, a spirit incarnate, even be possessed? I have too many questions, and I know they're all just distractions from how badly I miss Chela and Tía Lucía, and how worried I am that I'll never see Chela again.

"'Samatta, kid?" Tolo asks, nudging me back to the world with a little too much oomph in his elbow.

"Overthinking everything, no big deal."

He snorts. "Sounds about right. We ready to get this dead-people party started, Baba Johnny?"

Baba Johnny and Iya Lisa put the finishing touches on a white table in the center. Besides the three original spirits of the island, ancestor veneration is probably the one spiritual through line we all have in common. Every house has a copy of that weird, often misquoted text *The San Madrigal Book of the Dead*, and every house, whether pirate, Sefaradic, or Santero, has a small area with pictures of our lost family members going back generations.

The interconnectedness of our dead is so sacrosanct that a tenet of our misas, our ancestral ceremonies, is that one member of each community must be present for the ceremony.

On the table, three candles represent the island's three peaks (never mind that there are only two now); rum, flowers, honey, and a few other treats are scattered around them to appease the ancestors. Off to one side, a tattered copy of *The Book of the Dead* sits open to a random page. The old Santero lights a cigar off one of the candles and nods, appraising the setup. "Básicamente listos, sí."

The rabbi is here, too, along with his wife, Aviva. Everyone is wearing white clothes, and most look like they're ready for bed or to pull a shift at the ER, but Tams sits beside me in a full club fit, like she's about to head to an all-white party. Of course.

Iya Lisa starts in on a long trilingual prayer, and Baba Johnny welcomes everyone, then spreads his arms to either side with a beatific smile. "Espíritus, antepasados, muertos de la luz que nos desean claridad y paz, les doy la bienvenida. La gente de San Madrigal es una, viva y muerta, y juntos buscamos la verdad y la gloria. Asé."

"Asé," we all say, and I'm ready, I swear I'm ready, to see my tía again, to see my true love again, ready for whatever. The last time I saw Tía Lucía, she was already a spirit. She appeared to me right after she was killed to alert me to her death. She was terrified and barely coherent, barely there. Okay, I'm not ready, I'm not ready. I take it all back.

"It's very important," Baba Johnny informs us as Iya Lisa rattles off a list of ancestors' names, "that you allow whoever wants to come through to come through. Don't hold back, don't second-guess. If the espirits want to pass on evidencia, information, through you, then let them, let it out. Don't hold back, eh?"

Everyone nods, but what will it feel like? How will I know? My own thoughts are going so fast, I don't see any way to differentiate between them and messages from the beyond.

"And we are here especifically to espeak to the espirits who may have evidencia acerca del tema de los acuerdos de paz y la separación de Okanla y Madrigal. ¿Correcto?" He turns to me, and I nod.

And then we wait.

And wait.

Iya Lisa finishes off her prayer, shoots Baba Johnny a curious glance, then closes her eyes in meditation.

For a while, no one speaks.

Is something happening? I have no idea, no way to know. Soon we're all peeking back and forth at one another.

Finally, Baba Johnny opens his eyes. He looks more somber than I've ever seen him as he turns and quietly confers with Iya Lisa. Both are shaking their heads, frowning. A few more moments pass, and then Baba Johnny turns to address us, face etched with concern. "I have been speaking with los muertos for my whole life, and they have always been there, even if it is solo para decir que no pueden decir nada." *Even if it's only to say they can't say anything.* "I have never opened the space to espirits only to have none show up." He shakes his old head. "Pero something . . . *something* very, very bad must be happening, mi gente. Because the spirits aren't just not *here.* They are nowhere. Completely gone."

CHAPTER TWENTY-SEVEN

CHELA

YEAH, SO, SEEING THROUGH AN ISLAND IS HARD.

Guess I figured I'd get the hang of it as I went, but the whole endeavor—finding the balance, going in, and staying in—it all takes focus. Trying not to get trampled by bambarúto on the march also takes focus, and I don't have enough for both.

Mimi and Odé Kan keep a pretty breakneck pace, considering one is a rickety old something-or-other and they don't get along.

Anyway, doesn't matter. Pretty soon we find what we're looking for. Or, more to the point, it finds us.

We're coming out of the jungle, approaching another area of the beach. We crest the top of a dune, and then the sound of automatic gunfire rips through the late-afternoon peace as pockets of sand burst upward. Three bambarúto get pockmarked and thrown to the ground in an instant. They're not dead—I'm not sure what it takes to kill these things, besides, well, me—but they're definitely jacked up, and there's no Mateo around to weaponize their injuries.

Everyone else drops into a commando crawl as more gunfire shreds the top of the dune.

And then the reality of what happened smacks into me like a late-running freight train.

We just got shot at.

I don't know why it hits like that, what the delay was, or why I'm even surprised—we *are* at war, after all. But there are no guns in Little Madrigal. I've never been shot at before. And it came out of nowhere; we could've been paste and never even seen it coming.

Doesn't matter that I'm near impossible to kill with normal mortal weapons. A familiar flood races through my veins—that prickling, hyperalert feeling of intense danger, the way the body suddenly becomes so alive when it thinks it's near death.

And this is *my* island. This is *me*.

They're the trespassers, whoever they are.

It doesn't matter who they are.

I'm only vaguely aware of Mimi's and Odé Kan's shocked expressions as I rise, shoving a whole mess of grit, earth, and sand up in the air as I go.

The island lurches ahead of me—roots, vines, dirt, even death maybe, all burst forward to clear my path.

Somewhere in there, the roar of rending land blots out the gunfire tapering off. Doesn't matter. Blasts of sand explode on either side of me with simple flicks of my wrist as I walk.

There are two large yachts docked in a small harbor off the beachfront. Thirty men with assault rifles huddle amid the sand dunes in front of me.

I raise one hand, and the dunes roll backward, crushing, shoving, burying.

These aren't some barflies off the Manhattan streets, though. These men are part of a seasoned death squad, if I had to guess. Or maybe just a regular army. They don't scare easily, and it's clear they knew what they were getting into when they showed up on our shore.

A tall guy with sunglasses and a precise mustache yells commands in a language I can't place. His men spread backward in some practiced formation and prepare for their next assault.

One tries to run up on me as I approach.

Shaaa! A spontaneous dune wipes him from my path. An arrow whips past my head, thunking into the shoulder of a man leaping out from behind a crate. He shrieks and collapses and then gets swept away in my sand tide.

More yelling and gunfire erupt, but this time from behind me.

Mimi's bambarúto have charged, with her front and center, leading the way with a howl.

The men behind me have rallied, and they're getting off whatever desperate potshots they can before the front line of monsters crushes them.

From the corner of my eye, I catch movement. Swing my hand out, sending a sudden deluge of wet sand blasting outward. The man collapses, tangled in his own net.

Another net.

More men come; they all have nets. No guns, just nets. I'm about to sweep them all away, when Mimi leaps on top of one from behind, her long brown arms clenched around his neck. Both collapse backward into the tide as it rolls in.

More gunfire; more yelling. The ones nearby aren't shooting— too close quarters, I guess. They don't want to risk friendly fire.

I have to reach Mimi before the enemy does, but there are two guys right beside her . . . and then a net slaps over me from behind, yanks me backward into the water.

I go under. That's when I feel it.

A pressure drop, like a hurricane approaching from within. Panic. It sweeps upward, sharp electricity in my veins, warps the whole world.

"Get her! Go! Go!" someone yells as I resurface with a gasp. In front of me, the men are kicking someone in the crashing waves: Tía

Mimi. An arrow finds its mark in one of their foreheads, throwing him backward. Then another, but there are still so many. Mustache Man yells irritably, and someone sprays the trees with gunfire.

I thrash in the net, sending splashes of soaking sand all around me. Mostly useless.

The bambarúto are all caught up in a skirmish farther up on the beach.

Finally, I slow my breathing.

These powers I have—I don't have enough mastery of them to be sure I won't hurt Tía Mimi.

But I can destroy things. I have precision. I know that now.

Destroy. I shove hard against the netting, feel it dissolve against my skin, and then I lurch forward, bounce once off the ground, and crash my palms into the mustached leader.

I grunt once, letting all that good training do its thing, and four clean red lines rip outward from where my hands rest on his chest. Then the four pieces of him collapse with a splash into the tide.

For a few seconds, everyone just stares in shock as the waves whoosh and thunder along the shoreline.

That does it, though. You can only train for so many wild scenarios, and your top guy getting quartered by a teenage girl with an army of giant monsters, well . . . it's hard to be tough in the face of that. The men turn and run, screaming and yelling back and forth as they go.

I pull Tía Mimi from the water—she's sputtering and gasping but still alive—and get ready to dive for cover.

But no one takes potshots as they go; no one throws any last-minute grenades. Instead, they stand on top of the far dune—the very one we were crossing when they opened fire on us.

Odé Kan emerges from the woods, sidestepping toward me with an arrow ready to fly at the men. Our eyes meet, and she walks alongside me, ever ready, as I stroll down the pier to the boats.

As the men watch, I reach out to either side, my hand touching the bow of each yacht. I hold their worried, wrathful glares as wood buckles outward, pipes burst, masts splinter, hulls collapse. Soon all that's left are two smoking husks.

The men turn and run for their lives.

CHAPTER TWENTY-EIGHT

MATEO

"WHAT ARE WE SUPPOSED TO DO WITH ANY OF THIS?" TOLO GROWLS, pouring himself some more coffee.

It's been a few hours since the no-show misa, and this is about the sum of things: no one knows anything. That wouldn't bother me so much if I had a better idea of what's going on with Chela. But, of course, it's all connected, and right now it just feels like an impossibly tangled spiderweb that we're all caught up in.

We're in the Hidalgos' kitchen. Tolo and Tams sit at the table, nursing coffees. I'm standing at the window, gazing uselessly into the darkness of the cemetery, thinking useless thoughts.

Chela was the one doing upkeep on this little graveyard. She set up solar lights and turned the whole place into a cozy, Gothic little nook, tucked away from the rest of the city. It's already looking forlorn and forgotten, as if the graves themselves know their caretaker is gone.

Shut up, Mateo.

It all keeps blipping back to me—the way she offered her cheek instead of her lips, her hand on my chest. What the hell happened to us? How did it fall apart so quickly?

"Mateo?" Tams is beside me, her hand on my shoulder. "Hey."

I shake my head. She wants to know if I'm okay, and I don't have an answer for her. It's almost midnight, and I'm not sure if I should go disappear into the skies or just leave Chela alone. I don't know anything.

"Mateo? Tolo!" Aviva calls urgently from the front room. "Come quickly!"

We're all up and racing through the house, pulses pounding. Tams reaches the portico first and lets out a startled yelp. Maza stands in the doorway, barely holding themself up on Aviva's shoulder; blood pours down their chin and stains their designer clothes.

"What happened?" Tolo grunts, lifting them up and clambering into the house. "Lock the doors. Where's Tío?"

"He went out to see one of our congregants," Aviva says.

"I'm okay," Maza whispers, sounding anything but. "I'm . . . I'm sorry. I didn't know where else to go."

"It's fine," Tams insists. "Don't apologize. Mateo?"

I'm already there, my hands ready as Tolo gently deposits Maza on the living room couch and stands back.

My eyes close; the song within Maza rises, a sultry bolero. I let that spiraling melody wrap around me, guide me as the world becomes color and sound and nothing else.

There.

The wounded flesh slips back into shape under my fingers, but a deeper hurt remains: Maza's pride is wounded, their heart on the brink of broken.

When I stand, they look up, face wide open. "Thank you, I . . ."

Tams sits on the couch, cradling them. "Please don't apologize again."

"Just tell us what happened," Tolo says with more gentleness than I've ever heard from him. "We're not mad at you."

"It was a gathering to try to sort out our differences. Just a small student thing . . . We thought . . . Maybelline thought we could start small and see if there was some common ground. I wasn't so sure, but I went along with it, and it was going okay . . . but then they came. . . . Just like that they were there—riot cops. . . . They burst in and started smashing away at people indiscriminately. I was running, and I tripped and fell into a wall. Clumsy."

More raids. Were they looking for me? Did they scoop anyone up? Were they tipped off? I have so many questions, but none of them feel right to ask. And anyway, there are wounded people out there, right now. I back toward the door, unsure. "Are they . . . ? Are the people still there?"

Maza shakes their head. "Everyone scattered, Mateo. Stay here, please. There's nothing you can do."

For a moment, I linger between running off to wherever and staying put right here, where I know I belong. And midnight approaches.

"What are you going to do, Mateo?" Tams asks sharply. "Track down everyone who got hurt?" She softens, seeing how lost I look. "I know it's what you do, heal, but you can't heal everyone, man. Sit."

I do. I'm glad to stay but still lost in the feeling that everything is falling apart around me.

"What did the cops want?" Tams asks.

"I don't know—they were gone just as fast as they came. None of it . . . None of it makes any sense." Maza sobs, and then Tolo's beside them too, and the three of them already look like some kind of wholesome, loving family there on the couch, bathed in the flickering light of the fireplace.

Quietly, I step out of the room and brace myself for whatever's next.

CHAPTER TWENTY-NINE

CHELA

"HOW IS SHE?" I ASK, PEEKING INTO A SMALL SIDE CHAMBER OF THE
synagogue where Odé Kan sits on her knees beside Mimi's sleeping
form.

Candlelight dances across the hunter spirit's somber face. "Still
out. How are you?" She points her chin toward the slim line of
emptiness on my arm.

My first instinct is to shrug and wave her off, but I breathe instead
and force myself to give the question the weight it deserves. Pretending something's no big deal doesn't make it that way, no matter how
good I am at it. Also, it matters to me that she cares enough to ask.

"It's a little longer, a little wider, but not as bad as I'd thought
it might be." And that's the truth. I lower myself to a squat beside
her, place a hand on her golden shoulder, breathe. "I'm sorry about
Mimi."

Odé Kan scoffs. "Tch. Sorry? For what? For saving her life? For
ending the fight for us?"

"No, I meant . . ."

She seems to deflate, shakes her head. "I know what you meant. Thank you. I'm sorry, too. All of this is . . . It's so much worse than I thought it could get. And you . . ." She turns to face me fully, her yellow eyes flashing with the tiny flames all around us. "You took a life today, probably several, eh?"

I nod, my gaze fixed on Mimi. "Not my first."

"Probably the first time you turned someone into four pieces, though, eh?"

"Well, yeah, that was gruesome. Didn't quite mean to, if I'm honest."

"It did the job."

"Mmm."

A few moments pass. Night rain lashes the stained-glass window over our heads.

I'm suddenly irritated. What was she getting at, then? Back in October, when I took out Gerval's bodyguard, Trucks, I thought I'd murdered a human being, not a bambarúto in riot-cop gear as it turned out to be. I struggled with it, stayed up nights wondering if I'd made a horrible mistake, become someone I didn't want to be; waited for his ghost to start haunting me. Waited to feel something I thought I was supposed to feel.

Truth was, I'd known with every part of me that the choice was either Trucks or Tolo. Gerval and his followers had been plotting against my cousin's life, and no amount of hiding or trickery was going to stop them from trying to take him out. And sure, my cousin is the best scrapper I know, but he's not bulletproof. I'd already lost Tío Si; I wasn't going to let the same thing happen to Tolo.

So I didn't.

And I don't regret it.

A death being gruesome doesn't change anything, not really. It was instantaneous; that's what matters. The dead are still dead.

"I don't . . . I don't feel bad about it," I finally say. "If that's what you're waiting for."

Odé Kan lets out a soft laugh. "Oh, I'm not waiting for anything, nor do I think you should feel bad for defending yourself. Surely you have met me, yes? You know this."

I relax some. She's right, and her arrows claimed their fair share of souls today, too.

"But here's what I don't understand," I say. "No one shot me."

Odé Kan cocks her head sideways. "This is a good thing, no?"

"It's great, sure. But why? I don't mean they missed. I mean they didn't take any shots at me at all."

Just give us the Destroyer and your little hunter spirit, hmm? Archibaldo had said to Mimi. I'd assumed he'd wanted us handed over so he could kill us. But . . .

She shrugs. "I try not to question blessings, you know?"

It's not that simple, and suddenly I'm standing, pacing between the candles. "Why haven't we been overrun, Odé Kan?"

She tracks me with those wide cat eyes. "Again . . ."

"It's not a blessing if it's a trap," I insist. "Think about it: they have enough bambarúto to overwhelm us in a second. It wouldn't even be a fight, just a massacre. They know where we are. Why not end this quick? It doesn't make sense."

"Get some rest," Odé Kan says. "I don't have answers for why they haven't come to kill us, and we all need to get ready for whenever they do."

CHAPTER THIRTY

MIDNIGHT

We rise.
Together, but a thousand miles apart,
We rise.

All along the edges of this plaza, over the broken,
bleeding bodies of the wounded, the dead.
Then up, up, past the clock towers until the
whole island spins into the darkness below.

Past concrete, plaster, pipes, tarmac. Over rooftops and
windows and the city becomes a smattering of lights and
then nothing at all as the darkness devours the world.

It's easier, this time, to find each other. Two shimmering
spirits in the night; the thunder of our hearts calls out,
awaits a reply, the reply is a beacon, and so we join again.

There are strange men here—

The dead are missing!

What?!

———◆———

I miss you.

Miss you, too. Even like this. At least this is something.

It's all we have.

Will it always be?

I wish I knew.

The men on the island . . .

Yes. Some are dead now. They hurt Tía Mimi.
She's . . . She's unconscious.
I don't know what'll happen to her.

Are you okay?

Yes. Just sad. And scared. And confused.
What happened with the dead?

We held a misa to try to get more info on your leads.
From your leads. But . . . no one showed up.

I don't understand what's happening.

Can I . . . Can I hold you?

Do you think it's okay like this? In spirit form?

I . . . don't . . . know. . . .

We can solve this together.

Yes.

Tell me what you need.

I don't know. I don't know how to tell you anything anymore.

Okay.

Mateo, don't . . . Don't pull away.

I'm trying not to.

See you tomorrow night?

Same Bat-time, same Bat-channel.

Yes. Please.

Goodbye, Chela.

Come back. . . .

DAY FOUR

There is no clock, no map.

There is no dictionary, no translation.

Spirit's time is not man's time—it isn't even time at all.

There is no language that can encompass, no phrase or song that can define.

Spirit moves through, saturates, slips away.

Never, always, a thing beyond.

There is no map.

—*The San Madrigal Book of the Dead*, Canto XII

CHAPTER THIRTY-ONE

CHELA

THE GIRL STANDS THERE STARING AT ME, PIECES OF THE ISLAND floating all around in a wild constellation of sand, trees, creatures.

Her expression is blank, but those eyes drill into mine with the fury of a thousand years.

I'm so close. I have to reach her.

I know, though . . . Somewhere deep inside I know that if I move, all will be lost.

But maybe if I can move fast enough, somehow bridge the space between us before the world comes crashing down . . .

She raises one hand, fingers stretched toward me—pleading? Threatening? Her face reveals nothing.

I take a step, plant that foot hard, and launch into a sprint. I'm fast, I've always been fast, plus I have the untold realms of power within me. Who knows what—

In the blink of an eye, the spinning shards of island around us flash toward me, like I'm suddenly the gravitational center of this weird galaxy. I'm bracing for their impact; it will surely crush me, and then I'm sitting straight up in the bell tower, gasping for air.

"Chela?" Odé Kan somersaults into a standing position, already by my side. "What happened?"

I shake my head to clear it; doesn't work. Rub my eyes and try to smile. "A dream. That girl, and . . . my own stress, probably; I don't know."

Beyond these tower walls, night still covers the world, but a gentle flush of dawn tempers the darkness. Birds and other creatures hoot and yowl back and forth in the forest nearby, and somewhere underground, an ever-growing army of bambarúto prepare for war.

I'm on my feet before I realize I've stood, my hand resting on the stone lip of the window, the cool night breeze against my face. "We need . . . We need to make a move, Odé Kan."

She puts her elbows on the edge of the wall, rests her chin on her palms, and follows my gaze to the remaining two mountains. "Ay, my sister. You know I want to end this as badly as you, yes? But our feeling of urgency does not change the fact that the little force we have isn't up to the task ahead. We're badly outnumbered. No attack plan will change that. Even with you and me fighting side by side."

I smile a little at the image: an angel of destruction and a hunter spirit blasting away at hordes of bambarúto beneath a mountain. It's like something from those old Dungeons & Dragons games Tolo used to be obsessed with as a tween. But I know she's right, too. And I hate it. "Every minute we wait, the army gets bigger. Time is on their side. Plus, I'm pretty sure there's a reason they're keeping me alive. That I'm . . . part of their plan somehow."

Odé Kan raises her slim eyebrows. "Plan, you say?"

I explain the parts Mateo told me, what we pieced together. When I finish, she looks stricken. "Do you know what it all means?"

"Not even a little, but still I don't like it, you know?"

Do I ever. But even as I nod, an idea begins forming.

Odé Kan must see it happen. "Chela? That look. I haven't

known you long, but I know when you're about to do something reckless that you won't be talked out of."

I have to smirk. "Why would you want to talk me out of doing the right thing?"

"Chela . . ."

"Look, we don't know their plan, sure, but someone on this island does. . . ."

"Ah, hmm . . ." She does the cocked-eyebrow thing, considering me with a slight smile.

"Whoever they are," I continue, "however vile their motivations may be, they're still human, and I have a feeling they'd rather not bed down in the midst of all those creatures."

"Hmm." She's warming to it, I can tell. And I'm suddenly wide-awake and fully wound up with the urge to go, to do something, anything besides sitting in this tower waiting to be overrun. "You are suggesting a petit raid on the survivors of our little soiree earlier, yes?"

"All we need is one guy," I point out. "I'm suggesting a snatch-and-grab."

"It is the same thing, no? To snatch and to grab? You want to do the same thing twice?"

I exhale. "It's an expression. I think. Anyway, it is now. And I think I know exactly how to do it."

———◆———

I'm starting to get the hang of this dual-vision-while-I-move thing. Now that it's just me and Odé Kan—no army of bambarúto to trample me at any misstep—I can relax into our steady stride and slide more easily into the consciousness of the island.

We jogged silently through the empty city in the predawn darkness, dipped into a foresty area that led down toward the beach, and now we're skirting along the far edge of the Port District as I scan the nearby coves and embankments, searching, searching.

"There!" I whisper as the last flickering embers of a dying camp-fire appear over the crest of a grassy hill. I lead Odé Kan along the edge of the water, and then we climb through the jungle. She nocks an arrow, and I take a deep breath, centering myself for whatever lies ahead.

I'll be honest—it's excitement rippling through me right now, not fear. I don't want to take any more lives; it's not that. But these past few days—hell, maybe my whole life—it's been a whirlwind of being stuck in small rooms, in this small body, with these small disagree-ments and doubts. I am a being of air and water, the very essence of creation and destruction, balance. I am the expansiveness of the sky and the tiny grains of sand. What interest is math homework to such a creature?

I haven't been honest; I just crammed myself into these little boxes for the sake of the world around me, other people's comfort.

I could say I didn't know, and on paper that's true. But really, deep down, I *always* knew. I always felt the breath of spirit moving in and out of me when I quieted my mind, the fire that builds and tears down, the very sparkling embers of life itself dancing at the tips of my fingers.

So what my whole being is excitedly anticipating is not murder—although if that happens, oh well. It's the knowledge that here on this island that is me, in the delicious chaos of the battle that's about to unfold, I will embody myself fully, outside of morals and schedules and all the neurotic little intricacies that Odé Kan calls "human crap."

"Ready?" I whisper to the hunter spirit at my side.

Up ahead, about a dozen men share a bottle around the camp-fire. Their automatic weapons are on the ground nearby. I recognize some of them from the beach. A few supply crates sit nearby. One of them fusses with a satellite radio, but all he gets is static.

I raise one hand, reaching inside myself, inside the earth. Feel the island's consciousness meld with my own, the tingling blades of grass, the swoosh of the wind, the stomp of boots.

Odé Kan breaks into a run.

I clench my fist.

The land rises beneath her feet as she goes. I feel the rending within me, but it doesn't shock my system anymore; it's just natural, like breathing.

The rumble startles the men; they stand, grabbing their weapons. Too late, too late.

First arrow catches one of them in the shoulder; the second pins his foot to the ground. Gunfire rattles out, but they're firing over their shoulders; messy splatters of it thunk against trees and boxes, rip through the flesh of the one who couldn't follow.

Dammit.

The man we were going to grab lies dead, a shot-up mess of flesh by the dying fire.

Odé Kan has already earth-surfed past the campsite; her yellow eyes flash in the darkness, catch my brown ones. We trade a nod: *The plan goes on anyway.* We'll just have to take a different man.

The men have regrouped quickly, their training kicking in now that the shock has faded. A barrage of shots shreds the woods where Odé Kan stood seconds earlier.

She's already up in the trees, though. I see that telltale swoosh of grace and ferocity; the moonlight glints ever so slightly along the contours of her golden skin, her antlers, her drawn bow.

I let her get off a few shots into the screaming cluster of men. They don't even know where to shoot, and confusion soon bleeds into panic again. That's when I walk out into the open.

It's only been what—a day or two I've been out here? But I must look as feral as the horned spirit who hunts them. My clothes are filthy, my smile wide as I stride forward.

Guns rise in clenched hands, but their leader hoarsely yells something I can't make out. I'm sure he's telling them what I've suspected all along, that I'm not to be harmed. He's the one I want. He has a meticulous mustache, and he looks both more competent and more stressed than the others.

One of them fumbles with a net, trying to wrangle it into some kind of launch mechanism. These vile men and their toys. I send the soil cresting toward them with a sweep of my arm.

Odé Kan's arrows catch the leader as the others scatter. One in his shooting arm, the second in his thigh. He drops, squealing, and tries to crawl deeper into the forest. That's when my foot lands on his back, flattening him. Then Odé Kan steps beside me, and we both smile down at him.

CHAPTER THIRTY-TWO

MATEO

CHELA WATCHES ME FROM UNDERWATER.

I must be in an aquarium; it's so dark here. The shadows seem alive; they seethe and writhe. I can't take my eyes away from Chela, though. Chela spins in slow motion through the endless waters; tiny dapples of sunlight ripple across her face and arms, and over the flowing silky fabric surrounding her.

I know she can't drown. Know she'll be okay. But this glass wall between us—it's invisible and impossible to breach. It holds back the ocean; a crack would become a fissure and then an explosion, and then ten million pounds of water would issue forth and wipe me from existence.

I get a running start and hurl myself toward it, fists clenched . . . and a faraway, urgent pounding shoves me back into reality.

I'm out of bed—Chela's bed—glancing around the room, confused, a mess, and then the yelling starts. It's downstairs—outside. But even muffled, I know the cadence of a cop who's not getting what he wants. I'm pulling on my jeans, grabbing my go bag, when a thought hits me so hard it stops me in my panicked tracks: this is how Tía Lucía died.

It wasn't cops who came to the door that day, but what's the difference? The guys who killed her didn't have badges and uniforms or protocols to dip and dodge around; there was no paperwork to invent justifications on. But it's plenty clear the empire pirates have inside pull at our precinct and sent the sledgehammer of the law slamming into my life.

Very well.

I head down the Hidalgos' ornate staircase, readying my fingers to heal and then whip the pain back on the attacker. Violence is imminent; I can practically taste it on the prickly night air. The pounding and yelling get louder as I approach. I won't let the people who are protecting me suffer for it, won't let Chela lose someone the same way I did.

"Come this way *now*," a hushed whisper says from the shadows. I'll be honest, it startles the crap out of me. I barely manage not to yelp. Glad I don't, because it turns out it's Aviva, and she has Tams, Maza, and Tolo with her.

"What's going on?"

"We're taking you to the tunnels," Tolo says. "Don't make it complicated."

"But—"

"They're here for you, Mateo," Aviva says, her warm hand gripping my arm. "That's all. *You* need to get out. Tolo will take you." She sees the dismay etched across my face, the panic. *"Go."*

"If you don't open this door, we're knocking it down, Rabbi!" the muffled voice yells. "And then everyone's getting locked up for resisting arrest! You hear me?"

"Come on," Tams whispers, brushing past me after Tolo and pulling me along. I glance back at Aviva one more time, catch the worried look in her eyes, the determination in her set jaw. Then I turn and follow my best friend through a dim corridor to a trapdoor in the floor.

Tolo's already disappearing into the darkness below.

Tams signals me to go first, and I find my footing on the ladder and start descending. Not far away, the rabbi relents. "Very well, very well. I certainly hope you have a warrant!"

The shadows surround me as I hear the front door unlocking, the hinges squeaking. Tams crawls down the ladder after me. Heavy boots clomp across the floorboards. The trapdoor closes overhead, blocking out the last bit of light.

CHAPTER THIRTY-THREE

MATEO

BACK IN NOVEMBER, I FOUND OUT TUNNELS RUN UNDER THIS WHOLE neighborhood. I don't even know why I was surprised—pirates are gonna pirate whether they're in Tortuga, Shanghai, or . . . the borderlands where Brooklyn meets Queens. Tolo's dad, Si, had them built, from what I understand, and used them for his backroom dealings and to help him scare off the gentrifiers. A good chunk of the pirates' operation involved smuggling all kinds of weird and archaic merchandise, particularly relics from San Madrigal and the various cultures that helped form it. And they needed some way to move those items from one place to another.

At the tail end of that terrible week last year when the empire pirates and their bambarúto ruled these streets, the vast tunnel system became our salvation. And now we find ourselves once again under siege in our very homes, the tiny sliver of this world we lay claim to. This time it's not monsters roaming the streets but men with guns and badges, busting through our doors and yanking us away from freedom, our families. In a terrible way, they still win, even if they don't catch us, because being on the run like this is its own form of prison. Nowhere is safe, everyone is compromised; what kind of life is that?

"You comin'?" Tolo asks from the darkness ahead.

I'm lost in my thoughts again. Still trapped by my own disbelief and spiraling. I hurry after him, Tams, and Maza, catch up to them at a turn in the dank, dimly lit corridor.

"You don't think . . ." I start, and then don't finish because I hate what I was about to say.

"What?" Tams says, sensing my discomfort, knowing me better than I know myself, as usual. "That Tantor dimed us out? Uh-uh."

"I don't think so, either," I say. "I just—"

"Don't know who to trust," Tolo finishes. "Yeah, same. And obviously I don't trust the old guy, either. But having heard him out . . . I can't explain it, but it doesn't track for me. You staying at the Hidalgos' from time to time isn't exactly a secret, you know? They probably—"

"Oh God," I gasp, a lump forming in my throat. It hadn't even occurred to me until this moment. "They probably went to my parents' house, didn't they?"

"Yeah," Tams says. "But shifty as both our dads have been acting, I don't think either is capable of ratting out their own kids. No, I think it's like Tolo said. The cops were gonna come knocking on the rabbi's door eventually one way or another."

The notion of my parents talking to the cops makes me want to throw up. My dad must've been blinking through the anger he already felt toward me. My mom is probably even more of a mess. In short, everything sucks.

"Whoa," Maza says from up ahead. "There's a . . . problem."

We round a corner, and all come to a stop. Cement rubble and centuries-old shattered pipes cover the ground, blocking our way. The ceiling of the tunnel has partially caved in; messy slivers of streetlight from above seep in, cast an eerie glow on the debris.

"What happened?" Maza asks.

"Another one of those weird fissures that's been opening up all over town," I say. Wonder what that means is happening on San Madrigal.

Tolo grunts. "Guess we gotta go around, huh."

———◆———

It takes a while, but the tunnels eventually wind back to where we were headed—the wide-open hall beneath Tolo's club. This is where the army of golems waited silently after Mimi sent them over shortly before the island sank.

We figured they'd all been smashed to smithereens when the club collapsed. But what we find when we step out of the tunnel into the vast hall stops everyone in their tracks.

"They're gone," Tolo gasps. "They're just . . . gone."

In the center of the room, the ceiling has opened, letting in a landslide of smashed plaster and rubble. But as big as the club was, the underground hall was bigger, and besides all that mess, the place is simply empty. No golems, nothing.

"How?" Tams asks, blinking at the space where they had stood stock-still for years until the day Chela sent them leaping into murderous action against the empire pirates.

"No idea," I admit, because I'm stunned myself. "Guess she never deactivated them. But . . . where did they go?"

"Well, here's some good news, at least," Tolo calls from the other side of the wreckage.

Tams, Maza, and I all hurry over, hungry for something positive amid all this gloom.

Tolo greets us with a rare smile. In front of him, a pile of old books lies scattered in the crumbled cement and plaster. They're covered in dust and debris but look otherwise intact. "We might be able to help Mateo do his little research project after all."

CHAPTER THIRTY-FOUR

CHELA

OUR PRISONER HAS PASSED OUT BY THE TIME WE GET HIM BACK TO the synagogue, so we tie him to a chair and get some training in while the sun rises.

"You sure he's not gonna die on us?" I ask Odé Kan as she sends another plate whizzing through the air at me.

"Nah. I didn't use my murder arrows, and I didn't hit any vital organs. He's not actively bleeding. Probably scared, is all. Let him sleep it off."

I greet the plate with the palm of my hand, neatly bisecting it. "Murder arrows?"

Odé Kan wiggles her eyebrows at me. "Just added a special concoction to 'em, is all. It's saliva from the giant lizards that lounge around down by the beach. Effect is kind of like rabies—makes you a bit mad and frothy, but not for long because pretty soon you're dead, eh?"

She whips two plates at once; I easily handle them both. "Oh my."

When I look up, she's glaring at me, hands on her hips. "Time for something new, you know. Clearly you need a challenge."

"I'm listening."

"Well, you're getting better at messing with the island, and destruction is not a problem."

"I don't like where this is going."

"Why don't we try out your creation skills, eh, Miss Madrigal?"

Because that seems like another person. Because the notion of it somehow nauseates me and I don't know why. Because I'm terrified I'll fail at it. Instead I just nod gamely and say, "Sure!"

"Okay, I'm not an expert, eh," Odé Kan admits. "Like you, I'm better at destroying things. But I figure we start small. You said you did make the life-giving thing work once, yeah?"

"With the golems back in Brooklyn, yeah, but . . ." How do I put this? It didn't work at all the first time, and that nearly got Tolo killed. And when those giant stone warriors did snap to life, it barely felt like I did it; seemed like I'd stumbled onto the right mindset and movements. I skip over all that and get to the thing that really burns me up. "The only other time was when some spectral bambarúto figured out how to use my powers to become incarnated. Without my permission!"

"Ew," Odé Kan seethes, and I appreciate that she immediately gets what a foul violation that is.

"How are they better at using my powers than *I* am?" I demand.

It was more of a complaint than a question, but Odé Kan goes ahead and answers anyway. "Because they believe in them."

Immediately, I want to fight her. Not physically, but . . . how dare she . . . be right. "I didn't know about them! How was I supposed to? No one told me! No one knew!"

Her smile is sad. "Don't have to tell me, hermana. I'm with you. Whole thing's a hot holy disaster."

I calm, then laugh. "Problem is, now I do know, but I don't . . . I guess don't totally believe? It's like I know it intellectually—that I'm Madrigal—but it doesn't fully feel true . . . yet."

"Well, we start small!" Odé Kan says, gathering some mud into her golden palms. I want to cry—she's so hopeful and believes in me so easily. I just wish I felt the same way.

She fashions the mud into a little lump, then uses a twig to poke two eyeholes and draw an alarming smile for a mouth. Finally she snaps the twig and puts one half on either side of its little mud head. "You see the resemblance?" She cheeses, holding it up by her own face.

"Cute," I admit, then narrow my eyes, ready to get down to it. If I'm gonna figure this out, at least I have an actual spirit on my side to help. "All right, here we go. One living, breathing mud Odé Kan coming up."

I exhale, inhale, lift my hand, imagine a million particles of sparkling life essence charging through it. Touch. And . . . nothing.

Nothing at all.

Then more nothing.

Half an hour later, the sun is glaring down at us over the walls around this grotto and I'm soaked in my own sweat, holding a lump of mud in my palm, yelling hoarse curses at it while it wiggles ever so slightly.

"I hate this," I mutter as Odé Kan laughs.

Then someone else laughs, too—a cruel, throaty sound from the far end of the courtyard. "Stupid girls," our prisoner chuckles as Odé Kan nocks an arrow and sends it zinging so close to his head he probably felt the whoosh of displaced air as it passed. "Gah!" he yelps, eyes wide, smirk effectively wiped away.

"So he speaks," I say as we approach side by side. "Fantastic. We have some questions for you."

The man recovers his composure quickly, though he's clearly still in pain from Odé Kan's earlier marksmanship. He makes a big show of shrugging, then flinches, regretting it instantly. "Ask me whatever you want, girls. I don't care." His speech is accented, but I can't place where it's from.

"Name," Odé Kan demands.

"Serial number is all you get," he brags. "Five-five-seven-eighteen-sparrow."

"All right, Sparrow, then," I say. We stand facing him, and I can't help but wonder what terrible decisions in life would lead a man to be tied up in a chair on a mystical island, bleeding from two holes in his body that a forest spirit inflicted. No time for his autobiography, though; we just need some simple facts. "What organization are you with?"

"Can't tell you that, I'm afraid. If I did, I'd have to kill you."

"I would honestly enjoy watching you try," Odé Kan says with genuine thoughtfulness. "You have done a very poor job of it so far."

"But anyway, you're not allowed to kill me," I point out. "Are you?"

Sparrow gets serious, his face suddenly tense. Then he horks up a huge loogie and splats it into the dirt at our feet. "Demonas!"

Odé Kan side-kicks him in the chest, tipping his chair backward. He lands with a grunt and is wise enough to tilt his head forward so it doesn't crack on the cement. We stand on either side of him, looking down.

It wasn't Spanish, what he spoke—some adjacent language, I guess—but it's pretty clear what he meant.

"Yes, demon girls, that's us," I say. "Is that why you're not supposed to kill me?"

"Doesn't matter why," he grumbles. "I follow my orders."

"Orders from who?"

He shrugs. "From the boss, okay?"

Odé Kan looks at me. "We're not gonna get anywhere with this. Can I kill him?"

He glances at her, then me. Pretty sure she isn't bluffing and, more importantly, so is he. Sparrow squirms, trying to hide his discomfort.

"Or better yet," Odé Kan continues with a wily smile, "why don't you quarter him like you did that other guy?"

"Hnghhh," he moans, against his will. That did it.

I hold up a hand for her to wait. "What are your orders, besides don't kill me?"

He swallows, then blinks up at me. "We're here to examine the merchandise." With a jaunty, nonchalant head wobble, he goes on, already back to his baseline cocky masquerade. "If it's good, we purchase, yes? If not: Boom! Island go gone. That's all. No one knows it's here anyway; no one will miss it."

"Who is we?"

He smiles. "International coalition, yes? From all over the world. Very hush-hush; nobody needs for to know."

"What merchandise?" Odé Kan asks.

"Unstoppable soldiers. Impossible to kill. Don't know fear, only give it to others. Murder machines, they say. To put down rebellion, protest, dissent everywhere." He's laughing now, a truly tragic and deranged sound, with a few tears mixed in. "All this work, just to put myself out of a job, ahahaha!"

CHAPTER THIRTY-FIVE

MATEO

"ALL RIGHT, PEOPLE," TOLO SAYS IN FULL COMMANDER MODE, "here's what we're looking for: anything pertaining to the peace accords, which were in 1810. That means Cabildo record keeping, personal diaries, scrapbooks, whatever. Also, any references to something called the Divine Council, pull 'em. And of course, anything about Mateo's creepy ancestor Archibaldo will help, but I doubt there'll be much beyond the official story of his music career."

He gestures to the debris-covered mountain of books we've pulled from the rubble. "Obviously, all my meticulous organization of this stuff has gone to hell, so this won't be easy."

"Oh, love," Tams says, dropping a kiss on his cheek.

He squeezes her hand, eyes closed to receive the condolences, and then nods. "Right. Let's get to it."

Maza and Tams head off together to start in on a stack. I'm digging through some random books when Tolo takes me aside with a gruff "A word?"

"Of course." We dip into the shadowy corridor. Tolo's face is wide open; already I notice his eyes reddening. What happened?

He meets my gaze, and, man . . . I can see how this guy is able to run a criminal enterprise at his young age. Even when he's vulnerable and run-down, Tolo Baracasa looks like he could kill a man without thinking much about it. Sure, he's worried, confused, heartbroken, but behind those watery eyes a wolf stalks back and forth, ready to strike. "I'm, uh, ready."

"Huh?" I say, and then it hits me: his mom. "Ah," I quickly add to save him the trouble of having to explain something he's only barely able to put words to.

"Don't sugarcoat shit," he warns.

"I think the bambarúto kept her alive all that time, same way they did Archibaldo. And it's . . . It's changed her. Like, she has some of them in her now."

"So, she's . . . She really betrayed us all for Vizvargal and the empire pirates?"

I shake my head. "She did for a time, sure, but she went against them at the end. That's why the island fell instead of Vizvargal rising. She led Chela and me there as spirits, and Okanla brought the island down on top of the demon to seal him beneath it. That was all Mimi. And she sent the golems here, too, although she seems to think we were supposed to have returned them when we came back. . . ."

Something in Tolo is breaking. His face looks like a little kid's—brows raised, eyes blinking back tears. He just wants a straightforward story about who his mom is, what she's done. He should know better than any of us that nothing's that simple, but this has nothing to do with knowing things. "But . . . the bambarúto protected her even after that?"

"The ones that are on our side, yeah. Or . . ." I try to remember how Mimi put it. "Bambarúto are born from fear. That's how your mom explained it. Most of them come from the nightmares of regular Galeranos: persecution, enslavement, oppression, all that.

But the empire pirates have their own terrors, and that's how those other bambarúto emerged—the ones who protected, still protect, your mom."

Tolo takes all this in with a stern face. He's probably bouncing it against the reams of other island lore inside that big, full brain of his. "I barely remember her," he finally says. "Mostly just her smell, her chin for some reason, and the way she'd smile at me. I remember her temper, too. Small things would set her off."

"Still true," I say, and then immediately hope I haven't crossed a line.

Tolo lets out a rueful chuckle, so no. "I bet. Decade and a half underwater will do that to a person."

"I didn't ask, but I'm hoping she wasn't, like . . . awake that whole time."

He grunts noncommittally. "Look . . . you know this smuggling thing comes with some benefits. I have a team—well, a few teams—primed and ready to go at any time. Say the word and we're off—completely under the radar, of course."

I blink for a second, catching up. He arranged my trip back to the island, but it still seems wild, this guy my age carrying so much responsibility, coordinating so much, owning so much. "You have a plane. Several planes. Sometimes I forget that about you, man."

"Yeah, yeah, they belong to the outfit, not me, but I do run the outfit. Point is, we both have people we want to see on that island, and while both of them can surely hold their own, they also could probably use a hand. . . . Hell, we could go right after we're done here. Things are getting a little too cop-flavored in Little Madrigal for my liking, anyway."

We could leave now. Be there in a handful of hours. For a few moments, I imagine stepping onto that beach again, seeing Chela, holding her. Feel myself swept away by the vision. Then I shake it off. "She told me not to come back until I have answers, and I gotta respect that. But . . . soon. And thanks for the offer, man."

Tolo nods, but he's wrapped up in his own daydreams and nostalgia, I see. "Dad didn't talk much about her. Got the feeling they'd split over a number of things by the time I came around. Probably part of why he ended up in Brooklyn before anyone else. She didn't seem like someone you wanted to be too near to if you were on her bad side." He catches himself. "*Doesn't*. She's alive." Then a sob escapes him. "She's alive," he says again. And then he's draped across me, bawling like a baby. "My mom . . . What the hell . . . ?"

I close my arms around his big, heaving back and pat it gently. I've always respected Tolo . . . from afar. My respect wasn't based on fear, but the kind of long-distance awe you have for those folks who seem to move effortlessly through the world with that indomitable cool. *Seem* being the key word, I guess. Once I got to know him better, the real Tolo came through; it's not that he was putting on a performance—he really is that dude—it's that there's so much else to him. At some point, my faraway respect turned into a kind of brotherly love, and I know—I've known for a while now—that I'd put my whole life on the line for this man who is barely older than a boy, follow him into the gaping maw of hell and back out again if he asked. And it's not in spite of moments like these, when the lost, confused Tolo shines through—it's because of them.

He doesn't even bother getting himself together before going back in to see his two partners. He just pats me lovingly on the shoulder (almost shattering it, but that's okay) and nods once, his eyes locked with mine. Then he struts through the door, walks directly to Maza and Tams, and starts explaining to them, still tearfully, what we talked about as they comfort him.

Truly love to see it.

Anyway, while the triple threat is having their moment, I'll take the time to comb through this mess of historical tomes and see if I can get an answer to my own problems.

I find a metal bucket in the debris, flip it over, and make myself as comfortable as I can on it near the biggest pile of books.

The Baracasa family collection is no joke, I already knew that. I saw it when it was in its full glory, all organized and pretty on the shelves of Tolo's office. But somehow seeing all these old books splayed out and scattered gives the whole of it even more girth and weight. It's like spotting a tiger in the wild after only seeing them in pictures and zoos all your life. Rubble and disaster or not, these books have power.

The first bunch I pick up are way off-topic—Cuban recipes, pirate-themed nursery rhymes, a collection of praisesongs for the ocean spirit, Yemonja. (I have to resist the urge to get lost in that one—focus, Mateo!) Tolo did tell me once that Madrigal lore is famously interconnected—tidbits about sacred ceremonial procedures will pop up in margin notes of a bestiary; a single musical phrase forms the basis of a love song, a funeral hymn, and a children's lullaby; and on and on. I'm sure that's both maddening and thrilling for a researcher like Tolo, who simply lives to nerd out about this stuff, but I don't have time to read every random volume hoping to stumble on an offhand link.

So I set them aside and keep going. Almost immediately, a name stops me in my tracks. My name. Well, my last name. The book is called *The Last Fugue of Maestro Archibaldo Medina*. I pick it up, dust it off. The going story on Archi is that he was one of the greatest composers of Madrigal history—which is saying a lot for an island of music-heads—but then he lost his mind and created all these chaotic symphonies no one could make sense of. But when I got my hands on them, it turned out he wasn't mad at all; he was sending coded messages, including the name of his demon god, Vizvargal. So of course the melodies seemed unhinged.

I'd never explored his earlier work, though. I flip through the pages, and immediately I know something is off about this. It's supposed to be a fugue, but a fugue is characterized by counterpoint—two dueling melodies, basically, with one filling in the gaps left by the first, a tangled-up call-and-response that usually follows a bunch of archaic, annoying protocols about which direction the intervals can move and by how much. But there's only one line of music here. A single melody.

Second thing is—I hum a little bit just to be sure, and yep: it's a scaled-back, modified version of that horrible Vizvargal song. Gross.

But where's the other line of music? The piece opens with some long whole notes that take up entire measures and recur periodically throughout, so you'd think that's where the other melody would go. But it's nowhere. I flip to the back—maybe there's some text explaining it or a B section that's supposed to go there—but nada.

All right. That's irritating, but I have to keep looking, so I shove the book into my bag and start on another pile. Pretty soon I come across a dark blue gold-trimmed volume containing handwritten Cabildo meeting minutes. It's from 1843, three decades too late, but now I know the look of the thing, and I immediately spot a few more just like it in the dust.

1856; no.

1831; no.

They are *gratingly* meticulous; whoever the scribe was, they took their job very seriously. That'd be great news for me if I could find the actual year I'm looking for. Apparently, a good chunk of pre-1810 Madrigal history was wiped out—I guess the result of whatever war happened—which means there shouldn't be too many more of these.

1814; closer . . .

Here! I wipe away a layer of debris and then blow off the dust, immediately sending myself into a coughing fit. "I'm fine!" I yell to the others even though they're not paying attention. "Don't worry about me!"

The fete happens every October, and the first one came from that Cabildo meeting after the peace accords, Chela said. I start at the end of the book and work my way back, flipping through the giant stained pages of careful script.

Here. October 25, 1810. Pronouncement about the Grande Fete; no explanation about why. This is waaay more vague and sparse than the other entries. *Agreement about the universal need for peace on the island,* blah, blah, blah . . . *after so much death, unity, nunca conquistada,* etc., etc., yeah, yeah . . . This is weird: *That it may never occur again, and although we know it will, when it does, it shall be done in accordance with the express wishes of the Divine Council and thus fully within the natural order of the world, of our spiritual trinity, of San Madrigal, amén and asé.*

Never occur *again*? But they know that it will?

The text doesn't state what exactly it is they're talking about, of course. My first assumption is that it just means war, but I'm not sure they'd wage one in accordance with a divination. Or if they did . . . I don't think it would be preordained like this. . . . And what was the divination, anyway?

"Hey, power throuple!" I call, still reading and rereading the page.

"What is it?" Tams asks, already strolling over with Maza and Tolo in tow.

I roll my eyes. "First of all, I can't *believe* you actually answered to that."

Tams shrugs, peeks over my shoulder. "It's accurate."

"Whatchya got?" Tolo asks.

"Ooh, old bureaucratic crap!" Maza chirps, handing me a tattered old book from the pile they were looking through. "Fun!"

"What's this?" I ask, thumbing through the messily scrawled-upon pages. "Looks like an angry diary."

"Pretty much. Imelda Fabula's journals. She was better known as Mother Fabula and—"

"Oh, she was on the Cabildo," Tolo jumps in excitedly. "Back in the day! Back then, probably!"

"That's what I was about to say," Maza points out. "It says so on the cover: *Cabildo Years 1801 to 1836.*"

"Nice! Thanks." I put the book carefully into my shoulder bag to peruse later, then hold up my own dusty tome. "The Cabildo meeting notes from the 1810 peace accord," I report. "First of all, it's extremely vague!"

Tams crosses her arms over her chest. "Aren't all minutes vague on purpose so if someone has a problem with something they can always go, *Well, it's not really clear, oddly?*"

"Sure," I say, "except that all the other Cabildo meeting minutes are *excruciatingly* precise. Well, the bunch I read from other years, anyway. This one doesn't even say who the participants were."

"What else?" Tolo asks, scouring the page with those intense black eyes. "Looks like a bunch of slogans and jargon."

"Exactly!" I point them toward the line that's bothering me.

"*Again?*" Maza asks. "What *again?*"

"Exactly, exactly!" I repeat. "Tolo, would they have done a divination about fighting a war?"

He looks dubious. "Maybe, but . . . not in the Cabildo. I don't . . . I don't know, to be honest. That is weird."

"*Although we know it will,*" Tams reads aloud, "*when it does . . .* That's a bit grim, isn't it?"

"Doesn't have to be a bad thing," I try. "But . . . yeah. What's something they wouldn't want to happen but know will?"

"Bad weather," Maza suggests. "I mean, that's technically what took out the island years later, am I right?" We all flinch a little, and Maza throws up their hands. "What? Too soon?"

"What if this is it?" I say as the uneasy notion rises within me. "What I've been looking for. But that's all there is. . . ."

"You mean, what if it's about you? Or Chela?" Tams asks.

"Or me *and* Chela," I say, feeling ill. "And how we're not supposed to . . . I don't know."

"Tolo," a throaty voice says from the corridor entrance, startling all of us.

It's Safiya, and she looks grave. "Your uncle . . . They took him."

———◆———

"What do we know?" Tolo growls as we all strut back through the tunnels toward the surface.

Safiya shakes her head. "Not much. Aviva called me from the precinct. Said she and the rabbi were stuck at home for hours while cops tore up the place. Seemed like the cops thought you all would come back if they waited long enough. Finally, they got frustrated, booked the rabbi on a bunch of trumped-up charges, and dragged him in."

It's November all over again—the kidnappings, the random bursts of violence. The pirates are making another move, and we're powerless to stop them. Chela's gone. I'm stuck dashing from one shadow to the next. How is anyone supposed to live like this? We're not; that's the answer. That's the whole point.

I notice myself clenching and unclenching my fists, trapped somewhere between rage and despair.

"Anyone else been picked up?" Tams asks.

"Actually, yes," Safiya reports, checking a list she'd scribbled down. "Mrs. Barrero called me to report her husband had been arrested, also for BS. And, apparently, he was in a group with a few others—they all got hauled in. Also, Tantor Batalán."

"What?" I gape. "He was . . ." He was *what*, though? He was just playing music with us. He was just feeding us useful info about the empire pirates, which is exactly why he's locked up now. It's all happening so fast—I can barely wrap my head around people being with us and then so suddenly in the cold embrace of the system.

"Well, I guess if we had any doubts about his loyalty, this squashes them," Tolo allows glumly.

We stop by the collapsed area of the tunnel. Nearby, a rickety staircase leads to the basement of Pancho's Frutería, and out its doors the street awaits. But the street isn't friendly anymore; it isn't safe. And I realize very suddenly I have nowhere to go.

"What are we gonna do?" I ask.

For once, Tolo looks absolutely caught off guard. "I . . . I don't know. Not yet."

"I mean . . . we're gonna break 'em out, aren't we?"

He scoffs, and it hurts, but I know he's right even before he elaborates. "Break 'em out? And then what? Plastic surgery and fake documents? Charter a plane to Brazil? Over the past two days, you've gotten a li'l taste of what being in hiding is like. You think the rabbi's up for a lifetime of this? Running through tunnels and ducking around corners? How 'bout ol' Tantor?"

He's right, he's right, I know he's right. I just hate it.

"This isn't some rival pirate crew holding them, Mateo. It's the New York City Police Department. Even if it's the empire pirates who somehow made it happen, they're in the system now, and the system's got sharp teeth and a memory that won't quit, not ever."

We head up the stairs toward the sunlight, but I don't even know where we're going or why; it all seems pointless.

And then my phone starts buzzing with all the calls I missed while we were underground.

It's my dad again, about a hundred times. I'm about to roll my eyes and pocket my phone when I see his text message and the whole world falls out from beneath me.

Mateo, come home immediately.

They arrested your mom.

CHAPTER THIRTY-SIX

CHELA

WE LET SPARROW FLY AWAY.

Truth is, keeping him around was going to be more stressful than it was worth, and, despite our cruel front, neither of us cared much for the thought of executing a prisoner.

Anyway, between the two arrow holes Odé Kan put in him, I don't think he'll be much use in battle. We broke both his trigger fingers just to make sure, though.

Lucky for us, they don't have a Mateo on their side to heal him up and turn his injuries into weapons.

Mateo.

His face returns to me as I wander the synagogue grounds, trying and failing to clear my head.

Mateo on the night we stood outside my house and I asked him to make sure I was okay. I knew I was; I wanted to feel him feeling me, to know what it was like for the people he healed, to have him that close. He looked so startled and confused at first, like maybe I'd read his mind, and I hoped I had. And then when I opened my eyes, his face was so calm; a gentle tide of serenity had washed over both of us, and I knew I could tell him anything.

And I could. And I did. For the next two months, we spent most of our time telling each other things. Deep realizations we'd had about our weirdo lives, sure, but also, and maybe most important, tiny ridiculous things: which lines we'd memorized from our favorite movies, who we'd had crushes on at school, what songs we secretly loved to rock out to even though they're the corniest tunes ever. It felt like we had a whole lifetime of goofy crap to catch up on, and things in the world around us were so serious—*are* so serious—so deadly, the only way to survive was to just . . . be. Just be, together. Just be together.

And now it seems like that's the one thing we're not allowed to do.

It's not fair, I think with so much force that a sharp crack opens along the stained-glass window I'm tracing with my fingertip as I walk.

Crap. Sorry, Dad.

Add it to the list of repairs we'll have to make when all this is over. Because somewhere, deep inside myself, I still cling to the fantasy that there's a version of the world in which we all come back, we're all safe and okay, and we set to work rebuilding this place together. But the idea that there will be an *over* is probably the real fantasy.

The corridor stretches ahead of me in a series of glum shadows cut by sudden shards of sunlight from openings in the wall or broken windows. There are already too many pieces to this puzzle, and we still barely have a fraction of them, I'm sure.

Nothing makes sense and someone else made up all the rules a long, long time ago—rules we're all beholden to. *It's not fair,* I think again, taking care this time not to touch anything fragile.

I round a corner into a darker part of the corridor. Up ahead, the entrance to the study room looks like the gaping mouth of a cavern. It reeks of mold and something worse—something dead maybe, but it's a room I haven't explored yet.

Archibaldo has had the run of this island. He's been lurking in its cavernous undercity for centuries, undetected. And I barely have a grasp of my own father's synagogue. None of this is fair.

And Archibaldo had that book—*The San Madrigal Book of the Dead*. It's a common enough volume, one of those books most people keep a copy of even if it goes largely unread—a household item we collectively have. I think the Santeros use it at their ancestor parties. What was Archibaldo doing with it?

Maybe there's a copy in here, I think, stepping into the dank expanse of the study. Can't see the ceiling for all the shadows, can barely see beyond what's in the little triangle of light in the entranceway. There's a dim miasma in the air, the thick smell of decay. If it were an actual body, though, that stink would be much worse. This staleness . . . It's probably just rotten paper, all this lost lore and wisdom dripping off ocean-eaten pages.

If Mateo were here, we'd laugh about this, and maybe scan a couple of volumes just to make sure they weren't important, and then we'd run off to find a better method or just leave it all behind and be together.

That's not true. If Mateo were here, he'd figure out a way to light this place, then he'd go through as many tomes as he could until he was absolutely convinced none were salvageable while I nagged and threw things at him to distract him.

I start skimming the shelves; time slows down, then speeds up again as the caws of gulls and swirling ocean all blend into an ambient hush. It must've been such a peaceful, inspiring place once. I wish I could remember it.

I'm about to give up when a slim volume catches my eye. The copies of the *B.O.T.D.* everyone has are relatively recent ones, printed at the one press they had here on the island. But it's an old book, I believe.

When I pull it down off the shelf, the weathered tome feels like it's about to crumble in my hands. The cover has too much give; it's probably mostly mold. But when I open the book and thumb through the pages, most of them are surprisingly intact. Small miracles indeed. I flip back to the title page and smile. "Bingo," I whisper, taking in the elegant illustration of a cemetery gate, complete with scattered bones and grinning skulls framing the words *The San Madrigal Book of the Dead.*

As I walk back down the corridor, book in hand, a sad melody reaches me on the early-afternoon breeze. I follow it, daydreaming only of Mateo, the living embodiment of music, a walking melody. But this is a girl's voice, I realize, working my way down a spiral stairway toward it. Of course it's not Mateo. I knew that.

Of course it's the only other conscious person here: Odé Kan. I find her in a meditative crouch beside Mimi's slumbering form. The hunter spirit has a beautiful voice—pure like a church bell, perfectly tuned to the glistening gloom around us. I don't know the song; it's in Yoruba, I think. The melody dips and dives, and from the intonation, it sounds like a call-and-response that Odé Kan is doing both parts of.

I slide into a squat across from her, and for a few moments, we hold the space of my strange lost aunt.

———◆———

"All right, here's what we got," I say, jumping over a table and slapping another plate into the ether midair.

Odé Kan hurls three more. "I'm listening."

Mimi's bambarúto wander the synagogue grounds listlessly, waiting for their leader to recover, I guess. A light rain hovers in the afternoon air; it's that gentle tropical kind of rain that makes you feel like you're being spritzed with body spray. Refreshing amid all this . . . crap we're trying to sort out.

"This international consortium of jackasses is here to purchase bambarúto as shock troopers to put down rebellions around the world." *Bang! Smash!* I land in a somersault and leap up to smack the last plate. "We're gonna need to raid another nearby house for more dinnerware pretty soon."

"Check." She unsheathes her bow. "Plates are boring, though. Let's try something different."

I skid to a halt on the muddy obstacle course. "Whoa, whoa, whoa—you're gonna shoot arrows at me?"

She lifts one shoulder. "I'll use the ones with blunted tips."

"Is this like when you had me do something you thought was impossible so I could do the hard thing more easily? Because I'd rather just keep trying to do the really hard thing."

"You'll be fine," Odé Kan assures me, nocking an arrow and taking aim. "Keep talking me through the data points, eh."

I hurl myself out of the way as an arrow whizzes past. "I hate this!"

"Keep going!" Odé Kan encourages cheerily.

I do, leaping over another arrow and onto a nearby rope swing. "They came to examine the merchandise, but Sparrow said the merchandise isn't looking so hot. And it's not! The bambarúto I saw looked like hell. Oof!" I leap from the rope to the far platform and barely make it. Then I duck, and an arrow bounces off the wooden platform right behind where my head just was. At least it didn't go in—guess she really is using the blunt tips. "What else? If they don't get satisfying results, they're gonna nuke the island, so that's exciting. But also, they have no boat to get away in."

"Thanks, Chela!" Odé Kan chirps, firing two arrows at once.

I launch off the platform and barrel-roll behind a picnic table. "But also, *we* have no boat to get away in!"

"Thanks, Chela!" Two arrows thunk against the table, fall to the ground.

"Yeah, yeah, yeah!" I sprint to the next stop on the obstacle course: a bunch of rusted bicycle wheels splayed across a muddy expanse. "And they have orders not to harm me, so yay!"

"But probably because they need you for something horrible, eh? Boo! Anything useful in that ratty old book?"

I skimmed most of it up in the tower while Odé Kan sang old Yoruba healing prayers to Mimi. "Mostly archaic poetry and riddles."

"Ugh."

"Some recipe-type things, though. And spells. And . . ." I stop midway along the course. *"Death calls the dead . . ."* My mind is dancing down too many impossible corridors to keep up with. "What if . . ." That rotting bamba corpse by the mountain . . .

"What?" Odé Kan demands.

"What if he was doing a summoning?"

"Huh?"

"That corpse I found . . . it had flower petals stuck to its decomposing flesh."

She frowns, sliding down from her perch. "Gross, but so?"

I sprint over to the table where the *B.O.T.D.* lies open, its pages flapping in the warm wind. "And that sound of screaming nearby. Flower petals were part of one of the spells . . . a summoning spell. But it used a guinea hen and some other stuff, too. . . . Does that sound familiar?"

"This is a dead-people thing," Odé Kan informs me solemnly. "Not my area of expertise, eh?"

"But if he . . . somehow has phantoms on his side . . ." I wave my hands around, trying to shape the theory into something logical as it forms. "I dunno, conquistador ghosts or something . . . and then he gives them form using the island, you know?"

Odé Kan wobbles her head back and forth, considering. "You would like for us to go check it out?" She idly picks at one of her antlers.

I find the page. *The Only Summoning Spell*, the title announces sanctimoniously. It's more super-random poetry, and then a list of ingredients. *The most important part of this spell is the dead. Death calls the dead. It is the only way.* Some of this stuff I've never heard of; other elements would be gone, swept away in the wind within an hour. But white flower petals are to be sprinkled on the site as the final step. "If we can get to the bambas before they become incarnate, destroy the place he's holding them or something, I don't know . . ."

"Destroy his army before he can use it!" She gives no warning before, as fluid as a splash of water, she sends one arrow and then another zinging toward me. "I like this!"

I'd had a feeling she might keep shooting. I dodge the first easily and extend one hand filled with all the pure destructive energy I can muster. The arrow disintegrates against my palm. "Or maybe it's not that. Maybe it's something else entirely. But either way, we have to find out!"

Odé Kan's smile is resplendent. "In that case, what are we waiting for?"

CHAPTER THIRTY-SEVEN

MATEO

I DON'T KNOW IF I CAN GO HOME.

I don't even fully know where home is, besides Chela, and she's miles from here in several different ways.

But the place where I live . . . or lived until my dad kicked me out. The place where my tía was murdered. The place I've been standing around the corner from for ten minutes, freezing my indecisive ass off. I don't know if I can go there.

Are they waiting for me? Watching the building from an unmarked van across the street?

Somehow, I'm getting the sense that this is no longer about me. Or at least, no longer just about me. How many Galeranos have been arrested in the past few hours? It sounds like plenty. Before I headed out, Tolo got a text about Baba Johnny being snatched up. At this rate, who will be left to stand with us when everything falls apart? I guess that's the point. And I guess when everything falls apart is right now.

Nothing to it but to do it.

I round the corner, glancing at every parked car to see if any surly silhouettes lurk within. Half a block away, someone comes out of the bodega at the corner, and I freeze. An old guy I don't recognize; he wanders off. My heart hammers away in my ears. I make it to the stoop, the familiar whine of the door opening. Are they waiting in there? Was it even my dad who sent the text, or some cop who grabbed his phone? I go up the stairs, my hands shaking.

There, in the hallway leading to our apartment, Galanika shimmers, frail and dying, always dying. He reaches out. I don't have time for this crap. He can either tell me what he wants or get out of the way. Actually, it doesn't matter, since he's just a hallucination. I walk straight through the chilly visage, feel my own barely-there tendrils brush against my skin. Slide my key into the lock and shove open the door.

My dad stands in the middle of the room looking broken. I know we have unfinished business between us and he kicked me out, but all I can do is walk over and wrap him in a hug. He puts his face on my shoulder, sighs the sigh of a man who thinks too hard about details he knows don't matter.

Then we retreat to the kitchen, and he slumps into a chair and groans.

"What happened?"

He shakes his head, still stunned. "They just showed up at the door. Asked for you, and when we told them we didn't know where you were . . ." He shoots me a sharp look. "We did, by the way." Leave it to him to make sure I *know* he lied to the cops to protect me. Thanks, Dad. "Or we figured you'd be at the Hidalgos'. Point is, one of them checked something on his phone—a list, I think—and then they said they were taking Sandra instead, and . . . they did. They cuffed her and everything."

"That's it?"

"I demanded they tell me what the charges were, and they *laughed*! Said we could make up whatever charges we wanted—that's what they were going to do anyway, so what did it matter?"

Now I sit. The thought of Mom being hauled away by those men, fingerprinted and photographed and shoved into a cage . . . I don't know where to put the mix of sorrow, horror, and pure wrath that's welling up inside me. It feels like it'll bubble over, explode out through my nose and mouth, pour from my eyes and ears, and flood this small room, the building, gush down the streets of Little Madrigal until our whole world is drowned in it.

"This is . . . This is all my fault," my dad says, putting his face in his hands. He's either making this all about him when it's blatantly not, or he's confessing to something I don't know about. I'm guessing the first, but I keep my mouth shut to find out. "I should've . . . I should've . . ." He sits up straight, like it's all becoming clear to him, scratches his scalp, looks at me. "I should've listened to you, Mateo."

"That wouldn't have changed shit, Dad. But thanks, I guess?"

"No, but . . . you were right." He slams a fist on the table, his gaze turned so deep inside himself it's a hundred miles away. "I didn't forgive the empire pirates. I didn't then, and I don't now. I thought . . . I thought if I said it out loud, it would come true. And I thought it would change something. Bring us together."

"Yeah, none of that is how forgiveness works."

A wild impatience grips me out of nowhere. We don't have time for his pity party. Then again, I have no idea what to do. A thousand tiny pins seem to be poking through the skin of my face, my gut. I want out of all this. I want Chela in my arms and my mom home safe.

"You're right, Mateo. I just wish I'd listened."

I want my dad to shut up. "Okay, but you didn't," I say, trying not to snap. "It's easier to beat yourself up about whatever mistakes you made yesterday than to deal with what's in front of us right now, because this is so, so bad. But this is what we got. And you didn't cause this. This was coming no matter what. All you did was give them a little more cover while they got the last pieces of their plan in place. And we still don't really know what that plan is. But we have to find out."

He blinks at me, and I'm not sure if he's going to cry, or storm out of the room, or just sit there looking lost for the next hour. All options are the worst option. Instead, he takes a breath. Then another. My dad's famous deep breaths, back in action.

After the third one, he chuckles a little, which I take to be a good sign. Who can tell? "You're right again, Mateo. And . . . I know it's too late, but I am sorry. I'm sorry I didn't listen to you, or to Sandra, and I'm even more sorry I kicked you out. That was . . . That was not okay."

"Well, I wasn't really interested in staying here after that BS at the Cabildo meeting, to be honest. But yes, it was messed up. So, cool—you're sorry. What are we gonna do about Mom?"

My dad stands, his face suddenly a mask of righteous fury. "Well, I'm going down there, of course. I was just waiting for you to get home before we go."

I'm sure my mouth has fallen open. "I'm sorry, did you say *we*? What makes you think I'm going anywhere near the precinct full of cops who have been trying to arrest me for the past two days, along with everyone else we know?"

"Well, no, I think it's important—"

"You want me to turn myself in? Get locked up like Mom? Is that your plan?"

Dad looks like he thinks he's about to win this. He's started pacing, and now he turns to me, one finger raised triumphantly. "They have no evidence against you, Mateo. Not even a charge. They can't do any of this, and we'll make sure they don't!"

"HOW?" I yell. Comes out louder than I mean it to, but I've lost all patience. "How do you plan to stop the people who are deter-mined to destroy us? By hearing them out? Pretending to forgive them? By arguing with them? With logic? Reason? None of that applies here."

"Mateo." My dad is already putting on his coat, looking for his keys. "Aren't you the kid who proved to the world that these empire pirates existed in the first place? I saw the clips of you on vote night." Oh God, he's gonna start singing. "I was so proud of you, Mateo." Here it comes. *"She's oooooour deeeeestroyer,"* my dad moans in his worst imitation of Auto-Tune. A clip of me went viral and got turned into a terrible song last year, and I'll never live it down, ever. And now I'll never get the image out of my head of my dad singing it terribly while our world is crashing down around us.

"That was different, Dad. I was talking to the community. To *us*. That's the only reason it worked—because Galeranos, for all our problems and infighting, by and large still believe that consorting with slavers and empires is *bad*. The people we're up against do not feel that way; *empire* is literally in their name."

This jackass looks like he's about to argue even more—infuriating, to be honest—when my phone rings. It's Tams. She's crying. "They took both my parents. It was guys they knew, Mateo. Our own people."

"I'm so sorry, Tams. Where are you?"

"With Maza and Tolo at some apartment that's part of his smug-gling operation. We're safe. A-are you okay?"

"Yeah, I'm with my dad. You're on speakerphone. He wants to march down to the precinct and demand that everyone be released because he says so."

My dad shakes his head at me. "That's not—"

"Wait," Tams cuts in.

"Please tell me you're not entertaining his ludicrous idea," I demand.

My dad looks hopeful, like a goober. He doesn't know my best friend that well, clearly.

"Absolutely not. It's stunningly naive, even for someone who thought pretending to forgive the twerp who caused all this was going to bring the community together."

Like I said.

My dad looks like he's been slapped, which, basically, he has. "How did you know I was pretending?"

Tams wisely ignores that question. "I'm just saying, if he's dead set on going down there, we might as well turn his bad idea into a good one and see what information we can gather."

"I already chewed him out for suggesting I go with him," I growl. "Please don't make me do it again."

"No, you absolute ham." Tams already sounds like she's feeling better now that a plan is coming into place. "I'm talking about wiring him up so we can hear what's said when he goes in. I happen to be in love with a tech expert and they're sitting right beside me."

I look at my dad, who just blinks at me, lost.

"Send the address. We're on our way."

CHAPTER THIRTY-EIGHT

CHELA

THE MOUNTAIN THAT MATEO AND I SHATTERED—IF IT WAS actually because of us—slid sideways into the sea. The thing basically became an avalanche. The westernmost edge is still somewhat intact; this is where Mimi went in our shared memory of the day the island fell, where the empire pirates were holding their secret ritual to raise Vizvargal.

And it's where Odé Kan and I hear the screams.

It must be someplace underground—I first heard them when I was down in the caverns; surely all these tunnels are interconnected, a whole city. But maybe, if we approach from this side, we can breach through, or at least get a better look at what's going on.

We leap from boulder to boulder, bypassing the rotting bamba corpse, and make our way toward the small cavern entrance that was once hidden away and is now just about all that's left of the mountain.

The gentle rain lets up, and the sun is dropping quickly into a purple-orange splatter of sky as another Caribbean twilight sets in.

A few seabirds hover over the waves, looking for dinner. Swarms of tiny insects flit around the carcasses of fish that washed up and got trapped in this rocky embankment.

Beneath the buzzing flies and crashing waves, the screaming drones on from somewhere below, a never-ending wail.

"Hate this, eh," Odé Kan grunts, speaking for both of us.

The Iwin emerge, tiny flickering glows lighting up the newly dark sky, just as we head through the cavern entrance into the shadows.

"This is where they gathered," I say quietly. Wax from a thousand different candles forms grotesque, impossible statues on the rocks. Weird, cryptic paintings cover the walls, as well as what's probably blood.

"Eh, the fools didn't even have the decency to do their satanic-death-cult stuff deeper in the tunnel," Odé Kan snarls. "Lazy."

The screaming only gets louder as we descend a steep, circular incline and then creep along a narrow passage. Then we're in an open chamber—torches send out a dim glow at various intervals along either wall. I can feel a slight gust against my face, and the air seems thicker somehow. The noise is almost unbearable.

So many voices; I can hear them more clearly now. There are hundreds, maybe thousands, of raspy, desperate screams rising and falling in the darkness somewhere nearby.

Odé Kan wraps a warm golden hand around my arm, and I glance to either side, assuming it to be a silent warning.

But no. The only form here is hers, and when my eyes find her clenched face, she sniffs once, then scowls. "I will be honest, my sister. I am struggling with this."

I nod, because I know exactly what she means, and squeeze her hand. Even without being able to see whoever's screaming, even not knowing what it's all about, this is very hard to take. The voices blot out everything else now; the ocean, the constant drip-drops of the cave, even our own beating hearts fade into nothing beneath that ongoing shriek of terror.

There.

I point to the far end of the cavern, where something flickers in the darkness—movement, maybe. We head toward it, arrow and blade at the ready.

A roar rises above the howling; a huge figure races toward us through the shadows. Then it rears as I run to greet it, my blade flashing in the torchlight around us. An arrow whooshes past my head, then another. Both find their mark—of course! it's Odé Kan—but the bambarúto doesn't seem to mind much. It slams one chitinous arm into the dirt beside me, then another. I spin, chopping and slicing as I go, and while the appendages don't sever completely, I know I've cut deep as shiny blood issues forth from each mangled chunk of flesh.

Another creature is scrabbling toward me from the far side of the room. Either there's an entrance somewhere over there or . . . these monsters are just lurking in the shadows. I lunge past the one closest to me while it's still reeling from the kiss of my blade. Hack at it again, once, twice, and with some gusto on the third since I get a chance to really wind up.

Ichor splatters my face, my shoulders.

The bamba writhes and squeals but doesn't go down.

More are coming.

The screaming, louder now that I'm that much closer, beckons to me like a siren song.

"Go!" Odé Kan yells from somewhere in the darkness. "I'll keep them busy! See what's over there!"

No point in arguing. This is why there are two of us. I sprint across the shadowy hall, trying to block out the shrieks and thunks of arrows finding their mark in that foul flesh.

At the far edge, I skid to a halt before some kind of sizzling, bristling barrier. It's not unlike the one I saw in that memory that swallowed up the girl—it's as if someone took the static from a broken TV and made an impenetrable wall out of it.

I reach out to touch it, and a tiny current meets me; not painful, but definitely a warning.

Still, it must fall. It's only been a few days, but I'm not the same girl I was then. My powers have grown, sharpened.

The screaming has taken over the world now; there's no blocking it out, no hearing anything else. I have to squint against it; the sound seems to bleed into all my other senses, blot out whatever dim light there is.

If a creature attacks me now, I'm toast.

But I know Odé Kan has them under control, and I have to let her handle them.

I have to focus.

I only have one shot at this, that much I'm sure of.

I take a deep breath, channel all the destructive energy I can muster into my right hand.

Open my stance and bend my knees so I'm good and grounded.

Pull my arm back past my chest.

Then shove it forward, directly into the wall of dark static, yelling as I release all that destruction, all that chaos, all that—

With a whoosh, the part I'm touching gives way and I stumble forward. Icy, barely-there fingers wrap around my wrist on the other side.

The dead.

This is the grip of the dead. I try to pull back, but the grip holds tight.

Archibaldo has somehow captured the dead of San Madrigal. And he's using their fears to make bambarúto. That's why his bambas are shambling zombies: because they're made from the fears of the dead. And that's why he needs living people here—to bolster his ranks with more powerful creatures.

"Odé Kan!" I yell, but the screaming has become even louder with the breach; it's everything, everywhere, an impossible open sky of holy terror opening up within me, blasting outward like an atom bomb.

He must be using the creation properties of the island to fashion the creatures from the dead's fear.

But every time he does, it makes another blighted cavity in the soil.

The island is a limited resource. One day—at the rate he's going, it won't be too long—the island will be a wasteland.

So he needs a way to bring his monsters to life that won't run out. He needs me.

"Odé Kan!" I yell again as more fingers find my wrist, then my arm, and I'm yanked forward, my face smashing into that buzzing current of the wall. I feel it tremble and start to give against the pressure of my body, the unstoppable force of destruction that radiates from me.

With the last bit of strength I have left, I turn my head just enough to catch sight of Odé Kan sprinting toward me, her yellow eyes wide and terrified, monsters scrabbling in her wake.

She reaches out, leaping through the darkness.

Then the static opens around me, and I'm yanked all the way through into a world of frozen hell.

CHAPTER THIRTY-NINE

MATEO

"UH, HI," MY DAD SAYS GOOFILY ON THE COMPUTER SCREEN. "I'D like to speak to the officer in charge." I'm doing my best not to cringe so hard I turn inside out; it's not working.

Tams, Tolo, Maza, Safiya, and I are in a mostly empty apartment over a butcher shop on Fulton Street, one of Tolo's smuggling safe houses. Four of us are huddled around a laptop. Safiya is over on the couch, talking into a satellite phone in hushed, urgent Ladino.

My dad is a few blocks away at the precinct, trying not to ruin literally everything even more. "Hello?" He finally adjusts himself into the position we practiced so the tiny camera on his lapel can show us what he's looking at.

"Hmm?" Desk Sergeant Valdez looks up wearily from his paperwork. He's physically fit, but the man has all the charisma of yesterday's oatmeal. He just oozes self-sabotage and neglect.

"I said I'd like to speak with the officer in charge," Dad repeats, frustration singeing the edges of each word.

"Oh yeah? What about?" Valdez can barely be bothered to open his eyes all the way. My dad and his requests are simply not worth the trouble.

"My wife was arrested today, and I need to make sure she's okay. Along with a number of other people."

"Hmm, oh. What were the charges?"

"That's exactly the problem," Dad insists. "There were none! It's a disgrace to the law enforcement profession to arrest someone without charges. My wife is a well-respected doctor in the international community, and furthermore . . ."

"This was a mistake," I say as he rattles on and on.

"Are you kidding me?" Tolo scoffs. "This is the only way we're gonna get any answers. Cops hate this kind of chatter; they get all worked up and try to shove chests back, and that's when secrets spill out."

"Yeah, this guy looks real worked up," Tams quips.

Tolo snorts, undeterred. "Just wait. Ol' man Medina is doing exactly what he should be."

"Finally," Dad continues, possibly getting to the point, but who knows, "you have in your custody a much loved and respected pillar of the Galerano community, Rabbi Hidalgo, and—"

"Now hold on there, buddy," Valdez finally interrupts. "Did you say Galerano?"

"I did," Dad assures him. "But I hardly see—"

"Why didn't you mention that before? All the Galerano arrests in the past few days have been part of the community policing task force set up by the late Anisette Bisconte shortly before her death."

"The *what*?!" all four of us say at once.

"I—I'm sorry," my dad stammers, right along with us. "The what, now?"

"You didn't know? It's been in the works for a few months, but I guess they didn't deploy street patrollers until the past day or two. Go figure."

"What . . . What is it?"

"What's it sound like? A task force that polices the community."

"But . . . but . . ." It's wild to hear my dad struck speechless. I wish it was under better circumstances so I could enjoy it more. "We've always done our own community-justice work in Little Madrigal. That was the whole arrangement that—"

Valdez lets out a haughty scoff. "Heh. And that's what you're still doing, buddy—policing yourselves. Only now it's under the watchful auspices of the New York City Police Department. Oh, and ICE, from what I understand."

"ICE?" Dad nearly coughs. "Wha . . . Why?"

"You guys are immigrants, ain'tcha? Why not ICE? It's a joint task force. You're welcome."

A sick feeling settles over me. It's not just that this has gone from bad to worse; it's not just that the sergeant hasn't gotten even remotely thrown off his game. It's that the implications of ICE being involved have made this much, much bigger.

"Some kid named . . . Let me see." Valdez checks something on his computer. "Vedo Bisconte is the community liaison." He shrugs. "Huh. Wonder if that's a relative of hers. Is Bisconte a common name for you weirdos?"

Of course Vedo is elbow-deep in this. I knew it, we all knew it, but the confirmation still feels like yet another kick in the chest.

"I want to see my wife," Dad says, his voice pure steel. Suddenly, I'm both proud of him for sticking with all this and heartbroken that he's in the belly of the beast. I wish we had a mic in his ear so I could tell him, *Just get out of there, we'll find another way to reach Mom.*

But the joke's on me, anyway.

Valdez lets out a crude belly laugh. "Oh, you won't be doing that anytime soon, buddy."

"Why is that?" Dad demands.

"She was part of the Galerano roundups, right? Yeah, they were all deported as of three hours ago. They're well on their way to . . . let me see . . . San Madrigal! As we speak!" He chuckles. "Go figure!"

CHAPTER FORTY

MIDNIGHT

Up, up, over rooftops into the sky.
Out across the clouds, cruel winter wind;
City becomes a splatter of lights, then nothing
as darkness takes over the world.
The ocean stretches on and on below. . . .

Darkness, darkness, darkness.
Shadow and spirit, fluttering gasps of chilly air.
Then nothing.

Nothing. Even the walls are dead here.

Small islands stretch out amid the waves. More
lost, impossible places, too small to make the
maps, barely there at all. A bonfire marks one
of them; the rest are just smudges of black on
the black sea, the absence of cresting waves.

Darkness, darkness, darkness.
The sliding grasp of displaced air,
a tendril and a gaping mouth.
The dead. They scream.
Rising, rising, rising . . .
Breach. Just a sliver of me makes it out. Milky-gray
swirls and here and there, a tiny sparkle.
Night birds glide past.
The sky!
Mateo . . .
Wait for me. . . .

Where is she?
How will we make it without her?
The sky churns, wind howls.
Everything feels impossible, lost.
Loved ones cast about once again on the tide of history.
Everything is lost.

MATEO!

Chela?

This place is so cold.

Chela? Where are you? What's happening?

———◆———

Chela, I don't know if you can hear me, but . . .
I finally found some info about the Cabildo meeting.
It's not much; only weird thing was that they were worried about
something occurring again, and they know it definitely will.

Didn't say what.
Maza found a journal from one of them, which I'll be checking,
but that's all I've got so far. . . .

It's . . . It's . . .

Chela? Can you—

It's so cold; and the screaming never stops. . . .

I can barely hear you, Chela.
Tell me how to reach you! Tell me where you are!

No! Mateo . . . no . . . No one else must come to this place.
Keep them away. Keep everyone away from the island!

Chela? That's not . . . That's not possible anymore. . . .
Can you hear me, Chela?

So cold . . .

Chela!

Chela?

Please . . . I need you.

DAY FIVE

Open all the doors, shatter each window.

Welcome the unknown with arms wide.

Spirit calls, trembles, revels through the night.

With sharp teeth, steely blades, fists made of fire,

We march,

And as we thunder through the battlefield,

Language is reborn within us.

—*The San Madrigal Book of the Dead*, Canto **XV**

CHAPTER FORTY-ONE

MATEO

THE CITY LIGHTS TWINKLE BEYOND THE CLOUD OF MY BREATH rising past my face. Brooklyn seems so peaceful; in the distance, the reflections of Manhattan skyscrapers ripple in the river.

Inside, I am shattered.

She's gone; out of reach. Lost somewhere in that monstrous island that we come from, that we created, that created us. I left her alone, and now she's somewhere cold and surrounded by a never-ending scream that still pierces through me, long after our midnight connection has vanished.

I had to just sit and slow my breathing after her voice faded. Wandered back to myself, body racked with anxiety. My mom is somewhere between here and there, along with Rabbi Hidalgo and countless others. Parents, loved ones, best friends. All ripped away from their homes, gone. Desaparecidos.

And Chela, too. Trapped somewhere. I've never heard her sound so scared, so lost.

It's ripping me in two, the memory. I don't know how I'll ever leave it behind. Even if we find her and she's okay, that fear, the screaming all around her, that desperation in her voice—it will haunt me.

Shakily, I stand.

She said no one else should be on the island. But she doesn't know our families are already en route.

She told me not to come until I'd found answers to that impossible spirit riddle of our history and what it means.

I have no answers.

But I have no other choices, either. I pull out my phone, releasing a long, frosty breath into the night. The city sparkles; ice shimmers along the rooftops, orange lights caught in their tiny prisms, and sends dazzling rays in every direction. The beauty of it all is almost overwhelming. I'm so frazzled, pretty much everything is almost overwhelming.

"Yeah?" Tolo says over the phone.

"That cargo plane you mentioned . . ."

"Already gassed up and ready to fly."

"It's time."

"I'll tell the crew. Be outside in ten."

———◆———

I crack open the door and peek at the empty streets of Little Madrigal. A gentle snow sweeps down; nothing else moves. Safiya idles an SUV right in front of our building.

"She's here," I tell my friends, and I'm about to make a dash for it when a squad car glides around the corner onto Fulton, quiet as a shark. "Hold up."

The others stir behind me, wanting to know what's happening. I shush them with a wave of my hand.

The cops maneuver around the SUV and head off into the night. I glimpse them laughing about something, the blue glare of their onboard computer illuminating their wide smiles and rosy cheeks. Wonder if they're the ones who brought in Mom, or was that some other crew? Does this community-policing crap come with its own badge and uniform, or is it just paper pushers up in an office somewhere, sending heavies out to do the dirty work?

Doesn't matter.

Right now, all we can do is go get our loved ones from the island. We'll deal with the rest later. Until they're safe, the empire pirates have us by the throats.

"All right, let's go," I hiss once the squad car's lights have turned down a side street. "C'mon."

Tams slips past me, then Maza and Tolo. All had go bags packed and ready, of course. I turn to tell my dad that I love him—because I do, I really do—and I'll see him when I get back, which I hope is true.

Except something about his expression catches me off guard. Standing there beneath the unforgiving hallway fluorescents, he looks older than I've ever seen him, more ragged and worn-out . . . but there's something else, a light behind his eyes. I think he's . . . excited?

"Dad?"

"Look, son, I—"

"Please don't apologize again or make this somehow out to be all your fault, Dad, I'm begging you."

"Wow, no, not that."

"Okay, good. Look, I love you and I'll see you when I get back."

"When *you* get back? No, son. You'll see me on the way and the whole time you're there."

"What? Dad, no . . ."

He arches an eyebrow like he's about to report the cleverest fact of them all. "Sandra was my wife before she was your mom, I'll have you know. And you may be a mighty healer spirit, but I'm a doctor."

He had to get a little dig about my spirit powers in there along with the corny dad joke, huh?

But then he finishes, "Just imagine what we could accomplish if we worked together for once."

Damn. That got me. Wasn't ready. I hold up my hands to signal defeat, and he takes the opportunity to hug me.

"Anyway," Dad says as we walk out into the snowy night together and pile into Safiya's SUV, "I haven't been home in fifteen years."

CHAPTER FORTY-TWO

MATEO

THE PLANE IS ONE OF THOSE BIG OL' CARGO JOINTS THAT BAD GUYS always get thrown out of at the end of action flicks. It rattles irritably along the runway that Safiya drove us to in some deserted corner of Long Island. Then it lifts and we're off into snowy skies, retracing the path I've been sending my spirit form along these past few nights.

No one says much; there's not much to say. We have no idea what we'll be up against, what shape the island will be in. What shape our enemies will be in.

Tolo, Tams, and Maza huddle close to one another against the cold; Safiya checks her phone, then sleeps; my dad conks out as soon as we're airborne, snoring away.

A melody comes to my lips, slips crookedly out of me, and it takes a moment before I realize it's that horrible Vizvargal "fugue," the one that is a response without a call. Feels like it's infected me, somehow, for it to just seep out like that. Wish I'd never heard it. Some other song will replace the earworm—one of the old

Cuban-style rumbas that repeat over and over; that should do it.

I watch the darkness outside stream past the contours of my own reflection. I feel like Chela's with me, even though she's more absent from my world than she's been since we first became close. I can't explain it, don't understand it, but I guess I don't have to. It's not like she could reach out and say something to me, not like in our midnight meetups. But I feel her. So I say her name quietly, just to myself, a near-silent prayer that slips from my mouth and fogs up the window.

Then I pull out the book Maza found: Mother Fabula's journal. I've been saving it for a quiet moment, and those have been increasingly few and far between. In the dim light of the cargo hold, I flip through the age-old pages to October of 1810.

There's a whole lot scribbled in here; Mother Fabula definitely leaned into the minutiae of the job. I'm about to give up when the words *Divine Council* jump out at me.

They insisted it was the only way to maintain balance, that they had read and reread the letters through various divination systems, and that was that. The pact preserving Galanika's and Madrigal's eternal lives was sworn on the living island itself and sanctified by an Icharracht. To my knowledge, there is no greater binding power on Earth, and so I must be satisfied, though I admit to a certain unease with the arrangement. It feels quite abrupt. There is so much we do not know about what occurred at the harbor yesterday. Rumors and horror stories abound, each more terrifying and implausible than the last. But we are still rebuilding and burying our dead, and we will be for quite some time. Thus, as the Council said in their final missive: onward.

My pulse quickens as I read. Our immortality—Chela's and mine—is sanctified in an object of some kind. That means we can keep it safe. It also means it can be destroyed. But what the hell is an

Icharracht? And what happened at the harbor that had everybody so shook? It must've been the end of the fighting, but no one wrote anything down.

"Tolo," I hiss across the plane. He looks up groggily from his little polycular slumber party. I wave my head in a little circle to summon him.

"Better be good," he grumbles, sliding gracefully onto the bench beside me and crossing his arms over his chest.

"Excuse the interruption, Cuddles."

He raises a single finger and doesn't even have to warn me never to call him that again. It's just clear.

"What is an Icharracht?"

He immediately slides from gangster mode into Professor Baracasa. "Mythological creature that is created to function as a vessel for something."

A creature, not an object. That's super weird. "Mythological from where?"

He shrugs. "Just Madrigal, far as I know. A thing of legend; not sure if they ever existed."

"Isn't that strange?" I ask. "Most Madrigal things were from somewhere else first, right?"

"Some, sure. Coulda been lost to history. Who knows?"

"How would I find one?"

"More like how do you make sure one doesn't find you. They're horrific things, man—always depicted as having many arms and legs sprouting from their back, sort of like a spider but also muscular and hairy."

The . . . the creature . . . back on the island. I'd seen it, fought it. It almost killed me. Could it have been the same thing?

"Mateo?"

Pretty sure I'm looking off into the distance with wide, haunted eyes. I try to explain best I can.

"Uh," Tolo says when I finish. "None of that sounds good, but I'll keep my eyes out for it when we get there. Just can't promise I won't be running the other way when I see it." He pats my shoulder and heads back to his little cocoon of intimacy.

Archibaldo is holding our immortality hostage.

That's what it comes down to.

The one thing in this world that guarantees my safety, Chela's safety. That ensures we won't be cut down in all this hellish fighting, that we have a chance. It's out there, the embodiment of some long-ago pact, and my damn ancestor has turned it into his attack dog.

But that's all right. When we get to San Madrigal, I will find the Icharracht. I'll free it from Archibaldo's clutches, and I'll get it somewhere safe. And then I'll be safe. *We'll* be safe. And we can figure out how to love each other again.

That's the plan. It'll have to do. I try to stay focused on it, because whenever I don't, my thoughts slip into brutal imagery of all the terrible things that might be happening to Chela right now.

Eventually, I let myself drift off to sleep.

———

A few hours later, clanging and rattling knock me out of a vague and horrific dream. The others are all peering out the windows to the sea below, where day is breaking over the crashing waves.

There's an island ahead—Tolo's refill station, I'm guessing. It's not much more than a mile or two in each direction, mostly taken up by a runway and a couple of buildings and docks. A long, sleek boat waits a little ways away from it.

"What's happening?" I ask, nudging in beside Tams.

"Not sure," she reports. "The pilots are talking to the crew on the ground, and it sounds like some kind of standoff."

The plane swings sideways, and I feel my stomach lurch as we start to descend. "Guess we'll find out soon enough."

———◆———

Just a few days ago, Barnabas Toby had captained the small ship that brought me and Chela close enough to San Madrigal that we could head off by ourselves in a motorboat to find it. Now he struts toward us across the landing strip, his gregarious smile as wide and unvarnished as ever.

Tolo reaches him first and wraps the burly, dark-skinned captain in a wicked hug. "The hell's happening with that yacht out there?" Tolo grunts.

Barnabas drapes an arm over Tolo's shoulder and pulls him close, turning to face us. "Welcome to Saint Barnabas's Treasure Cove! It's named after yours truly, in case you were wondering. And you!" He points a finger at me, mean-mugging, and for the next few tense seconds I catalog all the possible ways I might've messed up and offended him after all the nice things he did for me. "How the hell are ya, kiddo?"

He shoves Tolo out of the way and catches my palm, pulling me into a warm embrace. "Last time I saw you, you were desperate to get back to Brooklyn. What happened?"

I shake my head. "Long story, man."

"Yeah, I bet." He chuckles.

"Barnabas . . . the yacht," Tolo presses.

"Right, right, come on, I'll show you."

He leads us through a wide-open hangar to a control room, where some of the other crew from our earlier journey are checking readouts and prepping weapons. "Figured you'd need a boat to get where you're going, since you said you'd be landing the plane here. All our crews are out on runs, so . . ."

"Good thinking," Tolo says. "This the first vessel to come by?"

"There's been activity all night. Chopper went past a few hours ago, then a medium-size barge. This one, though—it's been lurking in these waters for hours. We signaled 'em to come this way, but they just parked up out there like they tryna wait us out or somethin'. Must've gotten wise to our ploy."

"Why didn't they just cut and run?" Tams asks.

"Oh"—Barnabas laughs—"because we told 'em we'd blow 'em out of the water if they tried."

"But you won't, right?" I say, because all I can imagine is my mom bound up in the cargo hold of that yacht as it explodes. "You can't. Our . . . What if our people are . . . ?"

"Don't think it's big enough to be carrying too many folks," Barnabas says. "The one that went by earlier was more like a transport ship, so they'da probably been on that, if I had to guess."

"They're waiting for reinforcements," Tolo says. "Especially if they're with that group of mercenaries the empire pirates have been working with."

"So . . . what you want us to do?" Barnabas asks.

"You can't blow them up," I insist. But these are pirates, and pirates hate having their bluff called. Even if it started as a bluff, if someone calls 'em on it, they sometimes go ahead with the threat to save face.

"No one's blowing anything up," Tolo growls, opening a heavily locked storage bin in the corner. "There are other ways of taking over a ship." He pulls out one large rifle, then another, which he hands to Tams.

"Whoa, whoa, whoa," my dad says, both hands raised, face creased with alarm. "Let's just . . . Now, hold on. . . ."

I gape at my best friend. "Tams, when did you learn to—"

"Shoot?" She grins whimsically. "Tolo's been teaching us over the past couple weeks."

"But the . . . the no-guns thingy . . ." The whole no-cops arrangement came with a very simple caveat for our side: if a single shot was fired in the boundaries of Little Madrigal, the whole deal was off.

"The shooting range is out in Queens," Tolo says, handing yet another rifle to Maza, then Safiya. "Maza's a natural."

"I don't like this," Dad insists, and for once, I agree with him. I hate guns, and I hate the idea of my friends running into the line of fire to take over a yacht. Even if they do know what they're doing. Someone's definitely going to get killed. Of course there's going to be fighting ahead, but this just seems so sudden and unnecessary.

"There's enough here for you to take one," Tolo says, ignoring my dad. "I can show you the basics."

Dad shakes his head. "I'll have no part in those things. I am a doctor, and I took an oath: do no harm. I've lived my life by that oath, and I take it very seriously. You all have your spirits and credos, and I respect that; all I ask is that you respect my covenant in return."

I know there was a dig at me in there. He didn't say it, but he's heard about what went down—the fighting, my role in it. He probably can't fully grasp how my powers work, but he understands enough to know I was inflicting plenty of pain on anyone who got in my path. And even though his words are directed at Tolo, the fact that I'm catching strays—no pun—when I was on his side, it just doesn't sit right.

Anyway, I have a better plan, and it's not one Dad's going to like any more than this one, so that makes it a double win.

"I'll deal with 'em." Everyone turns to me. "Alone."

"Mateo, what are you talking about?" my dad demands, suddenly very much a dad. The others are all chattering and incredulous, too, but Dr. Jorge Medina is the loudest.

I stare at the low-res video image of that boat against the breaking day. It's probably carrying some of the people who kidnapped our families. It might carry our families, too. "Just trust me."

I'm an immortal.

Time to start acting like it.

I turn to Barnabas, already heading for the door. "You still got that li'l motorboat?"

CHAPTER FORTY-THREE

MATEO

As the motorboat peels through the waves toward that yacht, I keep reminding myself of the moment I placed both hands on Maestro Gerval's chest and shoved the death of Tantor Batalán directly into it.

I'd been keeping that little memento for exactly that purpose, like a bullet with my former hero's name etched into it.

I knew there was no way Gerval could survive a direct hit from the very essence of death. And if he did by some anti-miracle survive, then there was the fall through a skylight, through a wooden stage, and straight into the basement of Tolo's club that came afterward. That, surely, would kill anyone, especially someone who already should be extremely dead.

But it didn't. It didn't.

That jackass crawled out of the rubble in one piece, stronger than before somehow, and proceeded to be a problem. Why? Because he was like me: Immortal. Undying.

It took the death of another immortal, me, my death, to end him for real.

So unless they've got another one of me on board that yacht, which I doubt, they can hurt me, but they won't be able to take me out of the game for good, no matter what they do.

At least, that's what I keep telling myself.

My brain has believed this body to be 100 percent mortal just like everyone else's for the past sixteen years, though, so it's having a little trouble catching up.

Especially now that I'm getting close and a slew of burly dude-bros in aviators have shown up at the side of the yacht pointing automatic rifles at me.

It's one thing to know you won't die. It's a whole other thing to feel like you won't. And I don't feel it, not right now.

Anyway, undeadable or not, getting shot still hurts, according to my sources.

"Whoa, whoa, whoa!" I yell, both hands up, trying to look some-how both innocent and confident at the same time. Probably only achieving a blurry kind of anxiousness, but hey—it's worth a try.

The lead guy, a gym rat with spiky hair, starts yelling commands in some corny made-up language that sounds like dollar-store pig latin. I don't know if he's talking to me or his guys; he's just blurting things out.

"I come in peace and all that!" I say.

The guy keeps yelling, and the other ones are getting all wound up, and any second now they're gonna blast me out of the water, clearly, so I just jump in. I'm close enough to swim to the yacht, anyway.

The cold water shocks through me, and muffled gunfire roars overhead.

Panic is a wild animal within. It can't be reasoned with or tamed. When bullets rain vicious trajectories all around me, that animal takes full control. I don't know what direction I'm going, where the boat is. I just know *away*, and my body tries to find that. But the bullets are everywhere, in front and behind, and then suddenly charting their brutal paths *through* my flesh and bones, chopping arteries, cleaving meat, muscle, tendon; bursting back out into the ocean as the devastation they wreaked issues forth.

Pain explodes through every limb; my torso is on fire, lungs pierced. Panic roars through my brain, blindingly white noise, an impossible scream that blots out everything else.

Except this one word:

Under.

Through the pain, through the terror, the word becomes a thought:

Under the boat.

My only salvation. I'm so close.

The firing has let up for the moment. Reloading, maybe. It all happened in the span of a few seconds.

In a few more seconds, it'll all happen again, much worse.

But I'm only a few seconds away from safety. I push through the pain, the torn muscles and shredded tissue; taste of my own blood in the water. (Will it bring sharks? Can't deal with that now, Mateo.) One thing at a time. One thing at a time. And that one thing is to get under the boat. I surface just long enough to gulp air, then launch myself into an agonizing dive as more bullets burst into the water around me.

And then I heal myself.

There isn't much time. I don't know what'll happen when I run out of oxygen, but I'd rather not find out in the middle of a firefight.

But healing comes easy. I've done it countless times now. I feel the tingle of each cell regenerating and sliding back into place as my hands pass over the ruptured flesh and shattered bone.

My own song rises within, a distant, wistful lullaby that grows into something bigger, wilder with each repaired part of me; now a bolero, strong and somber; now a rumba, cataclysmic and relentless.

And so I shall be: the tragedy blown back on the masters of war. A reversal of fortune embodied in a boy.

One hand emerges from the waves on the far side of the yacht, then the other. My newly strong arms haul this long, muscular body from the ocean to the deck, and I catch the first attacker as he's turning to see what that thud was.

The thud was me, soaking wet and unwounded, with rage gushing out of every pore and the flesh-shattering brutality of each gunshot wound tingling at my fingertips.

With that kind of arsenal, I don't need to put much effort into my attacks—just a flick of my wrist will carry the destruction out of me and into them. But Bonsignore always taught us to put everything we've got into whatever we're trying to accomplish, so I do. I do.

The man hasn't even turned all the way around before I've wound up and cracked him across the face with all my strength plus a hearty helping of gunshot wounds.

With a squishing crackle, his jaw flies off and clatters to the ground. He collapses in a heap, somehow alive but thoroughly unconscious.

Okay, maybe I don't need to put *that* much effort into it.

The others converge, but I'm already too close for them to get any more shots off. It's a simple matter now—I cleave through them, spreading the devastation they themselves wreaked as I go. Men fall to either side with shattered limbs, gaping holes in their hands, missing fingers and arms, a splatter of blood from a wide-open mouth.

In seconds, they lie on either side of me, and I'm looking for one to interrogate when the crackle of gunfire sounds nearby and pain lances through my torso. I stumble back a few steps from the impact and glance down at my shredded stomach.

Up on the bridge, the spiky-haired leader is staring at me with his mouth wide open, automatic rifle smoking in his hand. "What the hell are you?" he demands, but I'm already lunging forward in a sloppy, off-kilter stagger, barely upright, and he's blasting more holes into his boat where I had just been standing.

I throw my back against the wall directly below him, panting. Slide one hand over the hemorrhaging mess of flesh and watch it smooth over, feel the rumba rise within me.

I've barely caught my breath when Spiky Hair comes leaping over the bannister, already taking aim.

Cataclysmic and relentless, I rise to meet him, letting carnage loose from both hands. It rips through him before he has time to shoot, mangling, bursting, pulverizing flesh, vessels, bone, and finally, brain.

He lands at my feet, dead.

I'll be honest: a part of me, a large part of me even, wants to leave him that way.

And I'll say this, it's not mercy or compassion that moves me to crouch beside his shattered body and let the song rise, the tissue repair, the heart pump again. No, I'd be lying if I said it was. We need information, is the truth of it, and this guy is the one most likely to have it. Plus, having an extra death in my pocket is probably a good idea for whatever lies ahead.

When he blinks back to life, gasping for air, I'm standing over him, frowning. "Tell me everything."

CHAPTER FORTY-FOUR

MATEO

IT'S ALREADY MIDAFTERNOON WHEN I STOMP BACK INTO THE control room ready to curse someone out.

I brought the damn yacht over to the docks, dragged ol' Spiky Hair off while Tolo's crew tied up the others.

And then it was questions and preparing and this, that, and the other—just a flurry of seemingly useless but actually probably important little things.

But none of those little things were the one thing my entire body was screaming to do: get on our damn way to damn San Madrigal.

There'd been no prisoners on the yacht.

Spiky didn't give up much info that we didn't already know. But sparing him was worth it if only to have a mortal blow tucked away. And once my adrenaline and wrath had cooled, I was very, very glad I hadn't taken another life, even if it was one that had been hell-bent on taking mine.

But then the boat had to be checked over, and the crew had to be secured somewhere, and supplies had to be prepped, and, and, and . . .

And now precious hours have passed, and I've had it.

"We have to go," I say to Tolo and Barnabas and my dad, who are all huddled around a monitor. "Now." I do my best to keep the growl out of my voice, but it doesn't work.

"About that . . ." Barnabas says, turning to me with a regretful frown.

"No." The growl *is* my voice now, no pretensions otherwise. "I've *had* it with delays, with prep."

"Mateo," Dad says in that excessively reasonable voice that makes me want to punch him in the throat on a regular day.

"Don't *Mateo* me, Dad. Our people are on that island. Chela is on that island. Mom is on that island. We go. Now."

"We can't," Tolo finally says, gruffly putting a fine point on the whole thing.

"Why the—?"

He's ready for that question; nods at the monitor they'd been huddled over. "See that bright red monster?"

Can't miss it. Looks like someone emptied an artery onto the display.

"That's a storm," Barnabas says with a sailor's awe for all the word entails. "Big one."

I blink at it. "How . . . ? If we hadn't—"

"No," my dad says, and I know he's not just saying it to calm me down. "There is no *if we hadn't*, son. The things we did had to be done, and anyway, if we *had* headed in earlier, that gale probably would've dropped out of the sky on us, and it may well have wiped us out."

"Chela . . . Chela can . . ." It's all I can get out because my breath isn't there when I reach for it. "Chela can . . . Chela can . . ."

Before I realize what's happening, all three of them are around me, guiding me to a swivel chair, easing me into it. "Whoa, Mateo, hey," Tolo says with gruff gentleness. "Hey."

"Chela can . . . Chela . . ."

Dad rubs my shoulders. "We're here, kiddo. You've been through a *lot*." Part of me wants to shove his calming hands away; part of me wants to pull them tighter around me. I still can't breathe, though, so I do neither.

I just sit there and let the hell of being stranded here wash over me again and again like the tide.

Chela can bring storms is what I want to say. She's in trouble. She needs our help. But who am I kidding? What use am I to someone who can send a whole land mass to the bottom of the ocean?

But anyway, everyone else there needs our help, that's for sure.

And all we can do is sit around and hope the storm passes? Feels like a massacre in my heart.

"We are monitoring it," Barnabas assures me. "And we're ready to move the second it dissipates. Mateo? You hearing me?"

I close my eyes. Finally find air in these lungs. Pull it in, let it out. My dad keeps rubbing shoulders. Time keeps passing.

Breathe, Mateo. Breathe.

CHAPTER FORTY-FIVE

MIDNIGHT

Up, over this tiny island of steel and concrete,
over blinking lights and somber preparations
for the battle ahead . . .
Over crashing waves and the endless sea,
And then . . .

Nothing.

Chela?

Chela!

CHELA!

Nothing.

Sea and sky and endless night.

Chela . . .

DAY
SIX

A pinch of ash.

Blood of my blood.

Three drops of holy water.

Fresh anise.

A watermelon.

Splash of rum.

Placed at the foot of the banyan tree.

Set fire to the world.

—*The San Madrigal Book of the Dead*, Canto XVIII

CHAPTER FORTY-SIX

CHELA

CHELA.

Mateo?

The world smashes back into existence around me, but everything is still darkness, screaming, darkness, screaming. . . .

And pain.

A senseless, horrific stabbing pulses through me, like I'm being turned inside out every few seconds. The screaming is me; I am screaming.

But no . . . When I pause, it's all around me, too.

Right. The dead. The dead are screaming. Terrified.

Everything fades, returns, fades, returns. . . . Time slips and slides around me; there's no way to keep track.

The dead still scream, but is it . . . ? It might be a little quieter now; it might have lessened since I first felt the rush of gravity take me as I plummeted through this icy darkness. I landed more than once, must've cracked against several surfaces as I fell.

Everything within me must be broken.

I don't even know where I begin and the darkness of the cavern ends. We are one. Whenever I try to move any part of my body, the answer is only more pain—endless, senseless, reckless stabs of it ratcheting up and down whatever remains of me, like I'm being carpet-bombed from within.

But . . . Mateo? That was his voice saying my name. It wasn't a memory. I felt him.

Is he close? Has he come to get me, despite all my warnings and pleas? The thought of that boy's beautiful face suddenly appearing in the darkness makes me heave with a sudden wrenching sorrow. He's nowhere near here; he has good sense. He's a thousand miles away, safe, where he should be. Maybe having hot chocolate with my mom and dad in the warm glow of the kitchen, snow falling outside.

Hrrrrgh . . . The notion brings another stab of pain, because my chest keeps rising and falling. Because I'm sobbing, I realize. I'm sobbing.

My body is shattered.

And I'm not Mateo. Healing power is its own special gift. But I can regenerate things, no? I can bring forth life. Make matter where there wasn't any before.

If I concentrate.

But the physical agony of each breath . . . I can't concentrate on anything but that.

There's no point in even trying.

I should've trained harder.

Should've accepted my own nature, the lost shard of my identity. Instead, I fought it because I'm stubborn and it didn't feel right. Didn't fit. I'm not a puzzle with a missing piece, and the very idea that there was a part of me I didn't know about but other people did . . . I hate it.

And now I'm paying the price.

I should be dead. I know that.

That fall would've claimed a mortal, no question.

Gotta tell Odé Kan I've finally accepted I'm one of her kind. If I ever get out of here.

I'll never get out of here, though.

That much is clear.

I will rot, alive and awake and in infinities of agony, I will rot, bit by bit, at the bottom of this cave, surrounded only by phantoms screaming in terror.

Except the screaming has faded for real now—it's only barely there.

Maybe they do it in waves, take a long collective breath before they start again.

Maybe it's because my brain is rotting first, and I'm losing my sense of hearing.

Or maybe they really have cooled it; maybe my presence is finally registering with them.

Maybe they feel . . . hope.

That would be rich.

But maybe there is something I can do.

Creation work is too hard with this much pain, but if I can get the island itself to lift me . . .

I try to breathe past the pain, go inward. Reach for the now-familiar feel of the island, its warm soil, that quiet murmur of growth, water, life.

I find nothing.

I'm not sure if it's me or . . . No. It's not only agony blocking my focus. It's this place. The walls, the darkness. It's a dead place. Different. It won't respond to me because it's not part of me, not part of the living island.

And I'm trapped here.

Mateo, I try to say, but my teeth are shattered; my jaw might be, too. Just the breath exiting my mouth leaves behind a fresh explosion of brittle aches and burns.

All that comes out of me is a gurgle of blood and spit and some horrific gasping noise.

You know, a familiar voice says from very, very close to the shattered remains of my face, *I owe you an apology, Chela Hidalgo.*

Through even more slices of anguish, I open my eyes.

Those big, rosy cheeks, that impeccable makeup, even in death.

Painfully, painfully, I rasp out a shattered cackle. "Tía Lucía?"

CHAPTER FORTY-SEVEN

MATEO

DAWN.

The world is just a gray cloud. Rain speckles our faces as we watch from the deck of the yacht, waiting, waiting.

Lightning crackles across the sky somewhere up ahead, and then the fog seems to part like a giant gate. San Madrigal emerges from the mist, a mighty, glacial behemoth in the twilight.

Around me, the whole boat gasps at once. I forgot that I'm the only one who's seen the place recently. Tams, Tolo, and Maza probably barely remember it at all.

Plus, there are only two peaks now.

"Well, I'll be damned," Tolo mutters. "Never thought I'd see it."

"Y'all really did knock down a mountain with your love," Tams says, but her tone is all awe, no snark. "Nice work."

"Ah, hate to ruin the excitement . . ." Barnabas cuts in from the upper deck. And before he finishes, we all know what he's about to point out.

Screams and growls rise in the early-morning air. On the beach, we can make out tall shapes colliding and collapsing as clouds of sand burst around them.

The Battle of San Madrigal has already begun.

"Who's fighting?" Dad asks as the others click and clack their weapons ready and strap on their tactical gear. "Can you make anything out?"

"Ehh . . ." Through the binoculars, it mostly just looks like a damn mess. "Lotta bambarúto. Gotta be Mimi's in there going up against Archi's." Some of them look weird, though. Incomplete and desiccated, they shamble across the beach in uneven, deathlike trances, swiping at anyone who gets close. "And a bunch are, like, rotting and shambling around. . . . Zambarúto."

Dad ponders this with a nervous hum. "How interesting."

"That's one way to put it. I don't see any people, though. . . ." Something golden flickers through the chaos. "Wait a minute." A girl. Tall. With some kind of wild headgear—antlers or something. She's whirling amid the huge fighting monsters like it's all some ballet, letting loose arrow after arrow.

"What is it?" Dad asks.

Each shot finds its mark; zambarúto crash into the sand whenever they get in her way. While I gaze in awe, the girl races up the back of one towering creature, shoots an arrow straight down into its head, then leaps off it as it falls. She crashes into the chest of another with both feet and launches herself sideways, letting loose more arrows into it as she flings through the air. She comes down in a tumble and is already taking more down as she rises. "She's like . . . if Legolas had a hot sister who was also half elk?"

"Okay," Dad says. "I have no idea what that means, but we're getting close, so . . ." He gestures to the smaller boat, which everyone has piled into. We must look like some kind of wild militia, rolling up on the shores of this forgotten island with a bunch of high-powered rifles and SWAT gear. Dad and I forgo the guns—for opposite reasons, of course—but we both strap on the vests as Barnabas guides the boat through the waves to the shore.

And I'm glad we did armor up, because before we even land, more gunfire rattles out, speckling the water around us with tiny explosions. Some of those mercenary dudes must be here, too, and I'm sure they're not happy about us showing up unannounced in the middle of their takeover.

We haven't even started fighting yet and I'm already tired of getting shot at. Heart racing, I ready myself to dive back into the ocean and probably get sprayed with a bunch of bullets once again. Instead, Barnabas cuts a hard right with the boat, swinging us sideways. Tolo and Tams have already raised their weapons, and then the sound of shooting is everywhere as they unleash barrage after barrage at a makeshift driftwood barricade I hadn't even noticed.

No idea what they hit or didn't hit, but it was enough to give us a few minutes of peace.

Up ahead, the bambarúto fighting has rumbled up closer to the forest edge and taken a vicious turn; several monster body parts lie in pools of blood across the beach.

Our boat touches land.

"Keep the medics inside our circle," Barnabas instructs. Clearly he has done this before. As we step into the shallows and race onto the shore in a messy dash, it finally hits me: we're at war. We're rolling up on our homeland, trying to snatch it back from the clutches of these horrible monsters and men who want us dead. We're walking the same path so many before us have taken. So many have been cut down while doing exactly this.

Immortal or not, I am terrified. For myself, for my loved ones, for my home. Both my homes. The weight of my entire world, every-one I love, rests on the shoulders of these moments, the decisions we make, the ferocity and ingenuity we bring to this fight.

There's no turning back. Not now.

"Do we chase down those shooters or head for the monsters?" Tolo asks, and I realize he's looking at me. The great gangster wants to know my thoughts on the matter. And it makes sense—I know more about the situation on the ground than anyone else—but it still catches me off guard.

Anyway, the answer's easy. "Follow the bambarúto. We don't have many allies, and the few we do have are about to be over-whelmed. We need someone to keep an eye out for the shooters, though."

"On it," Tams and Maza both say at once, then grin at each other because they're so totally on the same wavelength, and I can't lie, it's cute. I'm just happy anyone can figure out how to smile in the midst of this hell.

"All right, bet," Tolo says with that gruff warmth of his. "Let's move."

I can barely see through the bodies encircling me. The bodies of my friends, there to protect me, to literally take a bullet for me. And I get it—I'm the one who'll undo their wounds. Sure, I can't die, but it'll be hard to heal anyone if my brains are splattered on a palm tree. Still . . . I'm not used to this. To any of this.

The sound of roaring bambas and zambas gets louder, and then there are trees all around us. Tolo lets out a war cry—he's ordering us to charge, I realize. We run, all our feet pounding the sand, the soil, and suddenly, with a crash and a clatter, we've entered the fray.

The first thing that happens is shooting, so much shooting.

The *rat-a-tat* of those automatic weapons becomes all there is for a few moments. I think some shambling zombie bambas probably charged right back at us and got wasted real quick. Yes—I glimpse their writhing forms, smoke still rising from their wounds as we pass.

I hear yelling up ahead, and someone stumbles backward into me—Maza! They're okay, just startled, but then a zambarúto crashes full-weight into our little party, its rotting flesh sloughing off as it gargles and gasps. The circle is broken. Tolo blasts away at the fallen creature, but we're scattered now.

I don't see Dad. Monsters charge through our ranks, slashing and swinging those decrepit claws as they pass.

Gunfire bursts out of the mist nearby; people are panicking. At this rate, we'll be cut down by our own friendly fire as much as by enemy attacks.

"On me!" Tolo hollers through the woods. "Stay close to me!" I see him amid the trees, machete out, rifle slung over his back. A zamba is shambling up from behind. There's a fallen one nearby, so I slide toward it in a crouch, pull some of the damage from its festering, collapsing body, and leap toward Tolo.

He locks eyes with me, understands. Sidesteps just in time for me to hurl myself past him, arms outstretched. I let loose the devastation onto the attacking zamba, and it crumbles at my feet.

They're every-damn-where, though. And our party is still scattered. Tolo pulls a flare from his vest and snaps it. "On me," he roars again. "Come on!"

"Dad!" I yell, hating how I sound like a lost kid. "Tams? Maza!"

"Up here!" Maza calls. "Tams is hurt!"

We sprint up a tree-covered hill to where Tams lies bleeding from a slash wound while Maza swings a machete at three attacking zambas.

"Hrahh!" Tolo yells, unslinging his rifle and then letting loose on them.

A hand lands on my shoulder as I squat beside Tams. I glance up and almost burst into tears: my dad's smiling down at me. "She okay?"

"I think so," I say, squeezing his hand once and then turning to Tams.

"I am," she insists. "Just got a li'l cut."

"I got you," I tell her, already sliding my fingers along her blood-stained shoulder, letting her song rise as the tissue mends. "Come on." She grabs my outstretched hand and I pull her up, and then we're on the move, back in formation, with Barnabas and Maza watching the rear, Tams and Tolo in front.

"Here!" a girl calls from up ahead. "Humans! Up here, eh!"

It's the girl with the antlers. She's standing in a tree, waving like a little kid. "You guys are less useless than I thought you'd be—I'll give you that!"

CHAPTER FORTY-EIGHT

CHELA

"HOW DID YOU ALL . . . ?" I MANAGE TO SAY WHEN THE EARTH-quakes of pain from my laughter subside.

Get here? Tía Lucía scrunches her face in disgust. *Ay, mi madre—un desastre. Este tipo—Archibaldo—he set a trap.*

"It was a summoning. . . ." The words come out of me in a strained gargle. "The dead bambarúto."

He combined the summoning spell con algo más siniestro—a cry for help. It went out to todos los espíritus de Madrigal, a desperate plea from deep within la isla. A child's voice, urgent, terrified, begging for someone to come . . . What were we going to do, eh? Bueno, pues, we all came running . . . floating. Ju know. When we arrive, qué va—la isla! It was newly risen, our home.

She's crying now—glistening spirit tears slide down her glowing face as she shakes her head. *We streamed forward, a desperate, overjoyed procession. The day had finally come. We would save whoever was in trouble and then enjoy our long-lost homeland, eh? We followed the cries here, a este lugar muerto. . . .*

"And?"

One sad little espíritu was here, screaming in terror. As we tried to find out what had happened, Archibaldo sealed the entrance, and we were trapped. You must understand, sin la luz, without contact to our living kin . . .

"You eventually vanish."

Eso. The terror took over one and then the next and then all of us. There has been no stopping it, no reasoning. Fear is all we know here. Until you came plummeting into our midst.

"And he's been using your fears to make bambarúto. So . . . many . . . questions . . ."

Claro que sí, m'ija, Lucía assures me hurriedly. She's fussing with something, but I can't move my head to see what it is. I can't move anything. *Pero we don't have much time, eh? Got to get you moving.*

"Thought spirit time wasn't the same as people time," I mumble.

Tía Lucía's irritated face is usually aimed directly at Mateo, not me, and wow. No wonder he's able to look down a charging bambarúto without flinching. *You must be all right if you can make little jokes, eh?*

"I am not feeling all right, no. But . . . what am I supposed to do? I can't . . . I can't . . ." I can't do anything, can't even move, and definitely can't repair myself. But I also can't seem to speak that truth out loud.

Bueno, ju may not be Mateo, digo, Galanika, pero . . . you can create, no? Ju made this whole place, hmm?

"No, Tía, I . . ."

¿Cómo que no? Claro que sí, muñeca. Es simple que—

"I can't create!" I finally moan, cutting her off. "I've tried. I . . ."

Pero tú eres Madrigal. La Creadora.

"It's not that I *can't* can't. It's that I suck at it. In my human state, I just . . . I've always known myself as Okanla, even before I *knew* knew. . . . I always felt that part of myself, the Destroyer. But whenever I've tried to learn the creation part, it just . . . It's like I'm cut off from it. From . . ." Even as I speak, an answer forms within me. Well, no, it's like the ghost of an answer. A possibility—fleeting, like a shadow. Barely there at all . . . But it's enough.

Bueno, I can't pretend I'm not disappointed, m'ija. La verdad es que I'm not totally sure—

"Tía Lucía," I say, with just enough snap to get her attention but not get lectured about my tone.

¿Qué cosa?

"You can move through history, right?"

She does that pensive frown that elders do, considering. *Sí, a mi manera. Los muertos are not beholden to the same rules of time that you living are. Pero we cannot—*

"You can't change anything, I know. Passive witnesses to the past, yeah? And you can only move through times you lived in, right?"

Eso. But collectively, we can journey together as far back as any one of us has memories.

"Look, Tía, I need . . . There's a moment I need to find, and . . . I think I need a guide, an anchor point. Can you . . . Can you find . . . ?" My voice trails off as I realize that for the first time since I fell down here, the screaming has stopped. I'm not sure when it happened—at some point it faded some, and it must've gradually tapered off while I was talking to Lucía. Then I make out the misty contours of other forms, faces, hovering in the darkness around us.

Tell us what you need, niña, Tía Lucía declares, *y los muertos de San Madrigal will do whatever we can to help you.*

CHAPTER FORTY-NINE

MATEO

"YOU MUST BE MATEO," THE GIRL SAYS, WALKING UP TO ME WITH her hand awkwardly outstretched. It takes a second before I realize she expects me to shake it. "The one who Chela is always daydreaming about even though she pretends not to be."

That gets a smile out of me, but then the reality of everything going on slams back to being all I can think about. "Where is she? Is she okay?" I shake the girl's warm golden hand. It seems like a gesture she learned from watching people but has never tried.

"Chela got pulled into a cavern under that mountain you guys broke. I think the dead are trapped in there with her, but— Mateo?"

She stops because I'm already heading that way, battle be damned, good sense and reason be damned.

Then I stop, too. Because much as I want it to, the world does not revolve around me and Chela. Also, she is probably the one person in this situation who can truly take care of herself. And our families are who knows where. . . . I nod. Turn back.

Everyone's staring at me, but not with accusation in their eyes. They get it; they all have people somewhere on this island and are all probably fighting the urge to run off on a mad quest to track them down.

"Thanks for not making me shoot you," the girl says with a wicked grin that lets me know she's only half kidding. "Anyway, I'm Odé Kan. Please stop staring at my antlers, everybody." Everyone's eyes quickly find somewhere else to be. "Yeah, thanks, great, super awkward. To catch you up, eh? A convoy arrived late last night with a ton of you human types all trussed up in plastic handcuffs. The men holding them—some kind of private army, best I could tell—were trying to make it to the caves with your families. But I kept harassing them—well, shooting them—ah, the army guys, not your families—so they gave up and set camp near the edge of the city to wait out the storm."

"Are they—?" Tams asks, but Odé Kan quiets her with a swipe of her hand.

"Best I could tell, everyone was okay. I don't know how they are now. When the storm broke, we were ready for them. I took some of what you guys call bambarúto, and we were trying to bully the captors toward the synagogue, where the rest of our forces are. And by *forces* I mean a handful more bambarúto. But then those shambling deathlike monstrosities showed up and we got caught in a spat with them, and that's when you guys made a dramatic entrance. Thanks for that, eh? And now you're all on the same page."

"Odé Kan," Tolo says from behind us, startling everyone. He steps toward her. He's drenched, bloodstained, mud-covered, but his usually grim face is wide open. The hunter spirit stares at him with undisguised awe and sadness. "My mother's santo," he whispers.

With a tiny gasp, Odé Kan steps forward and embraces him. "Tolo, coño, I never thought I'd see you again. But there's no way you can remember me! You were—"

Tolo shakes his head, holding her at arm's length as if to take in a long-lost friend. "No, but Pops told me Mimi initiated, told me how a hunter spirit saved her life." He makes like he's going to drop into an elaborate Santero bow. "Do I— Do I salute?"

She pulls him up, embarrassed. "No, please. We're at war, kiddo, relax."

No one, to my knowledge, has ever addressed Tolo as *kiddo*, nor told him to relax, and certainly not in the same breath. But here we are: wild times indeed.

"Is she . . . ?" Tolo asks without having to finish.

"Wounded," Odé Kan reports. "But alive and stubborn as ever, even while unconscious."

Tolo nods, wiping an errant tear away. "Okay . . . okay . . ." Tams and Maza both put hands on his shoulders.

"My thought," Odé Kan says after introductions have been made and everyone's taken a moment to catch their breath, "is that we head for the synagogue; your families may be there, depending on how things went with the remainder of my forces."

Tolo and I glance at each other, since we seem to be sharing leadership duty, more or less. Everything in me wants to run off to that pile of rubble where the mountain once was and rocket through the tunnels till I find Chela. But I know . . . I know that ain't it. I give him the nod and he looks at Odé Kan. "Lead the way."

CHAPTER FIFTY

CHELA

I CLOSE MY EYES, SEND MY CONSCIOUSNESS STREAMING BACKWARD through the caverns and soil, the rising and falling pathways of this island. Somewhere nearby, a vicious battle rages, but I cannot . . . I *cannot* get caught up in that; I'll lose myself searching for loved ones. And I can't do anything to help them, not like this, so I'd be stuck watching—an even greater agony than the physical one that rips through my body with each breath.

No.

Anyway, the ancestors are with me; a great group of them placed their chilly, barely-there palms on me before I went, and I know they wouldn't stand for distractions.

So I veer my mind away from the rumble of earth and growl of monsters. Let time flatten and swerve around me as we all dip into the realm of memory, history, the great lost-and-found bin of the world.

When I glance up, we're in the central plaza of Madrigal City, and it's bustling with life. There's a fruit market, a butcher. Birds crisscross the sky, and all three peaks glisten in the warm Caribbean sun. A soft melody plays, a conjunto rattling off one of the classics from the bandstand nearby. I long to just stroll, learn what life was really like back then, take it all in.

But Tía Lucía stands beside me, and behind us, a whole retinue of spirits waits.

"Let's go," I say, and we do, marching through space and time as the years and cobblestones and sea-soaked facades become a blur around us.

You said you had questions, Tía Lucía prompts somewhere around the early 1950s, from what I can gather by the passing fashions around us.

"You said you had an apology," I prompt back. "Elders first."

Ha! Bueno . . . I told Mateo never to trust ju, back when he first became interested. I saw it in his face back then how he felt—before, I think, even he did. But I was afraid you were perhaps behind some of our problems . . . or would be trouble for him. She pauses, considering gravely everything that happened next, I'm sure. *I was so very wrong.*

"Thank you, Iya," I say. "But you weren't wrong."

She glances at me. *Oh?*

"I mean, obviously I'm the best thing that's ever happened to Mateo—I don't mean that." She chuckles, and I quickly add, "Besides you, of course."

Por supuesto.

"But you weren't wrong not to trust me. At that point, it was every Galerano for themself, as I recall. No one knew who was on what side or what it all meant. I'm not even sure if Gerval realized he was Vizvargal at that point. What were you supposed to do, see the future?"

She sighs. *Sometimes that's exactly what I do, ju know. But I was caught up, eh.*

Mateo fills my mind: the feel of his body wrapped around mine, the smell of him. It seems impossible we've only really loved each other for a few months—in our human forms at least. I hope he's okay.

Questions, Tía Lucía prods again. I suspect she knows I'm getting lost in my thoughts about her nephew.

"Archibaldo," I say, almost spitting the name out of my mouth. "What do you know?"

From what I have gathered, he began as a simple priest of Vizvargal and evolved into a powerful sorcerer in his own right, something beyond. Vizvargal was a means to an end for him, just like everything else. His magic lies in the striking of deals; without it, he can't do much. El problema, como siempre, es que many have been willing to do business, even at great personal cost. And others who weren't so willing were persuaded by coercion, blackmail, threats. . . .

"I don't understand. . . . He was a businessman?"

Spiritual deals, Tía Lucía amends. *The bambarúto that are in his thrall, por ejemplo. It's the result of a bargain of some kind that he made with them long ago. His unnaturally long life, otro negocio. Y así va, carajo. He has an otherworldly magic that few understand. That's how he trapped us. That's how he continues to work his machinations against us.*

"Vile" is all I have time to say before time begins to slow around us. A tall figure in all white steps up beside me. Imelda—I recognize her from the Cabildo meeting. She nods serenely, but the wear and tear of these past few days is clear in her faded, tired face. *There,* she says softly. *That is what you seek.*

Up ahead, time itself has slid to a near standstill as the Cabildo members argue and simmer in their elaborate chamber.

Without a word, I stride into the thick of them, then beyond, into a misty opening and then the vast ocean, where smoke still spirals upward from the wreckages of that invading fleet.

And then that vast, impenetrable shield rises up once again over the world, blotting out everything else, the one that seemed to swallow that little girl.

Closer, closer; the dead cluster around me as I approach the barrier. I feel their probing curiosity and wonder, their worry and doubt.

I raise one glowing spirit arm, place it on the trembling static of the wall.

We have long been puzzled by this anomaly in our midst, an old woman says solemnly. *We have tried to dismantle it with all our combined powers, y nada.*

I push forward a little, testing my strength.

What makes you think, the old woman demands, *that you can succeed in destroying this thing, eh?*

"Because," I say as two massive cracks burst open in either direction from my hand, "I'm the one who created it."

CHAPTER FIFTY-ONE

MATEO

WE SCRAMBLE FROM ONE BUILDING TO THE NEXT IN A CHAOTIC huddle. The smooth formation we'd fallen into so naturally early on . . . it's gone. Knowing our loved ones are close, that they may be alive but are still in danger . . . The impossibility of our situation now blitzes like electricity through our veins. We are a desperate mess, no matter how stern we make our faces, how well we still the trembling in our hands.

Will I have to heal my own mom? Will anyone be beyond healing?

"Mateo, stay alert!" Tolo growls. I look up—I've been lagging. That frantic hurry . . . Somehow it ended with me falling behind. And just when I break into a dash to catch up, something sharp clobbers me from the side.

"Mateo!" It's my dad's voice I hear as I drop; it sounds so far away.

But I got this; I survived getting shot to hell *in the ocean.* When I reach for the throbbing pain in my head to heal it, though, a sharp kick cracks my ribs and shoves me farther into the mud. Then everything is a tumbling, splintering tangle. When some kind of bubbling, ichorous skin slides off onto me from my attacker, I know I've been tackled by a zambarúto. The damn thing is fast; I can barely catch my breath or see straight, and the whole world has turned to mud.

All I know—and this is bad—is that I've already been shoved far away from the others, and there are more zambarúto around us. I can hear them stomping, their gnashing teeth and the eerie, sibilant grunts that these half-dead ones have—the air whistling through their malformed skulls, I'm sure.

I finally roll to a stop and regain full control of my limbs. Scramble to heal the bleeding flap of skin on my head, but too much is still happening for me to get it. The other zambas have already caught up to me, and now I'm trying to skitter away, but everything aches, every move opens a new continent of pain across my body.

When I finally scrabble into a standing position, arms wrap around me. Human ones. I whirl around and find myself face-to-face with a grinning tanned guy with perfect teeth and an obnoxious goatee.

"Caught one," he says with a smirk; a shorter guy next to him secures plastic restraining cuffs over my wrists before I realize what's happening.

I can barely stand up, barely make sense of anything. The zambas have already shambled off to find more prisoners to thrash. When I reach up to find the wounds on me, they're everywhere. I'm a walking bruise. At least I won't have to go looking. But I'm yet again interrupted before I get a chance to heal—this time when someone leaps off a nearby rooftop. My dad, as a matter of fact.

The goateed guy is leaning over to light a cigarette. It takes some work because it's still raining, and several of his fingers are in splints, I now notice. He rises back to his full height just in time to catch the full weight of my dad landing on him. The short guy makes a move for the pistol strapped to his hip, but I get to him first, shoulder-checking him into the mud.

I land on top of him, catch a wild punch across my face, but it doesn't have much force to it—the guy's just flailing. My cuffed fists come down together on his brow, once, twice, a third time, and then he lies still, a bloodied mess in this puddle.

When I look up at my dad, he's whaling on the goatee guy with the broken fingers, smashing away with both fists. "Dad!" I yell, stumbling to my feet and running over. "Dad! Enough! Ya!"

"Don't you ever!" Jorge Medina snarls, getting in whatever hits he can before I pull him off. "In your goddamn cursed life! Lay a goddamn! Other hand on my son! You coward!"

Jeez.

"Dad!" I yell, yanking him to the side. "I'm okay! It's done! It's done!" We're both panting, catching our breaths, and then my dad grabs me so hard for a second I'm worried he's attacking me in that same frenzied delirium. But no, this is a hug. A very intense, ter-rifying hug for the men of the Medina family, which I could quite frankly do without, much as I'm glad we're both okay.

I still haven't had a chance to heal myself, and my dad's about to rupture some important organ, I'm sure of it. "It's okay, Dad, it's okay," I whisper, hoping he'll relent some.

So much for "do no harm," I manage not to quip. But it's there; just know that it's right there, ready for the day I need it.

"Please stop squeezing me, Dad." My friends are running up now; this all must've happened so fast. They come to fuss and check on us, then fall back into position, guns ready. Tolo slices off my handcuffs with that bolo knife of his.

"Are you gonna . . . do your thing on them?" my dad asks, still shaky but a little more together now.

I can't tell from his tone what answer he's looking for, but I guess it doesn't matter. "Yeah," I say quietly. "But only enough to ensure they live."

He blinks a few times, furrows his brow. "You okay, Mateo?"

I find a smile, but it's a broken one, I'm sure. Shake my head. "Nah. But I will be. And you will be, too."

He nods, trying to believe me.

"We will be."

I give myself a quick once-over. By the time Finger Splints and Shorty are moderately healed and fully tied up, the whole of Madrigal City seems to grunt and groan with zambas; it's crawling with them.

We head off for the synagogue in silence, pausing every couple of steps to duck behind a house while a grunting, shambling squad of zambas passes.

When we round the corner onto the little plaza in front of the synagogue, four full-bodied bambarúto charge straight at us. Archibaldo must've been keeping the fully alive ones for special duties, like protecting the synagogue. Rifle blasts come from either side as I launch myself toward the monster directly ahead of me. There isn't time to duck and dodge, and I'm tired of people I love being in danger. I leap into the air. Human injuries don't fully trans- late onto bambarúto bodies, but they're not useless, either; anyway, I have more than simply injuries in my chamber.

The creature swings at me, but I'm already too close, so I just catch the bristling, slimy side of its arm as I clamber up its chest. Both my hands find its nasty head and wrap around it and I let all my built-up wounds fly, followed quickly by the death I've been sav- ing since we took over that yacht.

The bambarúto collapses backward in a heap, and I roll away through the mud as Tams and Maza open fire. The other monsters lie in steaming piles around us, some trying to crawl away with terrifying howls and chitters.

I glance to either side, regaining my breath, my shoulders rising and falling, my whole body aflame.

If I stop to think, what's happening will come crashing in, and it's too much to wrap my head around right now; I'll spiral. All we can do is keep going.

But besides those four bambas, the plaza is oddly empty. This is where I tangled with that huge creature a few days ago—there's the house we smashed up in the fighting.

"Don't like this," Odé Kan says, arrow poised.

"Nuh-uh," Tolo agrees. "We going in?"

No easy answer to that one. Seems as likely to be a trap as a blessing. But I'm not gonna wait outside all day, either. Whatever's in there, we'll meet it with all we've got, and between the seven of us, we got a whole lot. "Cover me," I say, walking straight up to the front gate and pushing it open.

"Aha, finally!" Vedo's voice crows as I step into the courtyard. That little tremble in it tells me he's more nervous than he's trying to let on, but that doesn't change the situation. "Took you long enough!"

The others file in behind me, and we stand face-to-face with about three dozen of our friends and family members. Their hands are bound behind their backs, and they're lined up with automatic weapons pointed at them from all sides.

CHAPTER FIFTY-TWO

CHELA

THE BARRIER BREAKS INTO QUARTERS AND THEN SIMPLY EXPLODES into a billion particles of dust. The crew of skeptical dead people behind me lets out a collective, and extremely satisfying, gasp of awe.

I can't help it: I glance back at them, and there's still a little smirk left on my face. But come on! I did that! Tía Lucía gazes at me with unabashed pride; most of the others are still trying to wrap their ghostly heads around what just happened.

Then I turn to the newly unlocked world ahead of me and find myself looking directly into the wide, haunted eyes of the girl who led me here the first time.

The ancestors must've noticed her now, too, because a sudden hush sweeps over them.

You . . . You can't . . . come in here, she whimpers.

I step forward, trying not to look threatening. "It's okay. It's okay."

You can't know. . . . You're not allowed to know . . . any of this! Her watery eyes gaze at some far-off tragedy. *It'll all go wrong again. . . . Can't know me, can't know my name . . .*

"I already know it," I say, another step closer. That stops her cold. Her gaze locks back on to mine. "Madrigal."

Behind me, the ancestral chorus gasps again. I try not to roll my eyes. "And Okanla," I say, keeping my focus tight on the girl.

How? she says, those big black eyes wide.

I admit it was a guess, but it was an educated one. When Mateo was trying to reach me through all that pain and darkness last night, I caught a little sliver of info: the Cabildo members were worried about something happening *again*. Something that definitely *would* happen again. It wasn't war; it wasn't destruction. It was *us*. Our spirits taking physical form, embodying ourselves. Somehow, it had happened back then, and whatever transpired afterward had thrown everyone for such a loop they did whatever they could to make sure things would go down differently next time—including dividing my very identity in half. We must've been torn from our vessels so violently the memories were lost to us as well. Or some foul sorcery robbed us of them. I don't know, but the little girl's answer confirms it all. "It doesn't matter how," I say, because who could explain any of this?

She shakes her head but doesn't move. *Not anymore, no . . . No, just Anabela now . . . I lost all that.*

I reach out my hand. "Show me."

An eternity seems to pass in the span of our stare. I pray none of the old fogies behind me open their big dead mouths to ruin the moment. It all hangs by a thread.

Finally, Anabela extends her own little hand and tucks it into mine.

Nods.

And leads us down a dark corridor to a small bedroom overlooking the bay. It's late, a thousand stars across the clear skies, and a whole fleet of ships makes its way silently through the darkness toward the island. Anabela sits on the bed across from a boy about her age with sandy-blond hair and dark brown skin.

Rolando, spirit Anabela whispers to me, her voice full of love and loss. *Rolando Batalán.* She says his name the way Mateo says mine: pronouncing each syllable with precision, with care, like it's a tiny love song, a prayer.

They're playing a game, totally unaware of the approaching invasion. She flicks her fingers, and a little light floats upward from her hand—an Iwin! The boy jumps up, trying to catch it, but the small spirit keeps whizzing out of reach.

It flits toward the window, and he's going after it, but she grabs his shirt, pulling him back to her.

He's seen the boats, though, and knows what they mean.

At first, she doesn't understand why he won't give in to her playful tugging; then she follows his gaze down to the harbor and lets out a little gasp just as the urgent call of the shofar sounds across the city.

Anabela's spirit hand tightens in mine, and she guides me out the window, down into the hell of battle as the sun rises and artillery fire burns across the sky, explodes across the Port District, sends shards of wood, metal, and body parts cartwheeling through the smoky air.

We soar above it all, take in the vastness of the attacking fleet. They carry no banner, seem to have no single nationality—a coalition of imperials joined together to overthrow this tiny hideaway.

I had always understood the fighting of 1810 to be a civil war . . . but this memory was blocked from the world. It's clear from the Cabildo meeting that they were preparing to rewrite the history. Archibaldo must've given the invaders access to the harbor. And I know, I know we were never conquered—no one ever shuts up about it—but still, this bombardment is real. The screams of terror and pain, the fire already ripping through some of the warehouses by the docks . . . It all feels impossible. How did we recover from this? Did we lose, submit, and just hide it from history somehow?

Another shofar sounds. A counterattack launches, but the first few ships get chopped up by cannon fire almost immediately.

Anabela tugs my hand, yanking me down, down, down till we're sweeping over one of the half-demolished docks. The wrecks of our proudest boats spew smoke into the dawn sky on either side; bodies litter the boardwalk, some charred but still writhing, screaming.

I see two pairs of feet stride purposefully through it all as they make their way to the edge of the dock. Anabela and Rolando walk hand in hand, sidestepping the devastation and death. They are not coolheaded or uncaring—they're terrified. Tears stream from their wide eyes; their fingers tremble in each other's grasp.

They reach the end of the dock and set to work. I can tell they know exactly what they're doing—they've trained, they have expertise. A strange little part of me is jealous; it's absurd, I know, given what's probably about to happen, but it's there, nonetheless. They had mentors and guides; they learned how to be what they are. And they are so clear and confident in that truth.

Anabela sends blistering destruction from her fingertips; it blasts through ships, soldiers, the cannons they wield. With his feet firmly planted, Rolando gathers the injuries of those all around them, the Galeranos who were cut down before they could even fire a shot, and sets them loose, raining more devastation on the invaders.

It's an amazing first volley, but it's not enough. Artillery shells shriek through the air. Bullets whiz by, thunk into the wooden docks, then find flesh, bone. Anabela stumbles back, shocked, blood on the hand she's placed against her suddenly shredded shoulder. Rolando hasn't been hit, but his eyes go wide at her injury. He can heal her—he knows it and she knows it—but they're thrown now, off their game. As he tries to use his power on her, more bullets rain down—they clip him, cut through him, and then they both are running, arm in arm, carrying each other along.

Overhead, artillery shells arc into the night sky, scream toward them.

Bloodied and stunned, Rolando and Anabela make it to the beach beside the docks. The bells jangle midnight; artillery keeps falling, blasting the wreckages of ships into explosions of splintered wood, nails, bone.

The two kids turn to each other. More cannon fire screams past; bullets burn through the air around them.

Anabela and Rolando stand inches apart, stares locked. They both take a breath, both raise their hands, palms out, and press them against the other's. The artillery shrieks toward them. They close their eyes.

And light explodes outward.

The burst covers everything: the docks, the wrecked ships and howling wounded, the blood-tinged waves, the dead, the fleet, the world. An unimaginable burst of unfiltered ruin surges outward and blots out the sea and sky. Then there is simply nothing, just pure light.

CHAPTER FIFTY-THREE

MATEO

"HERE'S HOW IT'S GONNA WORK," VEDO SAYS, EXCEPTIONALLY pleased with himself.

I'm empty. That's all I can think about as Vedo grins triumphantly at me with that big ridiculous smile and those irritatingly perfect teeth. I've got no injuries stored up, no death hidden away. I emptied both chambers into that last bambarúto, like a damn fool, and now everyone I love besides Chela is in one place with heavy firepower aimed right at them.

"You're all going to put down your weapons, or I'm going to tell these men to murder your loved ones."

There's my mom, trying to look strong but clearly terrified. There's Rabbi Hidalgo, and Maybelline, and Baba Johnny. So many lives in the balance.

And I'm just empty.

Vedo's smug smile lands on each of us, one by one. "And here's the beauty of it. These men don't care much if I live or die, and I don't care if they live or die. Isn't that right, lads?"

General mutters of assent from the military bros around him. There are six of them. I don't recognize any, so they must be part of that outside group he's been dealing with—the same ones we forcibly borrowed the yacht from. With these numbers, we could easily overpower them, but not without a good chunk of people getting killed or hurt. And there's only a small window of time in which I can bring people back. With automatic weapons in play, casualties could skyrocket out of control, and go with—well, nothing is promised.

"They'll still do what they have to do, regardless of what happens to me. But each of you does give quite a damn about someone in this crowd, hmm? So you're going to do what I say. Is that clear?"

I barely have any fight left in me anyway after dealing with those monsters all morning and worrying about Chela and everyone else the whole time.

Vedo's face goes somber, faux remorseful. "You have three seconds."

Empty and exhausted. Just when I most need to make sense of things and figure out what to do.

Tolo, Tams, Maza, and Barnabas glance at one another, then put down their guns. My dad raises both hands; then so do I.

"Watch that one," Vedo says, pointing at me. "Do not shoot him, and don't let him get close to anyone who's injured. We'll deal with him some other way. For now, just go get those guns away from them."

Four of the men come forward to collect the guns, their own weapons pointing languidly around the courtyard, fingers on triggers.

There'll be a moment here when they'll be distracted, their hands busy, but I don't have any move to make that won't guarantee someone else getting killed. Someone I love. And then it'll just be chaos.

"Ah, excuse me," an old, raspy voice says from the crowd of prisoners.

"Quiet!" Vedo barks.

"Hey, hey, kid, no need for all that. I used to babysit you, man!" Tantor Batalán shoves his way to the front of the group and then steps out into the open space between them and where we stand so he can face Vedo directly. The two military guys who aren't picking up weapons start looking antsy, glancing at Vedo for direction.

"Tantor, get back with the others!" Vedo barks, and immediately, I know what's about to happen. And I hate it. But it might be our only chance.

"Hey," Tantor croaks, "I gotta use the men's room. Whaddya want me to do, eh? Hold it? I'm not a young hopper no more, kiddo."

Vedo advances on him, furious. "Get back, Tantor! I will have them shoot you."

"No, you won't, you li'l twerp!" The old guy moves with surprising agility, I'll say that. Before Vedo can react, Tantor lunges forward, closing the distance between them, and delivers a devastating headbutt. You can probably hear the crack of Vedo's nose breaking all the way back in Brooklyn. This isn't part of what I had imagined when I said I knew what was about to happen, just an added bonus. The guys raise their rifles, but Tantor's too close to Vedo to give them a clean shot.

Then Tantor makes a break for it, sprinting in that ungainly old-guy way directly at me.

The shooting starts immediately, and they clip him in the shoulder and arms with the first few shots. But Tantor keeps stumbling and ducking toward me.

"Wait!" Vedo shouts, his voice muffled by the hands clutching his newly re-shattered nose. "Don't let him—"

But it's too late. With his last bit of strength, Tantor Batalán launches into the air, catching a splatter of gunfire from each side as he goes. I only have to step a few feet forward to catch his tattered, shot-up corpse in my arms. The song rises instantly—I've already brought him back once, after all. Don't even have to look for it.

"No!" Vedo yells. "You can't—"

But I can, and I do. Tantor's already taking his first breaths as I lay his body in the dirt, and I'm already letting loose with both hands as I rise. The guy nearest me was still trying to carry Tolo's and Tams's weapons, so his hands are full when I blast a cascade of sheer ruination into his legs; he collapses, screaming, the guns clattering around him. The two who shot Tantor are trying to make sense of Vedo's desperate pleas not to shoot me. One swings his gun around toward the hostages, and that's when I slap him with a barrage of broken cartilage and flesh across the back of his head. He falls with a whimper. The other man charges me—in desperation, I guess—and all I have to do is hold out one hand to greet his attack with the last of Tantor's wounds full in the chest.

By now, Tolo and the others have scooped up their dropped weapons and surrounded Vedo and the other guards. Even before I can glance around to make sure everyone is truly handled, my mom wraps her warm mom arms around my neck and pulls me in for the tightest hug I've ever gotten in my life. "Mateo, mi hijo, coño . . ." she whispers. "I didn't think . . . I didn't know. . . ."

"Shhh," I say in her ear as her words dissolve into sobbing. Then my dad's there, too, holding her, apologizing, carrying on.

I know this ain't over, not by a long shot, but I still have to take a moment to step back and let our small victory sink in, however fragile, however ridiculous. Around me, family members embrace and cry and hug.

Tantor Batalán slinks past with a wild grin on his face, looking pretty jaunty for a man who just got shot to hell. "Told you I'd make it up to you, ay!" he hollers, and all I can do is grin and point, because what do you say to that?

CHAPTER FIFTY-FOUR

CHELA

THE LOUD CLACK OF DRESS SHOES ON WOOD BREAKS THE EERIE silence. A figure approaches along the boardwalk. He's tall, in a black overcoat and top hat. Long fingers dance incessantly at his sides as he hums a quiet melody, that off-kilter song they used to summon the demon Vizvargal.

The spirit Anabela huddles close to me as he passes; she watches him with wide eyes. Behind us, the ancestors hiss and tremble.

The wrecks of those longboats still smolder, gently sloshed around by the waves. All that's left of the men inside are charred skeletons, their empty eye sockets glaring at the peaceful, starlit sky over their forever-clenched rictuses.

Down on the beach, Archibaldo delicately pulls up the legs of his suit pants and squats between the broken, burned bodies of the two children, Anabela and Rolando.

She's still alive, I realize with horror, as Anabela's little spirit hand squeezes mine. The Anabela in the memory is still alive, but just barely. Her small chest rises and falls with a sickening clicking sound and the slightest wheeze of air.

"You know who I am, the god I serve," Archibaldo says.

Ever so slightly, she nods.

"Then you know I can make great miracles come to pass, hmm? Yes. Yes, you do. You fear me, and you're right to. But at this moment, I am the only person in the world who can help you, so you'd do well to listen up, eh. What would you do for the chance to live forever?"

I want to run screaming at them, to yell at her, *No! Don't listen to him!* But it's the past, it has already happened, all of it, and who am I to tell a dying girl what to do, anyway?

To my surprise, she closes her eyes, and when she opens them, they're angled at some point in the distance. She has accepted her own death.

"And what if I could offer eternal life . . . to *both* of you?" Archibaldo leers.

Her eyes dart back to him, linger.

"Mmm . . . What would you do for that, hmm?"

"Anything" comes the choked, barely audible reply.

Archibaldo's grin spreads across his whole face. "That's what I thought you'd say, my dear. Well, it's very simple. Here are the terms. I know the spirits that reside within you. I know how they move and the power they hold, especially when they have entered human forms, and it is to them I am making this offer. You must never ever join forces with each other again when incarnated. You must swear to it. Or suffer the consequence of a great and dire chaos being released upon this world."

Anabela stares up at him.

"And you must wipe this memory from the history of Madrigal. Block it entirely so that no one may access it. Most of the witnesses are dead anyway. Close it off. It will be for me to decide what the world learns of your stories; the history, the very soul of this island shall be at my disposal. Swear this vow, and your incarnate forms shall live forevermore, hmm?"

I'm launching across space and time, through the pristine morning air, reaching, grasping with all my might to stop her from agreeing. The dead can't change history, but I am not the dead, and I can't just watch this happen.

It's no use.

Anabela nods, then winces.

"Very well," Archibaldo says gravely, placing one gloved hand on the sand between the two children. He hums his horrible little song as he works, and I wonder if that's a family trait, like how Mateo needs the music to perform his healing. "We will all touch hands to seal it, and so it shall be. We swear it on the island itself, your flesh and terrain, San Madrigal."

He slides his own hand over so it grazes Rolando's motionless gray fingers; then he directs a pointed stare at Anabela. "Eternal life, my dear. Think of it. All this pain will be so far away."

He hums his horrible little song as she closes her eyes. I'm just a flutter of breeze against her skin, but with everything in me I reach, claw at her cool flesh. Then I see more hands, spirits of the past and present, grasping at her, begging, digging their ghostly nails into her burned skin, anything to get the girl's attention, to get her to stop.

No! I shriek as Anabela reaches toward Archibaldo's hand. For a moment, she glances around, as if she heard someone calling to her on the wind. Then she shakes off the feeling and places her finger on Archibaldo's, tears streaming down her face.

As Archibaldo's tune gets louder, a barrier begins to form and grow.

The sand between them caves in on itself, and something with too many legs emerges from the depths, clawing its way onto the beach. That's the creature he was riding when they came for us at the synagogue!

"Your immortality lives in this beast," Archibaldo says, rising. "This Icharracht." Anabela blinks her terror at him as the enormous orange spiderlike monstrosity skitters past. "It will be ready for you when you next incarnate human forms, Madrigal and Galanika."

"I . . ." Anabela gasps.

"You what?" Archibaldo is already walking away, his dress shoes clacking on the wood once more. "You thought I meant immortal life for *you*, Anabela? Oh, no, no. . . . I never said *that*, my dear. The spirits who inhabit you will be torn from your body as you perish, and they'll remember none of this. When they next take human form, those incarnated beings will be immortal, so long as they uphold the covenant. And not to worry, my dear . . . I'll be sure that they do."

Anabela lets out a gut-wrenching, dying shriek, but Archibaldo is already gone, the many-legged creature rattling along ahead of him.

CHAPTER FIFTY-FIVE

MATEO

WE KNOW OUR VICTORY WILL BE SHORT-LIVED, THAT WE BARELY made it through, and anything, everything could come next. That fragile joy, it makes us savor it. Families hug one another and cry. Rabbi Hidalgo comes running over and scoops me up like I'm not the same height as him. "How many times are you going to save me, Mateo?" Then he turns to my parents, who are still in shock from it all. "You've raised a very special boy, you two. I hope you are very proud."

I don't know what to say to that, so I stay quiet, which is probably for the best. But then I catch Odé Kan signaling me from the entrance to the bell tower. Tolo sees, too, and understands—he cuts off his conversation with Safiya and makes a beeline for the hunter spirit. I tell Mom and Dad I'll be right back, tug on Rabbi Hidalgo's arm, and we head over to the stairwell, climb into the darkness behind Odé Kan's graceful strides.

"Is it . . . ?" Tolo says quietly. He doesn't have to finish, and we don't have to answer.

This is the room Chela was laid out in when we first came. Now it's Mimi sprawled on the cot, that same green glow emanating from her.

Tolo gets to her first, drops to his knees, eyes wide and watery. "I . . . She . . . Mateo, can you . . . ?"

I crouch beside the cot; my hands hover over Mimi's troubled face. I finally have time to do more than just the quick, lifesaving heal, a moment to breathe and really focus, and I plan to make the most of it. I'll need it. It's easy when you can see exactly what's wrong. But with Mimi . . . I'm not so sure. The sounds of celebration and worry below, Tolo's and the rabbi's anxious breaths, and Odé Kan's more measured ones . . . They all seem so loud as I try to grasp the slightest hints of a thready, faraway melody.

Mimi is a little beyond human at this point. I knew as soon as I saw her—the strangeness in her countenance, the glow—that her whole energy is just different. But it's even clearer now that I'm sweeping through her inner workings. Her song has hints of the strange, throaty warble that the bambarúto share, but it's also so familiar, a variation on the theme of Madrigal. She's more like her niece than either of them would probably like to admit.

Once I lock on to it, everything clicks into place.

She took a bad hit, a couple of them. Her brain took some jangling, bounced off the skull, started sending all the wrong messages to the rest of her body, so she's been breathing in weird off-rhythms for a few days, sending random hormones and cortisol bursts into an already taxed and confused system. The balance is all off. I'm sure if Mom and Dad ran her stats and levels, they'd be a mess.

I'm used to dealing with more instant problems—sudden violence and all the urgent, devastating ways the body tries to cope with it. This is something else altogether. But I will fix it; I will. This is what I do.

Her song weaves through me—I'm sure I'm humming it—as

I set out to find that sweet harmony, the equilibrium her different organs and interconnected systems have been craving, reaching for, and flailing at for days. Blood flow has been crimped here; it's too fast there. A whole splatter of activity around her liver was probably angling to become some kind of growth, but I sweep it away, feel it disintegrate as the melody fortifies, finds its groove, and another piece slides into place.

I don't know how much time has passed when Mimi Baracasa blinks open her eyes groggily. I'm covered in sweat; so is she. She lets out a wry, throaty chuckle. "Ahhh . . . Galanika indeed, eh."

Which must be what lets everyone else know she's awake. Tolo gasps from the far end of the room, rushes over. "Mamá," he says with a choked sob.

Mimi's sitting up by the time he reaches her, already crying as they hug.

When I look up, it's both my parents who stare back at me from the doorway, unvarnished admiration and awe in both their expressions.

"M-Mateo?" Dad says, like he's not sure what to call me. I wonder how long they've been standing there, how long I was lost within the tangled web of Mimi's damage. "I saw what happened on the boat, but this . . . This was different."

I nod, because that's me. I'm still Mateo, even if I'm also Galanika.

Mom shakes her head. "That was . . . How . . . ?"

I cross the room, let them fawn over me some. It feels good; I can't lie. Not in the told-ya-so way—well, a little in that way, yeah—but mostly because I hadn't realized how badly I needed them to recognize that what I do and what they do is connected. We're not on opposite ends of some corny spectrum. It's not science vs. magic, not a cut-and-dried debate, not a competition. All this time, I've just wanted them to see me, see what I do. Respect what I do, the way I respect what they do. Didn't even realize how bad I needed it until that moment their wide eyes met mine.

We step out of the room, because the rabbi has come back in and the Hidalgo-Baracasas need their moment. And the Medinas need ours. Except we don't get it, not really, because as soon as we make it back downstairs, I know something's wrong.

Everyone is muttering fearfully, and those who have weapons are prepping them.

Odé Kan calls to me from on top of the fortification wall around the synagogue, where she's perched, bow and arrow out.

I know it's bad from her voice, and I brace myself as I climb the ladder she's propped against the wall. But nothing I could've done would have prepared me for the sight of hundreds and hundreds of zombie bambarúto overflowing through the streets all around us. An entire horrendous army of the shambling creatures completely hems us in on all sides.

I exhale grimly. "We're surrounded."

CHAPTER FIFTY-SIX

CHELA

BESIDE ME, THE SPIRIT ANABELA MOANS, AND I HOLD TIGHT TO HER, wrapping my own spirit form around hers. Then I throw my head back and let myself cascade back into my body.

And an eternity of pain.

It throbs through me, now dull, now a thousand pinpricks and sword slices. It moves across my torso in a vicious wave, pounds each of my bones to dust, and regenerates them just to destroy them again.

I'm screaming, and the spirits have started their screaming again, too. It's a scream that encompasses all the pain and terror of being trapped in this hole, the sorrow of what I have witnessed, and the frustration at this impossible world. I know, too, that the stream of emptiness that began on my arm has expanded, reached all the way across to the small of my back and up my neck. I can feel its coolness; even through the agony everywhere else, I can feel it.

But it's Anabela's face that appears above me this time. Tía Lucía is somewhere behind her, along with the other ancestors who journeyed with me into the past.

Anabela, somehow, is smiling, and for a moment, I don't believe it's really her.

"How can you smile, seeing what we just saw?" I ask.

She shakes her head. *You don't understand; I never watched it before. I did not have the courage. For all these years, I've been trapped in that realm, alone. I made a cave out of my own fear and regret and hid in it; swore I'd hide there for all time if that's what it took.*

"I . . . I can't imagine."

But then you came along, Chela Hidalgo, Madrigal, Okanla. And you showed me what I had lived through; you stayed with me as it unraveled; you helped me feel strong enough to bear witness.

A strange feeling settles over me between the throbs of pain. It takes a few moments before I recognize it as a realization, like the emotion of it somehow preceded the understanding itself. The pieces come together.

"Alone, you said."

She nods. *Rolando was simply gone after that.*

"Tía Lucía," I say, my voice still a mottled, hoarse whisper. "The spirit who was already here when you—"

Tía Lucía's voice is warm and very, very gentle; a well of emotion hides behind it. *We have already brought him. I realized as soon as you . . .*

Rolando! Anabela yelps, and I see the flash of one spirit meeting another, then the two holding each other in an embrace so tight it's hard to tell who's who.

It's a very special thing, what you've done, Tía Lucía says, sliding into a sit beside me as the two long-lost friends sob in each other's arms.

"Urghh" is the first response that comes out of me, because every word I try to make still surprises me with new bouts of pain. "Just trying to . . . get us out of this . . . mess. . . ."

Don't downplay it, she chides. And then, with a kind of friendly, conspiratorial nudge: *Ju saw how they were moving, back in that lost moment, sí?*

"They were trained." It feels good that I wasn't the only one who noticed that. I try not to cringe too hard at the absurdity, the unfairness, of my envy over someone who was about to die a horrible death.

Eso, Tía Lucía affirms. *They did not know how to use their skills for war, no, because they were children. Pero sabían que hacer—con sus manos, sus cuerpos—sus espíritus—para hacer su arte.*

They knew how to move their hands, their bodies, their spirits, to perform their art. *Art.* That is what it is, even when it's a wartime art.

It's not just that moment he has taken from us, eh. It's entire traditions, ceremonies, methodologies.

"Man said, 'It will be for me to decide what the world learns of your stories.'" I shake my head, the pain suddenly somewhat dulled by the rage I feel. "I don't know if I've ever hated anyone this much."

This is the history of our island, Tía Lucía says sadly. *So much of it written by our enemy from within.*

The division. The words of the Cabildo meeting echo back to me. It's been him all along—the reason I can't find part of my own self, that I'm torn in half, divided within. He did that. Archibaldo did that. Because my power was too much for him. Because *our* power, mine and Galanika's combined, was something the world had never seen before. And they shamed us and broke us because of it.

No more.

Anabela, I call. *Rolando.*

The two spirits—so young and so old at the same time, casualties in these horrible wars of ours, and still so full of light—appear before me, arm in arm, determined never to be parted again.

Thank you, Miss Chela, for reuniting us after so long, Rolando says solemnly.

"You're welcome," I say, gritting my teeth through the pain. "I just have one small favor to ask in return."

They both perk up, ready to help.

"Teach me."

CHAPTER FIFTY-SEVEN

MATEO

LAST TIME I WAS IN THIS TUNNEL, CHELA AND I WERE HEADING OFF to the beach together.

Just a few days back, but it seems like a lifetime ago. It felt like everything changed when that mountain collapsed, but the truth is, there was dynamite inside us all along, waiting to blow. It was centuries in the making, and we were casualties of it before we drew our first breaths. Falling in love just lit the fuse. There was no stopping the carnage.

I wonder where she is, what disaster has kept her from our nightly meetings. Or did she simply lose interest, find something better to do?

Be here now, Mateo.

Be here now.

Problem is, the here and now is every bit as bad as my scattershot thoughts.

It's already almost dark out—we've whiled away hours fretting, prepping, and debating, all of us half-delirious with the impossibleness of everything. We finally landed on this half-baked, nonsensical plan to send out a small group through the tunnels to the beach, and then . . . No one seemed to know what was supposed to happen after that. I think we just wanted some way out, and we figured if we all wanted it desperately enough, it would somehow materialize when we took a few steps toward it.

That's how Tolo, Tams, Barnabas, and I all ended up down here, rushing like hurried wolves through this dank tunnel beneath the synagogue, hoping we don't get lost, hoping we don't get jumped, hoping some answer will show itself when we come out at the beach.

It won't, but we have to try.

"How is Mimi?" I ask Tolo, whose silhouette I can just make out in the dim shadows between torches.

He makes a noncommittal grunt, then takes a deep breath. "Alive. I still can't believe it. Doesn't make sense in my brain. Even with you telling me. But . . . I dunno. Thank you?"

I laugh because I get exactly what he means. Nothing makes sense. "Anytime."

We're rounding a bend, and I'm trying not to think once again about when Chela and I made this same trek, rounded this same bend, when scrabbling sounds come from up ahead.

A mess of clacking and clicking blots out whatever happens next as everyone except me raises their big fancy rifles.

"Easy, easy," Tolo says. "We don't know wha—"

A shambling zambarúto comes bursting through the shadows toward us; behind him, it's easy to see the bobbing heads of many more.

"Go!" Tolo roars. "Hold fire, just run! I'll cover the rear!" And he's right—if anyone else shoots, it'll be him and me who get chewed up first in this narrow, unforgiving tunnel. Tams and Barnabas sprint back toward the synagogue; I stay beside Tolo as he back-steps, opening fire with a deafening barrage. My hand is on his shoulder, guiding him, and the zambarúto are falling to pieces in the horrifying strobe of rifle blasts, their festering broken flesh collapsing into puddles of ichor and bone.

But there are so, so many. And they keep coming, leaping at us through the shadows, being blasted back even as more clamber over them, and they keep getting closer and closer.

"Wait!" I yell between bursts of fire. I launch forward, shoving my hands into the foul, still-trembling catastrophe at our feet. But it's a ridiculous idea—there's no time to figure out these creatures' mostly dead biology, no quick enough way to inflict their own damage on them. Anyway, more scuttle closer, claws extended, mouths open wide, and I have to lunge back behind Tolo as he lets loose once again.

"You guys okay down there?" Tams calls, her voice raspy with breathlessness.

"Gonna have to run for it soon," Tolo yells back. "Gotta change clips, and I don't know if we'll have time for that."

The direness of all this slams into me. It's not that I haven't been terrified up until now, but I dunno, some kind of wild adrenaline must've taken over, sustained me, sent me scrambling to do wild, impossible heroics. Yeah, well, that ran out, whatever it was. Tolo's words broke me out of it, and now the very notion of trying to outrun these things as they come clawing after us . . . It makes my knees turn to jelly.

"Ready, Mateo?" Tolo yells, blasting away again.

No. Absolutely not. "Yep!" I lie.

"Good. Go!" And with that, he stops shooting and runs like hell.

I'm out of breath as soon as we start. It's terror; it's eating me alive.

A stitch opens in my side just as we reach Tams and Barnabas. Tolo and Tams charge ahead, and so do I. Barnabas lets loose a flurry of shots, then runs behind me.

When we catch up to Tams again, she tags herself in and blasts away as we go. If she gets gobbled up, how am I supposed to save her? How many of them are there down here? And why is everything impossible?

I can't think with all the shooting and growling and running and panting, and that's probably for the best. A few seconds—or minutes, maybe, who knows—later, the shooting stops and Tams is running beside me again, smiling like a goober, and then we both barge up the ramp and into the synagogue, slamming the trapdoor closed behind us.

"What the hell are we gonna do now?" someone demands as I lie flat on my back, gasping for air.

"Not . . . that . . ." is all I can manage to reply.

CHAPTER FIFTY-EIGHT

CHELA

I DON'T KNOW HOW MUCH TIME HAS PASSED WHEN I FEEL THE LAST strand of organic material in my once-battered innards weave itself back into place. Could have been hours, could have been days—spirit time, people time, who even can keep track anymore? It's been what seems like an eternity of trial and error, learning, failing, ten steps forward, fifteen back. All the while, young Anabela's glowing hands guided my own, her gentle voice whispered in my ear: *A little more pressure, a little more light, just so, now here, easy, easy, weave, weave.* Other spirits gathered as we went, but Tía Lucía was there from the beginning, watching, encouraging, smiling, and cheering me on when I made progress.

And now, now I am whole. My breath moves easily through these newly repaired lungs—no more raggedy, rattling gasps. I can feel the blood coursing through me, each nutrient delivered, each organ enlivened.

But I'm not completely healed. The emptiness has grown across my skin, yes—what was once a tiny stream has blossomed into a series of rivers stretching the length of my body. I can feel those slivers of sheer absence crisscrossing my skin. Maybe it'll take me over entirely soon, I don't know. And in a way, I don't care. All that matters right now is what we just accomplished, and what we're going to do next.

You did it. Anabela grins down at me, my proud young mentor.

"*We* did it," I say, sitting up on my elbows, then easing myself into a cautious crouch. Not too dizzy. Not too weak.

Deep breath.

I stand. The spirits of San Madrigal surround me. There are thousands and thousands of them. Their glow lights up the sheer walls leading up into the darkness. I fell so far—so, so far. It must be at least fifty, maybe seventy-five feet. And there's something wrong with these walls—they're not regular rock like other parts of the cavern. Instead, that pale blight covers every surface, the same one that was in those spots around the island. The same one that's been slowly covering my body.

I remember my first anguished attempts to escape, the way the place didn't respond to me at all; it felt dead. It *is* dead. I don't know how or why, but it's clear I'll never be able to climb these walls, not without ropes.

What now? Tía Lucía asks. *How do we breach that barrier?*

I narrow my eyes at the darkness above, the spirits all around. "Leave the barrier to me. I just need some help getting up there."

I see the meaning dawn on her. "*That which is spirit must remain spirit,*" she quotes to me.

"Says who?"

"*The San Madrigal Boo—*"

"*Book of the Dead,* I know. And? Do you remember who I am? Who *you* are?" I shake my head, feeling the wind of what's about to happen wrap around me. "We don't play by their rules anymore, Iya Lucía. We *make* the rules."

That sweet, sweet smile I remember so well from the night of before her death slides across Tía Lucía's face. *Eso es.*

MATEO

Night.

The rows and rows and rows of snarling, grizzled zambas seem to go on forever in the darkness. The full moon sends gentle shimmers along their rotting carapaces, the drool and ichor sliding out of them.

"Maybe they'll all just get moldy and collapse on themselves," Tams says, walking up beside me in the tower.

I smirk, but there's not much humor left in me. Standing around is making everyone antsy. Rumors swirl, fears rise. We have a handful of weapons and too many people to protect. Making a run for it is pure suicide—worse, it would mean watching everyone we love die around us. My immortal ass would survive, sure, but my body would be shredded to pieces, and I don't know how I'd heal myself from that state. So, great.

"Did we fall into a trap?" I say, half to myself. "Or get outmaneuvered?"

Tams shrugs. "No way to know right now."

"But why haven't they overrun us and killed everyone yet?"

She shakes her head. "We're more useful to them alive, I guess."

"What if this is it, and we're just stuck? It's not like there's any help coming. They don't have to come kill us because we'll eventually run out of food." The thought is almost as chilling as the carnage that would happen if we tried to get out.

A distant rumble sounds from over the horizon. Thunder? Tams and I both glance toward the beach.

It's a clear night, and from the tower, it's easy to make out the crashing waves, the foam washing down the sand.

The rumble gets louder, becomes rhythmic, a pulse.

Now we're both squinting. Down below, an uneasy rustle sweeps the hordes of zambas.

Something emerges from the water—a towering figure. Then another.

"Is that . . . ?" I gasp.

The golems. All twelve of them stomp out of the sea and surge onto the beach in an unstoppable wall of stone.

The creatures below howl and snarl; they turn as one to face this new enemy as the golems vanish into the jungle.

The battle has shifted, but I'm not sure if it'll do us much good.

"Do you think we . . . we make a run for it?" Tams asks.

"Half of me does, but . . ." The idea of all our friends and family members being caught out in the open if the tide suddenly turns. "I just wish there was a way we could get the golems to push their fight away from us some . . . give us a chance to—"

I'm cut off when the sudden howl of a shofar bursts through the night from right behind us. "You mean like that?" Mimi says with a smug smile.

Tams and I gape at her, then gape back out at the island, where the rumble of battle has already tacked toward the far shore.

"How did you—?" Tams asks.

"I know a thing or two about a thing or two." Mimi shrugs, wiggling her eyebrows. "Anyway, glad they finally showed up. Took 'em long enough. Been days since I first blew the shofar to summon them, eh."

"To be fair, it's a long way to walk," Tams points out. "But either way—are we going to make our moves?"

This is our chance.

Tams has already started down the stairwell, and I'm right

behind her. In the plaza below, the cloud of doom has given way to confusion, the first glimpses of hope.

"What is it?" Tolo asks, hurrying over.

"The golems from your basement," I say, breathless. "They just showed up on the beach! And your mom can, like . . . control them. . . ."

Maza runs up, fully armed, and grinning for the first time in hours. "I'm ready."

I glance around. Families are helping one another up, gathering their things. Some will surely die; I won't be able to revive everyone. But we don't know if we'll have another chance at this. I meet Tams's expectant stare. "We need a plan."

"If only," my mom says, walking over, "you knew two people who happen to be experts at emergency management and disaster relief."

My dad, of course, can't resist joining in the smugfest, and for once, I'm not mad about it. "Who could that be?" he adds unnecessarily.

I always think of them as doctors—in part because they move through the world medical degree first, everything else second. Like, God forbid you call my dad Mr. Medina; you'll find out where the *Dr.* and *MD* go real quick. But hey, when you're the first generation of people from your tiny island to get a real medical degree, I guess you gotta flaunt it. Anyway, they're more than doctors. My parents have been in the thick of some of the worst disasters and war zones in the past thirty years. (Picture tiny me in a hotel a safe distance away, studying music to distract myself from all the horrible things that might be happening to them—music to make sense of the chaos of the world.) And they weren't there as tourists; they were there to actually do something, and the something they did, more often than not, actually made a difference.

And it's about to again. Before I can even roll my eyes, Drs. Jorge and Sandra Medina, MDs, have leaped into a logistical whirlwind of action—taking stock of what we have, who'll need help, how far we have to go to get to the beach.

Tams leans on my shoulder and chuckles as we watch. "That face they're both making . . ."

"Hmm?"

"That's the one you make when you get excited about a really great song."

CHAPTER FIFTY-NINE

CHELA

WE CLIMB.

Limbs find limbs; hands wrap around hands.

Surprisingly, the newly formed flesh of the dead is in fact quite fragrant, but not in a graveyard way—it's the smell of jasmines, lilacs, Florida water, fresh soil, washed linens. I guess we really *do* make the rules.

We climb—a towering, staggering ladder of spirit and skin—and when I make it to the very top, I place a hand on the barrier and feel it shatter satisfyingly around me. "We make the rules," I whisper as bodies clamber up onto the ledge and rush past me.

Soon, a bunch of those who are still barely-there phantoms float up to us and close their ghostly eyes as I lay hands on them, turning their glowing shadows into fully formed bodies.

It won't last, I don't think. There's a limit to this stuff, even with no rules/new rules, and I'm pretty sure none of them expect it to. But the ancestors stretch and sigh and take such a deep, stunned pleasure in finally feeling solid again—it's worth it just for that.

And now we are an army.

"Someone lead me to Archibaldo's lair," I say. "I have business with him."

This way! a spirit yells, and the others stomp through the dark corridor.

A small hand tugs at me as I'm about to run off with the others. *Chela.*

I look down into Anabela's big eyes. *You need to understand something. It wasn't the power of our magic that destroyed us.*

"What do you mean?"

It was the artillery. The guns. The enemy. That's what killed us.

"I . . ." I don't know what to say. "Why are you telling me this?"

Because, Anabela says softly, *I don't want you to make the same mistake we did. Our mistake wasn't using our powers or joining forces; it was waiting too long to fight back.*

I feel a smile cross my face. "That's one mistake I have no intention of making."

——◆——

Something is moving in the vast, dark cavern below.

Many somethings.

Of course.

This is where I first spotted that writhing horde of half-dead bambas. We stand on a ledge looking over the gloomy expanse. The creatures are still here, but something's different about their movements, their shapes. Then it hits me: these aren't the shambling zombified bambas—these are full-bodied, tall, and terrifying, like the ones we faced back in Brooklyn.

If my theory is correct, that means there are more flesh-and-blood people on the island. Maybe Mateo showed up with a badass team of misfits to drop hell on Archibaldo, despite my warnings. And maybe they got trapped somewhere. If there are new bambas springing up, it means there's fear in the air.

And then, very suddenly, all that becomes secondary. At the far end of the cavern, there's a sheer wall in the darkness; I'd figured that was an exit of some kind, because all the bambas are heading that way and vanishing into it. Except now the wall itself is stirring. The torchlight shimmers against it, revealing humongous legs that seem to unfold out of the shadows, an impossibly huge frame, a squinting, cruel face with a wide, grinning mouth.

I recognize it immediately. This is the creature that carries my immortality. The bambarúto surging toward it aren't leaving—they're vanishing because they're being pulled into the creature's girth, adding to its enormity.

And there, riding on top of it and laughing like a maniac, is Maestro Archibaldo Medina.

MATEO

"All right, listen up, everybody! My parents came up with a plan," I say to the assembled crowd. Faces full of hope, fear, and excitement stare back at me. "And I gotta be honest, it's about as cohesive a plan as we're gonna get given the circumstances. Okay, that sounded dubious, but it was meant to be a compliment!" Seems like everyone is here—Baba Johnny, my parents, Tams's dad, Maza, Maybelline, Tolo, Safiya, Bonsignore, Odé Kan, Mimi, the rabbi, Tantor Batalán . . . and so many more. All staring at me. "Anyway, here it is! We'll go in small groups. Each group will have a medic—either my parents or me—and—"

"Wait, wait, wait," Tantor interrupts. "No offense, Mr. and Mrs. Medina—ah, Dr. and Dr. Medina—but your son is a literal god of healing; I know, because he brought me back from the dead . . . twice! Everyone saw it! And you guys, what're you gonna do, CPR? I dunno, man."

I glance at my parents, and to my relief, they're both flashing good-natured smiles. And I can tell it's not forced diplomacy—they know he has a point. "You're not wrong, Mr. Batalán," Dad says. "I brought a bunch of emergency medical supplies that we'll have with us, but the truth is, nothing we do can compare to what my son is capable of."

I wish I could take this moment to relish what he just said, but instead I have to deal with war and death and zombie creatures.

Then my mom jumps in. "We can't do what Mateo does, but we can stabilize you until he gets to us, and that's going to have to suffice, because as you well know, there is only one Mateo."

"All right, all right, all right," I say, because I'm probably blushing and people seem pretty satisfied with that answer anyway. "Thank you, thank you, let's keep going! Each group will have a medic and two armed guards."

"What happens if—?" someone yells, but Bonsignore cuts him off with a sharp "¡Coño! Let the kid finish! Finish, kid!"

I nod at the best gym teacher in the world. "Thanks, Bonsignore! There are a *lot* of things that can and probably will go wrong. We can't plan for all of them. The goal is to get to the boats at the Port District. The yacht we came in on is still there, and—"

"Y'all brought a yacht?" someone else chimes in. "Damn!" Others chuckle and guffaw—trying to ease their own nerves, I know—but then Bonsignore growls, and they all shut up.

"—and the military guys we captured say the barges they brought everyone here in should still be there, too, though we can't confirm that from the tower, as they're behind some buildings and out of view."

"Boo!" Tantor jeers.

"Point is," I continue, hoping to get moving soon because I want this all to be over with, "we're heading to the docks. The golems seem to be keeping most of the zamba horde busy, but who knows what'll happen. If you get jumped and separated from others, it's your call whether to head for the docks or try to make it back here. Each group will leave one of their guards at the docks to try to hold off any surprise attacks there, and we'll keep rotating best we can until everyone's on a boat."

"And then?" an old lady I don't recognize asks.

"And then we get the eff out of here," Tantor answers. "And come back when it's not full of zombie monsters, eh?"

People laugh, but I can tell there's a lot of uncertainty. No one wants to leave their homeland a second time after fifteen years of it being gone. On the other hand, no one wants to be ripped to shreds or trapped perpetually in a besieged synagogue with dwindling supplies.

"All right!" I say. "Let's move."

CHAPTER SIXTY

CHELA

"STOP!" MY VOICE SMASHES ACROSS THE CAVERN, REVERBERATING along the dead gray walls, through the stalagmites and tiny canyons.

Archibaldo looks up from his mount, and his glowing pale green face breaks into a hideous snarl. "Ahaaa . . . Okanla!" he crows. "Welcome to the beginning and the end of everything! Have you come to your senses? Everyone does eventually, you know."

"You need me," I say, my voice calm as the last pieces of Archibaldo's hellish puzzle fall into place. "Not the other way around."

Archibaldo does something with his hand, and the hideous monster he's riding lumbers forward until it stands about ten feet away and the maestro is almost at eye level with me. Now that it's closer, I can make out the writhing horror of its flesh, made up of so many bambarúto's still-moving parts. "Is that so?" Archibaldo asks, and he sounds genuinely curious. "Do tell."

"You're selling bambarúto to these conglomerates and authoritarian governments all over the world. Shock troopers who know no fear and are almost unkillable, perfect for shutting down protests, intimidating voters, destroying movements, rebellions, dissent of any kind."

Archibaldo nods along as I talk, impressed. "Yes, yes, very good, very good."

"Bambarúto are created from fears. Our fears. Fear of empire, of authoritarianism, oppression. Fear of past traumas arising again, slavery, genocide, inquisitions . . . all the things Galeranos survived, escaped from. All the things we created San Madrigal to be a refuge from. You've been using that essence of creation—*my* essence—to build your private armies from the fears of all our ancestors, who you captured."

"Indeed, indeed, yes. And we have quite a few buyers lined up already. You'd be surprised!"

"But the fears of the dead don't quite make the same caliber of bambarúto, do they? And the island itself—it dies a little every time you use it to hatch one of these abominations, doesn't it?"

"Troublesome," Archibaldo admits. "But every problem is simply an opportunity to find an even better solution, eh?"

I ignore his unsolicited business advice. "The island is a limited resource, but I am not."

Archibaldo's smile stretches even wider. The Icharracht stirs and trembles. "That is correct, Madrigal. You go on forever, my dear. Thanks to me. At least"—he eyes the pale rivulets and islands of emptiness now visible along my neck and arms—"you would be unlimited if you would stop delving into the depths of this dying island."

"This island that is me!" I roar. The audacity of expecting someone to just calmly accept that you've poisoned a part of them . . . I barely have the words for my rage. Still, there are some things I need to understand before I wreck his world. "But that's what I don't get. You know I can't be killed by any mortal means, so why keep the commando bros from shooting at me? What difference does it make?"

Archibaldo spreads his arms wide to either side and cocks his head. "Why would I shoot at someone I'm about to go into business with for the most profitable venture of all time, hmm? It's bad form to take potshots at future partners."

"That's never going to happen."

"Of course it is," the maestro insists. "You think you're the only one with leverage here? This delightful ride of mine is the very embodiment of your immortality, my dear. And your beloved Galanika's as well." He's laughing, like this is some big bomb he just dropped. "And I have fused myself to the Icharracht, my dear. We are one now."

Okay, that *is* kind of a bomb. But it's still sort of hilarious that he thinks I give a damn.

"Do you even know the full extent of the bargain I struck with your previous young avatar, eh?" he goes on. "You don't. You don't know how deep it goes. What it allowed me to do."

I think back on his tapping fingers, that horrific little melody he was humming. "What have you done?" I demand, since he seems inclined to tell me anyway. But then, very suddenly, I know. Not even sure how it all snaps into place, but it does. The song, the pact, the way it was sealed. His long life and the power he wields. Archibaldo didn't just seal off the memory of what happened; it wasn't enough for him to simply hide the demon Vizvargal in the shadows of his own twisted version of San Madrigal's history. He used that music, that melody, to entwine himself inextricably with the very essence of this island, of our island, of the island that is *me*.

That's how he's gotten away with all of this, managed to conceal himself and his fellow worshipers for centuries, pulled off such audacious feats of magic. Because he was using mine all along. Leeching it as he wound the ever-lengthening fibers of himself deeper and deeper into the heart of San Madrigal.

"You've woven yourself into *everything* we are . . ." I whisper, aghast.

"Every story lives within its own opposite," Archibaldo proclaims haughtily.

Rage surges through me.

How dare he?

I take a few steps back, winding up. I'm already running toward the ledge when Archibaldo croons, "You wouldn't want to destroy the very thing that keeps you living forever, would you?"

"Please," I say, quoting the legendary poet Mateo Matisse as I smile. "I've probably been waiting centuries to do exactly that!" And then I launch into the air, one fist raised and bristling with all that good Destroyer energy.

MATEO

It's me, Tantor Batalán, and a handful of others in the first group out. Tams and Barnabas walk on either side of us, guns out, expressions grim. I'll have to get used to my best friend being this unstoppable badass on top of everything else that's amazing about her. We've already been through so much hell, and she seems to have been waiting her whole life for a moment like this. It's not that it doesn't affect her—more that she seems to know what to do with it, how to manage the chaos and uncertainty without letting it crush her. Pretty sure Tolo's been giving her tips since they started seeing each other. Either way, I make a mental note to check in and make sure she's really okay when this is all over.

When this is all over.

Don't even know what that means anymore.

What is my happy ending? I just know I want to live. I want Chela to live, my friends and family to live. Doesn't seem like too much to ask, but it's growing less and less likely by the minute.

Somewhere on this island, my creepy ancestor is holding the key to my immortality hostage—the ultimate leverage. Once I get all these people to safety, I'm going to find it, and find Chela, and we'll deal with Archibaldo and live happily ever after forevermore. Like, literally.

Easy.

"Aha, um, problem ahead," Tantor says with an uneasy chuckle.

Nothing is easy. I know that. But I can dream, okay?

We're about halfway down a steep slope. Lilac bushes cover it; we're, like, waist-deep in them, and that gentle aroma fills the air, totally contradicting every other thing about the night, which is full of monsters and the possibility of being shredded. It's like someone playing Sade's greatest hits at a public execution.

Tams and Barnabas already have their rifles raised toward where Tantor indicated with his chin—a scraggly tree at the foot of the hill. "What is it?" I ask.

"Movement? I think?" Tantor says. "I dunno, man. It's hard to tell in the dark. Just being cautious."

The sounds of snarling and thrashing come from another part of the island, but that's been going on this whole time. I don't see anything by the tree. "Maybe it was the wind?" I suggest, trying not to sound too nervous or hopeful.

But then a tiny light flickers through the branches, and then another and another join it.

"Iwin." It comes out of me in an awed whisper.

"Who's Ee, and what did he win?" Tantor asks. I probably would've rolled my eyes at any other time—old guys gonna old guy no matter how dire the circumstances—but somehow his crotchety dad joke hits me at just the right angle, and as the sky lights up with those bright bulbous spirits, I let out a loud laugh and then burst into tears.

Tantor looks concerned. "Oh man, my joke wasn't that bad, was it? I'm sorry, man. I'd forgotten about those little guys."

I shake my head and laugh and cry some more, and that's when I notice that they're not floating like they usually do, all wandery and aimless. The Iwin are on the move.

And they're not the only ones. Up ahead, huge shambling forms emerge in the darkness. They're all headed back toward the synagogue.

"What do you think happened?" Tams asks. "Is the attack back on? Were they waiting for us to leave to move in?"

I squint back toward the direction we came from, but all I can make out are a few more zambas rushing off through the underbrush. "I don't know. Take the others to the boats. I'm going to check."

Tams nods but shoots me a heavy look before heading off. "Don't get reckless, Mateo. There's worse things that can happen than death."

Don't I know it.

I'm over the hill and jogging along a windy path that leads back to the synagogue when a sharp crack snaps my attention ahead. The pile of rubble that was once our third peak suddenly explodes outward with a blast of rock and dust. Something massive bursts out of it, many arms flailing, and lands in a heap somewhere behind the walled-in plaza.

The Icharracht. Our one chance at getting out of this alive. But it's gigantic now—ten times the size it was a few days ago. The towering beast scrambles to its many feet and rears to meet an oncoming attack from . . . a tower of earth and rock that shoots straight toward the sky from the rubble, then veers sharply at the Icharracht. On top of the tower, I can just make out the tiny figure of the girl I love in full Destroyer mode, fists raised to strike.

No.

I break into a run.

I have to stop Chela Hidalgo.

CHAPTER SIXTY-ONE

CHELA

DESTRUCTION AND CREATION SURGE THROUGH ME AS THE EARTHEN tower rises, rises into the night, then lurches forward at my command. Below, the ancestors scramble out from the rubble and charge the stomping, flailing appendages of the Icharracht.

"You stupid girl!" Archibaldo yells in a frantic, high-pitched whine. "What are you doing? You can have everything you want! And still you fight? Do you love war?"

I will the tower beneath me to swing in a sharp upward spiral, carrying me alongside and then above the rearing monster and its rider. "I don't want anything you have to offer!"

This is taking too long, though, and the bambarúto keep piling forward, making this monster larger and larger no matter how much I trash it.

This won't do.

I know my powers, know my strength. I've tried precision, all that good training Odé Kan put me through. But this has to end for real now. I destroyed this island once before to stop Vizvargal. I can do it again to crush this vile little man. And just like that, I know what I have to do, how to do it.

He may have imprinted himself into the framework of this place, but it's still mine to control, mine to destroy if I must. Everything goes very still within me as I allow a supernova of devastation to build. I can't be sure Odé Kan will survive this; Mimi almost certainly will not. I'm not even totally certain *I* will. But I know it's what needs to happen. I would rather this island cease to exist entirely than let it become forever entangled in Archibaldo's foul schemes, a breeding ground for more empires of blood and conquest.

I refuse.

The destructive force grows and grows within me. When it's big enough to take out this whole cursed place, I'll simply let it go, and someone else's god can sort through the chaos.

"You didn't even let me finish!" Archibaldo screeches, breaking through my reverie. "Did you honestly think I had only one bit of leverage? What kind of fool do you take me for?"

"A dead one," I say, leaping off the tower and pointing myself straight down on a trajectory that will land me hands-first on Archibaldo. The power of absolute annihilation begins to erupt out of me. I let it seep forth in bits at first. Might as well inflict some pain before I call forth the apocalypse.

The damn creature is fast, though, even with the newly fleshed-out dead hampering its every step. It throws itself just far enough to the side that I land on an armored part of its thorax instead.

Still . . . plenty of damage to do here. I rain down blow after blow, each one carrying an infinity of oblivion. Shards of flesh and carapace explode into dust around me. The Icharracht roars in agony. I try to ignore the white lines of emptiness spreading along my arms and legs each time I pull on the island's power. Pretty soon, it won't matter anyway.

"Stop! Stop, fool!" Archibaldo yells. "Your family! All your friends! Don't you see? I will destroy them all!"

What?

I look up from the devastation just in time to see a gigantic claw swinging toward me. I leap out of the way, roll forward along the creature's squirming, bambarúto-infested abdomen, then hurl myself out into the sky as another claw comes down. The tower of earth and stone rises ahead, and I come down easily on it, then swing it far enough out of reach to catch my breath.

And, as I stand there panting, I take in the scene.

The Iwin flicker through the sky all around us; there are so many of them, and they're all congregated right here instead of spread across the island like usual. Their gentle glowing beauty lights up the night. The shambling, half-dead bambarúto swarm toward us from all sides, and there, nearby, a bonfire roars in the plaza behind the synagogue. People stand all around it, gazing up at us. My people. Galeranos. My friends and neighbors. I think I even see my dad.

The fight almost leaves me.

Can't even wrap my head around how they managed to get them all here. But it doesn't matter. I have to do what I can. Giving in to this monster won't save my family; that much I know.

"You see now, don't you?" Archibaldo calls from nearby. "You see that you've lost, hmm? There is no stopping me. No stopping the tide of history! You will—"

The sound of gunfire cuts him off. Down at the synagogue, a group of bambas has made a dash for the front door, but they're being cut up by snipers on either side. I guess Tolo's with them, then. I have to smile.

"Doesn't matter!" Archibaldo insists, although this clearly was *not* part of his plan. "They'll run out of ammunition eventually! And then what? What will your prec—?"

He stops because my tower is speeding through the air toward him, and with the mountains on one side and buildings on the other, there's nowhere for the Icharracht to go to escape my attack. If blowing this whole place up isn't an option, then I'll have to take Archibaldo and the Icharracht apart piece by piece.

"Stop!" Archibaldo shrieks, sending the creature into a clumsy lunge through some rooftops. I command the tower to sharpen into a pointed blade at the tip and then speed up, aiming directly for where Archibaldo struggles to pull the Icharracht from the buildings they've just toppled. Bambarúto swarm into the gap that's quickly closing between me and my prey. The tower cleaves them, sends ichor and body parts flying in either direction, but there are enough to throw off my aim and momentum.

Still grounded amid the ruins, the Icharracht lurches forward, plowing through the piles of bambarúto parts and gaining in size as it collects them into itself. I try to adjust course to hit my mark and end up hitting a pipe or well in the ground instead. The sudden jolt sends me flying, and suddenly I'm hurtling through the air, surrounded by peaceful little glow spirits.

"My armies will crush your beloveds!" Archibaldo is screaming when I tumble to a painful landing and gather myself. But he's still too close to the ground, and now my ancestor army has caught up to our melee. They go smashing into the rear guard of bambarúto, and a vicious brawl ensues.

I reach the Icharracht, stumble onto its huge squirming, fumbling form, but the damn thing keeps growing. Even with the ancestors' interference, more and more bambarúto stream in, collapsing into the carapace or joining the fight. I can't even make out where Archibaldo is, but I hear him laughing, laughing into the endless night.

CHAPTER SIXTY-TWO

MATEO

I'VE LOST TRACK OF THEM.

All I can do is follow the sounds of battle—squealing zambas and a strange, desperate song that seems to rise from the depths of the island. Who all is fighting over there besides Chela? The Icharracht collapsed somewhere behind some trees and rooftops, right at the foot of the middle mountain, and Chela vanished along with it. Is she dead? Is the monster? Would I feel it? Would I die, too?

I have no idea. I just know Archibaldo is a master of deceit and he's probably tricked her into destroying our only hope. I press forward along the path, skirting the edge of the synagogue and slipping between a row of houses that should bring me out to—

The mournful, defiant wail of Mimi's shofar breaks out across the sky, and for a moment, everything seems to stop. Then a rumble sounds. The golems. They're coming. Behind me, dust rises along with the growls and screeches of creatures locked in deadly combat.

"Mateo!" It's Odé Kan. She's racing along the rooftops above, bow in hand, arrow poised to fly. "Mimi sent the golems to run interference for us and keep the rest of the bambas away! Come on!"

"But . . . what about our families?" The whole escape plan hinged on the golems keeping the enemy busy. Sure, most of the bambas are swarming this way, but there are plenty to go around.

"Change of plans!" Odé Kan sounds jubilant, as unstoppable as the wind.

"What?"

"They're not leaving. They all agreed they'd run away from their home enough. It's time to stay and fight! And anyway, they want to make sure you and Chela get out of this okay!"

There's nothing to be said to that. If they're staying, they're staying. All it means is . . . we have to win even more so now.

I don't know if Odé Kan realizes what we have to do, that Chela must be stopped, and I don't think it's in me to explain it right now—we're heading the same direction, and that's plenty.

I'm about to dash forward when something heavy and snarling crashes into me from the side. The zamba and I tumble through the mud, the cold, nasty puddles, and then I roll out of the way, throwing myself against a wall to catch my breath. Scrapes and bruises cover my arms and chest, nothing more serious than that. As the creature stumbles to its feet, I hear a yelp from up above. Bambarúto—the full-bodied, fully alive ones—are clambering over the rooftops. Odé Kan has time to put an arrow through one of them, but then the others reach her and, with a fierce shove, send her flying off the roof.

The group swarms after her, squealing their delight.

"No!" I scream, and take one step toward where she probably fell. Then I'm clobbered from behind, and a sharp pain opens in my gut as I fall—the thing must've kicked me. I land in a heap, scrambling to heal myself and get away at the same time. I get nowhere, just kicked again, and this time a claw shreds a gash so deep across my torso that blood gushes out unabated.

From the mountainside, shrieking erupts, a hideous, earth-shaking howl that's probably Chela murdering the one thing that'll keep me alive.

No.

I will keep me alive. As long as I can anyway.

I roll out of the way, dodging the next kick by just a few inches, then stumble into a desperate, pathetic run. My hands slide up and down my poor torn-up torso as I go, barely mending anything at all, my own song a distant broken lullaby in the wind.

That zamba shambles along after me, relentless. I have to get to Chela and stop her.

I'm probably dying. And Chela is probably about to finish me off without knowing what she's doing.

Immortality is such a fragile thing.

I tried so hard to find a way to make us safe—it was right there, right in front of me. And Archibaldo's scheming is ripping it all away. Galanika flickers in the air up ahead, almost gone, mouth open, calling, desperately calling.

"Hrrgh," I grunt, shoving through the mirage of my own death just as the zamba roars up behind me.

I can't leave Odé Kan. Not after all she's done for us.

My song comes stronger now that I've made up my mind, but it's still nearly impossible to close this wound with my trembling hands and a creature just a few steps behind me.

I round the corner, and there's Odé Kan, trying to stand, trying to raise her bow. The bambas have already closed in on her. Before I can get there, they slash the arrow out of her hands, then bring their claws down one after the other. All I can hear is her screaming. And all I have is this half-healed wound within me.

It'll have to do.

I break into a run, the tear in my gut ripping open again as I go.

It sends a scream hurling out of me, unbidden, and all six bambas turn to look. To hell with the element of surprise, right?

Turns out, that's all the time Odé Kan needs. An arrow bursts through the head of one bamba, killing it instantly. I collide hands-first into the other, send the full force of my injuries into where I'm guessing its vital organs might be. Who knows with these things? It does enough damage to stun the creature, and that'll have to do. I shove it the rest of the way back with my own momentum and then leap off, landing in a wobbly squat beside the bamba Odé Kan already downed.

Two converge on me, swinging, as a third falls with two arrows in its back.

I lay my hands on the dead one nearby, absorb its shattered brain and punctured skull. Then I swing around and whip them at the other two, smacking one across the face with it and missing the other entirely.

That's all right—Odé Kan has climbed on top of that one and does her signature arrow-through-the-top-of-the-ol'-dome maneuver. The bamba drops to its knees with a bereft sigh, and Odé Kan stumbles off, then collapses into a pool of her own blood.

CHAPTER SIXTY-THREE

CHELA

I DON'T KNOW IF I CAN DO THIS.

Bambarúto are everywhere—the ancestors formed a solid wall to hold them off, but the creatures shattered it, and now the fighting's spilled onto the mud-covered chaos where this creature and I are fumbling through the wrecked houses.

And I still can't find Archibaldo.

The Icharracht finally raises its back half, and the sudden lurch sends me sliding off into a tree. I rise, already running, and leap onto one of its legs as it struggles to get the front part up. My hands deal a relentless barrage of destruction as I grapple my way up the leg, leaving only blistered, broken flesh in my wake. The creature falters, collapsing back into the dirt, but it lands partially on top of me, its crusty shell digging into my legs.

"Do you yield, child?" Archibaldo hollers from somewhere nearby.

I yank myself free, but one thigh is shredded right down to the bone.

Doesn't matter.

I am creation, destruction, the island, the girl.

I raise one palm, closing the wound enough to keep going. The pain still lances through me, but it doesn't matter.

I am creation, destruction, the island, the girl.

I climb back onto the Icharracht, stumbling toward where Archibaldo's voice came from. A bambarúto rushes me, and I slam into it first, obliterating the thing entirely before it can merge with the monster. More bambas approach, their claws extended. A group of ancestors rams into them from the side, and the fight explodes into a chaotic free-for-all as the Icharracht rises again. I drop down, clinging on to its slimy flesh.

I have to reach Archibaldo. I have to end this. His entanglement with the island means I can't wipe him out with one fell swoop without putting everyone I love in danger. So be it. But I'm running out of steam doing it the hard way.

The maestro lurks at the far end of the Icharracht; I can just make out those ancient arms flailing in the air over his head as he croons out that horrific melody, probably weaving each new bambarúto into place along the flesh of his horrible creation. My immortality. Mateo's immortality.

Where is that boy?

I drop into a squat for better balance. Push one hand down and release an enormous blast of death into the Icharracht just as I lift the other hand, raising another tower of stone and soil to skewer its midsection from below.

That does some damage. We immediately go cartwheeling back into the mud and bambarúto and ancestors and death. Everything becomes so loud and so quiet at the same time as I scramble to do the one thing I'm best at: destroy, destroy, destroy.

CHAPTER SIXTY-FOUR

MATEO

"I'M OKAY," ODÉ KAN INSISTS AFTER I'VE HEALED HER SHREDDED flesh and several broken ribs. "Come on."

I follow her through the muddy streets, but I'm limping still—I haven't managed to heal myself fully, and I don't want to stop now. We're so close.

"Look," Odé Kan calls over her shoulder, "when we get there, I'll keep it busy and you help Chela finish the damn thing off, got it?"

She doesn't understand. How could she? I'm dying; I'm sure of it. Galanika's appearances . . . that's all they can mean. Maybe it's just the spirit within appearing to let me know we did our best, it's over. Unless we can stop Chela. But I don't know how to explain any of this to the hunter spirit, and anyway, a cadre of fully formed bambarúto round a corner up ahead and charge us.

This time I have some injuries stored up, and I leap headlong into the fray as Odé Kan's arrows fling out on either side of me. The first bambarúto catches one of its fellow monster's skull breakages right in the face; the next loses an arm and then finds an arrow in its chest before it can get a second swing at me.

The world flickers away from me as the next creature lurches forward, claws extended.

A young girl with dark eyes looks me right in the face, the night sky exploding behind her, fire dancing across the dark water of the bay. Our palms meet in the air; we dream of a better world. An impossible burst of light flings outward from us, wiping out everything in its path.

My hands are on either side of the bambarúto's head, slamming pure pain into it; the monster crumples at my feet. Another one falls beside me, pierced by three arrows shot at once.

The next bambarúto drops on me from a rooftop, but my hands shove upward into its torso even as I fall.

A song calls to me—Galanika's song. I'm made of light, inside the flesh-and-blood body of a boy, realizing who I am, who I have always been. The song dances through each trembling part of our essence; the warm presence of Okanla glows nearby.

Ribs splinter, the beast howls. Internal organs rupture; it collapses onto me, dead.

I pull what injuries I can from it as I crawl out from under the body, accept Odé Kan's outstretched hand, rise.

Up ahead, the Icharracht howls, but I'm not sure what I'm supposed to do anymore, where I am.

Odé Kan pulls and lets loose another arrow. I follow its sharp path into the chest of a shrieking bamba. It falls at the feet of five or six others.

I break into a run, directly at them; everything slows; the world spins away.

I'm so, so old, and so, so happy. The room is quiet except for the crackle of fire and the jingle of wind chimes nearby. I am warm; I am loved.

This frail body, it's almost gone. Every cell knows it, every organ, too.

There is pain, but it's a gentle kind of throb, a quiet tide.

Here in this desperate night, my hands fling bone-shattering blasts of pain into the monsters all around me. A game of life and death, and death spirals closer and closer.

Death spirals closer, but it is a welcome kind of oblivion, here in this quiet room, the warmth of the fireplace, the song of the wind. The song of the world, the song of my beloved nearby. All that's left is to let my younger self know what this means, now that he has finally, finally let go enough to hear me.

Creatures collapse into the mud, splatter my already-soaked shirt with more blood, more ichor, more death. Arrows plunge through rigid carapaces, through skin, vessels, organs.

Up ahead, the humongous Icharracht writhes on its back, all those long appendages swatting the air.

The fire warms me; the wind whispers its song through the sonorous chimes. The boy will understand. My eyes closing, I turn to the woman I love, the woman I have always loved—her smile has always been in her bright, bright eyes, and it's there now, even though she's crying; it's the smile I see first. Our life has been very, very long together.

I find her hand on mine as my heart sends its last few thuds through my chest, against my palm, against her palm, and then the world finally slides away forever . . .

And I stand here in the mud, shaking, wounded, crying, laughing. And finally, finally, finally, I understand.

"Odé Kan," I hear myself say as she steps up beside me. "Get as far away from here as fast as you can."

CHELA

This goddamn thing won't die.

How many legs does it have? How many times do I have to destroy every vital organ I can find before it stops?

I crawl out of the mud; pain blisters through me, but I ignore it.

I am destruction, creation. The island and the girl.

I am tired.

And Archibaldo is still cackling out there somewhere.

Spirits swirl through the air, vibrating and chiming their gentle songs. Behind me, the Icharracht flails its many legs, trying to scramble back to its feet.

Someone comes running through the darkness toward me—another bambarúto? I ready myself for more murder.

It's Mateo.

Mateo Matisse Medina. Galanika. The boy I love even though I can't.

Except I can. And I will.

"Chela," he pants, stopping in front of me. He's almost unrecognizable—caked in blood and filth. There's a moment . . . a moment when we just stand there, and I know each of us is wondering what the hell happened to the other, what it all means, what the hell we're supposed to do now. I see his gaze fall on the lines that stretch across my skin.

"You're—" he starts, reaching out to heal me, I'm sure. To hear my song.

Mateo Matisse Medina. The only other person in the world who has powers that work like Archibaldo's do—through music.

I stop him. "There isn't time. I need you—"

Before I can finish, Mateo says, "I need you, too." His eyes are so wide, and he's been through hell—it's written across his harried face, his sweat-soaked, bloodstained clothes. He's been through hell, but all he sees is me. The world collapsing, a huge, hideous monster on the attack, our families in danger, but it's my feelings he's wondering about, our love that lights him up. And it's not like he's some goofball, ensorcelled donkey who's lost track of what matters. Mateo will do what has to be done; he'll get it done, whatever it is.

That night a week ago, all he was trying to do was tell me how he felt about me, move us forward, and I've been so caught up in trying to stay alive and take down Archibaldo, it's all gotten away from me. What we have, what we are. The fire between us. No archaic rules, no pact, no threats of imminent cosmic disaster can change that. No matter how far away or close we are.

Now he stands before me, panting. He's filthy and battle-worn and as wide open and unsure of our love as I've ever seen him, yet somehow, this is also Mateo at the height of his power. That bright, unstoppable heart of his, it doesn't shut down, doesn't wander away. Even when I've given him plenty of reason to think I'll break it, he doesn't miss a beat returning my affection.

Even when he misunderstands what I'm trying to say.

"I *do* need you, Mateo," I tell him with a weird giggle that I barely recognize. "But there's something more important I need you to do."

"Anything."

MATEO

"Escucha," Chela says, except it also sounds like Tía Lucía's voice. Maybe because that was her favorite word, her number one piece of advice. Or maybe, I realize, blinking through the twilight at a figure approaching from behind Chela, it's because it *was* Tía Lucía's voice along with Chela's. "Escucha a la isla."

"How . . . ?" I gasp, because Tía Lucía is flesh and blood, not a spirit, and that's not possible. It doesn't matter how, though, because now I'm hugging her, and smelling that Tía Lucía smell, and sobbing. I only allow myself a few seconds before I step back, and I know from their expressions that whatever this magic is that has made my tía whole again, it won't last long. In this moment, the how doesn't matter. Neither does the why. We have to get through this, and Chela's right: there isn't time. Off to the side, the Icharracht screeches, stumbles, and begins to rise.

So instead of asking a bunch of questions and blubbering, I nod, tears streaming down my face. Then I crouch and place a palm to the ground.

"Archibaldo has entwined himself with the island," Chela says as both her and Tía Lucía's hands land on my shoulders, bracing me. "We need to break the connection, at least a little, so we can—"

"I know what to do," I say, because I do—perhaps I've known my whole life, and all the many centuries of my existence have led to this one moment, to knowing exactly what I would need to do right now.

I listen. And once again, the song of the island rises.

But there's something else, too. Now that I know what to listen for, to focus on the silences between each lonely phrase, I find it: Vizvargal's haunting melody. That's what the final fugue was in call-and-response counterpoint to—the song of the island. Of course! Archibaldo is like me, more so than I'd realized or cared to admit. He heard the melody of San Madrigal echoing out from the depths of this place, and he hated it. He wrote his Vizvargal hymn in direct response to it, literally, and used that magic to entwine himself into the fabric of this place like a hidden thread.

But now that I've found it, breaking it is really no big deal. Even cursed, barely harmonious melodies have a way to them—a particular path, a cadence. I've gotten good at tracking down where a song goes off-kilter and fixing it. Causing dissonance is actually much easier.

So I do. I send my mind deep into the bowels of this place, beyond the sweet song of Madrigal. I latch on to Archibaldo's terrible, tangled fugue. And then, with precision and ruthlessness, I shatter it.

CHELA

He did it.

I don't know how; I'm not even entirely sure what *it* is, but it's done—Archibaldo's vise grip on the essence of San Madrigal is ruptured—and Mateo is why.

The whole universe seems to sigh as an impossible sense of heaviness is whisked away on the warm night breeze.

Now all that's left is to finish the job.

"You can't!" Archibaldo yells, flailing as the Icharracht stumbles to its feet. "You cannot!"

Mateo and I look at each other. Our eyes lock.

"We will throw off the balance of the world, you know," I warn under my breath.

Mateo glances at the devastation surrounding us. "What balance?"

"Chaos will rise."

He smiles, and it's a lopsided wonder, that smile. "Welcome, chaos."

We raise our palms just as the bells of the synagogue ring out across the spirit-lit sky.

CHAPTER SIXTY-FIVE

MIDNIGHT

The light enters the world from within us, between us.
It stretches out, out, out—a cataclysm.
Nothing exists beyond it; nothing exists within.
It simply is: an all-encompassing absence.
But, perhaps, like all empty things: a vessel.

A vessel . . .

Yes.

Before, the last time our palms met on this island . . .

Six days ago, wasn't it?

Sure. Whatever. Spirit time isn't man's time.

Chela, please.

The last time our palms met, we dreamed of a world

that would embrace us instead of trying to destroy us.
A world that would champion our love,
a world where we wouldn't have to
barely survive any given day,
explain ourselves, contain ourselves.

The dream brought down a mountain.

And my cousin's club.

Chelaaaa . . .

Now, into the emptiness of this divine
light that pours out of us,
that blasts through space and time,
shattering everything around,
into that vessel, we pour the same dream,
now bolstered with the sheer fire of who we are,
where we've come from.

We will not live forever.
We will not hoard all this power.
Immortality, released.
The island itself, released.
The two of us, released.

Archibaldo shrieks as the Icharracht
is peeled away, layer by layer,
and carried off in the wind.
He shrieks as our light disintegrates his
precious bambarúto one by one.
He shrieks as our light obliterates him,
each cell catches fire,

each flame runs wild,
devours each tendon and bone.
And finally, Maestro Archibaldo
Medina falls silent forevermore.
The final deal is done.

We have learned precision, we have learned to heal.
We have learned, most of all and against all odds,
to love.

And the future belongs to us.

DAY SEVEN

Where will we go when the world turns to ash?

When cataclysm comes, who will hold you close and tell you the truth?

We can only laugh through each spark and tinder.

A new day always begins with fire.

—*The San Madrigal Book of the Dead*, Canto XX

CHAPTER SIXTY-SIX

MATEO

IT'S FUNNY: I GAVE UP THAT IMMORTALITY THING, EMBRACED DEATH, even if it's a faraway one, and now . . . I've never felt so alive. Very Galerano turn of events, to be honest. But who knew? Well, I did, apparently. Or Old Guy Me did. Shout out to him . . . us.

Anyway, maybe chaos isn't so bad after all.

A melody moves through me as I saunter toward the festivities. I'm not sure where it came from, what it is. Never heard it before. Maybe it's a song about freedom. I'll have to keep playing with it to find out.

A wild bonfire rages in the middle of San Madrigal. Beyond the crackling flames, the rooftops and palm fronds, a fierce sunset covers the sky and sends stark crimson rays dancing across the waves.

It's been a day of cleaning up, healing, crying.

Everyone is still in some kind of shock; everyone is so happy to be alive. The world feels very broken, and very brand-new.

Archibaldo is no more—that tattered old body was already

nearly a corpse anyway, and our surge of power turned him to dust. I did what I could to rid his cruel, discordant melody from the fabric of our island, but it was like clearing wax from an ear—the more you dig, the deeper in some of it ends up. I'll keep working at it.

Vedo and most of his buddies made a break for it in the confusion. A bunch of them got chopped up by roving bambas, but some made it off the island in a stolen boat, including Vedo. Saved us the trouble of having to decide what to do with them, I guess. I barely care—just happy everyone's alive. The Cabildo members present had an emergency session and excommunicated all the empire pirates. Dad cut the kumbaya-with-people-who-want-to-kill-me shit, so the vote was unanimous.

And anyway, there were more important matters to deal with, like what the hell we're going to do now. Barnabas's crew already has a makeshift comms station set up. They also brought generators, an impressive food supply, and plenty of rum. It's been a week since we raised the island, less than twenty-four hours since we brought down Archibaldo and his Icharracht, and San Madrigal is already starting to feel like a place people could live in again.

Some folks—Tantor most loudly—have already declared that they're staying. Others plan to go back and forth. Mom and Dad, to my utter shock, seem to be leaning toward settling down here. They found the old house and started clearing out the junk and debris.

There's so much work to do, so much mess to clean up, so much healing that needs to happen, and it's not the kind I can just pull out of thin air with a melody. The healing we need is the kind that demands we face the past to face the future. Deal with all the ways we've broken ourselves and one another, take responsibility and move forward with all the compassion and ferocity the many fires of our history have forged.

There will be time for all that, but right now, now we need to celebrate, to toast, to dance. Somehow, against all odds, against a world dead set on destroying us, erasing us, pretending we never existed—we have survived. Survived and thrived.

And tonight, we dance.

There's the rabbi, laughing it up with Tolo, Tams, and Maza. I see Mimi stroll over, drink in hand, and join their revelry. There are my parents, huddled together beside the crackling flames. There are Bonsignore and Odé Kan, plotting the world's most sadistic obstacle course, no doubt.

The spirits are here, too, naturally. They're back in their floaty, glowy forms, mingling with us flesh-and-blood folks and the Iwin. Tía Lucía holds court to a whole enraptured audience of the living and the dead, forever a force to be reckoned with, as if death could've stopped that.

Chela's eyes find mine from across the bonfire. She nods toward the edge of the plaza and I make my way there, but she's nowhere to be found. I turn around twice with a skeptical squint since I'm positive she's watching me from somewhere.

Then I freeze because a gentle breath brushes my neck.

Damn, she's good.

Arms wrap around me from behind; I feel her smile against my back. "You gotta do better than that when you're dating an angel of death, buddy."

I turn around, wrap her in my arms, raise my eyebrows. "Did you say *dating*?"

She smirks, then pulls me along through the dark streets of San Madrigal. "Come on."

We enter a tall stucco house near the harbor district. Up some stairs, through the darkness, down a hall to a bedroom with floor-to-ceiling windows that look out on the bay, the vast ocean, the darkening sky. This place must have been lovely once.

For a few moments, we just take in the view.

Our loved ones' laughter and the wild strumming of a guitar can still be heard not far away, but the waves are louder, and the world feels so huge suddenly. There's so much to see.

"Do you want me to . . . ?" Mateo's voice trails off. He lifts my arm; his fingers hover over one of the many jagged lines that are now spread all over my body. They faded some overnight, and even more once Mateo did some extricating work on the island, untangling Archibaldo's song. But they're still there, these rivers across me. And now Mateo wants to know if he should erase them the rest of the way. Or try to.

I smile, guide Mateo's gentle touch along my arms, my shoulders and neck. Up my chin to my lips. "No."

He gives me the *Mateo has a question* look.

"These lines, they're not his work. These scars aren't here because of Archibaldo. He made the incursions on the island that caused them, sure. But they're there because of me. What I did. I chose to connect to this place that is me. I knew what it would do, and I did it anyway. And I'd do it again, Mateo. All these are is a reminder that I did everything I could to whup that old fool's ass and get us free." I raise one hand to his eye, where the scar he got fighting bambarúto back in Brooklyn will remain for the rest of his life. "Anyway, now we have something else in common."

"Ven acá," he says with a wicked grin.

"I'm already right here," I say, matching his expression.

"Closer."

———◆———

It's deep in the night when I wake, and the wild dance party nearby has simmered to a sing-along that's both joyful and nostalgic. Mateo sits at a small desk by the big window; he's humming and scratching his head, writing in a tattered notebook. Outside, the waves crash, and the Iwin float in the darkness like a slowly turning galaxy.

"What're you working on over there?" I ask.

Mateo looks up, startled. "Ah—something . . . new . . . actually." He puts down the pen, stands. "A melody that came to me, but I think it's more than that. . . ." He crosses the room and slips easily back into the bed. "A collection of songs, I think. I'll get to it later. It's not going anywhere."

"Neither am I," I say. "What's it called?"

He scrunches his face like he's still considering, then says, with finality, "*The San Madrigal Book of the Living.*"

"Perfect."

And for a few moments, he holds me in those big, loving arms while he hums this brand-new music.

Then, nuzzling Mateo's neck, I say, "Yes."

He glances down, draws me closer. "Which yes to what, huh?"

"Yes, I will be your girlfriend."

Now he tilts my chin so we're looking into each other's eyes. "When do we leave for our first date, boating around the world having adventures in mysterious ports and finding new creatures?"

My smile is as big as the whole dark sky and all its dancing spirits, and as the bells begin to toll midnight across our ancient outlaw island with its two perfect peaks and brand-new mythology, I say:

"Whenever we want."

GLOSSARY

The people of San Madrigal speak a mix of Spanish, English, Ladino, and Lucum. Here are a few words you'll find in the pages of *Last Canto of the Dead*.

Basura Spanish. Trash.

Bembé Lucumí. A sacred dance ceremony for the Orishas.

Bueno, pues Spanish. Okay, well.

Conjunto Spanish. A group, usually musical.

Coño Cuban Spanish. All-purpose curse word (means different things in different countries).

Demonas Esperanto. Female demons.

Desaparecidos Spanish. Disappeared, missing.

¡Desgraciado espíritu de mierda! Spanish. Goddamn shitty spirit!

Despojo Spanish. A spiritual cleansing.

Dímelo Spanish. Tell me, give it to me.

El Gorro Spanish. The Hat. (Arco Kordal's nickname.)

"El Manisero" Spanish. "The Peanut Vendor." (The name of a popular early Son-style song from Cuba.)

El problema, como siempre Spanish. The problem, as always.

¿Entiendes? Spanish. Do you understand?

Eso es Spanish. That's it.

Eso mismo Spanish. That's right.

Hermana Spanish. Sister.

Más o menos, sí Spanish. More or less, yes.

Ay, mi madre—un desastre. Este tipo Spanish. Oh, sweet mother—a whole mess. This guy.

Misa Spanish. A spiritual ceremony for the dead; also the word for a Catholic mass.

No se puede Spanish. It cannot be done.

Nunca conquistado Spanish. Never conquered.

Nunca vencido Spanish. Never defeated.

Pan barato Spanish. Cheap bread.

ACKNOWLEDGMENTS

THIS IS PROBABLY MY LAST ACKNOWLEDGMENTS PAGE FOR A WHILE, so I want to take the moment to highlight three really special people in the publishing industry with whom I've had the honor of working on this book.

Rick Riordan truly walks the walk and talks the talk. His gifts to the world are so many and so powerful, it's hard to even know where to begin. As an author, there are the beautiful stories he's told, the vivid characters he's created; the way he keeps us on the edges of our seats, turning pages, desperate to know what happens next; the profound truths about life that each of his books sheds light on. As an advocate, Rick is a truth-teller who knows that you can never really speak *for* other people, so the best use of a gigantic platform is to hand over that mic and let other voices rise. He has proven himself unafraid to take a stand, to fight for what he believes in, to have our backs, even when it's uncomfortable and not the easy path. I'm so grateful and happy to have been able to take part in this imprint and joined the Rick Riordan Presents family.

Next up, Stephanie Lurie: Stephanie brings so much wisdom

and compassion to the process of creating books. It's in her blood and her bones; the curation of great stories is simply a part of who she is; it imbues everything she does. Plus, she is a true joy to be around. To sit across the table from Stephanie is to feel like you can say absolutely anything at all, and know she'll take it in, ponder it, and reply with grace and honesty. I knew the second I met Stephanie that I wanted to work with her, and it took a few years before it happened but wow, it was absolutely worth the wait.

And finally, to my agent, Joanna Volpe—you are such a brilliant mind, heart, strategist, consiglieri, genius, innovator, master planner, and, most importantly, friend. Everything changed for me when we partnered up, and it's been the pleasure of my career to get to work alongside you and watch you revolutionize this badly tarnished industry with precision, empathy, and pure fire. Thank you for all you've done and all that's ahead.

Also, a huge shout out and THANK-YOU to coeditor Rebecca Kuss. It's been so great getting to know you and having you on board this project!

Thanks to the whole crew at Hyperion: editorial director Kieran Viola; Guy Cunningham and his team of copy editors, managing editor Sara Liebling; Marybeth Tregarthen and her production team; Matt Schweitzer, Holly Nagel, Dina Sherman, Danielle DiMartino, Maureen Graham, and Jordan Lurie in marketing; publicist Crystal McCoy; and Monique Diman and the entire sales force. And extra special thanks to cover artist Bastien Lecouffe-Deharme, map artist Virginia Allyn, and cover designer Phil Buchanan. You all have done breathtaking work in bringing the Outlaw Saints duology to life!

Thanks also to all the great folks at New Leaf, including Pouya Shahbazian, Jenniea Carter, Jordan Hill, Abigail Donoghue, and Meredith Barnes. Thank you all—there's no one in the business doing it like you are.

To Tito, mi hijo, watching you become who you are has been the most incredible experience of my life. You have made my heart bigger in the best way, and you have already changed the world.

Brittany, you continue to amaze me more and more with each passing day. I've simply never met anyone as incredible as you, and I'm so proud to be your man. I can't wait for the world to read all the amazing stories you've been conjuring up. I love you.

And thanks always to my whole amazing family: Dora, Marc, Malka, Lou, Calyx, Paz, and Azul. Thanks to my godmoms, Iya Lisa and Iya Ramona, and to Patrice, Emani, Darrell, Jair, April, Iyalocha Tima, and my whole Ile Omi Toki family for their support; also thanks to Oba Nelson "Poppy" Rodriguez, Baba Malik, Mama Akissi, Mama Joan, Tina, Jud, and all the wonderful folks of Ile Ase. Thanks also to Tracy, Ayana, Ron and Leslie and the girls: Sam, Leigh, Sorahya, Alaya, and Lauren.

Baba Craig Ramos, we miss you and love you and carry you with us everywhere we go. Rest easy, Tío. Ibae bayen tonu.

I give thanks to all those who came before us and lit the way. I give thanks to all my ancestors; to Yemonja, Mother of Waters, whose asé I have proudly carried for more than ten years now; to gbogbo Orisa, and Olodumare.

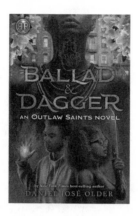

"Evocative and enchanting. Older has created an intricate, sometimes unforgiving world that weaves a vital narrative and provides a feast for readers' imaginations."

—J. C. Cervantes, *New York Times* best-selling author of the Storm Runner trilogy

★ "In this engrossing duology starter, the Riordan imprint's first YA offering, Older explores themes of diaspora, colonialism, and identity via a vibrantly conceived, folklore-tinged fantasy that never loses sight of its immediate human elements, including a strong sense of community and blossoming attraction between its sixteen-year-old protagonists."

—*Publishers Weekly* (starred review)

"This first entry for YA readers from Rick Riordan Presents offers the same heart and adventure that work so well in the imprint's middle-grade titles, with the addition of Older's finely tuned teenage voice and world-building details that will make readers long for a place that feels believable enough to be real. The first book of the duology ends on a satisfying note, leaving readers excited for the conclusion. A new, magical world full of rich folklore and hitting all the right notes."   —*Kirkus Reviews*

"Older deftly combines fantasy with political concepts to portray a young adult's journey through identity, mental health, and romance. Older cleverly integrates languages, music, foods, and other cultural elements. The novel's political coups, supernatural forces, and thrilling action should leave readers eager for the second half of the projected duology."

—*Horn Book Magazine*